Hunter's Revenge

Khardine Gray

Faith Summers

Photographer- Michelle Lancaster

Cover Model- Tommy Pierce

Graphic image- Babelast

No part of this book may be reproduced in any form or by any electronic or mechanical means, including information storage and retrieval systems, without written permission from the author, except for the use of brief quotations in a book review.

It is intended for mature readers. All characters are 18+ years of age and all sexual acts are consensual.

Hunter's Revenge

USA Today Bestselling Author
Khardine Gray
writing as
Faith Summers

Also By Faith Summers

Series

Dark Syndicate

Ruthless Prince

Dark Captor

Wicked Liar

Merciless Hunter

Heartless Lover

Ruthless King

Dark Odyssey

Tease Me

Taunt Me

Thrill Me

Tempt Me

Take Me

Original Sins

Dark Odyssey Fantasies

Entice

Tease

Play

Tempt

Savage Legacy

Devil's Kiss

Duets

Blood and Thorns Duet

Merciless Vows

Merciless Union

Cruel Secrets Duet

Cruel Lies

Cruel Promises

Novellas

The Boss' Girl

The Player

Standalones

Deceptive Vows

Deadly Games

Iuramentum est vita nostra et mors nostra
R
RAVENTHORN
Blade
Cypress
Erebus
Iapetus
Boreus
Gael
Adriel
Amergin
Myrrdin
Erik
Raventhorn

Author Note

Please note Faith Summers is the Dark romance pen name of USA Today Bestselling Author Khardine Gray

Dark Romance Note

Dear reader friend ,

Thank you so much for picking my book to read. I hope you enjoy it.

I just have to warn you that this book is a dark romance.

It contains scenes that may be triggering to some readers

.

Best of wishes xx

Blurb

My monster. My hunter. My husband.

It all started with a chance meeting in a bar that was almost normal.

I was drowning my sorrows, and he was the deadly handsome mysterious stranger who walked in.

He had that dangerous air about him I was always warned to stay away from, yet like a moth to a flame I was captivated by his charm.

All it took was one touch and I couldn't resist.

When I'm with him he consumes me and our passion is enthralling.

Little did I know that behind Malik Volkova's fairytale prince smile lurks a monster.

A monster who belongs to the Knights, a notorious secret society.

And we only met because he was actually hunting me.

By the time I find out who he really is, it's too late, and he unearthed my biggest secret.

Out for revenge on the cartel he forces me into a twisted arrangement for my hand in marriage.

But our union drags me into a war and deeper into his obsession.

Soon it becomes clear there's something he wants more than revenge—*me.*

But I'm not sure if he'll be my destruction or my savior.

Prologue

Malik

Kazakhstan 6 years ago

In the dark enclosure of my hell, excruciating pain flows through my veins when someone lifts my head.

Apart from the cold stone of my prison floor, pain is usually the only thing I feel.

I've gotten used to the evil of my masked captors. Their ominous presence of death and doom always makes me wonder if my last moments in the world of the living are breaths away.

I expect another session of torture I might not survive, but then the familiar voices of my father and my uncle snap my mind back to reality.

I can't see anyone in this dark, but I can hear them, followed by gunshots and the screams of dying men in the distance.

The presence of my family must mean that they found me.

They actually found me and I'm being rescued.

God...how long have I been lost?

Months...

Years...

I don't know.

It feels like an eternity.

As my broken body is carried out of my prison, voices continue to muffle in my ears like a twisted cacophony of broken instruments playing in an orchestra.

Someone—I don't know who—is asking me if I'm okay, but I can't talk. I can't remember the last time I spoke words.

Then I see light. Daylight.

The sun greets me with the warmth of a close old friend you haven't seen in years. But when my gaze settles on the deep Prussian blue sea flowing before me—calling to me—that moment there... that's when I remember who I am.

I am Malik Volkova. A Knight.

Being rescued means I got the one thing I truly wanted above all else—a chance.

A chance to rain Armageddon and avenge the fallen who can no longer fight for themselves.

Watching my Navy captain Jim Davison die as he took a bullet for me was a blow to my soul. He had already lost Brian, his son, and my best friend, mere months before.

When I joined the Navy, he trained me with the same

aspirations and ambitions he had for Brian. I owe him everything I accomplished.

Now I have that chance to punish those who took his life and correct the wrongs that struck when the criminal world followed me.

I've waited and waited and waited.

Now, finally...

Today, I am the dark phoenix rising from poisonous ashes.

I will never stop hunting until the sky rains the blood of my enemies and the earth is nothing but red.

This is my rebirth.

I am destruction.

And I am death.

Chapter One

Malik

Wilmington, present day...

Her name is Gwen St. James.

She's a twenty-three-year-old fashion and design graduate. She's been managing her grandmother's restaurant while she runs her own online lingerie store with her best friend.

Miss Gwen St. James also happens to be number three on my list, but her large perky tits, shapely hips, and that round ass of hers bumped her right up to number one.

Not many women have captured the attention of my dick the way she has. So, my fascination with her is interesting.

I rivet my gaze to her body as she enters the bedroom,

completely unaware of my menacing presence beyond the two-way mirrored wall of her walk-in wardrobe.

The sweet magnolia scent of her perfume is stronger in here. It clings to her clothes hanging from the surrounding rails with invisible fingers laced with temptation.

I'm sure whoever designed the room never thought the mirror would come in handy for would-be stalkers or devils like me with fucked-up intentions.

I can see her, but she can't see me.

If she could, she'd probably scream at the presence of an intruder in her home, then run off and call the sheriff and his deputy. Neither of which could do a goddamn thing to me. I'd either be long gone before they got here, or I'd deal with them, and they would never see the light of day again.

But everyone is safe from me tonight.

Tonight, I'm just here to watch.

Watch and dig a bigger hole for myself because I shouldn't be watching her like *this*.

My fascination is bad for us both because if she's the woman I'm looking for, I don't want to feel anything for her.

Not even attraction. If she's not her, it's still bad.

Women like Gwen St. James don't belong with men like me.

Women in general are a distraction I can't afford. Despite that, this one caught my attention and I wanted a closer look at the beauty. Days ago, when I first saw her, I was much too far away. The pictures I got are breathtaking, but they don't do her justice.

They didn't capture the jade hue of her eyes or the bronze hint of her silky skin. They didn't pick out the lighter parts of her waist-length blond hair which is almost golden, and they certainly didn't capture her perfect body.

Tonight, Miss Gwen St. James is wearing a little red halter-neck dress that shows off deep cleavage and long legs. A golden braid falls over her shoulder and those pouty red lips sparkle against the room light.

The entire ensemble makes her look like a cross between a 1950s pin-up girl and one of those models you see in makeup commercials. She has that bouncy and flirty vibe. But something is going on with her that's taken the bounce out of her step.

Something that's not me—who she doesn't know yet.

Distress wrinkles her pretty face as she sets her purse on the desk by the window.

She gazes out to the shadowy mass of trees for a few moments before her shoulders sag with the weight of someone who's carrying many burdens.

Like she's in trouble. I haven't received any new information to suggest so, but the knack to sense trouble was encoded in my DNA alongside my off-the-charts ability to spot microscopic details the average human would miss.

Gwen turns back to her bag, opens it, and digs around until she finds her phone. She dials a number and presses the phone to her ear.

"I'm just checking in," she says in a soft-spoken voice.

This is the first time I've heard her speak. She sounds exactly the way I imagined.

"Tomorrow," she breathes, running a weary hand over her face. "The bank will call me before the end of the day with their decision."

That sounds like money worries. At first glance, her

finances seemed like they were in order, but I could be wrong.

"I'll let you know," she promises, then hangs up and places the phone back in her bag.

With a sigh, she drags in a deep breath. "Positive thinking, Gwen, positive thinking," she mutters to her reflection. "If you don't find a way, no one will. And you don't have a choice."

That sounds like a sensible mantra for a person in serious shit.

With a shake of her head, she takes off her clothes. When her dress floats down to her feet, revealing the fleshy globes of her breasts and rose-dipped nipples, all thoughts fade from my mind.

Her tits bounce as she rolls her panties down her legs, and my mouth waters when I see her clean-shaven pussy.

Then she turns and gives me the perfect view of her ass.

I smile to myself at the triumph of seeing her naked and run my tongue over my bottom lip.

Gwen St. James is by far one of the most beautiful women I've ever seen.

I would love a little taste of her.

A little taste might not hurt me or my plans, but then again, it could.

Her lush ass jiggles as she strides into the en-suite, and my mind switches back into focus when I can't see her anymore.

It's time to leave before I make any more foolish mistakes.

Or indulgences.

I back away and walk through the door behind me,

which leads out to the back stairs of this old creepy-as-fuck house that belongs to Gwen's grandmother.

Even though it's part of the area many movies and TV shows have used in their production, the house doesn't look that much different from what you'd find in a horror film.

Back home in Boston, there are houses like this. This place has a different vibe, though. Maybe because it's me who's the malevolent spirit haunting the woman inside.

As if I was never there, I slip past her dog, a fluffy white Siberian Husky who doesn't notice me.

When I'm on the road, I glance back at the house, wondering what tomorrow will bring. I've been in Wilmington for the last two days following a major lead in my quest for revenge.

Last week, after six years of searching for the men responsible for taking me captive and killing Captain Davison, I got a breakthrough.

It revealed that Manolo Navarro, the leader of the Navarro Cartel, orchestrated the attack. Unfortunately, he died two weeks ago, but that's not going to stop me.

When people fuck with men like me, you simply dole out punishment for the sins of the father. My fucked-up mind devised an equally fucked-up plan to get the sweetest revenge and retribution.

That's what led me here on a mission to find Santiago Navarro's daughter, the secret heir to the cartel and the multibillion-dollar fortune that comes with it.

Santiago Navarro was the founder of the Navarro Cartel. When he died, Manolo took over. Except, it wasn't his right. Neither does the right belong to his son Diego, *his* heir, who thinks he'll be the next in leadership.

I've taken it upon myself to fix that.

There's just one small problem. Nobody knows who Santiago's daughter really is. The cartel king hid her identity so well not even his own can find her.

With all my skills, technological resources at my fingertips, and experience of gaining military intelligence, I haven't been able to find her either. But there's nothing hidden so deep that *I* can't find.

Time might be my enemy, but it's also my friend because men like me don't rest until we get what we want.

I've gotten closer than anyone else who could be looking for her just for finding out she could be living here in Wilmington.

My list has been narrowed to three potential women who could be the woman I'm looking for.

Gwen St. James is one of them.

With the plan of destruction I have in mind, the parts of me that are still human hope for her sake that she's nothing to do with them.

She represents life and living and I am still death.

Like Hades in his Underworld, my darkness would steal the light and life from her world.

Chapter Two

Gwen

The bank turned me down.

God... what the hell am I going to do?

Seriously, what am I really going to do?

I set my trembling hands down on the bar counter and reach for the glass of vodka tonic Duke just made me. This is my second one. *I think.*

The haze covering my mind is screwing with my awareness.

After I take a swig, the hot flush that flows from the top of my head to the soles of my feet suggests this is more like my third or fourth drink—*here.*

I'd already had a few too many before I walked through the large cedar doors of Duke's Bar and took my seat to join the host of patrons who practically live here.

Duke, the said owner, is serving a young couple who look like tourists, but when I glance at him, he gives me the same sympathetic smile most of the residents have been offering me over the last few days.

They think I'm grieving.

Last week, Gage, my ex-boyfriend, who I hadn't seen or spoken to in close to a year, washed up on the beach with bullet holes covering every inch of his body.

It was truly horrific and the biggest scandal to hit Wrightsville Beach for years.

Unfortunately for me, the last scandal to turn the town upside down was my mother's death fifteen years prior.

To this day, there are still hushed whispers of how Mom overdosed on heroin and was found dead in the church confessional with a bible in her hands.

My mother was already talked about because of her renowned fame as an international model turned fashion designer. When she died, the word spread far and wide about her tragic life and death and the eight-year-old fatherless daughter she left behind.

Because Gage and I were seeing each other for over a year, people have automatically assumed his death is another blow to my heart.

But it's not.

At least not the way they think.

I kept the truth about our breakup close to my heart. I couldn't bear to be the talk of the town like I had been since Mom's death and all the other series of unfortunate events that followed.

People don't know we broke up because I found Gage cheating on me on my birthday with two hookers in the bed we shared. He thought I was going to be away for most of the day visiting my grandmother at the nursing home.

People also don't know that I had to hire a private investigator to track him down when I found out he stole my entire life savings and my grandmother's by getting me to invest in some cock and bull business venture he set up.

Worst of all, they don't know that two days after he was found dead, Conrad Duncan, one of the most dangerous men in North Carolina, with ties to the Italian mob, paid me a visit, letting me know I owed him a hundred thousand dollars with interest.

Me.

Me, of all the people, who would never even owe Dru, my best friend, a favor.

I don't know how I didn't die when Conrad issued me a copy of the loan agreement I apparently took out with Gage early last year when we weren't even in contact and no one could find him. The fucking agreement had my grandmother's house and restaurant down as security.

When I protested, the asshole pulled a gun on me, along with a copy of my driver's license, and pointed to my signature alongside Gage's on the loan agreement, knowing full well I never signed or agreed to anything.

I may be a year out of college and inexperienced in the ways of the world, but I know you don't fuck with people like Conrad Duncan. Not when they hold you at gunpoint in your own home and leave you begging for your life.

All he wants is his money paid in full with an interest of seventy-five thousand on top because Gage missed a few payments and now he's dead.

If I don't pay what is owed by next Friday, Conrad will take my grandmother's

House, her restaurant, and me.

Me. He'll take me, too, and threatened to either sell me on the sex market or keep me for himself.

You hear about these sorts of bizarre things on TV shows or read about them in books.

Not many people consider it could actually happen to them in real life. I certainly didn't.

One word to the police or anyone I could potentially seek help from means death. Conrad threatened to kill the people I care about. Starting with Grams.

My soul shivers at the memory of him saying those words with his fingers digging into my throat and his dark hawk-eyes boring into me.

So, no, I'm not grieving for Gage in any shape or form.

If he weren't dead, I'd kill him myself.

I'm not even supposed to be in Wilmington, but that evil bastard has managed to screw me over from beyond the grave.

I had so many hopes and dreams for my career that just shattered when I found out just how sick Grams is. And, *God*, now I feel bad for selfishly thinking about myself when she sacrificed so much for me.

Everything is just fucked up in such a shitty way I don't know what to do.

Since I have no money and no means of getting anything close to a hundred and seventy-five grand, the bank was my last hope.

I take another swig of my drink, and my throat burns, unlike the last time, but the buzz that comes after numbs my mind, making the scathing discomfort worth it.

Duke returns to me, lowering his brushy brown brows, his eyes filling with concern. At six foot seven his height and bulky frame has always reminded me of one of those depictions of Paul Bunyan.

"How about I fix you a milkshake, like the ones your grandmother used to make?"

I shake my head. "No, I'm not in the mood for milkshake."

"But it always cheers you up." His eyes crinkle with a kind smile.

Bless his heart. He still thinks I'm six. Duke and his wife, Marybeth—the town's busybody who doesn't like me—are my grandmother's closest friends. She and my grandfather grew up with them in Charlotte. They moved down here to the coast after Duke and Grandpa got back from serving in the Vietnam war.

Duke and Marybeth never had kids, so they treated me like their own. Duke, not Marybeth. Definitely not when she found out I decided to follow in my mother's footsteps to design and sell sexy lingerie.

Now she refers to me as a Jezebel filled with the spirit of the devil. Basically on track to ending up just like my mother.

She might be right with that one, except I'm not as famous as Mom was.

And since Grams kept me out of the media after my mother's death, if I departed from this world tomorrow, I'd barely be remembered as Scarlet St. James' daughter.

"Could I have a tall glass of whiskey, please?" My request is much to Duke's dismay. I'm aware his offer of milkshake was a subtle way of telling me he's worried I'm drinking too much. The small sigh slipping from his lips is another giveaway.

"Gwen, maybe you should go home. I know this past week has been difficult for you, but I don't want to see you drown your sorrows in alcohol."

I want to ask him where I should drown my sorrows when I have so many, but I think better of it. Comments like that will lead to him offering to be my listening ear so I can talk about things I can't.

"I'll be okay, Duke. I promise." I give him a little smile, hoping he doesn't use those fatherly instincts he's so good at to discern through my lies. "I'm still shaken up. What happened to Gage was truly horrific." Better to play the game and let him think I'm distraught over Gage's death. Only hardcore liquor will get me through the rest of tonight, and I don't want him to stop me from drinking.

"Okay. Whiskey it is." He dips his head, then switches his attention from mine when someone walks up to the barstool next to me, filling my surroundings with a deep, musky scent that reminds me of the forest. "Ice-cold bottle of beer for you?" Duke asks, the tension leaving his face.

"Yes, please. And I'm impressed you remembered." The sexy, deep voice coming from the man next to me forces me to look at him.

When I do, my eyes lock on a deadly handsome face that would rival every heartthrob in *every* movie, romantic or otherwise, that I've ever seen. I'm pretty sure Hollywood definitely missed out on this guy. Then again, the serious military muscles bulging against his long-sleeved black T-shirt suggest you'd never find him acting in a romance movie, or even in an action one. Those muscles are far too definitive to be just for show.

"You're practically a regular now," Duke chimes. "Hope you're settling into the beach house okay."

"I definitely am."

"Glad to hear." Duke chuckles heartily and the handsome stranger returns his smile, revealing deep sexy dimples. "Not many people like being on the other side of the beach. They think it's too quiet."

"That's what makes it perfect for me."

Listening to the conversation, I quickly realize that Mr. Handsome is the new guy staying in Duke's old beach house. It's a ten-minute walk from my place. I'd heard Marybeth talking about him from the day he moved in, but of course, she being her, she forgot to mention that the man is drop-dead gorgeous.

"Good, good. One bottle of ice-cold beer coming right up." Duke dips his head and saunters away, but I'm still staring at the handsome stranger. And I can't look away.

I'm the last person who should stare at anyone, let alone a man like him. The glance I caught of myself on the way here revealed that I look like shit. My hair in its high bun looked like I'd just rolled out of a barn, and my eyes, which are normally a vibrant sea-green, were red from crying so much last night. I even had the blotchy skin to match.

Remembering how I look, I try once more to turn away, but I'm hooked all over again when a dark blond lock falls away from his slicked-back hair and he straightens up, showing off more of his body.

I'm normally good at guessing people's height, so I peg him to be around six feet four. As there's no wedding band on his ring finger—and no indentation to suggest he's taken it off—I think it's safe to say he's unmarried. But that's not always an absolute indicator; neither does it rule out a girlfriend.

Marybeth never mentioned a girlfriend or anything relationship-wise. Only that she was happy to sublet the beach house so early in the year and she hoped he would stay for a while.

I wonder what this guy does and what brings him to Wilmington. The oncoming spring has attracted a lot of surfers and those who love our beaches and scenic views, but I don't get the feeling that this guy came here to surf or sightsee.

And I'm just staring.

And *still* staring. It's no surprise when he looks at me, but what I'm not prepared for is to actually lock eyes on him face-to-face and realize just how good-looking he is.

Rich brown eyes gaze back at me with open fascination, along with a spark of something deliciously dark that instantly makes me think of hot, sinful things.

Hot, sinful things that remind me how long it's been since I was intimate with anyone. Those hot, sinful things are the sort I definitely shouldn't be thinking about in regards to a complete stranger, and I shouldn't be wondering if that's how he looks when he's having sex.

The thought of having sex with a man like him sends a jolt of desire straight to my pussy and instantly I'm wet.

When my handsome stranger's eyes darken, I have the mortifying thought that he can read my mind, and even though it's entirely ridiculous, I think he knows I'm wet, too.

Embarrassed, I look away quickly, breathe slowly so my heart will stop hammering in my chest and finish the last of my drink. As I'm not normally like this, I can only assume the host of drinks I've had over the last few hours must be doing a number on my head and it's possible I'm drunk.

"Don't tell me you're drinking by yourself." The low timbre of his rusty baritone draws me back to him like a fish attracted to irresistible bait.

I'm looking at him again, but this time wondering if he's talking to me. That last sip of drink didn't help either, because my skin feels hotter than before.

"Me?" I say in a breathy voice, actually pointing to myself.

The corners of his sensual lips slide into a grin, and I resist the urge to drool like a dog hungry for a bone.

"I'm looking at you, Malyshka."

Malyshka?

Whatever that means sounds exotic and mysterious. I also detected the very slight undertone of an accent, but I'm not sure what it is since he mostly sounds American.

Deciding he's definitely talking to me and I'd look like some loser if I didn't answer, I think of something sensible to say.

"It's been one of those days." I attempt a polite smile.

"Ah, I see. Well, if it helps, things are never as bad as they seem at first."

It doesn't help to hear that given my situation is dire on many levels, but it's nice to listen to his sexy voice. It's a momentary distraction I'm soaking up like a sponge.

"You sound wise." I straighten, resting my hands back on the counter.

"I've been told I know a thing or two." He winks at me and lines of heat race over my skin.

Duke returns with our drinks and sets them before us.

He smiles at our new friend, but when he looks at me, he shakes his head.

"That's your last one." He tried to say that under his breath, but as nothing about Duke is quiet, my handsome stranger *and* everyone else at the bar heard him.

I don't answer Duke, but he leaves us knowing I got the message. It's times like these when it completely sucks beyond measure to be here.

I was so happy when I went to UCLA, but I dare not think of those days for fear of feeling bad about Grams again.

"Never figure you for a whiskey drinker," lulls that voice again. I look back at my handsome stranger, who is tipping his beer bottle to his lips while staring at me beneath hooded eyes.

"What did you think my drink would be?" I'm interested to know.

He takes a sip of his beer and sets the bottle down. "A sexy cocktail."

I stare back, completely enthralled, and realize it can't just be me who feels that intense pull of attraction.

"A sexy cocktail?"

"Yeah, something like..." He thinks for a moment and gives me a wicked smile. "A margarita. Or Sex on the Beach."

I'm not sure which woman could hear this man say the words *sex on the beach* and not think of having sex on the beach with *him*.

I'm about to answer when Hazel, Duke's skanky barmaid, comes up to us and steals Mr. Handsome's attention away from me.

Dressed in a low-cut tank top which shows off the depth

of her cleavage and surgically enhanced breasts, she looks like she'd be more at home in Hooters.

She tosses her dark tresses over her shoulders and flashes my handsome stranger a seductive smile.

I went to school with Hazel, so I'm well versed in that smile. She was born with it. That smile is the same one she uses to lure many men away from their wives and girlfriends, and it looks like she's got her eyes set on our newcomer.

"I just thought you should know I finish in an hour, if you want to hang out," she coos in her deep Southern accent most men find sexy.

I don't have that accent even though Grams does.

"I'll bear that in mind."

"You should." She pushes out her breasts. "I'm the girl who will definitely show you a great time."

Great. What a fucking bitch.

Feeling defeated, I grab my whiskey and take a few gulps. The alcohol gets to my brain quicker this time, and I feel a cheerful buzz wash over me, making me feel like I could fly. My mind numbs, and I no longer remember how terrified I am of Conrad and his threats.

But rage washes through me when I look at Hazel flirting her ass off with my handsome stranger. She's always done shit like this, but this time, I'm so infuriated I want to rip the hair off her head and claw out her eyes as she bats her lashes at Mr. Handsome.

"See you in an hour, handsome." She gives him a little wave, issues me a filthy look, then walks away with her hips swaying as if she's got a tune stuck in her head.

I look back at him, watching him looking at her walk away, and I wonder if he will hook up with her in an hour.

There are very few men who have turned Hazel down. He's probably thinking about her promise to give him a good time.

Wait a minute... what am I thinking? I saw him first. Why the hell would I let him go off with her when I want him?

I can almost feel those big strong hands running over my skin and those lips kissing away my worries as he pounds into me.

"I'm available now?" I hear myself say. At least I think the words are coming from me.

"Excuse me?" He looks at me, and I stare back at him.

"I'm available now." I'm actually aware this time that I'm speaking, and what I'm saying feels like the perfect thing to say.

"Available for what exactly?" He rivets his gaze to mine.

"I want to fuck you." The words fall out of my mouth and I know I shouldn't have said that out loud.

He glances at my whiskey glass and leans closer. "That's awfully tempting, but out of principle, I don't fuck drunk women I meet at bars."

As the words fall from his lips, my stomach plummets, and the sinking feeling of raw humiliation pulls me under like a tidal wave.

At first, I'm stunned and I don't know what to say. Then pride kicks in and pushes me to save myself.

"I'm not drunk." My voice is barely a whisper.

He gives me a full smile and nods. "Yes, you are, sweetheart. So, maybe next time. That way, you'll remember being with me, Malyshka."

With another wink, he turns and walks away, leaving me

staring after him while his potent words rattle around in my mind.

What just happened?

What the hell did I just do?

Did I seriously proposition a stranger at the bar for sex, then get turned down?

But not?

Oh my God.

Feeling utterly disgusted with myself, I grab my drink again and down the rest.

My head spins, then I have no idea what happens next.

Chapter Three

Gwen

Bright lights beam down on my face, making me screw my eyes together tighter.

My head…

God, it hurts like someone hit me with a sledgehammer.

Maybe they did.

"Gwen, wake up." That's Dru, but she sounds like she's far, far away.

Where am I?

The thought brings my awareness to the forefront of my mind, and when I manage to prize my eyes open, I see Dru is actually standing right next to me.

The bright blue of her camisole top is way too intense for me, so I close my eyes again.

On my next attempt to look at her, her tall willowy frame expands and shrinks to a blue blob as if I'm looking at her through one of those crazy mirrors at the carnival. It takes a moment before my eyes adjust and she looks like the normal fashionable Dru I know.

And I see that I'm downstairs in my living room.

At *my* house.

I'm home, but I have no idea how I got here. The throbbing in my head is screwing with my mind's attempts to remember.

"Dru," I mumble, my voice sounding hoarse and thick.

"Gwen." She dips her dark head as she looks me over, and the blunt edges of her long bob brush over her shoulders. "Are you okay? I was so worried. I've been calling you for eons." Her bright blue eyes bore into me, amplified by the worry she speaks of.

She rests her hands at her sides and straightens.

When I sit up and realize my grandmother's tartan blanket is draped over my body and I'm naked underneath it, I pull in a sharp gasp.

"What the hell?" I shriek, dragging the blanket closer. "I'm naked."

"Sweetie, you just noticed that?" Dru winces and folds her arms. "What the hell happened to you? After we spoke, I thought you'd come back here, but you didn't."

"I...couldn't." I sigh and bring a hand to my head as the catalyst that pushed me into this debacle enters my mind.

The bank.

The loan I hoped to get from them.

The loan I didn't get from them.

Conrad and his threats.

Jesus. It's a wonder my head hasn't imploded.

I vaguely remember heading to Duke's Bar after I spoke to Dru, but nothing more.

Dru is more than a best friend to me. We grew up together from birth, so she's family. The same way I couldn't keep the truth about Gage from her, I had to tell her about the situation with Conrad.

I called her straight after the bank informed me of their decision, but I was crying so much, most of that conversation probably sounded like muffles.

"You look like you went on a college bender."

"I think it was a lot worse than that." I'm not sure if it's sufficient to tell her I got wasted. *Wasted* is too meagre a word to describe what I did. It was like I was on some self-destruct mission.

"Do you remember what happened?" Dru presses her lips together.

"No. How long have you been here?"

"Five minutes tops. I was trying to wake you."

"Please tell me my car isn't parked outside." I pray to God I didn't drive home in whatever state I was in. Not only would that have been completely irresponsible, dangerous, and so unlike me, but the last thing I want is trouble with the police or anyone who saw me driving under the influence.

"It's not parked outside."

Well, at least that might be good news. It means my car could still be at the restaurant. It's a few minutes away from Duke's. At least I had the good sense to walk there after my first two cans of beer.

But if my car is at Duke's, that still begs the question of how I got home.

"I don't think you should go to the restaurant today."

"I have to. It's Friday, right?"

"It is, but friend to friend, you look like shit."

"Oh, God." Knowing she's right, I shake my head in disgust. "I have to go in, regardless. There's the stock take and the new orders to do."

I have to do it. If I don't, it will mean I have to get Gilman, the restaurant's manager, to work extra hours, and I can't afford to pay anyone any extra anything.

I can't afford anything now, tomorrow, or in the future.

"Dru, I have to find another way to get that money."

She huffs. "It's tearing me up that you can't tell Sheriff Donovan what's going on."

Under normal circumstances, going to the police would be the best thing to do. Just not in this case. Not with a man like Conrad Duncan. You would need to have serious ammunition to go up against him and put him behind bars. Even then, it might not be enough.

"I know, but I can't take that risk and put myself and Grams in that sort of danger. For all we know, he killed Gage."

"I thought about that." Her skin pales. "Do you think he did?"

"I don't know, but why wouldn't he if Gage wasn't paying the loan?" My voice quivers and I think of the possibility. "That asshole probably did kill Gage, then came after me to get the rest of the money."

It's clear I'm terrified, but I'm not sure if she knows just how much.

Maybe it's because I've had to be strong all my life and she thinks I can just switch over to being that person she's used to. I might be able to if I still had Grams to be my backbone. Grams was the person who picked me up when I fell down. Now she can't.

These days, Grams can just about remember who I am. The doctors warned that as her dementia gets worse, those memories will fade with her.

That, by itself, is shattering my heart.

"Okay let's not think about that too much." She composes herself with a quick breath and smiles. "I have some ideas and good news."

"*Good* news?" My eyes snap wide at the prospect of such a thing.

"Good-ish. Yesterday, after you called, I got down to business and looked over the plans we have for the new line." Her face brightens with mischief because the new line was her idea.

It's called 'Welcome to the Dungeon', and the line is inspired by the raunchy type of lingerie you'd expect to wear in a sex dungeon.

After college, when we both returned to Wilmington, we went into business together and set up Brash, our online lingerie company. I design and create with a small team of ten people who follow my lead, but Dru gets the word out about the business.

With her marketing and advertising degree from Brown University, she's the ideas girl of our duo, but she was always my MacGyver.

"What did you do?" I bring my hands together hoping like hell she came up with something that can help me, but something that's not too crazy.

"Your best friend just made twenty-one thousand dollars and secured another twenty grand."

I suck in a sharp breath. "What?" How the hell did she do that? "Just last night?"

"Yeah, just last night." She nods with enthusiasm. "It was a long shot, but I took it. And there's more so please don't get mad. I figured desperate times called for desperate measures."

"Why would I be mad? That's over forty grand." And more than what I did. It's a drop in the well compared to the money I need, but I'm deciding to see it as my glass is half full.

"Well, I think when you find out what I did, you might be a tad pissed off." She bites the inside of her lip, and I just know she's probably going to be right.

After twenty-three years of knowing this girl, I'm used to her shenanigans.

"What did you do, Dru?"

She releases a little sigh and flutters long, thick lashes at me. "As our customers are already freaky, frisky, and psyched up about the new line, I thought we could pair our lingerie with other stuff. A.K.A sex toys."

If I wasn't pale before, I am now. "You what?"

"You heard me and I think it was a good call. I took the reins and partnered with Mistress Layla's Wild Nights. She's new and looking for business. I agreed to give her thirty percent on every sale. Last night, I sent out an email to the subscribers on our mailing list, and we got a thousand sales and five hundred preorders on the lingerie line itself."

I stare back at her in disbelief. I want to be mad. But I can't be. The news is phenomenal and way more than we've ever made on any of our launches.

We've been in business for nearly two years and our average earnings is twenty grand a month, half of which is deducted for expenses and the wages we pay our staff. So, her overnight success is a tremendous deal.

Screw everyone—*Marybeth*—to Hell who thinks that I'm the devil or that I've gone over to the dark side.

Where are those who judge me when I need them?

Not here, or anywhere.

"That is amazing, Dru. Oh my God. Thank you so much."

"It's nothing."

"It's not nothing, and please take your cut."

She laughs. "No, the whole thing is yours. Now we just have to figure out how to get the rest."

We.

Hearing her say that simple word makes me feel like I'm not alone. I've never been when it came to her. She's always had my back, and I've had hers.

That's the kind of friends we are. It's just that on this occasion, I feel so very foolish for the way I trusted Gage.

I'm normally so perceptive and careful. I should have spotted his deceit and lies from a mile away. But he had me wrapped around his finger so tightly I couldn't see for shit.

I thought I knew him. I thought I loved him at one point but I was a fool.

Even now, I'm still trying to figure out where I went wrong.

Where did I make that left turn and allow him to blindside me?

"I'm not sure what to do about the rest." The only money I have is what I put aside for my grandmother's medical treatment.

I get an income from the restaurant, but it varies every

month depending on how well we do. That was one reason I didn't get the loan.

"I might have an idea for that, but I'm really not sure if it will work."

"I'm open to anything at this point." Beggars can't be choosy.

"Great, because I was pre-approved for a loan of a hundred and forty thousand."

"Oh, my God. What? You got a loan?" I don't know how, but I stand. At first, I'm ecstatic that she would think to get a loan for me, but then my senses return, and I realize why she's doing it, so I shake my head. "No, wait. I can't let you do that."

"Gwen, stop it. This is not up for discussion. I'm going to do it. The loan is pre-approved. As I have a full-time job at the marketing agency, I thought I'd apply and see what happens."

Being self-employed without a steady income and my primary source of income being tied to my grandmother's care was the other reason the bank turned me down.

"I just need a homeowner to stand guarantor before I can go on to the assessment stage." Dru rubs her hands together. "You have the power of attorney over your grandmother, so that gives you access to this house. You would do the same thing if you'd gotten the loan from the bank, but we're basically applying for the loan together." She looks more hopeful than I feel.

"You're acting like you owe me again."

"And you're acting like I don't, when we both know I do."

She holds my gaze, and pain fills her eyes. I don't have to ask what she's thinking about; I always know.

It's her parents and the accident that took their lives when she was fourteen.

After losing my mother, I knew how she felt, but I didn't see my mother die.

She saw her mother take her final breath.

With no hesitation, my grandparents took her in and cared for her when her aunt, the only family she had, rejected her, wanting her to live in social care.

That's why Dru believes she owes me.

"Gwen, please don't argue with me. This is a really fucked-up situation. We don't know what Conrad is capable of, and I'm sure we don't *want* to know."

"No, we really don't." I lower my voice.

"Exactly. So, if I get this loan, it fixes the problem, and hopefully, you'll never have to see Conrad again."

"It's a lot to ask of you."

"But you didn't ask." She gives me a bright smile. "I offered. There's a big fat difference. And I figured with how well we're doing, there should be no problem paying everything back in a few months."

I nod with determination. "I promise I will work so damn hard to pay it off. And get us to our bigger goal."

"The bigger goal would be great. I'm so ready to leave this town behind."

"Me too."

That damn goal to have our own store in a promising city like New York or L.A. was what got me in trouble in the first place with Gage. He lured me in when he said he had a friend who could get us a deal for a store on Santa Monica Blvd. if I invested the money to refurbish the place.

To scam me out of everything I owned, the asshole even went as far as taking me to the site to show me the store, then, when we returned, he set up Zoom calls with the contractors' team leader for progress reports and all sorts of shit I believed.

"One thing at a time," Dru says, pulling me from my sordid thoughts before I go down the river of doom again.

"Thank you so much. This means everything to me."

"Thank me later. We have forms to fill out and various other things. If you could stay back from the restaurant today, that would be great, so we can get started on the pre-orders."

"I will absolutely sort something out." Maybe I can go later tonight. "What is—"

My voice cuts when the thud of heavy footsteps sounds on the floor above us. It's coming from my bedroom.

"Is someone here?" Dru rasps, keeping her voice low.

"No." I shake my head, but we hear the sound again, and that definitely

suggests someone *is* here.

This time, the sound is louder and followed by the patter of soft dog feet. That

would be Sebastian.

Given the circumstances with me owing money to a dangerous loan shark, Dru and I both start for the door when the footsteps come down the stairs. But we freeze, when a shirtless god-like man descends like he's walking straight out of a fantasy.

The instant I see him, my jaw drops, and I remember him as the seriously hot guy from Duke's Bar.

The seriously hot guy I propositioned at the bar who told me he didn't fuck drunk women.

He's in my home, half naked and exceeding the fantasy I conjured when I first saw him.

As he locks his gaze on to me with those sharp eyes, I look from his face to his hard muscles and then the tattoo on his left pec of what looks like a leviathan dragon with a sword running through it.

My eyes flick back up to his, and time stands still for what feels like eons.

When he reaches the bottom of the stairs, Sebastian scurries past him and runs onto the floorboards, snapping me out of my daze.

"Ladies." Mr. Handsome dips his head as if this is completely normal and shrugs into the T-shirt he was wearing last night. I just noticed it dangling from his hands.

Sebastian tracks back to him, and he crouches down, speaking what sounds like Russian words.

To my surprise, Sebastian sits obediently and puts out his paw, which Mr. Handsome strokes before standing.

"I've fed the dog and took him for a walk," Mr. Handsome says, then looks back at me, raking his gaze over my body. Those dark eyes send scandalous shivers through me. "See you around, Malyshka."

With a wink, he leaves the room, and I watch him with my jaw still hanging as he continues to the front door and departs.

When the door swings shut behind him, I wonder if I'm dreaming.

I must be, right?

Right?

It's not until Dru tugs hard on my arm that I remember she's here, and I realize this is no dream.

"Gwen, who the hell was the hot guy?" Dru blurts.

I open my mouth to answer, but I don't know what to say.

Other than meeting Mr. Handsome at the bar and having that little embarrassing exchange, I have no idea who he is. Or what I did with him last night.

I don't remember anything.

Chapter Four

Malik

I can still feel the intensity of Gwen's eyes boring into me as I jump into my truck and drive away.

Last night, I parked on the road behind the house like I did on previous occasions. In a town full of busy bodies, it's best to stay as inconspicuous as possible.

I turn the corner and head down to the dusty road that will take me to the beach house, but those eyes that remind me so much of the sea continue following me.

I feel them on my skin and in my mind.

Judging from how Miss Gwen St. James looked at me and the devastating shock on her pretty face, I'm guessing she probably remembers nothing about last night. Maybe it's best.

I'm not sure if I was thinking with my head or my dick when I decided it was a good idea to cross the line and take her home.

Admittedly, I'd crossed that line well before that when I talked to her in the bar. When I walked through the doors, I instantly saw her sitting by herself, and like the moth to an open flame, I couldn't resist.

My mind will do all sorts of mental acrobatics to tell me my actions were part and parcel of my mission. I might even convince myself that I was just sowing seeds to get possible information, but my dick tells me otherwise.

My dick remembers her telling me she wanted to fuck me.

Those words have been ringing through my mind on repeat right from the moment she spoke them.

They bewitched me with some kind of magic and I decided I couldn't leave her at the bar as I watched her gulp down the rest of her whiskey and lose her mind.

When she got on top of the counter, started singing-off key, stripped down to her bra and panties, then offer sex to two guys who didn't say no, I stepped in.

Not because I'm one of the good guys. No. I can't state any claim to being good.

I stepped in because there was no motherfucking way I was going to let them have what I so chivalrously declined.

Duke was going to take her home, but I offered to do it.

When I got her there, the craziness really began, and Miss Gwen St. James started telling me about her passion for designing lingerie while she stripped completely naked.

That was the second time I'd been in the presence of the woman in all her goddess glory and didn't touch her decadent body the way I wanted to.

After straddling me with her tits bouncing in my face, she insisted on sleeping on her sofa.

While I was hoping she'd be the kind of drunk who spills all her secrets and hopefully confirm being Santiago's daughter, nothing of the sort happened.

Nothing else happened either. Now I'm hard as fuck with the memory of her body engraved in my mind.

I'm not going to lie to myself; I want to fuck her.

Seeing her again just now wrapped in that blanket made me want to unwrap her and take her up on her drunken offer to fuck.

Even with her friend there, I wanted to bend her over the table and fuck her brains out. It took everything in me last night to keep my distance. That's why I stayed upstairs.

Now I'm reconfiguring my mind and setting myself back on track to where I need to be.

So far, all I know is Gwen *could* be Santiago's daughter, which would make her my ticket to getting what I want. That's what I need to remember.

I continue down the road for another ten minutes, then verge onto the path that will take me down to the beach house.

When I told Duke the place was perfect, I meant it. The beach house is far away from everyone and near the caves. It's essentially private. As the weather is also temperamental, I still have some time before the surfers, sailors, and fishermen populate the rest of the beach.

Like any sailor, I love being at the sea. Wrightsville Beach is perfect for an ex-Navy man like me, but as I hope to wrap up my mission sooner rather than later I don't have time to explore.

I pull up at the two-story beach house minutes later and jump out of my truck.

Sand and gravel crunch beneath my boots as I walk up to the door, which is already open. That means Zakh, my brother, has been out early.

I'm more than grateful he agreed to accompany me on this trip. He's my best chance of success.

Although I could track my assailants back to the Navarro Cartel and found out Santiago had a daughter living here in Wilmington from an email I hacked, the way my brother works is unique. I don't know anyone—not even me—who can hack a system the way he can.

I was an intelligence analyst and cryptologist in the Navy, but Zakh is a world-class hacker with skills no one has ever seen or dreamed of.

It was he who narrowed the possibilities down to Gwen and the other two women.

The email correspondence I found had all sorts of encryptions, but I got through them. Attached to the message was a copy of Santiago's revised will labelled exactly that and stating that his daughter should be the sole beneficiary of everything he owns. It then went on to list his assets.

The body of the email stated that if and when he died her name and address in Wilmington would be forwarded to them.

That's all it said. It was plenty to set me on my path but still not enough information.

Neither Zakh nor I could establish who the message was sent to.

When we tracked the IP address it went to a remote location that was probably hidden with more encryption at the time of receipt so it couldn't be tracked.

I can only assume that something must have happened to

the person who received the message, and no one else besides Zakh and me have seen the email Santiago sent. The Navarros are aware of his daughter's existence and of the will change but as far as I know none of them have ever been seen in Wilmington looking for her.

According to the will's provisions they would have definitely wanted to find her if they knew she was here. That snip bit of being in Wilmington was however in the email not the will itself. Another clever device of the cartel king.

The fact that we couldn't find more than what we did showed the lengths Santiago went through to keep his daughter off everybody's radar.

It was clear that as much as he'd left provisions for her to inherit everything, he knew the danger she'd be in if people knew who she was and he wasn't around to protect her.

I also thought that maybe he didn't want her to be part of that life.

Hiding her away here in this quiet town makes me believe it even more.

Wilmington is the last place anyone would look for the long-lost daughter of a Mexican cartel king. Of course that's if she's still here.

I hope for my sake she is.

When I walk inside the house, I hear Zakh talking in the living room. He seems to be on the phone.

I peek in and see I'm right. He's sitting on the small black leather sofa with his phone in his hand. The mellow voice speaking from it belongs to his wife, Lorelai. I can also hear the sweet chortles of Liberty, my nine-month-old niece.

I still can't get used to my brother having a wife and

child, but family life suits him. He seems to be a better man for it.

As he's on FaceTime, I don't say anything, but I meet the peeved-off expression he greets me with and smirk.

That look is because I was away all night. And because of my fascination with Gwen.

"Baby, I gotta go. Looks like Malik's finished thinking with his dick." Sarcasm ripples from his voice as he shakes his head at me.

"Hey, little ears are listening." Lorelai laughs.

"Just sing her a lullaby and she'll forget. Call you later."

"Say bye-bye to daddy," Lorelai says in a sing-song voice, then she and Liberty start with their usual ritual of insufferable cute kiddy sounds I've had to endure since being here.

Zakh hangs up moments after and zeroes in on me.

"And what time do you call this?" Zakh locks his eyes on mine when I sit opposite him and the coffee table, which has documents scattered all over it.

"Sorry, *Father*," I taunt, using my best rendition of our father's voice.

"Father wouldn't give you the courtesy of a question; he'd most likely shoot off your dick if he thought it was getting in the way of your common sense."

I smirk again. "Yeah, he most likely would have."

We do this sometimes—talk about Father as if he's still alive.

Cold silence and the dullness of grief pass between us for a few seconds.

Grief not just for losing our father, but for our Uncle Leif, too.

Because of the savage plot orchestrated by our mother

and brother, Viktor, to get the Volkova empire, both Father and Leif were murdered.

They're all dead now. All that remains of the Volkova line is Zakh, our older brother Desmier, and me.

Father and Leif's death took its toll on us in different ways, but for me, I remember how they saved me in my darkest hour in Kazakhstan. Neither stopped until they found me and brought me back from the abyss of Hell.

I always feel like shit that I wasn't able to do anything to save them in return.

"I'm not saying you can't have fun." Zakh changes the subject back to Gwen. "But we're not here for fun. You can have fun later when we're done."

"I know. Believe me you don't have to remind me." I straighten. "I made use of my time and looked around Gwen's house. I didn't find anything but at least I got to review the place and make some tweaks to what I'd already set up."

The other night when I was there, I bugged the place and the phones. Zakh did the same at the other women's homes. We figured with Manolo's death, there might be some conversations about him. Just because the Navarros don't know where Santiago's daughter is it doesn't mean she won't be aware of them.

Unfortunately, there has been no discussion of any of them yet.

Our problem is, we're doing things the old-fashioned way and being too clean-cut. Almost like cops.

"Is that what you did all night?" Zakh raises a brow.

I give him a wicked grin. "She needed some help. Don't worry, brother, consider it an ice breaker if I need it." Last night was one hell of an icebreaker, if I'm calling it that, but on a serious note, Gwen knows me now, and I can use that to my advantage if I need to.

"Alright, well, you might need it because we have a problem."

Fuck. Things are already sketchy as hell. Problems are the last thing I need.

"What happened?"

"Manolo's funeral is next Thursday. The lawyers are going to transfer all the Navarro assets to Diego the day after. That means he'll take charge of the cartel as well."

I grit my teeth and ball my fists. Time was already a motherfucker, but this news places the clock right over my head.

Diego is set to become the next cartel king.

If I fail here, he will be.

Right now, because the legal heir is unknown and unable to be located the board of directors of Santiago's pharmaceutical company have the real control over everything including the cartel. They act as Santiago's executors. That limits control to a degree because they choose who runs the company and the cartel, but I'm sure they were under some influence by Manolo and Diego because they are Santiago's family. Having the real heir eradicates that and takes away all control from everyone.

"Damn it." I bite the inside of my lip. "We have to step things up."

"I know, and with that said, you'll be glad to hear I've eliminated Daisy Shaw."

She's one of the women on our list.

"Really?"

"Yeah, her father is the town priest the residents here believe is a prophet. He paid off Daisy's mother to keep her quiet."

Jesus. That makes me wonder what other sordid secrets are floating around this town.

"So, it's down to Gwen and Allyson."

Zakh nods.

Gwen is on the list because Zakh found an old picture of Santiago with Gwen's mother back when she was a model. The picture was taken on the beach. Allyson is there because Zakh found multiple footage of Santiago at her mother's house.

Both women had daughters who are roughly about the same age and have no fathers present on their birth certificates or any other records.

"Do you have any other ideas?" Zakh asks.

"Give me a few days."

I know what I have is essentially a very long shot because we could be wrong about both Gwen and Allyson, but it's a risk I'm going to take.

Since Zakh and I have been here, we've investigated each woman; the only thing I can do next is get close enough to them to see things I can't find by digging around or investigating.

"This mustn't get messy, Malik."

By messy he's warning me not to hone in on the ruthlessness known to men in our world that would tell me to take the two women, test them both to see which is Santiago's daughter, then dispose of the one I don't need.

Although I'm not averse to the idea of taking them, I'm

not that fucked-up yet to become the psycho who would kill the one I don't need.

"Don't worry. Whatever I do won't leave a mess anyone can track back to us."

"Better not." He reaches for a document on the table and slides it over to me. It's a printout of a police report. "Here's something you need to know about your girl, Gwen."

"What's this for?"

"Her ex was the guy who washed up on the beach last week."

Woah. I never expected to hear that. Also, Miss Gwen St. James didn't exactly look like she was grieving. Or maybe propositioning me for sex was her way of doing it.

"His name is Gage Miller. I did a check on him; he is one twisted motherfucker. It looks like he scammed his last scam. Gwen was questioned by the cops because she was his girlfriend. This report states she hadn't seen him in close to a year, but as the cops have nothing, they're keeping their eye on her and a few others."

"Meaning we have to be extra careful," I fill in.

"Exactly. Whatever we do next, we have to tread softly. I would prefer if we continued to keep up the appearance of being here on vacation."

"Believe me, that's exactly what I'm doing."

"Alright." He stands. "I'm going to get food. I'll be back in an hour, then we'll work."

"Sure thing."

He leaves. When the front door clicks shut, I gaze out through the sliding glass doors at the bright blue sea before me, allowing my thoughts to process and reconfigure my plans.

Failure is not an option for me.

I've come too far to entertain the possibility of such a thing.

I won't do it now that I know the most crippling way to punish my enemies the same way they did to me.

That attack that put me down like a dog was the criminal underworld crossing over into the vanilla life when I saw something, or rather some*one*, doing business I shouldn't have seen.

Coincidence was at work when I happened to run into Barabbas Jones, a black-market dealer, in a coffee shop in Uzbekistan. But nobody simply runs into a man like Barabbas Jones, who usually stays off the grid. When he saw me, he knew who I was straightaway, then he all but fled the scene.

He didn't recognize me for being a member of the US Navy.

He recognized me as a Volkova, the men in the Knights, one of the most powerful secret societies on earth who run their own Bratva Brotherhood—the Komarovski.

Barabbas Jones works with the Camorra, who are known enemies to most, including our family and anyone in the Bratva. So, the motherfucker knew I would investigate his presence, as he wasn't supposed to have allies in Uzbekistan.

That's exactly what I did, but I didn't get very far.

The attack happened two days later. Jim, who had no idea I was investigating Barabbas, lost his life, then they took me captive for two weeks shy of a year.

All that time, I never had a clue who my captors were, but I knew my captivity had something to do with seeing Barabbas. Someone didn't want me investigating the way only a Knight could, or drawing attention to whatever it was he was up to.

For the last six years, I've tried to track him, hoping to discover who took me. That breakthrough came last week when I intercepted his phone call to Diego.

On that call, I learned what happened to me as Diego assured him that his father's passing wouldn't affect their alliance. He assured him that everything would stand the same way it did when his father removed me as a threat six years ago.

That's how I found out Manolo was responsible for the attack.

I hold Diego equally responsible, but death is too good for him. So is life.

The Navarros have one of the biggest cartels in Mexico, but their greatest asset is their pharmaceutical company based in L.A.

Weeks before Manolo's death, they got FDA approval for a pain-reliever drug they've been using to create a new street drug on the underground the wealthy are paying millions for.

I'm not going to allow him to get the cartel and the billion-dollar pharmaceutical company, because *I* want it.

Taking the Navarro empire and adding it to my own in the Bratva alliance is the only thing that feels like justice to me for what Manolo Navarro did.

Conquering their empire is also the only thing that will make them all truly suffer.

But the only way for me to take it all is if I marry Santiago Navarro's daughter.

That's why I'm looking for her.

Chapter Five

Gwen

"Are you seriously going to shove this juicy news under the rug and not talk about it?" Dru gives me a wide-eyed glare. "At least the man was seriously hot. Like, seriously."

Dru and I are enjoying a late lunch on the roof terrace of the restaurant. We're sitting around one of the wooden bench tables at the far end, which has a perfect view of the pier and the sailboats coming in.

Ignoring her comments and question, I take a sip of my coffee. Definitely not the best choice of beverage to calm my nerves, but I need it to help me stay awake and focused.

I'm also hoping that maybe, just maybe, the extra dose of caffeine will jog my memory. Because I still can't remember anything from last night past Mr. Handsome walking away from me after my embarrassing rejection.

And I don't know how he ended up in my house.

"Dru, please. There's nothing more to talk about." The more I talk, the worse I feel about my new debacle with Wrightsville Beach's newest hunk..

My skin is still on fire even though the cool sea breeze is wrapping around me like a blanket.

It's just gone two. After Mr. Handsome left this morning, Dru made me tell her the stuff I could remember, which was hardly anything.

After we finished the paperwork for the loan, I got a little break from her when she dropped it off at the bank.

Now we're here again. We're supposed to be finalizing the work schedule for the designs, so the people who ordered the new lingerie line receive their items on time, but she still wants to talk about him. And it looks like she's not going to let it go.

"Did you see those abs?"

"Yes, I did see those abs." Since I woke up naked, I've been trying to remember what else I might have seen.

Mr. Handsome said I would remember being with him. But seeing as I don't, does that mean we did nothing?

Would I seriously have a guy like that in my house and not do *anything*?

I don't know, and I'm not sure if I want to.

What I do know is that I went college-wild and whatever I did before I got home was bad, bad, *bad*, because I got a mouthful from Duke when I arrived at the restaurant earlier.

He was already here waiting for me, looking like he was going to blow a fuse and steam would pour out of his ears.

He was supposed to come by anyway because we get our rum supply from him, and he was fulfilling an order.

I barely walked through the door when he started

chewing me out for my behavior at the bar. Duke has never spoken to me like that before. Probably because I've never given him any reason to.

The whole thing just made me feel more fucked up than I already am.

"Gwen, come on. This is ridiculous. You're not even trying to remember." Dru throws her hands up.

"Because we have more important things to worry about. Like fulfilling these orders. I also have to do the stock take."

"I told you I would help with that if we got done on time."

"Yes, but at this rate, we're not going to get anything done."

She pouts and pretends to be upset. "This is unfair. You spend the night with a seriously hot guy, and you won't even try to remember the juicy parts to tell me."

"How is that unfair? I could have had sex with this guy, and I don't even know his name." God, I sound like a slut.

"Plenty of people, including me, have done that." She waves perfectly manicured fingernails in front of me, brushing off the notion as if it's nothing.

"But that's completely not me. I just hope he leaves town soon."

She rolls her eyes at me. "That man is not leaving anytime soon. If he were, he would have rented a hotel room not a beach house. Plus, I hear he has a brother staying with him who is equally hot. So, the way I see it, there's one guy for you and one for me."

She's driving me crazy.

"*There* you are," comes a haggard drawl from behind me

that sounds like a bad version of Blanche Dubois from a Streetcar Named Desire.

I don't have to turn my head to know it's Marybeth.

She stomps up to the table, wrinkles her already wrinkled face at me, and sets her hands on her bony hips.

When I was little, I thought she looked a lot like Olive Oyl from *Popeye*. I still think so. Not only does Marybeth have the same hairstyle, she wears similar clothes, too. The only difference is she has the temperament of a witch from hell.

"Can I help you, Marybeth?" I put on my best business voice and act like I don't know this is part two of my chew-out session. This is one of the wonderful joys of living in a town with people who knew you as a child. They always see you as one.

"I heard about how you embarrassed yourself last night. I didn't think you could sink any lower, but you proved me wrong."

Since Grams went to the nursing home, Marybeth has taken every opportunity to criticize me. She's the kind of person who will kick you right into an early grave and carry extra dirt in her purse to ensure you're buried properly.

"I already apologized to Duke. And I am sorry for the way I behaved."

"Your sorry means nothing to me. Who the hell thinks it's okay to strip practically naked and dance on the counter of a bar, then ask men for sex when their ex was murdered a week ago?" Her eyes blaze, and Dru's widens even more.

I never told my friend about those parts of my evening.

"Everyone has their ways of dealing with grief." I know

that sounds lame, but what can I say if she won't accept my apology?

Besides, if she truly knew everything that was going on with me, I doubt she would care.

All she would say is 'like mother, like daughter' because Mom attracted trouble, too.

"Just don't run your grandmother's business into the ground," she adds in a high-pitched voice. "God bless Leila. She deserves so much more than you and your no-good mother. At least your mother did her dirty things in secret. You are a public mess."

"Hey! Watch it, lady," Dru cuts in, sharper than a razor blade, always ready to defend me.

"I will watch nothing." Marybeth switches her gaze from Dru to me. "Last night, you didn't just embarrass yourself, you embarrassed your grandmother, too. You couldn't even get yourself home. What a complete disgrace you are."

I would defend myself if I had the strength. And if I didn't see that on this occasion, Marybeth is right. That's why I say nothing when she shoots Dru and me the dirtiest look she can muster before she marches back the way she stormed in.

Marybeth might be a bitch, but she talks a lot of hard truths people don't want to hear sometimes.

My skin feels hot again. This time from shame.

I have become a pathetic public mess, and I need to fix it somehow.

I need to fix me.

It's just that I feel as if I can't breathe until this mess with Conrad is over. Everything is too uncertain.

I never saw this shit with him coming any more than I did Gage being a fraud.

"Don't take any notice of her." Dru reaches across the table and taps my knuckles.

"Dru, please. She's right." I dip my head, and my shoulders sag with the weight of my worries. "I was a real mess last night. The bank turned me down, and I'd had enough. I just needed something to help me deal with whatever was going to happen next, which I still don't know."

"Keep your fingers crossed for the loan."

"What if I don't get it?"

She presses her lips together. "Let's hope it works out. If it doesn't, then the only thing you can do is speak to Conrad. Or worst case scenario the police. You'll have to do it and hope there's no repercussions. This is extortion, Gwen. It's not legal, and it's not right."

"I know." I blink back tears, remembering how Conrad held his gun to my head. I don't know when I'll ever be able to forget that.

"Try to be strong. Fingers crossed you get the money so this can be over." She nods with conviction.

"Fingers crossed." I drag in a deep breath and allow the crisp, salty air to soothe my mind. Mentally, I cross everything—my heart, my fingers and my toes—and pray to anyone who will listen for all the luck in the world to flow my way.

"In the meantime..." Mischief returns to her face and brightens her eyes. "It sounds like a certain hunk got you home safe and sound last night. That same *hunk* walked and fed your dog. That's bonus points. I'm just saying that might warrant some sort of thank-you, seeing as all you did was gawk at him this morning."

I blow out a ragged breath. Trust her to bring the conversation back to my mystery man.

"It would also be nice if you had a name." She chuckles.

"You're right."

"Of course, I'm right. If it were me, I'd want to see him on my own terms and talk." She gives me a sassy shrug. "I'd hate to run into him in town or something and experience that awkwardness. He was at your house and took care of your dog. That means you have a pass to his place. It's not like you don't know where to find him. Just saying."

It might not hurt, and it will be one less thing for me to feel bad about.

"Okay. I'll see him if I finish up here early enough."

She gasps and claps her hands with excitement. "Really? You'll do it?"

"Yeah. If it will get you off my back."

"Oh, please, this is my job as the best friend. If I don't encourage you to do these things, who will? I should also inform you that last night happened because you have no sex."

I'm surprised when I laugh. "Are you serious right now?"

"Yes, of course I am. You make all this sexy lingerie, yet you have no one to wear it for, which is your fault, by the way. I'm the marketing brains, and I see way more action than you."

"I'm just being careful."

"So careful you stripped and danced on the countertops of Duke's Bar."

"Hey, that's not fair."

"I actually think it's hilarious. I can't believe I missed it, but it ended well. Who knows? You really might have ended the drought."

I shake my head at her.

She continues with her lighthearted humor, and we laugh while we work as if nothing else is going on and we're just having a regular day. But I know she's doing the best-friend thing again by distracting me and making sure I don't fall into the chasm of worry.

The day wears on, and with Dru's help, I'm able to get everything done quicker than I imagined.

I even get home at the reasonable hour of eight o'clock to undertake the task of visiting Mr. Handsome.

To make things more lighthearted as well as take the heat off me a little, I decide to take Sebastian, who is more than happy to go for a walk.

Night fell long ago, so the two of us walk under the moonlight and take the scenic sandy path to the beach.

My little dog has been in my life for over ten years. It was my grandfather who got him for me after my mother died. I was so distressed I shut down and hardly spoke to anyone, if at all. The grief was unbearable. It still is because my mother was my world.

I adored her to no end. She's the reason and my inspiration for becoming a designer.

She inspired most of my earlier designs, and I even set up a line which is purely dedicated to her creations.

Although I saw her addictions and watched her change, she wasn't the troublemaker Marybeth and all those two-faced bitches make her out to be.

I was eight when she died, and I know I probably got a jaded version of the truth, but that's what I remember.

Those memories are possibly my best. Not that my grandparents mistreated me. I just got to know them more during a sad time when they were devastated, too.

Things were sad again after my grandfather died, and the strength he gave my grandmother and me died with him. Life was never the same after.

Hope returned to me when I went away to college. I thought I was going to spread my wings and be who I was destined to be, but those hopes died when Grams got sick.

It was like taking down the queen on a chessboard when all your other powerful pieces are gone, too.

There's a possibility that I lost my mind last night and went wild because things have been bad for so long. I have Dru, and I know she's that ride-or-die friend people dream of, but she has a life, too, which can't involve saving me.

The beach house comes into view when we walk down to the sandy shore.

The sight shoves my thoughts out of my mind, and nerves steal the moisture from my throat.

When I was little, I used to play here with the other kids who lived nearby. It fascinated us that the sea and the surrounding caves were a stone's throw away. Of course, back then, it didn't have a super-hot guy living inside it whom I might have slept with.

God, I still can't believe I got so drunk I only remember the little I do. It's nearly been twenty-four hours, and nothing more has come back to me.

The closer I get, the more I wonder if this is a good idea. Maybe it wasn't.

What if Mr. Handsome is there with a woman? Like Hazel.

Ughh. That would be icing on the cake.

I would hate that, and she would never let me forget it, either.

There's a truck parked out front, and when I approach, I see the front door to the house is open.

Feeling slightly thrown, I look around to check if he's outside. It would be awkward to go up to the door and look inside the house. That would just be weird. Weirder than me being here.

Sebastian runs ahead to the side of the house. Then he barks with excitement.

I stop in my tracks when he skips back around the house, and I hear the familiar rumble of a deep male voice speaking Russian words I don't understand.

Then Mr. Handsome emerges from the shadowy path, stepping into the combo of moonlight and the outside lights of the house.

Both light him up in a sexy glow, showcasing his masterpiece body. His hair is wet, slicked back, and dripping with sea water. And he's only wearing shorts which display long powerful tattooed legs. I'm amazed by how many tattoos he has. Also, how artfully designed each one seems to be.

When he comes closer and I scan those muscles again, I think of one of those sculptures in Rome or Greece, of the mythical gods of legend. Someone like Poseidon—God of the Sea.

With his eyes on me, Mr. Handsome walks over to the truck and tosses Sebastian a squishy ball that was on the ground. That's when I see Poseidon's mythical trident inked across his entire back.

Wow, at least I'm right about something, or close enough.

Sebastian doesn't hesitate to grab the ball and plays with it. Mr. Handsome straightens, says something else in Russian, then looks back at me.

"I've never spoken Russian to my dog before, but yet he understands you," I say. It's baffled me all day.

"How old was he when you got him?"

"A year old."

"My guess is the breeder or someone around him before you must have spoken Russian."

"Is that what you are?" He sounds native when he speaks Russian.

"Yes, although I was born in the States."

"That's cool. I um... just speak English."

When his gaze flicks down to the sandals covering my feet, then travels back up my body slowly, I feel like I'm naked again, and my entire being flushes.

His gaze settles back on mine, and those words I wish I never said to him float back into my mind—*I want to fuck you*.

Did I?

Maybe this really wasn't one of my best ideas.

"You still can't remember a goddamn thing, can you?" He smirks.

"No," I confess coyly, bringing my hands together. "And I'm sorry to drop by unexpected. I felt I should come by to thank you for taking me home and let you know I'm not normally like that."

"No?" He chuckles, deep and low. It's a pleasant sound any woman with ears could get used to.

"Not at all. So, I apologize for, um... coming on to you at the bar." I'm grateful it's night. Although where we're standing is well lit, it's dark enough to hide my blush.

"That's a real shame." His lips curl up into a sensual smile that has me thinking of those sinful things again. At that moment, I realize the high content of alcohol in my system last night had nothing to do with the potent cocktail of sexiness I felt from him.

All of it really was him. The man screams of sex. From that mystery lurking in his eyes to the dominant way he carries himself, he has that air of a man who always gets what he wants.

Sex appeal is oozing from him right now as we stand here inches apart, and I'm having the hardest time concentrating on what I'm supposed to say next.

"You think that's a shame?" I mumble, now wondering if he's saying that because it really is a shame, or because we really slept together and me apologizing makes it seem like I never meant for last night to happen.

"Depends on which way you look at it."

Now I'm more confused, so I need to just come right out and ask him. "Did we sleep together?" There, I said it, but the amused smile he gives me makes me wish I hadn't.

"I told you you'd remember being with me." The deep rasp in his voice sends a jolt of need straight to my core and brings an array of scandalous images to the forefront of my mind.

"So, we didn't?"

"No, Malyshka."

"Oh." I blink a few times.

"You sound disappointed." He tilts his head.

"No," I say quickly, even though I question whether or not I am. "I was just wondering why I was naked."

"You took your clothes off." He smiles.

My nerves spike. "Was that at the bar?" Duke said I stripped down to my bra and panties. He never said I was naked.

"No, it was when I took you home."

My eyes snap wide. "In front of you?"

He leans in, and his smile widens. "On me."

"Oh, Christ." No darkness on earth can cover my embarrassment.

"Don't worry, you gave a good show, and I liked what I saw."

"Oh my God. I am so sorry. I really am not like that."

"I'm not exactly complaining." He sets his shoulders back and runs a hand through his hair, causing the remnants of water to trickle down the side of his neck.

I watch him keenly, feeling that undeniable energy between us again, along with something else lurking in his dark gaze that looks dangerous.

It makes me wonder if he is.

No. I shouldn't think that. My thoughts disconnect when he steps back and opens the door of his truck to take out a rucksack.

When he looks back at me, an awkward silence drifts between us. The sort that probably means I should say goodbye now. But suddenly, I want to know more about him, especially if he's not complaining.

"How long are you in town for?"

"I have some business to take care of. I'm here for as long as that takes."

"With your brother?"

He smiles again. "Word travels fast."

"Around here it does." I relax my shoulders a little. "I have a restaurant on the other side of the beach, right by the pier. It's called The Spot. I've been told I make the best apple pie. You are welcome to drop by sometime for a meal on the house. I definitely owe you for last night."

He raises his brows. "Thanks, and pie sounds great. But what if I want a taste of something else?" I definitely don't miss the meaning behind his words, or the way he's looking at me.

"I have an extensive menu with a variety of food choices."

"Alright, Malyshka."

Malyshka. He's called me that several times. I definitely need to know what it means.

"What does Malyshka mean?"

"It means baby girl in Russian. Like it?"

I'm not sure who wouldn't. "I do." The flutter of butterflies in my stomach is unexpected, and I know, given my circumstances, I should catch myself before I go deeper down this rabbit hole. But whatever spell he has on me keeps me rooted to curiosity. "What's your name?"

He sets the bag over his shoulder. "Malik."

"Nice name." Now I can stop calling him Mr. Handsome. Even though I still think he's ridiculously gorgeous. "I'm Gwen."

"I know, Malyshka."

A gust of wind picks up my hair and blows it in my face.

Malik steps forward to get closer, personal space close, but he feels like an invited guest. Then, as if it were the most natural thing, he takes a lock and allows the ends to curl about his finger.

I look up at him, into those dark eyes which seem like pools of coal against the moonlight, and the desire I witness makes me almost think he's going to kiss me.

I nearly believe it, until he inches back, breaking the momentary spell.

As my hair floats away from his finger, I look down at his hand, and the tattoos on the underside of his wrist catch my attention.

One is a Viking rune, and the other, which is just above it, is the Greek Sigma symbol.

While those tattoos aren't uncommon and I've seen loads of people with Viking runes and Greek symbols tattooed on their bodies, that specific combination on his wrist triggers something in my mind. Something I feel I've seen somewhere before.

And not in a good way. The recognition revives that previous vibe of danger I sensed from him, but when he rests his hand at his side, removing the tattoo from my view, my thoughts break.

I catch myself, so I don't look so obvious. Then the echo of footsteps at his door turns us toward it. My gaze lands on a man as tall as Malik and just as muscular.

I assume he must be his brother because they look extremely similar. Although Malik has dark blond straighter hair, and his brother has black loose curls.

He stands in the doorway for a breath before he's gone,

but he definitely carries that dangerous vibe, too. I felt it all the way over here.

That's probably my cue to not just leave, but stay away.

"I should go," I say. "I have some work I have to do."

"Alright. See you around, Gwen." Malik's eyes hold mine.

"See you around, too." I smile, tamping down my obvious attraction to him. And my nerves.

I snap my fingers at Sebastian, and he runs over to me, leaving the squishy ball to roll down the path.

For good manners' sake, I throw one last smile over my shoulder at Malik before Sebastian and I leave.

I don't look at Malik again, but I can feel him watching me as we walk back up the beach.

The deadly cocktail of attraction and temptation follows me with his gaze, but so does that sense of danger.

I could be completely wrong about his tattoos, meaning something sinister.

Lord knows I've had my fair share of being wrong lately, and the man is covered in tats.

Maybe the sense of danger I feel is that sixth sense again rearing its ugly head. It resurfaces from time to time because I could never tell anyone who I truly was. Or rather, who my father was.

But given the circumstances of the past, it's understandable why no one could ever know that Santiago Navarro was my father.

The ability to smell danger comes with being the daughter of a former cartel king.

I wish I could say I never picked up that vibe on Gage,

but I did. I just refused to believe it at the time and look at what happened to me.

If I am right about what I sensed about Malik and his tattoo, I definitely need to stay away.

Even if I liked how he made me feel.

Chapter Six

Malik

Captain Jim Davison rests a hand on my shoulder. "Make sure you take a decent break when you're home, son. It's going to be intense once we're back on duty." His voice is firm but carries the carefulness of a concerned father.

"Decent break? What's your definition of decent, Jim?" I smirk.

He's about to answer when an explosion shakes our surroundings. Then masked men rush in through the door and open gunfire on us.

Jim pushes me out of the way and a bullet pierces his heart.

I'm about to get up and fight when everything fractures around me like already broken glass being smashed into more pieces.

Darkness surrounds me, then electricity spreads over my body in painful, rippling waves.

The intense torture my masked captors inflict on me daily is their pleasure.

"Bratva scum." Someone spits in my face, and they administer another dose of electricity to my body.

This time the pungent smell of burnt flesh assaults my senses and I feel death is at the door. Another powerful jolt of electricity shakes my soul and the darkness around me becomes thicker, stifling, suffocating. I can't breathe.

Then the cold metal of a gun is placed at the side of my head.

Click-clack.

I jump out of the darkness and into the bright morning sun spilling through the bedroom window.

My gaze darts around the room, searching every corner. Although I'm sitting on the bed and can see my surroundings quite clearly, it takes a moment for my brain to process where I am.

Or rather, where I'm not.

I'm not in that prison anymore, and the men who took pleasure in torturing me are no longer breathing.

I'm in Wilmington. Here to get retribution.

That's where I am and what I'm doing.

With that realization, my breathing and the wild beat of my heart steady.

I glance at the clock on the wall and see it's nearly ten in the morning, which means last night was one of the rare occasions when I slept straight through.

Apart from that nightmare, I almost had a normal night's sleep.

After I was rescued, nightmares and PTSD were the least of my worries.

There were moments when my mind would suddenly slip, and it was the hardest thing in the world to convince me that I wasn't back in Hell. In my waking hours, I found it hard to distinguish between what was real and what wasn't.

When I was asleep, the nightmares would rip my mind apart. I'd have dreams within dreams and horrors within horrors and wake up in the in-between, unable to steady my mind to get back to reality.

The nightmares would always be the same. A mashup of Jim talking to me just moments before he was shot, then everything would switch to my tortuous captivity.

Being captured by my enemies reduced me to the one thing I loathe most—*weakness*

That was where my Uncle Leif came in and helped me to find my strength.

He knew exactly how to heal my mind because out of everyone in the family, I'm most like him. Leif was the adventurer and lover of the old Viking seafaring life who taught me how to swim and sail.

To fix me, he took me on a quest where we sailed around Europe for six

months. By the time we returned I had a new found strength that gave me the energy

to get back on track, and more importantly to never stop until I found the motherfuckers responsible for fucking up my life and killing Jim Davison.

Leif understood how I felt more than anyone. It was he who introduced me to Jim and Brian.

This mission of mine is important to me because it's for the both of them.

If Brian were still alive, he'd want to avenge his father's death. As his best friend I owe it to him to do what he can't.

Years ago if anybody had told me I'd have to live in a world where Brian and Jim only existed in memory, I wouldn't have believed it.

I was eight when I met him and his father. Because I was obsessed with the sea Leif thought it was a good idea to introduce me to his friend from the Navy who also happened to have a son my age who was equally obsessed.

That day Brian and I became kindred spirits, inseparable as Jim taught us everything he knew.

I have a close relationship with Zakh but Brian was different because he loved sailing just as much as me. By the time we were sixteen we started entering every boat race we could across the country.

Then we joined the Navy and had a good run of service until Brian was killed in a car accident two days before Christmas. He'd lost control of his wheel and his car ran off the edge of a cliff. Just like that, he was gone.

Months later Jim was killed.

It's all sad and unreal but I feel like I can't move on with my life until I have some form of justice. Then maybe I'll find the peace I need to quiet my demons.

I get off the bed and drop to the floor for my usual morning routine of push-ups.

I'm planning to start my day the same way I did yesterday—in the presence of Gwen St. James.

Her visit last night was a win I didn't expect. She

entered the dragon's lair on her own with her sass and her curves, and that scent in her hair that drove me wild.

The first thing I'm doing is heading to the restaurant to take the beauty up on her offer.

It's kind of hard to think of anything else besides getting the woman in my bed, but I realize that to get close to a woman like Gwen, you can't just fuck her. In a town like this, I also can't flirt around with her, then do the same with Allyson—not that I want to.

Luckily for me, Allyson and her boyfriend own a water-sports store in town. It's been easier to get close to them both as a customer because of my genuine interest in sailing.

I stand when I finish my push-ups, and my gaze lands on the printouts on my desk of the loan information I got from the bank on Gwen. It has details of the massive loan she was turned down for.

I noted the date was the same as her wild spree at Duke's. That explained her behavior.

The loan rejection also confirmed my thoughts on the financial worries I suspected, but also that there was something more at work.

If her finances didn't look as clean as they do, I wouldn't be suspicious, but when I dug around and found that her friend, Dru, had applied for a loan hours before Gwen came by and Gwen was standing guarantor, I suspected something else is up that felt like trouble.

The kind of trouble where you need a shitload of money quickly to get yourself out of it.

That made me wonder if the loan had something to do with Gage Miller's death. The thought occurred to me when I found payments to a private investigator more than a year ago who was supposed to be looking for him. It seems Gage scammed Gwen out of a lot of money.

If that didn't happen a year ago, I'd believe it to be the reason for the loan, but her attempt to get one feels like something new. Something that could still be connected to Gage because he died last week.

Perhaps it's something I'll find out eventually. Or not.

It would be odd for Santiago's daughter to be in such a dire situation where she needed a loan of that amount. But maybe that's just the way things are.

Maybe the money he gave her family dried up, and the only thing left, if she finds her way to it, is the cartel.

Or the woman I'm looking for isn't Gwen.

I guess I'll find that out, too.

Hopefully sooner rather than later.

* * *

There she is.

Dressed in a sexy-as-fuck skater dress which shows off her finest assets, Gwen waltzes onto the restaurant floor, completely unaware of the male attention she's garnering.

She's not mine, but the possessive asshole inside me wants to cut out the eyes of every man who's looking at her like he wants to devour her for his next meal.

Her hair in a high ponytail emphasizes exotic cheekbones and those pouty lips I would love sucking my cock.

Fuck me. This woman has seriously worked some magic on me I don't want to resist.

Now that I'm here in her restaurant and she's parading in front of me, I want that taste again.

I purposely sat in the back booth so I would see her the moment she came out of the staff entrance.

Where I'm sitting, she should see me, too.

The Spot is definitely my kind of restaurant. Its bistro style is perfect for every meal of the day. It's just gone eleven, so customers are filing in and filling up the nearby tables. I was probably lucky to get a table at this hour with a prime view of the sea and the surrounding pier.

According to my research, this place was set up by Gwen's grandparents in the seventies, so it's been around for a very long time. People know it far and wide for its great food and homey service.

Gwen struts across to the maître 'd to speak to him. When she turns, she sees me.

She's about thirty feet away, but the flush of the color rose creeping down her elegant sun-kissed neck is alluring. Like any man, I love watching women react to me.

This one just fascinates me more because she's the first to tell me she wants to fuck me.

While she might explain the request away as a drunken mistake, based on the way she's looking at me, I believe she still wants to.

That would be no problem since I want her, too.

Like a would-be gentleman, I dip my head, and she smiles.

She says something else to the maître'd then makes her way over to me.

Her cheeks grow rosier when she approaches, and she sets her little notepad at her side.

"You're here." Her voice is breathy, and she looks genuinely surprised to see me.

"I am. You told me about the extensive menu, so I thought I would check it out. I wave my hand across the menu on the table and her smile widens.

"Have you found anything you want?"

"I have." I grin, and from the tone of my voice, she knows I mean her.

"Can I get it for you?"

"How about I start with coffee, and you join me?"

The light of interest dances in her eyes as she contemplates the idea, but I can see she's also wary of me.

And I know exactly why.

I caught her looking at the tattoos on my wrist last night. The symbols mark me as a Knight. So, whatever her natural instincts warned her about me was completely correct, and she's right to feel like she should stay away.

Those who recognize the tattoos and their meaning are usually from the underground or the circles we travel in. But someone like Santiago's daughter might recognize them for what they are and know I'm a dangerous man, but I can see good old curiosity is getting the better of her.

Finally, she sighs and shifts her weight from one foot to the other. "I would really love to join you, but I should probably get ready for the lunch crowd. I'm down a waitress today."

"Ten minutes." I hold up my fingers and set my hands back on the table.

She contemplates again and then nods. "Okay. Ten minutes. I'll go grab us coffee. How do you like it?"

"Surprise me."

She chuckles and sets off to get the coffee. Minutes later, she returns with two large cups of steaming black coffee. She places mine before me and then sits opposite with hers.

"Black coffee felt like the safest option." Nervous laughter escapes her lips.

"Fine by me." I nod. "So, you look fully recovered."

"I am. I promise I am more myself today than any other day."

"That's good to hear. Maybe I can find out some more about you."

She laughs. "You might find this shocking, but I'm really not all that interesting."

"I find that hard to believe."

"Thanks." She takes a sip of her coffee. "What did you want to know about me?"

If only I could just ask her what I need to know. "I noticed that while you look like you work hard here, you don't exactly look like a restaurant owner."

The other night, I got the full history of fashion design, so talking to her about something she has a passion for will make her feel more comfortable around me.

"I'm not exactly. The restaurant belongs to my grandparents. Well, my grandmother now. My grandfather died a few years back."

"I'm sorry for your loss."

"Thank you. This place was my grandparents' life, so when my grandmother got sick a few months back, I took over. But really, I'm a fashion designer and own an online business. I design lingerie."

"Wow, that's impressive." I try to sound like it's the first I'm hearing this and as if I haven't researched her life. "I've never met a fashion designer who designs lingerie before."

"I run the business with my best friend. You saw her the other day. Her name is Dru. Our dream is to have an actual store someday in a big city. That's what we're working toward."

"That definitely sounds like a good dream. Good luck with it."

Her smile brightens. "I'll need it. What about you? Do I get to know more than your name and that you're here on business?"

I think of what I can tell her that won't make her more wary of me. "I was a lieutenant in the Navy."

Now she looks really impressed. "Oh, wow. You look too young to have accomplished all that."

"I'm twenty-eight. I enlisted the second I turned eighteen."

"My grandfather was a pilot in the Air Force. He enlisted at eighteen, too, and served in Vietnam."

I give her a fascinated smile, again pretending I don't know that about her grandfather. "Now, that's impressive."

"Thanks. What made you leave?"

I knew this question would come, and I can't think of the answer without my mind running over Jim Davison's final moments. And the way my attackers ambushed us to take me.

It's not exactly easy to penetrate a military naval base. It's even harder to capture a man like me. I've considered them having help, but if they did, I haven't found evidence of it yet.

Their ultimate goal was to kill me, but they wanted to mess with my head first. That's why I was captured.

"An injury took me down," I say after a moment too long

of silence. I won't go into details about how fucked-up my left hip was, along with any hopes of returning to the Navy.

Even though the injury has taken nothing from my brute strength or capabilities, the fact that my hip plays up sometimes robbed me of eligibility for active duty by the Navy's standards.

The brightness in Gwen's expression fades. "I'm sorry to hear that. Are you okay now?"

"I'm fine. It happened years ago.

"Sounds like you loved being a sailor."

"I did, and the beauty of it is, I still am." I wink at her, and she chuckles.

"Gwen," the tall Hispanic man who showed me to my seat calls her from the bar area.

Gwen nods at him and gives a little wave, then she returns her focus to me with a hint of disappointment in her eyes.

"That's my cue, and the quickest ten minutes ever."

"But it was good."

"It was." She rises to her feet and picks up her coffee cup.

"I'll plan better next time."

"Next time?" The desire returns to her eyes.

"Yeah. I might want to take you up on your original offer."

She blushes again, knowing exactly what offer I'm referring to. "Are you always like this?"

"Mostly." I love that she doesn't give me an answer.

"I'll see you around."

"Sure."

She saunters away with my eyes glued to her ass.

That little meeting was another win for me; I've successfully painted a picture of a man that I'm not just to get closer to her.

The human parts of me may not want Gwen to be Santiago's daughter because it's clear she's going through something and it's better she doesn't know me.

But despite myself, the selfish motherfucker inside me wants that taste I craved since meeting her and thinks it would be interesting to make the woman my wife just to claim her in every way and make her mine.

That part of me is already looking forward to seeing that perfect body of hers next time.

Chapter Seven

Gwen

I've just arrived at the nursing home to visit my grandmother.

I visit her every other week, but when I have more time, I'm here every week.

Usually, I worry about what condition I'll find her in. But today, a certain ex-Navy lieutenant has occupied my mind.

I know I shouldn't be thinking about him, especially after last night, when my instincts warned me to err on the side of caution, but I'm my worst enemy.

I'll even admit that if I'd known talking to Malik would have the ability to rid my mind of all my worries for those few minutes, I would have ordered a lifetime supply of those moments.

I certainly wouldn't mind a replay of the way he looked at me throughout the entire conversation.

Then there was what he said at the end. About taking me up on my original offer.

God help my poor mind when those wild images of a forbidden fantasy assaulted me, and I wished I could be as daring as Dru is always encouraging me to be.

It's not that I don't want to, or even that I haven't got it in me. I just know I have to be careful.

Dru came from a normal family who loved her right until the end. I came from secrets and was the child of a forbidden affair with a dangerous man that never should have happened.

Dru also hasn't been burned the way I have by Gage.

Gage screwed with my mind so badly, I'm not sure if I could ever trust anybody ever again.

But I suppose this morning was just a good distraction I desperately needed.

One without the enhancement of alcohol. It's also one I'm going to handle with care because I'm almost certain I'll be seeing my handsome ex-Navy Lieutenant sooner than I think.

When I see him, I need to control my attraction to him because even though he sold me the image of the ex-Navy lieutenant, I'm still not sure what he is.

Of course, when I got back last night, I tried to look up the meaning of his tattoos and groups that might have them. I found nothing, but you rarely tend to with people like that. If you manage to find something, it's going to be random, meaningless shit.

All I know is that somewhere in my mind is a memory of those tattoos. Honestly speaking, though, the other Russian mafia tattoos he had were equally worrying.

No matter how nice he is to me, or how sexy he is, getting involved with a guy like that—even for one night—would be begging for trouble.

I sign in at the reception desk and make my way down the beautifully decorated corridor, which takes me into the patient garden where a few of the residents have gathered with their families.

It's just gone six, so the sunlight is waning, creating a serene atmosphere.

I head to Grams' room, getting there at the same time her doctor, Dr. Perry, is stepping out.

Dr. Perry is also the lead doctor here. He's in his late sixties and has been friends with my grandmother since before she got sick. I've been fortunate so far to have him look after her.

I know he'll do all he can to make sure she's well cared for. At the same time, it's never a good sign when I see him like this.

Grams has been here for over a year, and every time I've run into Dr. Perry like this, it's been bad news.

"Ah, Gwen, I'm glad I caught you," he says, adjusting his glasses. "I was about to schedule a meeting with you."

"Is Grams okay?" I can't restrain the panic in my voice, and my heart trips over itself when concern fills his eyes.

"Do you have time for a quick chat?"

"Of course."

"Let's go over here." He points to the seated area by the floor-to-ceiling glass window.

By the time we walk over there and sit, my hands are sweating and my heart is galloping in my chest at such a pace my entire body aches.

"What's going on?" My voice is barely audible.

Dr. Perry pulls in a breath and leans forward. "She's gotten worse again. This time, her memory retention has significantly deteriorated."

"I was here only two weeks ago." I don't know why I say that. Grams wasn't any better then. That was when she looked at me like she didn't know me, and all she wanted to talk about was growing up on her parents' farm in Tennessee. At least she remembered that.

"Unfortunately, this is how dementia works. No one can predict when the changes will occur. The best we can do is prepare for them. With that said,

I'm thinking of changing her care plan and medication. I just needed your authorization to do so because of the potential side effects."

"Will it help her?"

"It will make her life more comfortable," he explains with hesitation. "That is all we can do at this point. I wish I could tell you something more positive, like I can make her better, but I can't."

"I know, and I really appreciate that."

"I'm glad. I also know you're financing her treatment yourself, so I need to check that everything is okay for the budget."

Money. It all comes back to that.

God. Everything is okay for the moment, but if I don't get that loan, the money for Grams' care is all I have. There's no way I can touch that.

No way. Not even if Conrad threatens to sell me to the highest bidder or keep me for himself.

With the lavish way I grew up, with money from not just

my mother and father, no one would believe I would be in this situation now.

"Yes, everything is okay." I wish I sounded surer, but I'm as sure as I can be.

"Good. Well, I'll let you see her and leave the paperwork at reception for you to look over and complete. If you agree to everything, I'll start the new care plan tomorrow."

"Okay, thank you." I nod.

We stand, and he dips his head before leaving.

I turn and look at my grandmother's room across from me, now worrying even more about what she'll be like.

I guess I'd better go in and see. Standing here in fear isn't going to help me one way or the other.

Shaky legs carry me forward, and I open the door to find Grams sitting in her wheelchair by the window.

Hearing my footsteps makes her look at me. When our eyes lock, I have a hard time not falling apart. She looks frail, like she might snap in a gentle breeze.

She didn't look this weak two weeks ago.

Grams is seventy-two. Although her hair has always been completely white, for as long as I can remember, people have always complemented her on how young she looks for her age. But right now, she looks like she could be a hundred.

I rush to her side, and when she smiles, hope fills me because there's recognition in her eyes.

"Oh, Scarlet, there you are." She reaches out to me, and I freeze.

Scarlet—that's my mother.

Grams thinks I'm her.

"No, Grams, it's me, Gwen."

Confusion fills her face, and she shakes her head. "Gwen...I don't know any Gwens. I don't know you."

No. *God, no*. I can almost hear my heart shatter.

This was the part I've always feared right from the moment she was diagnosed with dementia. This part where she'd look at me and not know me.

This day just arrived sooner than I thought, and I can see what Dr. Perry meant about her getting worse.

Calming myself, I take her hand and keep my gaze fixed on hers. "You know me. You just can't remember me. We love reading poetry together."

She smiles, narrows her eyes, then touches my face.

"Gwen. That's you."

"Yes." I nod and try to stay calm, but truthfully, I want to scream. "I'm your granddaughter."

She blinks several times, then something seems to come to her that I hope is recognition.

"I want to go home, Gwen." Her voice is small and careful. "I don't like being here. This is not my home."

"I know, but they'll help you here."

"Really?" She looks around with a frightened expression. "I don't like being away from home. I don't feel safe."

"I promise you're safe and everyone around you will take care of you."

"You promise?" She searches my eyes.

"I do." As I say those words and she squeezes my hand, I know I can't fail.

* * *

It's late when I reach home. Once I feed Sebastian, shower, and change for bed, I'm so drained that I should fall asleep straightaway.

But I can't.

It's come to the stage where I have to accept that Grams isn't going to come back to me. Everything will be harder from here on out, and when it ends, when she dies, there will just be me.

I have three cousins, two aunts, and one uncle. All of whom I don't really know and have only met at a family wedding and my grandfather's funeral. Our family was one of those with continuous arguments which drove people apart.

So, there really will just be me.

I get off the bed, kneel, and open the loose floorboards under the bed to retrieve my treasure box.

It's just a bit bigger than a shoe box. For safety and security purposes, I've always had to keep it locked away underneath the floor because it contains pictures of my father.

I sit back on the bed and take out the photo album I wasn't allowed to show anyone of my father with Mom and me.

The box holds several other trinkets from my mother, but this album always pulls on my heart.

I open it and look over pictures of my father holding me as a baby, then I flick through to the others of us as I got older. Dad might not have been as present as I wanted him to be, but he was with me as much as he could be.

My father took extensive measures so that no one would ever find out I was his daughter and Mom was his mistress. All to protect us from his enemies.

As far as I know, no one knows I exist apart from my father's wife, Esperanza, who was enemy number one.

It was she who threatened our lives. The whole thing was a messy situation that was wrong on all counts because my father cheated on his wife.

He promised Mom he'd leave his wife for her. The day came when he was supposed to, and Esperanza blackmailed him into staying with her.

They never had kids. She couldn't, but that wasn't why Dad got involved with Mom. His marriage to Esperanza was a business arrangement between families, encouraged by his father because Dad had the cartel.

It was Grams who told me the whole story on my sixteenth birthday.

When my parents were alive, I would have been too young to understand what had happened, but I'm not sure either of them would have told me anything anyway.

Despite Esperanza's threats, my father saw us in secret, and when we were together, it was magical.

I always believed Mom turned to drugs because she was so in love with my father, it hurt to live without him when she had to. It hurt me, too, because I could see just how much he loved us.

I'd see him a few times a year. Always, always on my birthday, then just before Christmas, and randomly when he could visit during the year. Dad would always get me whatever I wanted including my favorite cakes he got from Allyson Peterson's Mom. She was a supply teacher at our school who was always doing bake sales.

Mom met her and liked her at one event, but of course they didn't know my father was my father. They thought he was one of Mom's friends from the fashion world because he was always so well dressed. Whenever he came to visit he'd stop there first, get my cakes, then come to me.

The last time I saw him was at Mom's funeral. Then never again.

We found out from watching the news that he killed himself.

I've never been able to accept that as truth because he told me at Mom's funeral that he was going to take care of me. I still don't believe it now.

At eight years old, there was nothing I could do, and that's how I ended up living with my grandparents.

As for money, Mom blew all of hers on drugs. The maintenance money Dad gave my grandparents went toward my education and my life, then eventually toward the extensive medical care my grandfather received when he was diagnosed with a brain tumor.

The last of that money was put toward repairing the restaurant after the fire Grams accidentally started.

Prior to the fire, Grams cancelled both her business and health insurance, mistakenly believing them to be something else. It was then I found out she suffered from dementia and chronic heart disease. I also found out that she'd known for some time and kept it from me.

Suddenly, all finances were placed on me and I put a pause on my career plans.

We had to repair the restaurant because it was our primary source of income.

But had we known that Grams would need to go into a nursing home months later with the need for extensive medical treatment, we might not have done the repairs. *I* may have done certain things differently.

That includes being with Gage and trusting him with that investment money.

Although at the time I was with him for close to a year, I might have seen him for who he was and wouldn't have trusted him with personal details, like access to my bank account and Grams' savings. I might have seen through his shit and lies when he offered to help and take care of things.

There's so much grief and pain in my life that I actually fear happiness.

Every time I think I could be happy, something happens. It's like a big cloud of dark mojo is perpetually waiting around the corner and watching for the moment to strike.

Tears I've been holding back trail down my cheeks, and I put the album away.

I hate crying, but I allow myself the reprieve of breaking down sometimes because I need to.

Chapter Eight

Gwen

I start the next day with the migraine from hell.

It doesn't surprise me with all the crying I did last night.

Although I look like hell with my red puffy eyes, I do my best to look as decent as possible. It's a full-on busy day today where I'm going to be at the restaurant from open to closing time.

I need to be on my game, no exceptions and no matter that, I wish I could hide away in a cave and let the world pass by without me.

By lunchtime, I'm exhausted and so worried about Grams and the whole situation with Conrad, I can hardly concentrate.

I get some respite when Dru comes by for an hour to hang out and help me, but the moment she leaves, I'm a mess again.

It's obvious to everyone that I'm not myself and I'm not coping at all. There were several points during the day when people tried to ask if I was okay, to which I gave the usual faux assurance.

I barely held myself together when I gave Dru the update on Grams, so talking to everyone else would have been awful.

Miraculously, I make it to the end of the night.

We're an hour away from closing, and it's just the bars upstairs and downstairs that are open for the customers who want to mingle.

As the waitresses seem to have a handle on clearing up, I head to the bar, where Gilman is busy mixing cocktails for a group of rowdy women.

I slip behind the counter and start arranging the bottles of wine back in their rows, making a note of what needs replenishing.

I try to shove my angst to the back of my mind so I can concentrate. I don't want to lose track the way I did when I cashed up the register and had to start all over again.

When I reach the end of the row, I suddenly feel eyes on me, heated and so intense I'm not sure how I missed it before.

I turn right around and find myself staring straight at Malik standing in the crowd by the balcony on the upper level.

The sight of him throws me off kilter. A, because I never expected to see him, and B, because it's *him,* and despite worrying about Grams, I haven't stopped thinking about him.

He towers over the surrounding people with his height,

but even from all the way down here, his presence overwhelms me, heating up my body like a furnace.

Our eyes lock, and I sense something different about him tonight. Something sensual, predatory, and so potently mysterious that roots my body to the spot.

I would have waved or acknowledged him by now, but I'm frozen in his gaze as that secret something calls to my inner desires and needs, which haven't stopped fantasizing about how good it would feel to have him touch me.

Touch me and make me forget the way he did during those few minutes we spoke yesterday.

Except, I'm not thinking of talking now. Somehow, I have a strange feeling he knows that. After all, we started this... whatever it is we have, back to front.

Malik breaks eye contact, and his eyes roam down my body in such an overtly sexual way that sets me on fire. Wetness beads between my thighs, and the ache in my pussy grows as his lust-filled invisible fingers touch me everywhere.

Embarrassingly, my mouth waters like I've been starving for food for years.

What the hell is wrong with me?

I need to stop this. It's ridiculous. I know it is, but temptation holds me in the lure of him, and I check him out, too, because damn it to hell, he looks sexier than any other time I've seen him. Tonight, Malik is wearing a black button-down shirt with the sleeves rolled up his thick forearms and the top buttons undone, showing off the tanned skin on his chest.

Taking in his masterpiece body heats me up once more, and my mind goes wild. His eyes meet mine again, and several moments pass of staring at each other, until a warm hand rests on mine and I look away.

It's Gilman.

Earlier, he was annoyed with me because it was clear that tonight of all nights, we needed an extra pair of hands. The softer look in his eyes suggests he's back to his old self.

"Why don't you go home? The girls and I can do the rest and lock the place up," he offers with a sure nod.

Usually, I would decline such an offer, but I've wanted to go home from the moment I got here. "Are you sure?"

"Yes. You look like you're barely hanging on. You could use an early night."

"I could, and thank you." I give him a kind smile.

"A word of advice, Gwen, if I may. I can see you're doing your utmost best to keep everything going. I also know that in your grandmother's absence and illness, times are hard, but everybody needs a break. If I were you, I'd take tomorrow off and get Tony or Lilly to cover. I'm in all week, so I can manage the place."

I didn't want to take any days off or get extra staff to cover me, but I think I need to. My mental exhaustion is worse than the aches in my body from running around. If I don't take the time I need to rest, I might burn out sooner. Then I'll be screwed.

"Okay, I'll do that." I nod and give him a gentle smile. "I'll get Tony to cover."

"Good. Let me know if you need anything else."

"I will, and thanks for looking out for me." I always thank him for things like that. Gilman has been the restaurant's manager for years. Practically from the time it opened its doors, so he's part of the family.

"Of course." He gives my shoulder a gentle squeeze. "You're going to be okay, Gwen."

I give him a curt nod. It's all I can do because I'll believe that I'll be better than I am when I can erase Conrad Duncan from my mind.

"See you in a few days."

I turn to depart but quickly return my gaze to the balcony, searching for Malik. But he's not there.

I scan the area, looking through the groups of people who have gathered to talk and drink cocktails. But he's not anywhere.

Did he leave?

I know I had the spellbound moment where he mesmerized me and I couldn't do anything but look at him, but if he's gone, it was odd he didn't say hi.

Maybe the moment of fascination is over.

Or maybe I need to get a grip on my common sense and put my priorities in order. I know something isn't quite what it seems with him, so I should leave well enough alone and not seek to add more shit to my plate that I can't handle.

With that reasoning, I head to my office.

I just need to put away the invoices and documents I was looking through earlier, then I'm out of here.

Sebastian will be happy to see me. It's super late and will be close to midnight by the time I get home, but I may take him for a five-minute walk before I jump into bed.

I open the office door and leave it ajar when I enter.

I walk over to my desk and start packing everything away. Not a minute later, footsteps approach the door, and I look up to see who it is.

The only person who usually comes down here to see me

is Gilman because his office is at the end of the corridor, but since I just left him at the bar, I doubt it's him.

I'm right. It's not him.

The door swings open, and the hot Russian ex-Navy lieutenant walks in, tall, foreboding, and with an air of malice.

Dangerous heat simmers through me from the lust glimmering in his eyes. My blood spikes with the fire I felt earlier when I was watching him on the balcony, and my nerves jump to attention, setting off the colony of butterflies nesting in my stomach.

With his eyes glued to me, he proceeds with the confidence of someone who owns the place. My spine solidifies when he closes the door behind him and flicks down the little latch, locking us in.

The public isn't allowed back here. I'm sure he's aware of that, and since my office isn't exactly easy to find, I also don't miss the fact that it seems as if Malik has been around here before.

Before tonight.

Has he?

If so, why? Why am I suddenly feeling so wary around him?

Apprehension clouds my mind because this is bold, unlike what I've known him to be, and... daring.

Daring in a mysterious way that feels forbidden and dangerously sexy.

"Hi," I say, failing to keep the quiver out of my voice. I also fail to control my body's reaction to him. My nipples are diamond hard just for seeing him. And I'm wet again.

"Hello, Malyshka."

I usually like the deep baritone of his sensual voice and hearing him call me Malyshka, but just now, the endearment sent a chill through my nerves the same way I've felt when I see or hear something that gives me the creeps.

If I can think and feel like that, why am I seriously turned on?

I'm wet, and if he were to touch me the way I fantasize about him touching me, he'd know.

"You're... here." I carry on as if this isn't weird.

The corner of his mouth lifts into a grin that doesn't seem like one of humor.

"I noticed you on the balcony. I was going to say hi."

"Well, I'm here now." He steps closer. The room seems smaller, and so do I.

I'm standing behind my desk totally having an Alice-in-Wonderland moment where it feels like I'm suddenly small, small, small and everything around me is ginormous, especially him.

Remaining silent, he takes several more steps toward me, reminding me of a predator advancing on a prey it knows has no chance of escaping.

My lips part to say something, but my mind is frozen.

He gets closer, and it's not until I feel my back hit the wall that I realize I moved. I backed away without even knowing or feeling myself do so.

Malik's smiles and places his hand on the wall next to my arm, completely blocking me in. My only other escape is the window on my left, and there's no way I'm jumping two stories down.

That I even contemplated an escape route is a clear indication my instincts are going batshit crazy trying to warn me away from this guy.

At the same time, there's something lurking deep in his eyes that draws me to him like a magnet.

I don't know what it is, but it hooks me with some kind of power I'm not sure I'd want to resist.

He angles closer until he's a breath away from my lips, and everything inside me stills like the calm before a storm is about to hit and wreak havoc.

I swear my heart even stops beating until he moves to my ear and his warm breath tickles my skin. Then it speeds up and trips over itself.

"Are you scared of me, Gwen?"

The question throws me, and I'm not sure how to answer it because I can't say no. He does scare me.

I haven't seen this version of him before, but it feels like the real him.

I turn my face toward him, but he restricts my movement by coming even closer to plant a kiss on the side of my neck. It's just a kiss, and it's not even on my lips, but I feel it everywhere.

Another one follows, then another, creating a trail down my neck. My lips part from the ecstasy of having his lips on me, and my body, starved for attention, wants to feel those lips all over me.

"Answer me, Malyshka. Are you afraid of me?" His voice is more forceful, with such power, I know I don't have a choice but to answer with something.

"Should I be?" Hints of a moan ripple between my words, echoing the pleasure he's giving me with his mere touch.

"I don't want you to be." He brushes his cheek against mine, and when a flurry of seconds passes by, I realize he's assessing my every move and he's not going to actually answer my question. "If you are, you're going to have to push your fears to the back of your mind until I'm done with you."

God...*until he's done with me?*

"What are you going to do to me?" My voice comes out stunted, like when I've been underwater for too long.

"How about I show you?" Malik's lips brush over my ear, and my entire being shudders.

My heart just about stops, and my breath goes short in my chest when he trails his free hand up my leg, leaving fire on my skin. He lifts my skirt, rolling it up my thighs until he reaches my panties, then he cups my sex and pushes his fingers beneath the fabric. A thick finger swipes over the bare skin of my pussy lips and into my wetness, pushing against my swollen clit.

"You're so wet for me, and I've barely touched you." He's still at my ear, and his breath feels hotter. "Is that how badly you want me, Gwen?"

I don't get to answer. A raw dose of pleasure hits me as he pushes his finger into my passage and starts a slow steady pump in, then out.

Hot arousal simmers through my body, hotter than lava, and oh my God, that feels good. So good I've stopped thinking of what's right and wrong for me.

Uncontrollable moans I would never be able to hide fall from my lips in response as he continues to stroke me, giving my body the pleasure it's desperate for.

"Ma... lik... ahhh." My body arches against the wall, and I grab his shirt.

"I'm going to fuck you, Malyshka." His answer electrifies the air around us, paralyzing my mind and my last resolve. "I'm going to fuck you right here against the wall and own every part of your body.

My lips part, but I'm incapable of doing anything else but feeling his touch.

He moves back to face me with a wicked yet satisfied grin on his handsome face.

We're eye to eye now, and I realize I'm not actually breathing. I thought I was, but the air has completely left my body. All that's left is a void.

He stares back at me as if he knows, and that air of menace I sensed surrounding him thickens.

His smile grows, and he presses his weight into me, pinning me to the wall. I'm held captive by his body, his dominating touch, and his stare.

I lift my chin as another moan stirs within my chest, then suddenly, his lips are on mine, kissing me, setting me on fire.

It's a glorious, breathless kiss he deepens by sweeping his tongue into my mouth so he can take more from me.

He kisses the way he carries himself. With the sort of confidence shown by someone who knows they own the world.

He kisses me like he owns me and like he knows I'm not capable of resisting him.

Sweet pleasure dances under my skin. It's intoxicating, and I want more. More of him. And more is exactly what he gives me when he speeds up his pumps, finger-fucking me into the wall.

Our kisses become hungry, and so does his touch.

I'm barely containing myself as it is, but I fall apart in a mess of shivers when he adds another finger into my passage.

The beginnings of an orgasm pull tightly at my insides like rope, and spikes of pleasure ripple through me.

He moves faster, taking me higher and higher. I throw my head back, waiting for the climax to hit. I'm so close, and he knows it. He's touching me in all the right places, giving my body everything it needs. But then he just stops. He stops kissing me and stops touching me, and I'm left starving for more.

Malik pulls away, and his eyes darken. "I'm clean. Are you?"

The question allows an ounce of reality to seep back into my mind, giving me a chance to save myself. But God help me, I don't want to. Everything about this man seems to be an exception to all my rules.

Just for tonight, maybe I can allow myself to indulge in the fantasy I had when I first met him. Just for tonight, for this moment. However long it will last.

"Answer me, Malyshka." His voice runs over my skin like warm honey, smooth and strong.

"I'm clean."

"Birth control?"

"I'm on the pill."

"Perfect."

Claiming my lips again, he kisses me hard, pulling me flush against his body and the solid bulge of his cock pressing into my abdomen.

Just like that, he makes me lose myself, and I give my body permission to enjoy him. Screw the consequences and all my reservations about him. Damn it all the way to hell. I can deal with whatever shit follows me later.

He wants me, and I want him. My body, heart, mind, and soul want him.

Right now, that's all I need to know and all I need to feel in the turbulent storm my life has become.

I run my hands over the hard muscle of his chest while his hands roam down my ass, gripping me with sheer possession.

He pauses kissing me to lift my top over my head. I was wearing one of those tops with the built-in bra, so my breasts are exposed the moment it comes off.

He returns to my lips, but this time rolling his thumbs over my hard nipples, tweaking and squeezing.

Pulling away again, he undoes his belt and pushes his pants down his hips. My mouth goes dry when he takes out his cock and I see how big and thick it is.

It's definitely the biggest cock I've ever seen. He notices me looking and gives me a sexy grin.

"There's plenty of time to play with me later, Malyshka. I need to be inside you now."

Later?

He's thinking about later? And he *needs* to be inside me now?

God, I must have stepped into some kind of wild fantasy where I have a guy like this telling me he needs to be inside my body.

My thoughts snap when he pushes me against the wall again, lifts my leg to hook it around his waist, then moves my panties aside.

Taking his cock, he guides himself to my entrance.

I gasp as he eases into me. At first, he takes his time, inching into me deeper and deeper, but the instant my walls widen to take his size and length, he slams into me.

Pleasure explodes in my soul, and I cry out from the impact. Then he starts fucking me.

Time shifts around me and pulling me into a sea of pleasure where my orgasm rises like a tidal wave.

Malik pounds into me harder and faster, our moans and the wet sounds of our bodies filling the room.

All I can do is hold on to him when he fucks me harder into the wall. Then I come and it feels like I'll never stop coming.

He groans and tightens his grip on my hips, grinding into me as a savage groan rumbles in his chest.

From the hardness of his cock plowing into me and the thickness of the vein popping out on the side of his neck, I know he's close. I've been there all this time, coming undone as he pounds into my body.

Suddenly, he fucks me even faster and harder, taking me to the pinnacle of pleasure, and we both come together. Me crying out so loud I'm sure people would have heard me and him shouting through his climax.

The climb down from such a high scatters my thoughts like light chasing away darkness, and I'm dizzy from pleasure. He releases his grip on me, and I sink against the wall, barely able to stand.

Malik's forehead rests against mine for a few heartbeats, and I think of what I just did.

I didn't even care that we're at the restaurant—in my office. The window is even open, so anyone could have heard me.

In fact, I'm almost certain someone would have.

Lifting his head, Malik gazes into my eyes, and I wonder what he's going to say to me.

He moves closer, brushing his nose against mine. "Your place or mine next?"

He's not finished with me.

This is another opportunity to escape, but I get the feeling he wouldn't allow me to leave.

I wouldn't allow myself to go either because I want more, too.

"My place."

Chapter Nine

Malik

Holy. Fucking. Hell.

This woman has definitely done something to me that I can't shake. The worst thing is, I have no desire to free myself from the seductress' spell.

I'd be a madman to say no to a woman who's currently on her knees deep throating my dick like her life depends on it.

Gwen has one slender hand wrapped around my shaft and her other stroking my balls while her hot wet mouth works me, awakening every cell in my body.

I'm supposed to be the one with the power here, but she's usurped that power by owning my dick.

This wasn't something I planned. All I wanted to do was see her. That's it.

I saw her, watched her like I have been all this time, and realized I couldn't make it through the night without tasting her the way I've wanted to since I knew she existed. I watched her walking around in that little skirt, and I wanted to get underneath it to own her pussy.

I'm not the kind of man to see a woman he wants to fuck and let her get away, so this is one of those moments of weakness I had to allow myself.

The pupils of her sea-green eyes dilate, dark with desire as she stares up at me. She's looking at me like she wants my approval. It throws me because she doesn't need it.

The more I've gotten to know her, the more I've realized she doesn't know how fucking beautiful she is and the effect she has on a man like me.

A dangerous man like me who knows everything about himself and knows his life is too dark for her. Gwen represents everything good and is the complete opposite of me.

At the very least, she's a woman who would deserves a man who can tell her the truth. But there was no fucking way I would have been able to resist the temptation to escape in this goddess tonight.

She releases my balls but continues to suck me and runs a hand over her breasts, circling the hard tips of her tight nipples. The light pink color has changed to a dark dusky rose.

Watching her touch herself is fucking hot, but fuck me, my dick goes hard-as-steel when that hand of hers slides down to her pussy and she rubs her clit.

The erotic-as-fuck sight sends my pulse into overdrive and leaves my mouth watering like a man who's been given food after not eating for weeks.

My dick jerks, and my balls tighten, a signal that I'm

going to blow my load, but I don't want to come in her mouth.

It's late. In the early hours of the morning, late. We've been at this for hours, and judging from the tiredness in her expression, this might be the last time.

If it is, I want to be inside her. I want to come inside her and feel her wet pussy wrapping around my length as I fuck her and take back control of owning her body.

I pull out of her mouth and grab the hand that's stroking her pussy.

"I'm sorry," she whispers, thinking she's done something wrong.

"Don't be, but that's my job. As long as I'm here, you don't touch that pussy until I tell you to. Now, get on the bed on your hands and knees, your ass up." I need to see that ass while I fuck her.

Her face flushes at my words, and I know this good girl isn't used to my forwardness or my dirty language. It makes being with her that much more salacious.

She obeys getting on her bed, doing exactly what I told her. I'm on the edge of exploding but take a moment to admire her beautiful body before me, kneeling on blue satin sheets as if she's been served up to me to devour.

I position myself behind her and trace my hand down her torso. She shudders against me, then our bodies mold into each other when I press into her and she sinks into me.

I lower my mouth to her pussy and slide my tongue across her swollen clit, loving how soaked she is for me. The glorious scent of her arousal fills me, stirring the beast inside me that wants to possess her.

"Oh God," she whimpers, clutching a handful of the sheets as her back dips into an arch.

I suck on the nub harder, licking some of her juices, then I circle the tight rosette of her asshole, wondering if she's a virgin there. I would love to take her there, but I'll leave that for another time.

Sliding my hands up her body, I play with her nipples. Mindless moans of pleasure hum from her body.

"Malik, I'm going to come." Her voice holds pleasurable agony within every word.

Hearing her sound that way because of what I'm doing does something to me I can't describe and probably shouldn't try to.

I lick her some more, then stop because I want her to come when I'm inside her, too.

"Not yet, Malyshka. Not yet," I mutter.

I straighten, then guide my straining length to her entrance. Her body welcomes me, and I sink so deeply into her it's difficult to see where she begins and I end.

Blood pumps harder in my veins when the walls of her pussy tighten and I move inside her.

The sensation of being inside her again scorches every nerve in my body, and I let loose, pounding into her pussy.

"Oh, Malik... oh... oh!" she screams out.

I respond in Russian, telling her I want to destroy her pussy and do other dirty things to her body that would probably make her run from me. I know she can't understand a goddamn thing I'm saying, but I say it anyway, hoping she can feel how fucking badly I want her.

"Malyshka," I growl, pounding harder into her.

My heart is hammering in my ears, but so is the sound of us, along with the sweet smell of sex.

I slam into her sweet cunt repeatedly like I've unleashed the psychotic side of me. Her body spasms around me, unable to stop, and she comes.

The tightness of her walls squeezes my length, and I lose every ounce of control I had and come, too, flooding her passage with my hot cum.

Then it's over.

The life seems to drain from her body, and she collapses onto the bed, her hands still clutching the sheets.

Breathing hard with sweat covering my body, I sink next to her and slip my hand around her waist.

She turns to face me, giving me a lazy, dreamy smile.

"You're tired." I kiss the top of her shoulder, then fill my palm with her breast.

"No, I'm fine."

"Liar." I smirk.

Light laughter falls from her lips. I love the sound. "Okay, maybe I am lying. But I don't want to stop."

I press into her, feeling myself getting hard again, and suck her nipple. "Bad girl, you want more."

She moans, so I suck harder. "Is that such a bad thing?"

"Fuck no."

I pick her up and set her on top of me so she can straddle my hips.

Her beautiful breasts bounce up and down, looking ripe and juicy, begging me to suck them, so I feast on them.

"Ride me," I tell her, gripping her curvy hips.

That rose-colored flush returns to her cheeks but soon

disappears, and Miss Gwen St. James becomes the seductress again.

With my cum already inside her, she slides her glorious body down onto my dick, and I'm ready to go again. Seconds later, we're fucking. Fucking as if this is the very first time and we can't stop.

But that's not the last time.

The last time happens when I have her on her back and I'm fucking her into the mattress. Half the sheets are falling off the bed, and Gwen's hair is a mess of sexiness, her skin glowing with the light of pleasure.

I made the mistake of going into the bathroom to get a warm towel to clean her off, and when I got back, she was fast asleep.

That was five minutes ago, and I'm still here staring at her, looking at a woman I can't keep, no matter who she is.

If she's not Santiago's daughter and we have this fling, then that is all it will be. But if she is his daughter, she'll become a pawn in my game, and she will hate me.

Either way, I would lose this.

Personally, I don't think Gwen is Santiago's daughter. Her life doesn't fit what I would expect of a cartel king, but neither does Allyson's.

Maybe it's more about the innocent light of goodness I can see in Gwen.

The sound of something scratching against the door pulls me from my thoughts.

It's Sebastian. Since it's nearly six in the morning, I'm guessing he's probably used to coming up here and staying with Gwen until she wakes.

He did the same thing that first night I stayed here.

Quickly, I put my clothes on, then look at the beauty asleep in her bed one last time before I leave the bedroom, completely unsure of what I can trust myself to do when I see her again.

The dog gives me a hopeful look when he sees me coming through the door, so I spare another few minutes to feed him and take him for a little walk before I head back to the beach house.

Zakh is awake already.

He's in the living room and looks like he's been working for a while.

"You slept with her, didn't you?" He asks without taking his eyes off the screen.

I sigh and press my lips together. "Yes."

"Malik—"

"I know. Whatever it is you're going to say, I already know."

"Well, that was easy." He smirks.

"Sorry I was away. I didn't know you were going to be up working." When I left he was on the phone talking to Lorelai.

"Something came up and I had to check it out." He points to the laptop screen. "It might be nothing, but it's worth a shot."

"What have you found?" Hope rises in me and I move closer, pulling up a chair to sit next to him.

"I spoke to a guy Santiago used to hire when he was here."

My interest instantly piques. "How the hell did you find him?"

"Believe me, it wasn't easy."

"What did he say?"

"He and another guy did jobs for Santiago. The other guy was Santiago's driver. He used to take him to meet his daughter and her mother at the park a few weeks before Christmas every year."

"Does this guy have a name?"

"He's dead."

I press down on my back teeth in frustration. It's so fucking convenient that everyone who knew Santiago—who could help me—is dead or off the grid in some sort of way.

"Okay, so maybe we could get surveillance of the park?"

"Way ahead of you. Santiago arranged for the surveillance to be switched off when he was there. But I came up with another idea when I went to check out the place." He takes a breath, and I can see he's not entirely confident in whatever idea he's come up with. "The park has a custodian who I'm told has worked there for over twenty years. He's parked pretty much in the same spot that's allocated to staff. His vehicle has its own surveillance, which wouldn't have been switched off. Although he's changed trucks several times, he's kept the same security system. I already hacked into the digital files, and I saw Santiago in the park, but the recording of him was only for five minutes. The custodian left the grounds after that."

"Jesus, Zakh." This is where our talents differ in vast quantities.

"Don't get your hopes up, brother. Everything we're already doing here is a long shot, but this is an even bigger one, which I'm not sure will work." He sighs heavily.

"Just tell me what your thoughts are." I don't want to give up on something before we even begin.

"If we can get footage of his daughter with him then we know who to look for. We have pictures of both Gwen and Allyson as kids. Even if we can't get a clear image from the recording we can use facial recognition software to fill in the blanks. The problem is there's a lot of files to check through and as it's an old security system we can't do a quick search without running the risk of missing something."

"Let's just do it."

"Malik, this really might not work. So far, I haven't found any other footage of Santiago. Also, the custodian might not have been there on the day Santiago visited. Or, like in the one I found, he could have left for the day or left just as everyone got there."

"How many recordings did you get?"

"Two hundred. I've gone through ten. I've narrowed the time down to an eighteen-hour window. That covers a wide range, and we can skip through any surveillance that's not of the park."

"Okay, I got it."

"If we focus on this today and tomorrow, we should get through it. Allyson has invited us to a party later. I'm gonna go. You don't have to go. I figured you could stay here and keep looking."

"Sure, I can do that. That sounds like a plan."

An uneasy look enters his eyes, and I know he has more to tell me. I know my brother so well that I know whatever it is, it's not something I'm going to like.

"What else is there, Zakh?" I lean forward, resting my elbows on my knees.

"Desmier called. Aleksander wants us back next week if we're not able to figure this out."

My shoulders sag. Aleksandr Ivanov is the leader of the Knights and the Pakhan of the Bratva. What he says is the law. Desmier is the Sovietnik, his second-in-command, so what he says is the law, too.

"Fuck. We've only been here for five days."

"Malik, you know if we don't figure this out by next week, there'll be no point anyway, right? Diego is going to be chosen to lead the cartel after his father's funeral. We'll have fuck all to pursue if we don't find Santiago's daughter." He tilts his head to the side. "Alexander also doesn't fully support us being here. He doesn't think we have enough evidence to investigate either of the women, and he doesn't want us making a mess where we have no actual trail to follow."

"Well, he can go fuck himself." I mean it. I'm always and ever the loyal Knight, but I play by my own rules when I need to. "He of all people should know that sometimes you don't always get a perfect trail to follow. Sometimes, we have to start with minimal information and work backwards."

"He just doesn't want us to get anything wrong. Normally, if we see something we want, whether it's a person or a thing, we take it. We can't just do that here."

"I know. It's just that I can feel we're close."

"Maybe so, but I'm also at my limit with ideas. And I think looking through these recordings might be the last thing I can do for you." His voice holds regret. "You're going after the dead, Malik. I hate to say this, but maybe the fact that your enemy is dead has to be enough."

"No. It's not fucking enough." I grip onto the edge of my chair. "It's not enough, Zakh. Year in, year out, I go about like everything is fine with me, but I'm not. I say nothing to anybody because I know no one can help me, and I can't help myself. Then I found this lead like finding the proverbial needle in the haystack. So, this can't be the end of the line. Taking the cartel is the only thing that will give me justice."

"I understand. Which is why I'm giving this my all, but if we hit D-day next week, our attempts are fruitless and there's nothing either of us can do. Regardless of what is happening and how far you've come, or how close, the problem is Santiago didn't want his daughter to be found by anybody."

I nod slowly, completely agreeing. The man certainly didn't want his daughter being discovered by men like me, who would use her as a weapon.

"I'm sure you've guessed that he probably didn't want her to be part of that life. His new will and the ownership of the assets as they are now seem like a big fuck-you to his family. They know they'll never fully be in charge, but they have what they have. It's like leaving your empire to a pet."

"Let's try looking through the recordings. We might find what we're looking for."

He nods, but looks like he doesn't have much faith that we'll find anything.

I have to keep my faith going and believe that we will.

Otherwise, the thirst for blood will consume me and drive me insane.

This time, there won't be anyone to bring me back.

Chapter Ten

Gwen

I've been awake for a few hours now, just lying in bed daydreaming of Malik and all the ways he devoured me all night.

His deep, sensual voice is still caressing me with sweet nothings in Russian that only my soul understands, and my body is still humming with the pleasure.

He left before I woke up and it's okay. I expected him to leave. I don't have much experience but I figured men like him don't stick around.

Sure it dulled my mood but I accepted last night was clearly a one-night stand which resulted from our flirting over the last few days, and now he's gone.

The only trace left of him is the faint musky scent of his cologne clinging to the air. It's stark against the usual floral fragrances of my perfumes and bath things.

Being with Malik in my office was wild and so unlike me,

but when we got back here, that was when he rewrote every woman's fantasy and gave it new meaning.

I lost count of how many times he was inside me. I just remember that we couldn't stop and neither of us wanted to.

Sebastian runs in the room, hops on the bed and curls up next to me, looking me over with concern with his huge blue-silver eyes.

Sitting up, I realize the poor little thing thinks I'm sick. A quick glance at the clock on the wall and I gasp when I see it's two o'clock in the afternoon.

No wonder my dog thinks I'm sick. I can't remember the last time I was in bed at this hour. But then, I have a reason for that.

I can't remember the last time I had sex all night, and with a man who is practically a stranger. *Practically, Gwen?*

Just because I know the stranger's name and allowed the man to devour me doesn't automatically make him someone I know.

The normal me—the girl who works twenty-four seven and tries to be responsible in every way—would be going crazy by now.

She would be asking me why I thought it was a good idea to first of all, have sex in my office with the hot ex-Navy lieutenant without protection, then invite him into my bed.

That Gwen would ask me all sorts of questions I probably should acknowledge, but I'm putting her in the back of beyond because if given a choice to repeat last night, I'd do it again.

I'd do it all over again quicker than a heart can beat. Malik made me feel something more than what I've been feeling for too long.

I swivel my feet around, and the decadent ache between my thighs confirms Malik's promise that first night I met him —that I would remember being with him.

I do remember, and so does my body.

I get off the bed, pull on my dressing gown, then head downstairs to get some coffee. Sebastian follows.

When I get in the little area I've sectioned off for Sebastian's bed I see a new bowl of food has been put out for him.

Malik. He did this.

My gosh. Could this man be any more perfect?

But what will happen when I see him again?

How am I supposed to act?

What should I say?

It was he who sought me out last night. One look at him standing on that balcony at the restaurant, and I knew what he wanted.

I felt what he wanted well before he touched me, and like an addict hooked on their favorite drug, I wanted more and more and more when I gave in to him.

Malik was my first one-night stand.

I haven't been with anyone since Gage. Before Gage, I was a virgin. That was why catching him cheating on me on my birthday, of all the days, hurt so

much more.

He ripped out all the love I had in me for him in such a way that I still can't feel bad that he died in what could only be a brutal and horrific killing.

I release a little breath and gaze out the sliding doors in the sitting room as if the picture-perfect scene outside can tell me what to do next.

The moment is disrupted when I hear my phone ringing. The ringtone tells me it's Dru.

I thought my phone was upstairs, but it's down here. Somewhere. I follow the sound to the coat stand and find my purse with my phone chiming inside.

Quickly, I reach into my bag and grab the phone, answering before it can switch over to my voicemail.

"Hi," I say first.

"Hey, there." From the sullen tone of her voice, I know something's wrong straightaway. Dru has never been good at keeping things from me.

A lump forms in my throat. The only thing that could be wrong is the thing I want the most right now to fix my life.

"What's up?" My voice sounds faint, shaking as if it's on the edge of the wind.

"We didn't get the loan, Gwen."

My body collapses in on itself, and I sink into the wall, sliding down to the floor. Although I sensed the problem could only be that, I feel like I'm going to die.

"Gwen, are you there?"

"Yes. I...here." I swallow past the lump now swelling in my throat and take several deep breaths. "Thank you for trying."

"I'm so sorry I couldn't get it. The bank said that my earnings weren't high enough for the loan to be fully approved. My additional income from our business wasn't stable enough either. I really am so sorry."

"It's... it's okay." It's not okay, but I don't know what else to say. Every scenario of what could happen next is flashing through my mind, and it's all bad, bad, bad.

"Gwen, listen to me. Please hear me out."

"I'm listening." I take another set of shallow breaths.

"We have forty-one thousand. I just wired it to you. What you need to do is call Conrad's office and offer to pay that amount now. Ask if some arrangement could be made to pay the rest in installments or at a later date."

I'm listening to her, but I don't know if that will work. In fact, I doubt it will. On my last encounter with Conrad, he made it clear he wanted full payment with no exceptions. That was why I freaked out.

"Do you hear me, Gwen?" Dru asks in a shaky voice.

"I hear you." I can barely hear myself over the drumming of my heart in my ears.

"Please do that. If he could just give you some time and be reasonable, he'll get his money. If he can't, the only other thing to do is call Sheriff Donovan."

Call Sheriff Donovan?

I don't know which will kill me quicker. Doing that or doing nothing. I was told that people would die if I contacted anyone like Sheriff Donovan.

If anyone I loved died because of me, that by itself would kill me.

"Gwen?"

"I'm listening." I need to face the rest of this by myself. Dru has done enough for me, and it's not right to involve her in the situation anymore. "I'll do what you said."

"Okay. I'm going into Charlotte later. I have training there for work, so I'll have to stay overnight. I will call you, and please, for the love of God, update me on whatever happens. *Please.*"

"I will," I promise, even though I've already decided to tell her only what she needs to know.

"I'll speak to you later. Be strong, Gwen, be strong."

"Thank you."

We end the call, and my hand drops to the ground as if the life has been drained from it.

My heart speeds, galloping in my chest, and my lungs tighten with terror.

God... what am I going to do?

What the hell am I going to do?

My breaths come out ragged, and then it just cuts as if someone switched off the oxygen supply flowing into my body.

I'm having a panic attack, or maybe a heart attack. Maybe both.

Water, I need it. Lots of it.

I manage to stand and get myself into the kitchen, where I turn the cold tap on full blast and place my head underneath it.

The cold, cold water soothes my skin and numbs my mind, but it does nothing to rid my fears.

Once the panic is over, I pull my head back, turn off the tap, and try to think of how the fuck I'm going to get myself out of this mess.

Calling Conrad has to be a last resort. I'm still hellbent on finding that money.

Maybe I could go to the bank again and speak to the manager. I should have gotten the loan. My family and I have banked with them for years. We have business and personal accounts that they can access to see that I can afford a monthly repayment of a loan.

Maybe I should go and plead my case. I need to.

I have until Friday to pay Conrad. Today is Monday.

With that reasoning and threatening reminder, I dash upstairs, get ready, and leave. I jump into my car and head into the city, all thoughts of last night gone.

There's a lot of traffic, so it takes me well over an hour to reach the bank. Once there, it's another two hours before I get to see the manager because I didn't have an appointment. Then it takes him roughly ten minutes to deny me again. This time, I suppose I should be grateful that the rejection came with more explanation and an expression of sorrow that he couldn't help more.

I leave the bank like I've just been given terminal news and drive to a secluded spot on the beach. There, I sit in my car for another hour before I make the dreaded phone call to Conrad's office.

A woman with a New York accent answers the phone on the second ring.

"Hello, can I help you?" she says with more insistency when I don't answer straightaway. I really don't want to have this conversation, but I'm a little thrown that I've made it through to what seems like a secretary. I've never had to call Conrad before, but I expected to hear someone who sounded like a hell beast on the other end of the line.

"Yes. Hello. My name is Gwen St. James. I'm calling to discuss a loan repayment."

"Just a second. I'm bringing up your details on our system."

That surprises me, too, and makes me curse Gage all over again. That fucking asshole put me in this damn position.

Fuck him for doing this to me. Fuck him.

"I've got your details," the secretary says. "The records

show you're due to pay a hundred and seventy-five thousand this Friday. Are you calling to pay now?"

I almost laugh. I'm not sure how I don't. The question sounds rhetorical to me because I'm sure few people pay that kind of money days in advance of the due date when they never had it before. She'd know from the system that I didn't have the money when they first wanted it. I don't have it all now.

"No, I'm not calling to pay now, unfortunately. I was unable to retrieve all the funds in such a short amount of time. I have forty grand. I wondered if I could pay that now and pay the balance in installments."

I'm proud of myself for getting out the words without tripping over the other thoughts clashing in my mind. But the long pause I receive suggests my request is far from acceptable.

"I'm not sure Conrad will agree to that. Your partner, Gage, missed over five payments, breaching the contract."

"I didn't know about this loan." The tears raining in my soul echo in my voice. "I didn't take it out. Gage did."

"The evidence we have on file suggests otherwise." She might sound professional, but she's as crooked as Conrad.

"Look, please just ask him if that arrangement can be made. At least I have some of the money."

"Okay. I will pass on the message, and he'll get back to you later."

"Thank you." I've barely uttered my thanks when she hangs up.

I stare at the phone in my hand for a few moments hoping like hell Conrad could grow a heart.

I spare a few seconds to message Dru to let her know I've

contacted Conrad and am waiting for his decision. She messages back straightaway, telling me not to worry, but I know she's only telling me that because there's nothing more she can do.

There's nothing more I can do, either.

I rest my head against the soft leather of the car seat and wait. I don't want to go home yet with this angst lingering in the air, so I decide to wait right here for Conrad to get back to me.

When night falls and I don't hear from him, I start up my engine and head home, feeling worse than I did when I left earlier.

My legs shake when I get out of my car and walk up the path to my door.

My mind is so wrapped up in my worries, I almost miss that the door is ajar.

As in, it's... open. And not the way I left it.

The kitchen light is also on. It was daylight when I left, so I wouldn't have turned that on.

Oh my God.

There's someone in my house.

Someone is in my house.

I can't go in. I mustn't. That would be foolish.

I back away, getting ready to run back to my car, when I hear a little whimper.

It's Sebastian. The whimper sounds again, and my stomach flips when it hits me, he sounds injured. I can't leave him inside.

Without another thought, I open the door wider and walk into what could be my final doom or death.

Within seconds, I hear footsteps in the kitchen. Several of them.

I press down on my molars and clutch my chest to keep my heart from leaping out, then, with all the strength I can summon, I keep going.

One step follows the one before until I'm in the kitchen facing Conrad, who is sitting at the breakfast table drinking from my grandmother's teacup.

Dressed in full black, he looks like he just stepped out of hell. The light shines down on his bald head like a spotlight, almost making him seem younger. I don't know how old he is, and it's not easy to guess because he's built like a wrestler and his skin looks like it's been burned by far too many years of intense sun.

I've assumed he must be in the latter end of his fifties, but he could be younger than that. Dark eyes bore into me like he's going to rip me apart, and my skin heats like it might burn right off my body, turning to ashes so it can become one with the wind.

"Gwen St. James, I got an interesting message from you earlier." His gravelly voice sounds like it's filled with rocks and sand.

"I'm sorry I couldn't find the money. You have to understand that—" My voice cuts when one of Conrad's henchmen steps out of the sunroom carrying Sebastian.

Blood covers the fur on his neck, and he whimpers again when he sees me.

My soul falls through the earth at the sight. I rush forward to take him, but Conrad gets up so fast I hardly see him move. What I feel next is the back of his hand across my face. The impact knocks the life out of me, and I go flying backward, screaming as I connect with the floor.

Pain rattles my brain and body. No one has ever laid a hand on me. I've never even been in a fight with another girl at school, so this... this pain is one I've never felt before.

Conrad gets up in my face and grabs my chin. Tears pour out of my eyes from the pain as my body shakes uncontrollably.

"Listen to me, you little bitch." He tightens his grip on my face, digging his fingers into my skin. With his free hand, he pulls his gun from his back pocket and places it at my temple, just like he did that night the other week. I cry harder, and he runs the cold metal over my skin. "I don't have to understand anything. And I won't. The terms have changed, and the date has moved up. I want my money tomorrow."

"But I don't have it," I cry. "There's no way I can get it."

"Then you better pray God can help you. You have until noon tomorrow to find it. Fail to deliver, and your dog is the first thing to die. Then I'm coming for you, Gwen St. James. And since you've already pissed me off, I've decided your fine ass would be best placed in an auction to the highest bidder."

He releases me and rises to his feet, but I'm still shaking and crying.

"No, please."

"Don't beg. It's pathetic."

"But there's nothing I can do."

"That's not my problem." He cocks his head to the side, and the man holding Sebastian walks to the door.

I suddenly realize that they're going to take him. "Please don't take my dog!"

I try to get up, but Conrad points his gun at me, and I freeze.

"Noon tomorrow. Noon." He smiles back at me, revealing disjointed teeth. "Oh, and if you tell anybody about our little fiasco, you're dead, your grandmother is dead, and that cute little friend you have is dead, too. Got it?"

I nod vigorously, as if I've been programmed to do so.

Sebastian howls, trying to break free, but the man holding him tightens his grip. Droplets of blood fall onto the floor as they walk through the kitchen door. Conrad follows, keeping his gun pointed at me.

I stay in that frightened child-like position for what feels like forever, feeling like I've just woken up in a nightmare.

This can't be happening.

It just can't. Everything I feared is unravelling before my eyes, and I don't know what to do.

There's no way I'm going to find that money by noon tomorrow. No way. So, what do I do?

Let them kill Sebastian?

Then sell me.

With my soul shaking and the pain in my face spreading over my entire body, I stand.

My gaze lands on the picture of my grandfather dressed in his Air Force uniform. It's hanging near the fridge. Grams put it there because my grandfather loved her cooking, and her pancakes were one of his favorite ways to start the day.

As I look at the picture now, I see my grandfather's smiling face, but he makes me think of another military man I know.

I can't go to the police about Conrad, but there's someone else who might help me.

Maybe I can go to the ex-Navy lieutenant I've felt wasn't entirely who he claims to be. That tattoo of his means something, and he might be exactly the person who can deal with a man like Conrad.

Maybe in this instance, the devil I don't know can help me before the one I know destroys me.

I have to try.

Chapter Eleven

Malik

I take a drag on my cigar and blow out several rings of smoke. They drift outside through the window and blend in with the darkness of the night.

I suppose I blend in too. I'm sitting on the window bay with the lights out in the room. The only visible light is the glowing fiery end of my cigar.

I'm alone in the house. Zakh left for Allyson's party a little while ago. I could have gone with him but I decided to stay back and keep looking through the recordings of the park.

We spent the entire day searching through a total of a hundred videos and found nothing.

The day feels like it was wasted, but I'm going to keep going until the end. Only then will I accept that I tried everything.

I'm just taking a break now. And thinking about Gwen. St. James.

She's crept right back in my mind, along with the wildness we shared last night.

I'm fully aware I only dragged myself away from her body because she fell asleep. Chances are if she hadn't, I'd still be balls deep inside her.

Her slumber gave me the moment of reprieve to come back to my senses. But I haven't been able to shake her from my system.

I know never to mix business with pleasure, and what's worse is mixing business with the pleasure of a woman who's not from my world.

The unwritten rules imply never to do it, and the written ones dictate the same thing.

Even though my father allowed me to branch out and join the Navy, if he were still alive, he would have married me off by now to an heir of the Knights or a woman from the Bratva elite. That is the rules and the law of the Knights.

As a Volkova, it's also my legacy. I'm just not one for playing by the rules.

Since I'm planning to marry the heir to the Navarro Cartel and their pharmaceutical company so I can take over, no rules on earth or Valhalla apply to me.

No one can come and tell me having control over such a giant wouldn't benefit us in unimaginable ways many have never thought of attaining.

Of course, that's if I get it.

This is all taking too long for men like my brother and me who have technology at our fingertips. And I guess that's just the problem—technology can't solve everything.

People can still hide their secrets and bury them deep, deep in the earth where people like us can't find them.

Right now, I'm in this Pleasantville-looking town where everyone knows their neighbor and they're all too close for comfort. I've come to a standstill and I can't see my way around.

I'm not one to accept defeat, and I won't. Not when I've come so far. It's just that, as usual, time is fucking with me. It wants me to wait the way I did for that year in Kazakhstan when those motherfuckers made a game of me. And time wants me to wait like an idiot for another six years to pass before I get another breakthrough. Or nothing.

Everything is fucking with me, and now I can't bleed this woman from my mind, who I don't think is Santiago's daughter.

The sight of someone rushing toward the house snaps me out of my reverie. The person runs into the moonlight, and I realize it's Gwen.

She looks like she's crying or has been. The thought moves me.

I put out the cigar and rush downstairs.

I open the door before she can knock and confirm that she is crying, but worst

of all, there's an angry bruise on the side of her face.

Someone hit her.

Someone put their hands on her and hurt her.

My temper flares at the thought and I catch her face when fresh tears run down her pale cheeks.

"Please, help me," she stutters.

Something happens in my heart I never thought possible. I feel. I feel it beating in my chest, quickening with warmth in response to seeing her this way, asking me for help.

"Who did this to you?" I demand.

Her breath catches and tears roll down her cheeks. "I'm so sorry to bother you—"

"Gwen, who the fuck did this to you?" My voice comes out so harsh and loud she quivers in my grasp. I know she's afraid of me, but clearly not scared enough to stop herself from running to me for help.

"A man I owe money. He took my dog, and he's going to kill him and take me, too, if I don't pay by noon tomorrow."

Like fuck is that going to happen. "What's his name?" I speak through gritted teeth, my blood spiking with a lethal dose of rage.

"Conrad Duncan."

What the fuck? Conrad Duncan? I know the name because Zakh and I checked out the town for people like him who might be alerted to our presence.

Conrad doesn't travel in our circles, but he'll know who we are. If not by sight, then the tattoo.

He's small fry compared to me. Nevertheless, he's still a man you don't fuck with. How the hell did Gwen get mixed up with him? I knew she was in financial trouble, but how did I miss this?

I grab my jacket, which holds my gun, and shrug into it.

"Let's go."

She stares back at me with disbelief, as if she considered I might turn her away.

"Gwen, come on. Do you know where I can find him?"

"Yes. His office is at the edge of the city. He's open late."

I slip my arm around her and usher her to my truck. I

open the door for her to climb in the passenger's side, then I get in and tear out of the driveway.

"Thank you so much for doing this." She looks at me, tears still streaking her pretty face. "But please don't get hurt. Conrad has a group of men at that office."

"It's going to take more than that to hurt me." I glance at her, and her gaze switches to the tattoo on my wrist. Again, I think she has an idea of what it means. If she didn't, she would have gone to the cops about this problem of hers, not me.

"So, how have you come to owing this guy?"

She glances away, and for a moment, I think she's not going to tell me, but then she starts talking and tells me everything. I learn more about Gage and all the fucked-up shit he's done to Gwen.

The motherfucker is lucky he's dead. If he were still alive, I would tear the skin off his body, then make him watch as I rip his heart from his chest in brutal Bratva style and crush it in my hands. Men like him don't deserve mercy or compassion. They prey on whoever they can sink their lies into and drain them until there's nothing left. Not even the person they once were.

I speed down the road knowing Gwen is worried and scared for her dog.

She's stopped talking now, but she's still crying. She's looking through the window with her head slightly dipped in shame as teardrops fall onto her lap.

I'm compelled to reach over and tell her it will be okay, but I don't. I've already accomplished my mission with her, and she trusts me.

If I succeed, and she's not Santiago's daughter, or if I fail,

I'm leaving. I'll be gone without notice, as if I was never here. So, this thing between us, whatever it is, has to end here. Tonight.

"Over there. That's his office." Gwen points at the seedy-looking building in a complex with a pawnshop and a hair salon attached to it.

I turn into the parking lot, scanning the area.

A host of rowdy men hanging around by the wall on our far left look like they're ready to start trouble, and there are two women who look like hookers standing on the sidewalk under the lamppost.

Most of Wilmington has that safety I'm not used to, but I can tell from the locked doors on the houses and apartments nearby that this is a bad area.

I'd get Gwen to stay in the truck, but since I don't have backup and I don't know if Conrad's men are out here, it's best she comes in with me.

I jump out of the truck and open the door for her to get out. She has a shiner now on that bruise, which just pisses me off even more.

"Come on, we'll be okay," I tell her when she looks hesitant. "All you need to do is stay close to me until I tell you otherwise. You hear me?"

"Yes." She nods, pulling in a deep breath.

With that, I place my hand to the small of her back, ushering her across the parking lot until we're at Conrad and Co.'s door.

I push it open, and we walk in. There's no one around, but at first glance, the place looks like a normal office. There's a reception desk, chairs in the waiting area, and magazines stacked neatly in a rack for you to distract yourself while you wait.

But the faint scent of blood cloying to the air that only a guy like me can pick up opens the reality of what Conrad and Co. truly is.

I take that scent as the cue to retrieve my gun. When I do, Gwen stiffens beside me. I glance down at her, but she doesn't look at me. Her eyes are on the Glock in my hand, and I won't tell her she's not to be afraid of me.

A mixture of raised boisterous voices echoes off the walls in the back office. The sound amplifies the fear on Gwen's face, suggesting one of the voices must belong to Conrad.

I proceed forward, pulling her to my side when we get closer.

I walk up to the door. A guy with a buzz cut notices me first.

He stands and balls his fist.

"Sorry, pal, you need an appointment, and as you can see, reception is closed," he dares to speak to me.

Ignoring him and his dumb-as-fuck face, I walk into the room with Gwen at my side, finding three other men. One of which is Conrad. He's sitting behind his desk.

At first, he and his goons look like they're ready to kill, especially when they see Gwen. But when Conrad looks at me like he recognizes me, his face turns ghost-pale and he just about manages to signals his men not to charge at me.

I smile when I see that. "Conrad Duncan, a wise choice. You look like you know me, but we've never had the pleasure of meeting."

"I do, Malik Volkova," he answers with a cautious undertone lacing through his voice. He also looks at my arm with the tattoo on my wrist.

Gwen's eyes are on me the moment he does that. From his declaration and actions, I'm sure she's not thinking Conrad knows me because I'm new in town. She can also see Conrad looks like he's about to shit himself just for seeing me.

"Good. We can skip the formalities and the bullshit, then. Give me the dog now and show me the loan agreement."

Conrad stiffens, and his nostrils flare as he switches his gaze from me to Gwen.

"Man to man, I'm sure you can understand that—"

I raise my gun and fire a shot into the roof. That has everyone cowering.

"I'm not going to ask you again."

"How the fuck is this fair?" Conrad challenges, getting up and coming toward me. His third mistake of the evening. His first was what he did to Gwen, the second was pissing me off by challenging me.

"This bitch owes me a lot of money. I want it." The more he talks, the more I see he's not very bright.

And neither are his men. Out of the corner of my eye, I catch sight of the bulky one who looks like a bulldog reaching for his gun.

Before the asshole can take his next breath, I pull one of my knives from my jacket and throw it at him. The knife wedges his hand into his leg, sending him to his knees, howling with pain.

I whip around with one hand on my gun and one on

Gwen, looking at the shocked faces of Conrad and the other men.

Mentally, I mull over what other weapons I brought with me. I don't have my full ensemble, but I have enough, plus my strength.

"Conrad, I'm going to give you a piece of advice. Don't fuck with me. I'm not like my brothers. I will kill you." Everyone knows my brothers are ruthless men who show no mercy. What I mean by saying I'm not like them is they still have some humanity. Something that would stop them from killing meaninglessly. I don't have any such thing to stop me. If I ever had it, it died alongside the man I was in that prison. "One last time. Give me the dog and let me see the loan agreement."

With great reluctance, Conrad gives the man at the far left a nod. The man walks through the back door.

I keep my gun ready just in case he tries any shit. I don't want Gwen to get hurt.

Conrad opens his desk drawer, searches through some files, then sets an agreement on the desk.

"Now, we both know Miss St. James didn't agree to this." I keep my eyes and my gun on him. I'm glad when he doesn't protest and insist that she did because I would just kill him.

"Maybe so, but I'm out of pocket by a hundred and seventy-five grand."

"And you're going to stay that way. That strike to her face is payment enough."

"Are you fucking kidding me?" He steps forward.

"Do I look like I'm kidding? Believe me, Conrad Duncan, you don't want a problem with me. Since you know who I am, I shouldn't have to tell you it wouldn't be a good idea to piss me off."

His face turns to a stony mask of defeat, and he nods. "Alright, play it your way."

"Of course. Now, tear up that agreement." I wave the gun toward it.

He picks up the document and tears it in half.

"Good boy." I smile. "Now, what you're going to do is this: delete Gwen's name from your system and your mind. You and your people will not go to her restaurant, anywhere near her house, or her ever again. Is that understood?"

He looks at Gwen for a moment, then nods slowly.

At that moment, the other guy returns with Sebastian. Gwen rushes toward them and he hands her the dog, who I see is injured. Matted blood covers the entire right side of Sebastian's fur, and he looks despondent even though he's looking at Gwen.

Seeing that rekindles my anger, and I think of the perfect way to part with Conrad Duncan.

"One last thing, Conrad," I say.

"What? What now?"

"Which hand did you use to strike Gwen?" I give him a malicious smile.

He stares back at me with the fear of God in his eyes. "Why? It's done and dusted. I've agreed to waiver the loan."

"Which hand did you use to strike Gwen?" I ask again, emphasizing every syllable of my words.

"This one." He holds up his right hand.

He's about to say something else, but I fire a shot straight through his hand, showing him what kind of psycho I am.

Like his friend in the corner, he goes down. His shouts of

pain mix with Gwen's scream, and he looks at me with fear that I might take his life.

I'm not going to do that tonight. If I were, I wouldn't do that in front of Gwen. For now, I'll allow him to spend the rest of his life looking over his shoulder.

"Don't let me see you again, Conrad."

When he nods, I turn to Gwen, who is shaking and looking more afraid of me than she was before.

"Come on, we need to take Sebastian to the vet." I soften my voice on purpose to loosen her fears.

The mention of going to the vet seems to help, along with putting my gun back in my pocket where she can't see it anymore.

I put my arm around her for more assurance and guide her out of this hellhole.

"Thank you," she mumbles when we get back into the truck.

"Don't mention it."

She holds my gaze, searching my eyes as if she's doing her best to find something.

People say the eyes are the windows to your soul. If that's what she's looking for, she won't find mine.

* * *

Two hours later, I have her back at her house safe and sound from her demons and monsters.

One of the men cut Sebastian with a knife, so he got stitches and bandages. The wound wasn't too deep, but Sebastian was traumatized, as expected.

He's lying on Gwen's bed next to her while she strokes his fur.

It's time for me to go. It was time to leave when I got here, yet I'm still here.

I waited for Gwen to get cleaned up and ready for bed, and I even fed the dog.

It's hard to believe I'm standing here looking at them when just last night, I was rolling around in that bed with Gwen practically glued to my dick.

"Thank you so much for everything," Gwen says with a grateful smile. She looks exhausted, like she might fall asleep at any moment. "I don't know how I'm ever going to repay you. You have no idea what you've done for me tonight, seriously."

"How about I figure out how you can repay me and let you know?"

"That works. There is still pie."

I give her a grin. "There's that, yes."

Although she looks as grateful as she sounds, I sense her apprehension. She can't figure me out. I helped her, but what she saw me do was bad.

I went in by myself and dealt with Conrad and his men. She also knows I would have killed all of them without hesitation.

I know she has a million questions she won't ask me because she probably knows I won't give her answers.

Gwen tucks her hair behind her ear, revealing the bruise. Unable to help myself, I move closer and brush over her cheek.

Sebastian barks and shuffles over so I can touch his head.

I do with the best intentions at heart, but when I glimpse

the fascination in Gwen's eyes, my fucking dick hardens wanting to take her again like last night.

I shouldn't. As Zakh rightly pointed out the other day, I'm not here for fun. That means I should go now.

Allowing my dick to take charge again will make everything worse than it already is.

"I should head out. Can I get you anything before I go?"

A twinge of disappointment flashes in her eyes. "Just some ice for my face would be great."

"I'll go grab that for you."

I dip my head and go downstairs, where I grab some ice and put it in a cloth, then make my way back up to the room. But Gwen is fast asleep.

I saw it coming, so I'm not surprised.

I walk to the nightstand to set the ice down in case she wakes up and can still use it.

Sebastian wags his tail and knocks Gwen's handbag to the floor. Most of the contents fall out, rolling underneath the bed, so I kneel to pick them up.

When I reach under the bed to grab her lipstick, I notice the floorboards feel different. Like the ground beneath is hollow. A light tap confirms I'm right, and my curiosity piques.

This would be the only place in the house where I haven't been able to look because I didn't know about it.

I feel around the area for an opening, and when I find it, I lift the board and find a box inside.

I take it out and open it, finding a photo album.

When I open it, my hands still as I see a picture of Santiago Navarro posing with a blonde-haired baby on his lap. Scribbled on the side of the photo are the words. Daddy and Gwen.

Jesus. This is it. My God, this is it.

Fucking hell, I found what I was looking for.

It's her. Santiago Navarro's daughter is Gwen.

The evidence here speaks for itself.

I look at Gwen asleep on the bed and the sight of her innocence instills something in me I never expected to feel. *Guilt.*

I feel guilt as tangible as if it had taken form and slapped me in the face.

Sebastian is looking back at me. They both trust me. Dogs try to protect their masters, but this one will never see me as a threat. The same as Gwen didn't.

Falling asleep is the most vulnerable thing a person can ever do. She drifted off without worry because she doesn't fear me that way.

I keep my gaze trained on her, and I almost, almost wish I didn't find this box.

If I were a better man—the man she thinks I am, who she probably sees as her protector—I'd pack this album back up, return to the beach house and tell Zakh the mission's over. We failed.

But I can't do that.

The reasons I'm doing this are never far from my mind.

The dead can never avenge themselves. Taking over the cartel is the only way I will ever avenge myself.

Not only that, the dangerous, selfish part of me that was hoping my target was her just found a way to keep her.

The problem with that is, everything I do next will make us enemies.

I saved her from her monsters tonight, but there's no one who can save her from me.

Not even I can do that.

Pushing to my feet, I lower my lips to hers and plant a soft kiss on them, then I inhale that scent I've grown accustomed to and back away.

I leave the room and retrieve my phone to call Zakh.

He answers on the first ring.

"What's up? I'm back at the house," he says.

"It's Gwen, Zakh. She's Santiago's daughter. Get everything ready."

Chapter Twelve

Gwen

A deep sleep holds my body captive.

My thoughts drift in and out of the corners of my mind, trying to push through to the surface.

It's strange, although I know I'm asleep, I'm alert. I feel like I'm in that pocket of consciousness in between asleep and awake.

Dad used to tell me that's where dreams live, and if you're pulled from a good dream, you can easily slip back in. Like magic.

But this feels different. My body doesn't feel like itself.

There's a dullness in my being and a slowness in my mind that reminds me of the time I spent in the hospital as a child when I broke my leg. That was the only other time outside of my birthdays and Christmas when I saw my father.

I was lucky enough to have him for a few days before he had to return to Mexico.

I was seven years old. I'd fallen out of a tree in the park near Grams' house.

The pain was so severe that I got seriously strong painkillers that knocked me out.

This feels like that time.

But why?

What's going on?

Why do I feel like this?

I move my eyes, and finally, they open.

I blink a few times until the haze covering my eyes clears and I find myself staring up at an ornate white plaster ceiling with a Rococo centerpiece similar to the one in the living room.

Similar but not the same, and since I'm on a bed, I know I didn't fall asleep in the living room.

So, where am I?

The thought makes me sit up. My head spins, along with everything in the room.

When everything settles and stops moving, I take in my surroundings.

Within nanoseconds I realize I'm not in my bedroom and...

I'm not home. I'm not anywhere I know.

Satin navy wallpaper covers the walls of a room the size of the Presidential Suite at the Hilton.

Dark walnut wardrobes run down the full length of the wall to my right, along with a matching dresser. That curves into what looks like an en-suite bathroom.

The only thing I recognize is the little long-sleeved nightshirt I changed into last night. The thing hardly covers my thighs. Apart from my panties, that is all I'm wearing.

A look to the left shows an archway leading to sliding doors that are already open, showcasing an ornate stone balcony.

Where the hell am I?

And what happened yesterday?

My mind struggles to remember.

This is the second time this week that I've woken up not remembering anything. But it's certainly the first time that I've woken up in a strange but lavish room, not remembering how I got there.

Despite the grogginess weighing down my body, I make myself get up.

My bare feet touch down on the carpeted floor, and I walk on shaky legs out to the balcony, where I get more shockers.

Before me is the beautiful view of a beach with golden sand and a yacht moored by the boardwalk.

It's beautiful and looks like something you'd see on vacation somewhere in the Hamptons, but it's not Wrightsville Beach or any of the other beaches around Wilmington.

I know Wilmington so well I can spot the differences straightaway.

So, if I'm not in Wilmington, where the hell am I?

What the hell did I do to myself this time?

I turn and glimpse my reflection in the sliding door. The sight of the bruise on my cheek awakens memories.

Conrad.

The money.

Sebastian.

Malik...

Malik.

He saved me. He saved Sebastian.

I ran to him in my desperation, hoping he could help me, and he did. He got Conrad to tear up the loan agreement and made him promise to leave me alone forever.

The problem was solved, and I couldn't believe it.

Malik was ruthless with those men, who were obviously scared of him, and although it was awful to witness such violence, I didn't care because each of those men deserved what they got. Especially Conrad.

Malik took Sebastian to the vet, and we went home.

I had an ocean full of questions in my head for Malik, but I didn't ask any because I didn't need to. I realized I was right about him.

He's the last thing I remember. I asked for some ice for my face, then fell asleep.

Now this.

And what is this?

Did Malik take me somewhere? Why would he do that?

And where is here?

A wave of panic tightens my lungs, and I walk back to the room then over to the door to open it. If he's here, I need to speak to him.

But when I turn the handle, the door won't open.

It's locked.

Frantically, I rattle the handle every which way I can, but it's not opening, and it's quite clear someone locked it from the outside.

"Malik!" His name pours out of my mouth like the air leaving my body.

I slam my fist into the door, and suddenly, I'm calling for help.

Whatever this is, it's all bad.

Because I think someone has kidnapped me.

Through the hammering of my fists on the door, I hear footsteps on the other side, then it's my heart that's pounding against my ribcage.

The click of the key in the lock echoes off the walls of my soul, and I back away, suddenly very afraid of who is going to come through the door.

What if it's not Malik?

What if Conrad came back to the house and took me, and I'm being prepped for sale?

I step even further back, hardly able to breathe.

The door swings open, revealing Malik.

According to the thoughts I had not even a few seconds ago about Conrad, seeing Malik shouldn't terrify me.

But it does. A lump the size of the universe has swelled in my throat, and every nerve in my body is standing to attention, telling me to open my eyes and look at this man much closer than I have since I met him.

Dressed in full black with the sleeves of his shirt rolled up his arms, he hardly looks different from that night at the restaurant when he came to find me, but that night, he was different. It was like I was getting two versions of him.

He had a darkness about him that possessed me and crippled me.

That seems to be the version of him I'm getting now, and it feels like the real him.

"Where am I?" My voice comes out choked and shaky with a question that might not be as relevant as the millions of others waiting in line to be asked. That's just the one that came out first.

Without breaking that dark gaze, he lifts his chin, and if possible, I feel even smaller next to him.

"Boston."

Boston? What the fuck?

"What am I doing in Boston? Why have you brought me here?" I despise the way my voice shakes, but what I hate even more is that feeling in my soul telling me I've been played for a fool again.

Malik steps forward, and my instincts move me one step backward.

Unlike at the restaurant, I'm fully aware that I'm moving away from him.

Back then, my instincts were trying to warn me about him. But I didn't listen.

I didn't listen as the universe practically screamed at me to run from danger. Now, what am I up against?

"There are certain things we need to talk about." His voice is far too calm. It reminds me of the villain in those films about psychotic madmen who believe their bizarre actions are completely justified.

"The only thing I want to talk to you about is getting me back *home*."

"That's not possible. You're not going home today, or any time soon."

My mouth goes dry, and my mind stops working, as if someone pulled the plug on it.

A sheet of blankness covers my mind, and I can't move past it. All I see is him before me. Tall and foreboding, like a dark storm cloud drifting over the sea, getting ready to wreak destruction.

I stare at him, then, as if someone switched me back on, the gravity of the situation and what he's actually saying hits me, striking my being like a bolt of lightning.

All at once, everything important—everything that depends on me—pushes to the forefront of my mind.

Grams.

Dru.

The restaurant.

Sebastian.

"What are you saying to me?" I choke out, trying to regain control of my voice. "Why the fuck are you doing this to me? I have people and a business who depend on me. I need to go home."

"Let's just say you're needed here more." His eyes darken, clouding any emotion I might have previously seen in him. It's like a wall rises up, and it becomes impossible to preempt what he might do next.

"What do you want with me?" I cut to the chase, sounding braver than I feel.

He pushes his wide, powerful shoulders back and intensifies his stare. "I need you because of who you are. I know you're Santiago Navarro's daughter."

And there it is, the thing everyone tried to protect me from.

Truth hidden in a secret that was never supposed to come to light. Truth that only my father could have kept me safe from. If he'd lived.

I'm about to deny it, like Grams taught me to do if ever I met anyone who found out my secret, but Malik reaches into his pocket and pulls out a picture.

He holds it before me, and I realize it's of me and my father at the park.

I'm sitting on his knee, and we're smiling, pretending we're living a normal life where we hang out at the park all the time. That was the week before Christmas, the year before Mom and Dad died. On the edge of the picture are the words '*Daddy and Gwen 2008. This was such a good day. I will love you forever, my princess.*'

Mom took that picture, and Dad wrote those little messages to me, so I would remember those magical moments.

So I would remember him and how he loved me.

They were never meant to be used against me. But this is my fault again. I let the devil into my home. Into my bed, into my body. Into my heart.

I was the one who ran to him for help, not knowing he would discover my biggest secret that not even my best friend knows.

Malik was in my room when I fell asleep. I don't know how he found my treasure box when I hid it so well. But that's not the part I should be focused on.

Wilmington was my treasure box. The place where people who loved me hid me away from men like Malik.

Somehow, he found out where I was, meaning he was already looking for me that night we first met at the bar.

But he didn't know who I was until I all but handed him my secrets on a plate.

Silence has drifted between us, strong and deadly. He's looking at me, still holding the picture, and I'm staring back at him, trying to keep the ball of terror from rising in my soul.

He breaks the awkward moment by putting the picture

back in his pocket, then he brings his hands together and cracks his large knuckles.

"I'm sure you know my father is dead." I speak because I'm not sure what else to do.

"I'm very aware, and it doesn't matter. You're his heir, and that's what I need."

"For what?"

"To take over the cartel." His voice is blunt. "Your father left everything to you, including the cartel."

I shake my head. This must be some sort of fucked-up mistake. My father would never do that. "No, I would have known if he did. There's no way he would do something like that without me knowing."

"Well these things happen sometimes without our knowledge."

"It can't be true."

"It is. Your father left everything to you, Gwen, but no one knew who you were."

I can't believe what I'm hearing. Why would my father do that?

Why would he keep me away from everyone and then leave me everything?

Why didn't I know?

It's as vague and confusing as his death.

But that doesn't matter now. What matters is the here and now, and what this devil plans to do with me.

"I'm not part of that life." I pant. "You have to let me go home."

"I told you that's not going to happen."

"So, what do you plan to do? Keep me here and get me to sign over something I had no idea I owned?"

"Not exactly. That would have been the easy way." One corner of his mouth lifts into a sinful grin that melts my insides. I feel sickened that I could still be attracted to him.

"Then what are you going to do?"

"Marry you."

My eyes snap wide. "What!"

"Marriage is the only way for you to take ownership of your father's inheritance."

"No, I'm not doing it. No fucking way." I back away, shaking my head. Panic swells within me, cutting off the air in my lungs.

"Yes, you are, Gwen."

"No."

"I'm afraid I'm not exactly giving you a choice."

Oh my God. This isn't happening. It's just not.

My lips part to continue this one-sided argument where I'm trying to defend myself, but one look at the opened door behind him jumpstarts my instinct to flee.

Finally, I'm listening loud and very clearly to my instincts. So, when they tell me to run, run like hell and far away from this man I should never have trusted, I do.

I use every ounce of energy I can summon to dash past him. But before I can even make it to the door, one large arm secures around my middle and swoops me up from the ground with my legs dangling in the air.

I scream and pound against the solid rock muscles of his chest, but, of course, he's not going to let me go.

That knowledge doesn't stop me from fighting, though. I can't give up. I mustn't. There are people who depend on me, and then there's me.

I can't be part of this. This can't be another nail in the coffin of my fucked-up life.

While I'm giving as good as I got, Malik effortlessly moves with me across the room toward the bed.

He sets me down, or rather throws me down, and as I tumble to the ground, his gun falls out of his pocket.

When I see it, I see a way to get out.

But I'm not quick enough. He picks it up and smiles.

Like some crazy person, he taps the side of his head with it and runs the metal over his temple as if it's nothing.

His smile widens when he reads my terror.

"Gwen St. James, you're a quick little one, aren't you? I wonder if sweet little Gwen would have killed my ass if she'd gotten her beautiful hands on my gun?" He laughs. It jars me.

I've never heard him laugh before, but I find it odd that he would call my hands beautiful at a time like this.

"Why don't you give me the gun, and we'll find out?" I surprise myself with that answer and my obvious bravery. Maybe it's coming from that place inside where I'm sick of everything going to hell in ways I can't control.

A deep, scary chuckle rumbles from his lips. "You know what? I'm almost tempted to give it to you, but I'm more obsessed with seeing my plans through than I am with tasting death's welcoming kiss."

That answer surprises me even more. It's like he's not afraid of anything, and he talks about death as if they're old friends.

He's crazy.

I caught the attention of a madman who's going to wreak havoc on my life in ways I can't imagine.

"Fuck you. You fucking asshole. You know this is wrong."

"I'm sure you know I don't give a shit about right and wrong. But I'm going to give you a piece of advice you need to listen to. Don't piss me off, Gwen, or fuck with me in any shape or form. Don't do it. If you do either, I will punish you, and that's a side of me you don't want to meet."

I'm so scared by the darkness I see in him I can't say another word.

I can barely breathe.

It's hard to believe this is the same man who took such good care of me and my dog, and devoured my body like he wanted me.

It was all a lie.

All of it.

This is the real him.

He rises to his feet and glares down at me, a crumpled mess of fear on the ground. I expect him to continue his threat, but he doesn't.

"None of it was real, was it? Nothing you said, nothing you did, was ever real. Everything was a fucking lie." I don't know why I'm bothering to point out the obvious. "Why did you help me when you knew you were going to do this?"

"Malyshka, let's just say now you owe me instead of Conrad. I don't think that money or trouble you got yourself mixed up in should just go away. So, this is what we're doing, and in four days' time, you'll be my wife."

My jaw drops open in horror. There are no more words left inside me to speak.

I owe him now, and we're getting married in four days' time.

This maleficent devil is being even more of an asshole than he already was by telling me the price I had to pay to get Conrad off my back. He's acting like I had a choice, but I never did.

He turns his malicious stare from me and walks out of the room, closing the door behind him.

The rattle of the key in the lock sounds, then doom fills my soul.

Chapter Thirteen

Malik

And so it begins—*war*.

I've put the wheels in motion to start a war in my own home.

Gwen St. James and I are enemies now.

All the lighthearted feelings that came with meeting someone new and having off-the-chart chemistry are gone.

Just now she looked at me like she hated me. I expected nothing less. Everything I did, good or bad, led us here.

But no matter what she thinks of me, it was real.

I was real with her.

I can admit that. I've always promised myself to never shy away from the truth, and that's the truth.

So, I won't act like the sight of her heaving breasts in her little nightshirt didn't harden my dick with all the things I still want to do to her. Or that I didn't think of doing all those things to her just then.

My attraction to her isn't a lie. The temptation I feel when I'm with her isn't a lie.

None of what I did with her was a lie or part of the lie I created.

When I was with her, I was with her. She had all of me, something I've never given anyone.

But I can't be that guy or whatever vision she expected from me.

Now it's back to business, back to the plan, and I have to be me.

My steps sound heavy on the marble floor as I walk down the corridor.

It's nearly lunchtime. Zakh assisted me to transport Gwen here. We arrived about two hours ago. He left shortly after and I stayed back to speak to Gwen when she woke.

Now that I've done that, I'm going to meet with my brothers at Desmier's house.

I'm just going to speak to my staff first, then I'll be on my way. I have a lot of work to do today to make sure everything is in order so I can focus on the cartel.

Taking over a cartel the size of the Navarro is going to be one hell of a task.

As time is of the essence and I need to put this wedding together in a few days, my brothers have each been completing individual tasks to move things along as quickly as possible.

Once everything is ready, we'll make contact with Diego Navarro and set up the meeting of all meetings where I'll hand him his ass.

I make my way downstairs and into the living room. There I find Jeanne, my head maid and custodian. As she worked for my parents when I was a child, she's known me since birth.

After my rescue in Kazakhstan, it was clear that I couldn't go back to the Navy, so I bought this oversized house because of the beach and my need to be near the water. My father got Jeanne to work for me, and she practically moved in before me to get everything ready. My father would say it was his way of helping me find someone good who was used to managing large homes. But I knew he sent her and a few other members of his personal staff so I would have people around me I could trust.

Those members of staff consist of my guards Yuri and Vladmir, and Kelly, another maid who I grew up with. All have been in my life since I was born.

They live on the premises. Jeanne, however, has always been in charge.

She takes care of everything here, and best of all, since she knows our ways of life, she does as she's told and doesn't question certain things others would.

Like holding someone captive. She's fully aware and probably in complete disapproval of the fact that I've kidnapped a young woman and locked her away in my bedroom. But Jeanne will never express any of her opinions, even when I ask for it.

She looks at me when I walk in, pushing the ends of her graying ponytail over her shoulder as she straightens.

She was polishing the table that was already glossy but not perfect enough to meet her standards.

"Everything okay?" she asks, glancing through the door as if she can see up the stairs.

"For now."

"How long will you be gone?"

"A few hours tops." I'm not going to be out for too long because I don't think it's fair to leave Gwen for anyone else to deal with besides me. "When I get back, I have a few things to take care of, so I'll be in my office."

"Okay, that's fine." She nods, then her huge brown eyes become more open with emotion, which suggests she's concerned about Gwen. "What about the girl? What should I do if things become difficult with her?"

"Don't worry about her. Leave anything difficult for me. Right now, I think I'd be right in assuming that we have some level of understanding and she won't be *difficult* for very long." I didn't want to throw the Conrad thing in Gwen's face, but I needed something to hold over her so she'll comply.

Even though it has absolutely nothing to do with my plans.

If I had nothing to make a deal with, I would have just taken her and forced her to marry me anyway.

"Should I go up and introduce myself?"

I shake my head. "Not yet. Take her something to eat at lunchtime. You can introduce yourself then. I also want to limit contact to just you for the moment. I'll let you know when she can meet the others, and when she can leave the room."

Obvious discomfort enters her eyes, but she gives me a curt nod, agreeing.

"What if she tries to run?"

I smile, but I shouldn't. There is nothing humorous here. Gwen looked like she received my threats perfectly well, but I expect her to run again.

"Let's hope she doesn't while I'm away." If she runs, I want to be here because I'll enjoy the chase. And the punishment. Gwen has the perfect ass made for spanking.

"Okay, well, I'll make sure everyone else is clued in."

"Good. See you later."

Again, she dips her head. I leave and head outside.

Once I get to my garage, which currently holds six luxury cars and three motorcycles, I select the black Kawasaki and speed off the premises, leaving my pretty little captive behind.

I can just imagine what must be running through her mind now that she knows my plans.

She'll have questions. More questions.

All will be questions I'll have to spoon feed answers to.

There are things about me that would be easier if she learned gradually—like everything to do with the Knights and my family. Then there are other things I'll have to figure out as we go along.

So far, I've taken care of the important things, so no one in Wilmington will suspect she's in trouble. Based on what I've done, no one will miss her for at least a week. Past that, it will get to a point where suspicions will be raised.

Dru will be the first to suspect something is amiss, followed by the people at the restaurant. Duke and his irritating wife, Marybeth, will probably be the next because they're close to Gwen's family.

I'll have to think of a better excuse to explain her absence so it shuts down anything that will threaten my plans. But right now the primary focus is the wedding and keeping it under wraps until it's over. The less people who know the better, especially after we contact Diego. I don't want him discovering what I'm about to do.

Half an hour later, I pull up on the drive of Desmier's manor home and jump off my bike.

His butler answers the door and tells me Desmier and Zakh are already waiting for me in the office, so I make my way there.

I take the quick route, which leads me to the balcony overlooking the garden.

Sitting on the grass below on a wide picnic blanket are Desmier's wife Anastasia, and Zakh's wife Lorelai. Both are playing with their baby girls, my nieces, Mischa and Liberty, who wear matching pink dresses.

Normally, when I see them all together, I don't think deeper than what I see—my brothers' wives playing with their kids—but today is different.

When I look at them now, it hits me that in a few days, I'll have a wife.

Weeks ago, marriage was the furthest thing from my mind, and even though my father would have married me off at his first opportunity, I never really saw it in the cards for me.

The difference between my brothers and me is that they're head over heels in love with their wives. My marriage, on the other hand, will be based on conquering an empire.

My thoughts return to the plan at hand when I walk through the archway leading back into the house. Desmier's office is just ahead of me.

Throughout this entire thing, I've been grateful to have

him on board, especially where the Pakhan is concerned. I know Desmier has pulled a lot of strings to give me the time I needed to stay in Wilmington.

I don't think my plans would have run as smoothly as they have if Desmier weren't around. Viktor certainly wouldn't condone going to Wilmington and would have talked me out of the whole thing. He would have told me I should take Manolo's death as my win and leave it at that. Then he would have been an asshole and convinced Father and Leif not to help me. All because he would have been more worried about the disruption it would cause to the alliance by us taking charge of the Navarro Cartel. Some people in our alliance are not going to be happy about that, but this is where you tell them to either get the fuck out or fall in line.

Since nobody has ever declined working with us, they would have shut up and put up with whatever we do.

Desmier is only our half-brother, and he's shown more support for me than Viktor ever did.

Desmier has only been in our lives for the last few years. Prior to that, none of us knew of his existence. Just before my father died, the empire was supposed to pass to Viktor, who everyone thought was my father's eldest son. But Desmier flew in on the wings of revenge and took it from him.

Desmier's pursuit for revenge was the catalyst that unearthed many dark secrets in our family, including our mother and Viktor's evil scheme, which killed our Father and Leif.

Death and destruction pushed us together, forming a solid bond of trust I never knew I could have with anyone.

When I reach Desmier's office, the door is already

open, so I walk right inside and find them. Desmier is sitting behind the grand mahogany desk, and Zakh is to his right.

Although I'm dark blond and Zakh has black hair, the first thing people would comment on when they saw us together is how similar we look. But Desmier and Zakh could be twins.

"Hey, guys," I say, giving them a curt nod.

"Hey, there," Zakh replies, and Desmier nods back.

"Everything okay at the house?" Desmier asks.

"As good as can be."

"Did you get to speak to her?"

"Yeah. She's aware of the situation now. Obviously, she's not happy about it."

"That was expected."

"Well, everything on our part is underway." Desmier straightens. "I'll be contacting Diego once it's all sorted out and schedule a meeting for Monday afternoon at Volkova Inc."

"That's perfect."

"Good. We want them on our territory. I figured meeting on Monday will give them enough time to get to Boston on such short notice."

"That gives them and us plenty of time." That's six days, so it leaves room to fix things if something goes wrong, too. "I've got everything sorted out on my end, too and I've taken care of the DNA test."

Although the photo album is more than sufficient evidence Gwen is Santiago's daughter, the Navarros will demand hard evidence. As you need substantial living tissue for a DNA test and Santiago has been dead for more than a decade, the next best option was to get that tissue from Manolo's body.

Being Santiago's brother made him the perfect candidate, and it was pure luck that he's been dead for only a little over two weeks.

Because I'm me, I was able to get his samples. I sorted that out before we even left Wilmington.

"I should have Manolo's samples at our lab by tonight," I add. "Then it takes about three days to get the paternity test results."

I got Gwen's sample, which was a mouth swab, when she was asleep. The lab I'm using for the tests has the best technology, so I didn't need to take her blood.

"Well, things seem to be underway." Desmier nods. "I'll organize the wedding, and Zakh will take care of all the paperwork."

"Thank you for being on board with me." I feel I should offer my gratitude again. "It means a lot, and I know the task ahead is going to shake things up in the underworld."

"We're Volkovas. We'll be ready for it." Desmier smiles. "This is your legacy, and having the cartel will make our empire a force to be reckoned with. The Pakhan was blowing out of his ass before because he didn't believe you could pull this off, but you guys did it."

We did do it.

Now it finally feels like I can make that start to get my life back on track. The wheels have been put in motion for retribution, and that part of me that's been holding on to the guilt I've felt over Jim's death can hopefully start to heal.

"Now we just have to get everything ready for Monday," Zakh states.

"It will be ready. I'll take care of any obstacles we might encounter." The only one I can think of is the beautiful woman I left at my house, who's not going to give in so easily to marry me.

Judging from the understanding look in Zakh's eyes, I can see he's thinking the same thing.

"Alright, we just have to talk about the schedule for next week for the Bratva meetings and our work at Volkova Inc. Then we're done for the day." Desmier glances over some documents on his desk, then starts reconfiguring the schedule.

My mind, however, is on how everything is going to play out with Gwen.

If nothing else, it will be interesting.

Once she's married to me she'll be a symbol of defeat to the Navarros.

But she's also the spoils of war and I already know I'm going to have a hard time resisting that urge to taste her again.

Chapter Fourteen

Gwen

M*alik Volkova.*

Volkova.

That's the surname Conrad gave Malik.

His name rattles around in my mind like marbles being tossed onto the floor. I press my head against the edge of the bed. A fruitless attempt to soothe the ache of worry and terror tightening my scalp.

At first, when Conrad addressed Malik, I thought it was strange that I'd had so many encounters with him and never knew his full name. My next thought was that the name sounded powerful. Just like the man.

I got the memo about how powerful Malik Volkova was the moment he told me to jump into the truck. I just didn't pay attention to the right things.

Like how he just headed out to deal with Conrad by himself and how terrified he looked at him.

One man. One man with a gun and a damsel in distress at his side.

As if I have no common sense and I didn't just go through all manners of shit with Gage, I didn't pay attention.

Worst of all, I got involved with this man, none the wiser that he would be the worst enemy I could ever encounter.

Had I even thought to ask for his last name—if he'd told me the truth—I might have been able to look him up. I was curious enough about him to do so because I was already trying to figure out what his tattoo meant.

Maybe I would have found something. Something that would have given me a better heads-up that captivity was in the cards for me.

But here I am, sitting on the floor with my back against the side of the bed.

I'm pretty much in the same spot Malik left me. The only thing I've been able to establish in the few hours that have passed since I've been locked in here is that

this is his bedroom.

Debt or not, I started looking for a way out of here when the gravity of the situation truly struck me.

I have my injured dog at home, a restaurant to run, a best friend who must be frantic with worry, and most of all, Grams. They all need me, so I couldn't just sit down and give up.

As the only other door in here, apart from the main door, is the ensuite, my only option was to look through the wardrobes. I hoped perhaps they were like mine, with a back door leading downstairs. Of course, they weren't. All I found was his clothes—which I knew were his because of the style and the scent that lingered amongst them. His scent permeates the room, too.

When I didn't find any means of escaping—except over the side of the balcony and into the jagged rocks below in the sea—I felt even more stupid than I already do because *he* wouldn't be so careless as to leave any sort of opening for me. Even if there were some sort of door, it would be just as locked and inescapable as the main one is.

I got desperate.

I still am.

The worry over everything back home has increased a hundredfold, and it's making me sick to my core.

I can imagine Sebastian whimpering and looking for me to take care of him.

Gilman would have called me over a hundred times already, and Dru would have tripled that because the last thing she heard from me was that I was going to sort something out with Conrad.

When she realizes I am missing, she'll think he sold me, and I don't know what she'll do then.

Knowing Dru, she won't stop looking for me. I can count on her to look after Sebastian, try to run the restaurant and our company to the best of her abilities. I know she would even look after Grams.

But if she thinks Conrad took me and she goes anywhere near him, he'll kill her.

The thought brings tears to my eyes that I can't hold back. So does the next thought. The one of me ending up dead.

All worries aside, if I die, Grams is who I'm most

concerned about. I can't expect Dru to keep looking after everything and everyone for me forever. It won't be her responsibility. So, I have no idea what will happen to my grandmother.

Right now, all I know is that I shouldn't be here. If the one rule everyone made me live by was to never tell anyone I'm Santiago Navarro's daughter, I can only expect death to follow me from here onwards.

Even if I confirmed who I was, no one should have been able to find me in Wilmington.

So, how did Malik Volkova do it?

Who is he, or rather, *what* is he?

What sort of power does he have to take over a giant like the Navarro Cartel?

I considered him belonging to the mafia. Like maybe the Bratva, the

Russian mafia. I don't know, though. I think it's something more because of that. tattoo on his wrist.

The rattle of the key in the door steals the air from my lungs, and my entire

body tenses with trepidation.

He's back.

Not wanting to look as pathetic as I am, I stand, dry my tears, then gear my heart up to face the beast.

Except when the door opens, it's not Malik coming through.

It's an elderly lady with a long graying ponytail and model-like cheekbones.

She's a little taller than me with a slim build and wearing a full black uniform dress.

She issues me a little smile as I stare at her and wheels a trolley in with food that smells divine. Smelling it reminds me I'm starving. The last time I ate properly was days ago. It was the day I went to see Grams. After that, my appetite went to hell, along with everything else.

"Hi, there," the woman says in an accented voice. I'm guessing she must be Russian.

"Hello." My voice is heavy with despair and helplessness.

A guard with a machine gun steps up to the door, showing himself before he closes it as if to extinguish any bright ideas I might have of trying to escape.

The lady pushes the trolly to the desk before she turns to face me with a warmth in her expression I find irritating given the situation. How can she look so calm and comfortable, as if everything is fine?

It reminds me of when my grandfather was dying in the hospital and the doctors sent out a chirpy little nurse who kept trying to cheer us up.

I hated it, and I hate this now—whatever this is. This woman works for Malik, and she knows I'm being held captive here, so she can't be good.

"I'm Jeanne." She presses a hand to her heart. "I take care of the house, and I'll be taking care of you."

I think carefully before I answer. "If you want to take care of me, let me go. Let me go home."

Suffice to say, the warmth disappears from her face at my reply. Discomfort replaces any former emotion as she brings her hands together.

"I'm afraid I can't do that."

"Why? Did he tell you to keep me locked up in here?" I sound furious. I am. But I'm also terrified and clutching at anything I think will get me out of here, including what I think looks like pity in this stranger's eyes.

"I've brought you some lunch and a few other snacks, as you didn't have breakfast." She ignores my question and the pity fades from her eyes.

I stare back at her with a deadpan expression, unable to believe that anyone could sanction this craziness.

"If you require any more food, just knock on the door. There will be a guard down the corridor who will help you." More meaningless information.

When she moves away from the trolley to leave me, I panic and rush toward her, grabbing her arm.

"Please, don't leave me in here." I hate to beg, but I realize it might be all I can do to save myself. "You have to help me. I have a grandmother who's in a nursing home. She needs me. Please, we're all each other has."

More pity returns to her eyes, and she pats my hand. The gesture feels genuine, and for a split second, I almost believe she might help me. But then she shakes her head as if she read my mind.

"I'm sorry. I can't help you. All I can do for you right now is bring you food and tell you it would be best for you to comply."

My hands drop from hers like steel weights are attached to it, and the tightness in my body grows, making my skin feel as if it's going to snap.

Without another word, she walks away, opens the door, and departs. Although my instinct to flee is telling me to run, one sight of the guard holding the machine gun keeps me rooted to the spot.

I know he's not there to kill me. Malik needs me alive, so the guard isn't there to shoot me down like an animal, but there are worse punishments than death.

The door closes. And I hate, hate, hate it when I hear that dreadful click of the key turning in the lock.

Blowing out a ragged breath, I sink back to the floor in utter despair.

What am I going to do?

I've had to ask myself that question so many times over this past month that my brain is tired of hearing it.

And I'm tired.

I'm so damn tired. How much can one person take in such a short space of time?

I pull in several deep breaths to clear my head and gather myself. I can't fall apart. Not now. Not ever. I don't have such a luxury.

No matter what, I have to escape this house somehow, someway.

The only way I can do that is by taking things one step at a time.

That might start with eating.

Food is normally the last thing I'd consider when I'm distraught, but my hunger is screwing with my ability to think straight.

I get up and walk to the food trolley. There is a row of chicken and lettuce sandwiches on a little platter and some croissants on another plate. In the middle is a bigger plate that has a cover on it. I lift it and reveal the most delicious-looking chicken casserole I've ever seen. It's surrounded by boiled rice and has an aromatic aroma that makes my stomach rumble.

I unwrap the napkin next to the jug of water, not surprised to find plastic utensils.

Most of everything on the tray is plastic, nothing that can be used as a weapon. Except maybe the trolley itself. I'm sure, though, that if I could successfully throw it at Malik, he'd be able to dodge it or take it. It would probably bounce off those military muscles.

Military.

I don't even know if that was true. That he was in the Navy. If he's in the mafia, why would he have been in the Navy? I find that odd.

Swallowing my pride, I tuck into the food and eat the whole thing. I'm so full by the time I finish, I can just about manage a few sips of water.

But I feel better physically just for providing my body with some nourishment.

As my hands are a little sticky, I head to the bathroom to wash them and splash cold water over my face. I had to do that earlier when I thought I was going to have a panic attack.

The cold water on my face soothes me once more and gets my mind back on track to plan my escape.

I walk back out and glance over the room, wondering what will happen later tonight when Malik is back. Will he force himself on me?

Will he even see it as force when I gave him my body several times over this past week?

Fuck, it was me who propositioned him at the bar that night we first met.

Me.

But he only spoke to me because he was following me. Then he used me in one of the worst ways a man can use a woman.

In some ways, he was worse than Gage. But I only have myself to blame for falling prey to a beautiful devil and sleeping with a guy I hardly knew.

My stupidity aside, Malik is certainly worse than Gage for what he's doing to me now.

I rest against the wall near the bathroom door and yelp when it moves.

Whirling around, I realize it's a secret sliding door. Well, not so much secret now that I've discovered it.

The wall/doorway leads into another room. It's dark inside, so I can't see what's in there.

Curiosity, my good old friend, compels me to move forward and check it out, but the voice of reasoning warns me away. What if I go in and can't come back out?

But... what if this is another way out?

What kind of man has a secret door in the wall of their bedroom?

Maybe I'm about to find out.

I don't spare another thought. I step inside the room, my bare feet connecting with the cool surface of a concrete floor.

Automatic lights snap on one at a time, revealing the enormous size of the room.

It seems to be way bigger than the bedroom, which is already huge. That makes me wonder just how big this house is.

Rows of wooden shelves greet me at the door with an

assortment of different things, from books to tools neatly placed on each panel. It reminds me of a store.

I walk in deeper and stop when I come across pictures hanging in frames on the wall. The ones I notice first are all of Malik in his Navy uniform, so I guess he told me the truth about that.

There are a lot of him as a teenager with another blond-haired guy. The same guy is in a few others where they're older, and in the same Navy uniform, so I'm guessing this must be a best friend of sorts, or family.

Further along the wall hang more pictures of him as an adult in his uniform with the same guy and an older man who looks like the guy. There are a lot of the three of them together.

Then it switches to Malik with a man who has to be his father because they look so similar, and another man, I guess is a relative. Maybe an uncle because he looks roughly the same age as his father—if I'm right that other man is his father.

I tear my gaze away from the pictures and scan the room for a door.

That's what I need to look for.

There's a little curve to the wall, so I follow it and stop in my tracks when I see a blue knight's tunic hanging on a clothes rail. It looks like something straight out of the Crusades or...

Something snaps in my mind as I remember where else I might have seen such a costume. Like movies. This looks like something the Templar Knights would wear, but it doesn't have a cross on the front. It has a black raven.

My scalp tingles with fear that ripples down my spine in icy tendrils, but I still move forward to get closer.

Closer and closer until I find myself reaching out to touch the soft material.

"This is no costume," I say to myself.

"No, it's not," answers that deep rusty voice. *His* voice.

I turn with my heart in my throat and find Malik standing by the doorway, watching me.

Chapter Fifteen

Gwen

I don't know how long Malik has been standing there watching me.

Although it couldn't have been too long because I haven't been in here for more than ten minutes, the thought of him watching me without my knowledge is jarring. Especially when I'm clearly somewhere I'm not supposed to be.

This room... it doesn't have a good vibe to it. It's too personal, too private, too secret. Like him.

The air is thick with grief and something sinister.

Even though I don't know the story behind the things he's keeping in here, in some ways, the room feels like a shrine.

My eyes are glued to the devil's like the deer caught in the headlights, freezing up at that moment, not knowing what to do.

When a shit-eating grin slides across his handsome face,

I don't know what that means for me, and that fear I experienced earlier amplifies a million times over.

"Looking for something?" Malik keeps his gaze fixed on me the way a hunter would when it's tracking its prey.

"I..." Any explanation my brain would have conjured dies because it's obvious that, as a captive, I could only be in here if I was looking for a way out.

He walks in, the sounds of his footsteps rising like a tidal wave the closer he gets. My heartbeat becomes a staccato of terror with each beat out of cadence, and my legs tremble under the weight of his intensive stare.

By the time he reaches me, I don't know how I'm still standing, or how my lungs haven't exploded from holding my breath for so long.

It's only when his gaze switches from me to the tunic that I look away from those dark eyes and realize I'm still touching the fabric. Actually, it's more like I'm gripping it as if it can save me.

I release it quickly and take a measured breath in an attempt to soothe my burning lungs. It doesn't work. The potent silence between us is stifling, as is the suspense of wondering what he's going to do to me.

What if he's going to kill me now that I've come in here and seen that he's part of what looks like some secret organization?

Those eyes drift back to mine again, and there's a spark of something I can't quite figure out, but I know it's not good.

"Go ahead. Ask me." His voice is challenging. "I can see all those questions bouncing around in that pretty little head of yours."

At first, I think of keeping my silence, but since I need answers, I decide to speak and play his game.

"What are you?" That seems like the best question to ask. If I don't know what he is, I won't know what I'm truly up against. Or who I got myself mixed up with.

"What do you think I am?" He gives me a hard, daring stare.

I think carefully before I answer and decide to go with the simplest answer first. "Mafia. Bratva."

He smiles, revealing perfect white teeth. "Yes, but I'm a little more than that, as you've seen." His gaze darts back to the tunic. "Want to try again?"

I look at the tattoo on his wrist, and his smile widens. "Secret society."

"There we go. Now we're on the same page."

The confirmation sends an icy shiver cascading down my spine, rooting my feet to the floor.

"It's called the Brotherhood of Knights," he says in a matter-of-factly tone. "I am a Knight."

As I hear the name—the word *Knights*—it jogs my memory and I instantly remember where I saw those symbols tattooed on Malik's wrist.

It was years ago when I was a senior in high school. Dru and I went to L.A. for the weekend with some friends. On our first night, we went to a club. There a fight broke out between a group of guys. One of them—the one who won—had those tattoos on his wrist. He walked away without a scratch, while the paramedics had to be called in for the guys on the ground who were barely alive. I'd heard two of the bouncers talking just after the fight. One was telling the other not to go after the guy or file an incident report because the guy with the tattoos was a Knight and they didn't want any trouble. He'd said the Knights were the type of criminals no one would dare to fuck with. Those who did, disappeared never to be heard from again. Unless they turned up dead in the worst way imaginable. The Knights also didn't just punish you, they'd punish anybody close to you.

I'd forgotten that incident because it happened so long ago. Now here I am with my very own Knight in front of me.

"They own the Komarovski Bratva," Malik adds, cutting into my thoughts. "Of which I am the senior enforcer."

Enforcer, as in the guy you get when you need someone dead. But he's not just any old enforcer. This guy has so more letters to his name like the degree credentials of an esteemed academic.

"And you need me to take over a cartel?" I'm trying to sound like I'm not scared of him but the tremble in my voice and my body are dead giveaways.

"I do."

"But it sounds like you can find other ways of getting it all on your own." I feel like I'm reaching down deep into a bag full of tricks and coming up with nothing.

"You're a clever girl. You know that's not how this works, or you wouldn't be here."

His words sting deeper than they should, reminding me I'm just a pawn in his game.

"I'm sure you know you're not going to be able to keep me locked away forever. There are lots of people who will notice that I'm gone." I set my shoulders back and steel my spine to show him I'm not weak.

"I imagine they will."

"Good, because those same people know how reliable I

am and that I take my responsibilities seriously. In a place like Wilmington, it won't take long before they realize something bad happened to me. When they realize *you're* gone too, the first thing they'll do is put two and two together and come up with the answer." Most of the people I know in that town might be busybodies who make it their duties to know everyone's business, but that's what you need in a situation like this.

I was hoping to faze him, but he smiles again, as if everything I said meant nothing and he's privy to something I have no knowledge of.

"No one will come up with the kind of answers you're thinking of if they think you're perfectly fine."

"But they won't. Dru and Gilman will be the first people to miss me."

"At eight forty-five this morning, Gilman received a message from you letting him know you were taking some time off to sort out a large order for your business. You instructed him to get in as many staff as he sees fit to run the restaurant."

The Arctic shiver that covered my body earlier turns to icicles.

Damn it, and damn him. He messaged Gilman. Gilman knew about my order for my business, so he won't question that for one minute.

"Minutes later, Dru received a message from you."

"And what did it say?" My blood simmers with the hellfire of rage.

He reaches forward and takes a lock of my hair to twirl around his thumb. "You told her you sorted things out with Conrad and Malik connected you with a business opportunity you had to check out, so you'd be away for a few days."

Dru might suspect the business opportunity part if he didn't put his name to it.

Knowing my best friend the way I do, I'm a hundred percent sure that will translate to me hooking up with him. If she didn't hear from me for at least a week or so, she'd think nothing of it because she'd be so happy for me.

"My dog."

"Is taken care of."

"My grandmother."

"Is taken care of."

"How is my grandmother taken care of? I have payments to make and various other things to do with her care."

"And I've done it. Or rather, you have. You fully paid up for all her treatment for the rest of the year, and the nursing home knows to contact you if they need to."

I would say thanks because he's used his money to pay that, but as the gesture isn't coming from a good place, I'm still so enraged it's eating me alive.

God...I have nothing. I literally have fuck all to work with.

By the time anyone misses me, who knows what could have happened to me by then?

The air around me thickens as my lungs tighten, constricting as if a wrench is clamping around them.

This seriously can't be happening to me. It can't.

Is there really nothing I can do? And I don't know if I can actually believe him that my grandmother and Sebastian are taken care of.

"I have to see my grandmother."

"You heard me. She's been taken care of."

"I don't give a shit what you said. You're a fucking asshole." I know I should shut up because I'm getting worked up and I have nothing to fight with, but I can't calm myself. "This is some crazy bullshit, and I don't want to be a part of it. You need to let me go and find some other way to get what you want."

"I'm going to give you a pass on that one because you don't know me yet. I've told you all you need to know right now, so all you have to concern yourself with is being my wife. And doing what wives do." Although he releases my hair, he gives me an openly seductive stare that scatters my nerves.

"What is your definition of what a wife should do?"

That grin returns to his face. "Don't worry. We won't do anything too major that we haven't done already, but for the record, I love the way you ride my cock."

My face burns with the same shame experienced by thousands of women who have fallen prey to sweet-talkers and frauds who have charmed them out of their dignity.

What a complete asshole. But no... this isn't his fault. Not that part. Once again, it's mine. I was the fool.

"I am not your whore." I imbue my voice with strength.

"My dear Gwen." He leans right in, so his face is a breath away from mine. "You don't seem to realize I own you now. That means you'll be my whore whenever I want you to be."

As if someone added a dose of napalm to my hand, it springs up and connects with his jaw quicker than my brain can warn me not to slap him.

By the time any sort of signal takes fruition in my mind,

I've already left a handprint on his jaw, along with a graze where my fingernails pierced his skin.

Blood seeps out of the mark, and the sight fills my soul with dark dread.

Jesus.

Why did I do that?

Calmly, Malik touches his cheek, and his finger comes away with blood. When his jaw tenses, I know I've landed myself in more trouble.

"I'd say that's strike one."

Instinct moves me, along with the same panic I felt earlier when I tried to run. But unlike then, when I thought I could escape, I'm fleeing now because I don't want to find out what strike one means.

Like the lion playing with the mouse, Malik allows me to get a few more steps ahead this time before he catches up to me.

He grabs my nightshirt first, and because I don't stop trying to escape his grasp, it tears off my body like paper, leaving me in nothing but my panties. He grabs me with one arm and throws me over his shoulder caveman style.

"Running again was strike two." His voice deepens, and one large hand lands on my ass cheek so hard I cry out. He spanks me again, holding me tight as I try to wriggle out of the lock.

"Let me go!" I scream.

One more slap comes down hard on my ass, and another, before he walks out of the secret shrine with me just like that and back into the bedroom.

"Put me down. What the hell is wrong with you?"

He throws me onto the bed, and blinding panic races

over me when he climbs on, too, then presses his hard body into mine.

Before I can say another word, he catches my hands in one of his, pinning them above my head. Instantly, I think of worse things he could do to me than what he's already done.

Would he really force himself on me?

Why wouldn't he?

I'm naked and completely at his mercy. He's strong. There would be nothing I could do to stop him.

"Malyshka." I wish he didn't call me that. Hearing the stupid endearment reminds me of how much I liked it. And how much I liked him. I must be sick in the head if I can think of that now when nanoseconds ago, I was worried he'd rape me. "I warned you what would happen if you fucked with me."

"I'm sorry." The words tumble out of my mouth.

"It's too late for sorry, Malyshka. The last man to draw blood from me is six feet under." He speaks in a deep, low voice that heightens my fear. "What do you think I'm going to do to you?"

His massive erection presses into my belly, and he parts my legs with his knees.

"Malik—" My words cut when he releases my hands to cup my sex.

I gasp, and he doesn't give me a chance to recover before he shoves my panties aside and pushes his finger into my pussy.

"Baby, I'm not above fucking you into submission." He pumps into my passage and I can no longer move. "I just think it's so much sweeter when you come to me willingly, like all the other times we've fucked."

Holding me captive with his massive hard body, he continues pumping his finger in and out of me, then speaks in Russian. Of course, I don't understand him, and it's clear he doesn't mean for me to. But I can tell that whatever it is must be something completely inappropriately sexual, and it would frighten me more than I am now if I knew what he was saying.

"What are you going to do to me?" The high-pitched whimper of my voice carries across the room.

He smiles and answers in Russian, sounding scary and sexy at the same time.

"You...bastard." I grab his shirt as I feel the beginnings of an orgasm rising through my body on a wave of fire.

"Yes. But I'm the kind of bastard you like, Malyshka. Look at how fucking wet my naughty little designer is for me. You seem to be a good girl, but you like my fingers in your pussy. You like how I touch you, and you like being restrained." He grins.

"I... don't." My forced answer feels like the same kind of lies I hate telling myself.

"Your naughty little pussy doesn't lie, Malyshka. This cunt is soaking wet for me, and only I can please you."

I want to protest and tell him it's not true, but I can't speak. A stupid moan comes out instead, betraying me.

Smooth circles go around and around my clit, and I whimper in confliction because I want to hate it, but what I hate is that my body loves what he's doing to me.

I hate that his fingers feel so damn good inside me, and I hate it even more that I remember how his cock felt even better pounding into me.

Intense pleasure arches my body into the mattress, and I

moan out loud, unable to help myself against the scorching arousal coiling through me.

He's stealing all my willpower again, robbing me blind in broad daylight of my senses.

This is the time that should count the most because I know what and who he is. I know he's just playing with me and fucking with my mind, but no matter how hard I try to realign my mind and body in harmony with reason and logic, it doesn't work.

I can't fight back to regain control, and I can't resist him.

I can't deny my body of the pleasure that wants me to succumb to its power and allow it to possess me.

The worst thing about it is the wicked way he smiles down at me because he knows.

He knows.

He also knows that everything he said was true.

Malik slows down to a steady pump, knowing exactly how to touch me, and I come straightaway, whining like an animal in heat.

The sweet pleasure from my orgasm creates a buzz of fire over me that increases when he buries his face in my pussy and drinks up the juices from my arousal leaking down my thighs. His tongue licks me and thrashes around my clit, bringing more mindless moans of ecstasy from deep inside my core.

While he eats me out, he grabs my breasts, squeezing and kneading my nipples that are already painfully tight with arousal. Within seconds, I know I'm going to come again. I'm right there at the precipice when he moves away from my pussy, kisses his way up my body, and starts sucking my breasts.

He touches me and does everything as if he's speaking some secret language only he and my body understand.

What I'm not prepared for is his lips on mine.

After everything, I never expected to feel them again in this lifetime, or to kiss him back the same way he's kissing me.

I taste myself on his lips as our tongues tease and tangle in a dance of the forbidden who want each other. It's spellbinding and almost hypnotic, lulling me into giving him everything.

He takes my hand and moves it down to his hard erection, then forces my fingers to clasp his hard cock.

He breaks the kiss, leaving us both breathing hard, and stares down at me, but squeezes my hand around his cock tighter.

"Remember this every time you think it wasn't real." His words surprise me, throwing my mind out of sync. "But I also promised you a punishment, so you don't get to come twice."

Although I'm so damn desperate to come, his crass words yank me out of the sexual haze, and once again, I feel like such a fool.

I'm so humiliated by his words and the effortless ability to switch back to being the devil that all I do is stare at him, speechless in disgust.

Disgust at him and myself.

But I should have used those seconds to do something wiser—*anything*—because when he grabs my hands again and pins them over my head, it's too late. I thrash against him, and a second later, cool metal latches around my wrists. Then there's a click. Like a lock.

Frantically, I gaze above my head in horror to find my hands chained to the railed loops of the headboard.

What the fuck?

And where the hell did he get chains from out of nowhere?

"What the hell is wrong with you?" I glare at him as if I can incinerate him with my thoughts of how much of an asshole I think he is. "Release me now."

I flounder uselessly against the chains, looking like some kind of spectacle.

Malik backs off the bed and runs a casual hand through his hair to smooth out the tousled strands.

When he straightens, I expect him to give me that mocking smirk again, but his expression becomes more serious.

"It looks like you need some time to think, Malyshka. When you're ready to play nice, I'll think about letting you go. But if you strike me again and continue to fuck with me, we'll take our vows right here with you chained to my bed."

My mouth drops open. I know he's serious. He would do exactly that.

"I hate you, Malik Volkova." My voice is filled with so much venom, I don't recognize it. I've never told a person I've hated them before. I certainly wouldn't have thought to do so while feeling like my body is going to explode from a pleasure overload.

To intimidate me further, Malik gives me that mocking smirk, leans close, and plants a kiss on my forehead. "Gwen St. James, this would be so much easier if you actually hated me. But we both know you don't, and that's okay because I don't hate you either. It's just one more problem we have to figure out, my little wife-to-be."

Those words sting, cutting me deeply, letting me know I'm helpless.

He moves away once more, then without another glance, he walks through the door, leaving me naked and chained to his bed.

Chapter Sixteen

Malik

I'm in my boat garage. It's not that much different to Batman's cave.

After my encounter with Gwen, this place was the only solace that could distract the beast inside me who wanted to fuck whatever I feel for her out of my system.

I keep the three sailing yachts I've used for races in here. One of which is the boat Leif and I built from scratch when I was sixteen. I came down here to work on it once I'd finished up what I had to do for the day.

I've been here for several hours, but the taste of Gwen and her sweet nectar is still driving me wild, as is the knowledge that Gwen St. James is naked and chained to my bed.

So far, she's done everything I thought she would do.

She ran again, and I caught her.

She went snooping around my secret room, and I caught her.

She tempted the fuck out of me, and I caught her.

I trapped her in the bed chains I normally bring out when my darker desires take control. But the joke's on me because I still want her, and I'm cursing myself for depriving my dick of being inside her.

I came down here to take back control but it's only marginally working.

I'm allowing myself another hour, then I'll go check on my little captive and see if she's ready to play nice.

I smooth over the wood of the boat's hull with sandpaper.

I've done several repairs on this boat over the years. It's one of those things that has reached the end of its life many times over, but I do what I have to do to keep it going because of its sentiment.

It was made in the spirit of adventure between a boy and his uncle who wanted to do something amazing.

Making boats was what the Volkovas did right from the Viking age. That's why they got into the shipping business. But to Leif, the sea kept us in touch with who we were.

Brian and I had just signed up for a race, so Leif thought it would be cool to actually make a boat.

He was right. Now this old boat tethers me to all the good memories I've had of the people who created my adventures.

I'm hoping to take it out sailing in a few weeks with Desmier, who is also a sailor with nearly the same skills of working on ships as me.

If I didn't have other important things to do I'd lock myself down here and get the boat finished sooner.

"I'm surprised you're down here." Zakh's voice cuts through the still silence I've gotten used to.

I look up at the door at the top of the stairs and see him standing there staring down at me.

I didn't expect to see him again today, but it's good. It means he has something for me that will advance my plans.

"Where else would I be?" I chuckle.

"Well, with the girl being right under your roof, I assumed you'd be in bed. Or something." He smirks and makes his way down the wooden steps. "Jeanne told me you were down here working on the boat."

"I'm keeping my focus where it should be."

"Or distracting yourself?" He angles his head and stares at my cheek. The bruise is still there from when Gwen slapped me. I have to give her credit for the surprise attack. I never saw that coming, but her defiance only hardened my cock. "Back at Desmier's, you said you spoke to her, but the bruise on your face suggests otherwise. Trouble in paradise already? It's not even been a full day yet."

"This was never going to be paradise for either of us."

"I'm guessing she must have put up one hell of a fight."

"Of course, but I'll make sure she's as compliant as I need her to be. I have her exactly where I want her."

His face lights up with interest. "Do tell, brother. Looks like you have something else up your sleeves."

"She owes me Conrad's debt now." I'd told him all about my encounter with Conrad on the way back from Wilmington.

He chuckles. "Well played."

"Business is business."

"Of course, but...that doesn't make it a crime to like her. Especially since you already do."

Now that we've fulfilled the hardest part of our mission, the playful side of him I'm used to is showing itself.

"I know, but business needs to be business." That sounds more like me trying to keep myself in check.

Zakh deadpans me, then gives me that look he always casts my way when he thinks I'm bluffing. He's right because I am.

"Are you seriously going to stand there and tell me you're not happy that Gwen is Santiago's daughter?"

"Zakh—"

"Six months, Malik." He holds up six fingers, giving me a pensive stare. "Six months. That's it."

"I know." Six months is how long Gwen and I have to stay married.

"I'm just saying you've been on this quest for *six* years, and you accomplished the impossible. Of course, business always needs to be business, but maybe you can start loosening up a little and live. Especially if you like this girl."

Maybe he can see that I'm dead inside. The problem with that is, once you're dead like that, not a lot can bring you back. Sometimes, the damage is done, and you can't repair it.

"Maybe." I only say that to get him off my back.

"Cool. Brian would be proud of this, you know. If getting the cartel is sufficient justice for you for Captain Davison's death, I'm sure Brian would think the same."

"I appreciate that." Zakh is the only person I talk to about Brian and Jim, and those conversations are few and far between.

"I know. And with that said, my job is officially done. I just dropped by to give you these." He reaches into the inside pocket of his jacket and takes out two things. One is a brown envelope. The other is a little black ring box.

I fixate on the box because it contains Gwen's engagement ring. I asked Zakh to get that for me.

"Her ring."

"Yeah. I got something nice. I think she'll like it."

"Thanks." It never crossed my mind that Gwen may or may not like it, because I know she'll hate it as much as she's trying to hate me.

I pop the box open and look at the ring. It has a delicate oval cut diamond set in the center of a thin gold band. It suits her and even looks like it was made for her graceful fingers.

"Do you like it?"

"I do. No pun intended."

"Of course." He gives me a light laugh and holds up the envelope. "This contains the marriage registration documents. I need both of you to sign them and return them to me by tomorrow at midday."

"Consider it done."

He nods. "Good. Well, I'll let you get back to whatever it is you're doing." He looks over the boat and narrows his eyes. "What exactly are you doing?"

"Planning a voyage for a few weeks when I think I'll need a break." Once everything is done, I want to head out to sea for a few weeks.

"Aren't you worried this old boat will sink with you?"

I laugh. "It won't sink."

"Okay, see you tomorrow."

"See you."

Once he leaves, I look back at the boat and stare at the old grooves in the wood, getting lost in the pattern.

I planned to work on the boat a little longer but I think I should go see Gwen. I have one more ace up my sleeve today for her that might help her cooperate.

I need to prepare myself first, though, and see if she's taken the time I gave her to think about her situation.

I pack everything up, then make my way over to the little section in the corner with the surveillance cameras.

It's a duplicate of what the guards can see in their security office, but this one has access to the cameras in my bedroom. No one else but me gets to see inside there, and that works perfectly for times like today when I have the goddess of a woman chained to my bed.

I tap in the password that will bring up the footage of my room. The sight of Gwen's perfect naked body brings a salacious smile to my face.

No matter how many times I see her, I don't think I could ever look at this woman's body and not be satisfied.

I allow my gaze to travel over her, from the glossy pink of her fingertips and her hands secured by my chains, down to those ripe, gorgeous breasts I got to suck on.

My only regret is that I didn't take her panties off.

I lean back against the wall and take in the view that hooked me from hello.

Earlier, it would have been so easy to fuck her. She wanted it, too.

Now, the distressed look on that beautiful face of hers speaks of her helplessness.

She's sunken against the pillows with her head leaning to the side, facing the window.

Have I broken her yet?

Has the devil in me broken this sweet angel who should be anywhere in this world besides with me?

No.

She's not broken yet. That fire that draws me to her is still in her vibrant sea-green eyes. It's not something that can break easily, and it will continue to keep that hope lurking in her stare alive.

That's just the thing. I don't want her broken. I want her exactly the way she is. And while I'm admitting that, I'll allow myself to admit, too, that it wasn't the beast in me who wanted her.

It was the man.

The man who's supposed to be dead inside.

The man I haven't been in years.

I feel him when I'm with her, and for those moments, that is the only time I'm not death.

I'm not sure that type of addiction is good for me.

But like any good addict, I want to keep going back for more.

Those are the things I need to be careful of when it comes to Gwen St. James.

Whatever I do, I must never give her that type of control over me.

Chapter Seventeen

Gwen

It's just gone ten o'clock, which means I've been in this position, naked and chained to the bastard's bed, for the last eight hours.

Thank God, I'd had the good sense to eat the food Jeanne brought me and peed when I went to clean up in the bathroom before that encounter with Malik.

I also didn't drink any of the water or juice she fixed up. Although I planned to.

No one has come by to check on me.

At first, I thought that was a good thing, but then I realized how bad it was because I'm a prisoner here.

And look at me.

I remember watching several movies with Dru where some woman wanted to be tied up and live out a wild sexual fantasy. Dru was into all of that and even went to a BDSM club a few times with an old boyfriend.

I get it; it's kinky and exciting. But neither of the two apply to you when you're chained up for real and there is no safe word or compassion while you're left at the mercy of a sadistic bastard who wants to force you to marry him so you can take over your father's cartel.

God... it hurts just to think it, and everything else hurts, too.

There's nothing I can do, and I really miss home. On a night like this, I'd be curled up by the fire with Sebastian at my feet while I draw the inspirations that come to me for my designs.

I miss that, and I miss Dru so damn much it hurts.

I worry I won't see her again, and I can't even think about how scared I am about Grams.

Everything about this entire scenario is crazy, and I really don't want to have anything to do with the Navarros. Throughout the day, it's crossed my mind several times that I'm probably going to end up meeting a family I never hoped to meet. And Dad's actual wife, Esperanza.

I don't want to meet her and remember that I'm a child of an affair that never should have happened. I don't want the reminder that my father cheated, or that he could never really choose to be my father because of her.

I just want to go home, if that is even a possibility. Nothing was mentioned of when I might do that.

I know nothing more than what I've been told, which has all been basics to do with Dad and the cartel. I don't know anything else, but I'm assuming a man like Malik is not going to want to stay married forever. Or maybe that part doesn't matter. All he needs me for is to be his wife in name only.

If that's the case, what will happen to me?

What will happen to me, anyway?

Am I actually considering this?

Do I even have an ounce of a choice?

I don't believe I do.

From the way things look, if I don't comply, life will be harder for me or the people I care about.

But is this it? Is this how my life ends? Maybe this is the curse of my parents' decision to be together. Everybody loses, and I have to be the scapegoat.

The patter of little feet on the other side of the door makes me lift my head. It's the first sound I've heard since Malik left. It's also odd because it sounds like tiny feet.

When I hear a distinct bark, I sit up straighter—well, as straight as I can get.

Was that really a bark? Like a dog? But not just any dog. That was Sebastian's bark.

I'm sure of it, or maybe I'm delirious with worry and I've gone crazy.

When the door opens and Sebastian runs in, barking and looking so happy to see me, I suck in a breath, and my heart lifts.

Sebastian is here. Malik brought him.

It's an absolute shocker, but I don't care. Having Sebastian with me is one less thing to worry about.

I'm so happy to see him I try to reach for him, but the rattle of the chains around my wrists and the sight of Malik walking in behind Sebastian remind me of my current demise.

He locks the door behind him. Another reminder.

Sinking back to the bedrail, I stare at the two of them. Sebastian stretches up onto his back legs and places his paws on the bed next to me, while Malik keeps his gazed fixed to me.

He looks away first and focuses on Sebastian, giving him an order in Russian.

Fuck knows what he says to *my* dog, but my little furry best friend listens to him and sits on the floor, obeying as if Malik is his new master.

I haven't cried all day throughout this whole thing, even though my tears were never far away. But the sight of Sebastian taking orders from my enemy brings my tears that much closer.

Malik looks back at me, then allows his gaze to drift over my body with the same languid manner he used to touch me earlier before settling back on my eyes.

"You brought my dog to Boston?" My voice is so gravelly it sounds like it belongs to someone else.

"I'm not the kind of man to leave an injured animal without a master. He'll want to stay near you for comfort tonight."

It's hard to believe that such a devil can show any compassion.

In the spirit of seeking freedom, it also makes me wonder if I could reach this side of him and get him to see that I can't do whatever it is he wants me to do.

"Am I going to stay like this?"

His eyes settles on my breasts, and I hate that my nipples harden like they're begging for his mouth again.

"That's entirely up to you." He inclines his head, and a lock of his hair falls over his eye. "I don't mind sleeping next to you chained up."

"You're actually going to sleep in here?" The heat in my

blood rises.

"I'm sure you must have figured out that this is my bedroom."

"Yes, of course." My words are stiffer than Marybeth's over-sprayed hair on the Fourth of July.

"*Good.*" He borrows my tone. "So, this is where I'm staying, and the manner in which you'll sleep next to me will depend on whatever your answer is to my next question. If I were you, I'd choose my words wisely."

I want to lash out and tell him to go fuck himself, but I know I have to cool my temper down. Look where fighting back got me for the last eight hours.

"What is your question? And before you ask, I'm not fucking you." I'm not doing that. It's obvious that this man has some kind of hold on me. But that's just because my body is confused and my mind conflicted. Given enough time, I should be able to resist him with no problem.

A predatory smile spreads across his face, sending shivers down my body.

"If I wanted to fuck you, I wouldn't have to ask. I'd just do it. Like I did before."

While the flames of embarrassment heat my body up all over again, his gaze intensifies with such a force it could push me into the wall, but I regain my strength and lift my chin.

"What is the question?"

"The question is, are you ready to play nice?"

Play nice. I have no choice but to do so if I want him to undo my chains. "Yes."

He straightens and pulls a little key from his pocket. Leaning over me, he undoes my chains.

My arms drop like deadweights to my sides, and the blood rushing down to my fingertips is painful and numbing.

I shudder and curl inward, hugging myself.

He walks toward the wardrobe and pulls out a little bag I saw earlier when I was snooping around.

He brings it over and hands it to me.

"These are some of your clothes I brought for you."

How nice of him to remember to pack a bag when he was kidnapping me.

I take the bag and shuffle to sit up properly. "Can I go to the bathroom?"

"Of course."

I get up on wobbly legs as he watches me. He continues watching as I make my way to the bathroom.

When I'm inside, the air returns to my lungs, and I'm grateful for the moment of reprieve from him.

I splash water over my face, dry off, then open the bag.

He didn't bring many things. There's another nightshirt, a few yoga pants, some T-shirts, and a pair of ballet pumps. In the middle pocket are my birth control pills.

Not wanting to miss a day, I open the pack and take one, but the fact that Malik thought to bring them spikes my nerves.

Given the circumstances, I suppose I should be grateful to have my own clothes to wear and my pills to take, but seeing them enrages me further.

So does the sting of betrayal. It's been hitting hard all day, but seeing my things packed in this bag ignites it worse than before when I think of how Malik must have planned to take me. I'm not safe around him. No matter what he says or that he saved me from Conrad, I'm not safe.

How can any woman feel safe around a man who drugged her and kidnapped her? A man who watched her from the shadows with seedy intentions, while she was none the wiser until it was too late?

"Don't think, Gwen, don't do it," I mutter, speaking so quietly the words are barely audible. While most people give themselves a mental pep talk when they need it, I've always found that saying the words out loud has a better effect.

My words of advice don't actually help, but I need to do whatever I can to get through the night. Maybe I'll be stronger in the morning. My mind might be clearer and maybe, just maybe, I'll be able to figure my way out of this. A way that sees me back in Wilmington and on track to where I should be.

With that thought, I pull on the nightshirt and go back out into the room, hugging Sebastian before I do anything else.

Malik already has his shirt off and starts taking off his pants.

Unnervingly, I watch him until he's completely naked, and my gaze drifts down to his cock, which is already erect. It looks bigger and thicker than when I last saw it.

That was only days ago, and nothing will eradicate the memory of us from my mind.

"Get in the bed." He points to the bed.

"I thought we were going to talk."

"No more talking tonight."

Hearing that sends a pang of anxiety straight to my heart. There's no way I'll be able to sleep without answers to my questions.

"But I—"

"Gwen, we are going to bed. Remember, play nice." He hardens his stare.

"I have more questions."

"I've told you all you need to know for today. Now get in the bed."

At first, I look at him, the urge to scream and defy eating me alive, but I tamp down the overbearing emotions roiling within me and slide back into bed.

He switches off the light, and the moonlight takes over, spilling in through the window the way sunlight would on a bright morning.

I'd think it was enchanting and beautiful if it were under better circumstances.

Sebastian lies down on the floor next to me, giving me some comfort, but the moment Malik climbs into the bed with me, my nerves slip.

"Lie down." His voice is calmer than before.

I rest my head on the pillow with my back turned to him.

"You're not going to drug me again, are you?" I don't care if I'm not playing nice by asking him that. It's a valid question given the fact he did that before.

"Not unless I need to. Do I need to?"

"No."

"Then we won't have a problem."

I beg to differ. All the problems that exist are mine. Mine alone.

I'm the one who has to share a bed with the beast who kidnapped me.

Chapter Eighteen

Gwen

It took forever to fall asleep, possibly hours, but I made it through the night.

I woke to Jeanne tapping me on my shoulder with the instruction to get ready for breakfast downstairs, where Malik would be joining me. She explained that he'd taken Sebastian for a walk.

When she left, she made a point of showing me she was leaving the door open.

Open for me to go and come like a free person.

Seeing the opportunity to gather the information I'm so desperate for, I get ready as quickly as possible, dragging on one of my yoga pants and T-shirts.

When I make my way out of the room, my steps slow when I see the grandeur décor of the hallway. I look up at a high plaster ceiling with ornate cornices and a wrought-iron chandelier hanging above me as I walk on the marble floor.

Being trapped in the bedroom yesterday with the view of the sea below closed my mind off to everything else. Now that I'm out and seeing how huge and grandiose the hallway is, I can only imagine what the rest of the house must look like.

I've always considered Grams' home to be elegant and sophisticated, but it's nothing compared to this.

I follow the path to the landing, where I'm greeted with a wide sweeping staircase, like the kind you'd see in a stately home, or those TV shows that showcase homes owned by billionaire.

I'm stunned and definitely caught off guard.

My mind shifts back in focus when I reach downstairs and see Malik standing in the dining room smoking a cigarette.

He's dressed in a suit, like he's going to work, and looks so different from the attire I've seen him in. The suit makes him seem more mature and distinguished. Like the dark billionaire. It makes me wonder if he is.

He puts the cigarette out when he sees me and sets his shoulders back.

"Morning, Malyshka." He beams as if we're old friends and everything is wonderful.

"I would prefer if you didn't call me that." I keep my tone measured and without the disgust I feel for hearing the endearment again.

"You seemed to like it just fine when you first heard it."

"Back then, you were someone else. Not the devil or the fraud." I know that was way too harsh and I'm pushing my limits, but I can't act as if I'm just going to play along with his games and I'm fine with being a pawn.

A sinful grin spreads across his handsome face. "Do I need to remind you what happens if you don't play nice? Believe me, I have all sorts of wicked ideas for that body of yours."

"I remember very well, thank you."

"Good, then we can start today off on the right foot."

I look away from his intense stare at the large oil painting on the wall of a pirate ship caught in a tempestuous storm. The painting looks old and valuable. So do the ornaments on the wall and the solid mahogany table in the center of the room with the matching chairs around it.

"How many people live in this house?" I look back at him.

"Apart from us, there are five others. All staff. Jeanne is one of them. You'll meet the others today."

"How many bedrooms does this house have?"

"Ten."

"And this is your home?"

"Yes." He watches me closely and I look over his suit.

"Are you going to work? Do you even need to work?" For all I know, he could be meeting with a bunch of drug lords to discuss their next billion-dollar drop. Or it could be worse, like maybe he sells people—women. Women like me.

"I do work."

"What kind of work do you do? I'm guessing it's not with the government or anything to do with the Navy. Was that injury story even true? I mean, maybe you were called back to your *Knights*."

At my comment, something dulls in his eyes, and I can tell I've struck a nerve.

"If I hadn't been injured, I'd still be in the Navy. There

is no question about that." There's something about his eyes when he's telling the truth or showing emotion that lets me know what he's saying is genuine. It's like whatever guard he's placed up falls away and I can see the real him. "Now I work at my family's company, Volkova Inc. It's a shipping company. I take care of the fleet of cargo ships we have worldwide. Sometimes I'm here in Boston, at other times I'm in Russia or Norway."

I'm surprised he told me so much.

"What exactly do you do there?"

"Anything to do with finance and logistics."

It sounds so ordinary, like something you hear a normal businessman talking about. But he's anything but.

Malik points to the chair at the end of the table. "Sit. We're going to eat while we talk. I have a busy day ahead."

I make my way down to the chair but can feel his eyes on my ass with every step I take. Just to check, I turn and look at him. I see I'm right.

He's checking me out, and even when he sees me looking at him, he doesn't stop like most men would when they get caught. Malik Volkova shows he's not most men by continuing to stare at my ass, then oh-so languidly runs his gaze over my body as if it's his next meal.

My cheeks burn with the heat of arousal, and that wild combination of chemistry and attraction I've felt for this man since the first day we met stirs in my body like hot lava.

His eyes meet mine just before I sit, then he seats himself at the head of the table in the chair next to me.

We stare at each other for a few silent beats that fuel the deadly combination of everything I need to be wary about this man. This thing between us, this reckless thing I can't stop myself from feeling and he clearly feels, too, is real.

That makes him more dangerous to me for the simple fact that I've never felt that with anyone before. I don't want to feel anything like that for a man I can't trust—or specifically, *him*.

The moment is broken when Jeanne walks in carrying a tray of delicious breakfast food. The aroma softens the tense atmosphere, as does the warm smile on her face.

"All your favorites, Master Volkova," she says, setting down the tray.

"Thank you."

With a proud smile, she takes off the little platters containing the assortment of food and arranges them before us. There are scrambled eggs garnished with herbs, fried eggs, strips of bacon, herby sausages, slices of normal toast and French toast, and fried green tomatoes.

There's also a separate plate of croissants, which she positions nearer to me as she glances at me as if she secretly knows how much I like croissants.

"Thank you," I tell her. She dips her head respectfully.

I'm about to say something more when another maid walks into the room with a pot of coffee.

This maid is younger, probably the same age as me or slightly older, and very pretty with her red, foxy hair, piercing blue eyes, and a body the runway would love.

She looks at Malik and the smile on her face is enough to tell me she likes him more than just as her boss.

But then maybe that's why she's here.

"Good morning," she greets me.

"Good morning."

"Do you like your coffee, black or white?" She speaks with the same cultured accent as Jeanne. It crosses my mind that they might only speak English when they need to.

"Black, please."

Like Jeanne, she gives me a curt nod, then she pours Malik a cup, too.

Malik speaks in Russian to both her and Jeanne. When the new maid replies in Russian and he laughs, I feel something akin to jealousy, and it's not because they're talking in a language I don't understand. It's because of how he responded to her.

He says something more, and they both leave. New maid glances over her shoulder at him; he's already looking at her —something else that flares my temper.

This is just great.

I'm not going to be naïve and think he's not sleeping with her because he probably is. Most men like him do. In fact, they hire staff like her so they can have access to sex whenever they want it.

Instantly, I've lost my appetite. It's bad enough that I'm in this situation, but the thought of him screwing his maid hits too close to home because of Gage.

Malik looks back at me, reaches into his pocket, and pulls out my phone.

"That's mine." My eyes dart from the phone to him.

He hands it to me, and I'm so eager to take it the phone almost slips out of my grasp. But I bridle my excitement. He wouldn't simply be handing me back my phone without some stipulation.

"It's chipped so I can listen in on your conversations if I need to."

There it is. "Great. So, why give it back to me?"

"So you can establish proof of life."

My stomach churns. "Proof of life?"

"When we're done here, Jeanne will show you around the house and the grounds. Then you're going to make two phone calls. One to Dru and the other to Gilman."

Ughh. This just keeps getting better and better. "And what am I going to say?" Sarcasm drips from my tone.

"You're going to follow up on what I said yesterday with the business opportunity. You can also tell Dru an investor took care of Conrad's loan and you're paying them back once you get everything set up."

"And what is this business opportunity?" The whole idea sounds ridiculous.

"You're the designer, *Malyshka.* Create something." He emphasizes Malyshka, and I cringe inwardly. "You need to make them believe you're going to be away for a while, and you'll check in daily if you have to."

I stare back at him and summon the strength to tell him once more that this is crazy.

"Somebody is going to suspect something somewhere along the line. It will most likely be Dru. She knows me too well. She knows I wouldn't just up and leave to be away for any amount of time, and I would never get married without my best friend. If you let me go now, it should be fine. I can pay you back Conrad's loan in a few months once my line has launched."

He sits back and chuckles. "And how much do you think that loan is now that it's in my hands?"

I glare at him. "It was a hundred and seventy-five thousand."

"Unfortunately, it's no longer that."

My jaw drops. "You're seriously going to put interest on it?"

"In a manner of speaking, yes, but men like me don't always want money, because we have so much of it. We like to take payments in things like secrets and anything of value."

He gives me a cold calculative stare that displays the wealth of darkness in him, and I'm almost afraid to look into his eyes.

"So, you want to take me?"

"I do want to take you, Gwen St. James. In more ways than one. This is just one way."

I grip the edge of my chair and bite down hard on my back teeth. "This was never supposed to be my life. I want nothing to do with the Navarros."

He flicks over his palms. "Not even for the billion-dollar fortune your father left you?"

Those words short-circuit my mind. *Billion-dollar fortune*, what the hell? "What are you talking about? I thought this was about taking over the cartel."

"It is, but your father owned much more than just the cartel."

"Like what?" I search my brain, but surely, I'd recall if my father had something worth so much. Grams would also have told me. If she knew. And if she was told to tell me. With so many secrets going around, there's a chance she was told to keep it from me.

"Do you know the pharmaceutical company Astori?"

"Yes." Everybody knows that company. They're one of the biggest pharmaceutical companies in the world. Surely, he couldn't be saying that... "No way. Are you going to tell me my father owns Astori?"

"No. *You* do."

My eyes pop wide, and I'm frozen to the chair. "Me?" My voice comes out in a hushed whisper.

"Yes. You."

I shake my head. "How could I not know this?"

"The cartel is built on that company. It's almost like a front for the real business, but both are empires. Astori produces legit drugs that have FDA approval, and the cartel combines it with other synthetic drugs to traffic worldwide without question."

"Oh my God."

"Your father never named you in his will, but the provision was for his daughter to take ownership of everything. To do so, you needed to get married and stay married for a minimum of six months." He straightens and rests his hands on the table. "It is only through marriage that you would own the company and all his other assets, including the cartel, but in equal parts. That's how it works. If after six months, the marriage didn't work out, you would get to keep your share without the need to remarry. And obviously, if your husband died, you'd get his share, too. If your husband died before the six months, or wanted a divorce, you would be found a new one who would assume all the rights of the old one."

I'm hanging on to every word like I have rope attached to them. I can't believe what I'm hearing, and I'm even more confused now than I was before.

"I don't know why he would do that and make such a big deal about hiding me. Why would he give me everything and never make a way for me to find out?"

"I think you were supposed to find out at some point, but for some reason, it never happened. The company was left to you in an irrevocable living trust, which would take effect the moment you turned twenty-one. So, I think it was important for him to keep you a secret until that time. It seems to me that he thought someone was going to kill you. Am I right?" He's asking in a tone that suggests he already knows the answer but wants clarification.

"Yes. His wife wanted to. Esperanza Navarro. Hearing the news of this will makes me think his entire family would have supported her." It's not like I have to keep these details close to my heart anymore, so I decide to continue. "My father was going to leave Esperanza when he met my mom. They had an arranged marriage. She loved him, but he loved my mom and saw my mother in secret. Everything was a secret, including me. When I was born, my father got into some trouble and accidentally killed the brother of his enemy, but they didn't know he was the killer. Esperanza knew, though, and used that to blackmail him when he presented her the divorce papers. She had evidence and threatened to not just expose him but kill Mom and me, even though she didn't know who we were. My grandmother told me my father spent his life from that point on trying to fix the problem, which I take to mean eliminating the threat, but that never happened. Nothing was ever clear when it came to my father. When he died, everything else became more confusing. Like this. Leaving me everything was a sure way to start some kind of war. Esperanza would have never wanted that."

Malik might be the devil, but getting all that off my chest feels freeing.

"None of them would, and rest assured, it wasn't just me who would have been looking for you all these long years."

An icy chill rushes along my spine like fire tossed on gasoline. "They're looking for me?"

"Always, Malyshka. None of them wanted the threat of an heir. If they found you before you turned twenty-one, they would have killed you to nullify the will and your father's wishes for you. But if they found you now, they would marry you off to one of their own to keep the control, power, and wealth the way they want it to stay."

God, I was never safe.

But... I was. I was literally under lock and key, and no one should have known where to find me. Until he did.

"How did you know I was in Wilmington?"

"People like me have their ways." He doesn't blink while he speaks. As if he would have found me eventually, no matter how hard it was.

"What sort of ways? *They* never found me all these years."

"You don't need to know my ways. I will say, though, it was near impossible to find you. I think I did because I truly wanted to. But consider this: if *I* found you, they would have found you eventually. If that happened, there would have been no escape for you."

The more he tells me, the more my nerves tremble. Sometimes ignorance really is bliss, but not if you're in the dark about a threat that could uproot everything you know and change your life in ways you can't imagine.

But why now?

Something must have led Malik here. He wouldn't have always been looking for me.

"How has this just come about? My father has been dead for fifteen years. My uncle took charge of everything after he died." It sounds so strange to say the word *uncle* in reference to a man I don't know.

"Your uncle died three weeks ago. He was only placed in charge by the board of directors. Since your father's death, everything has been operating through the board. But being the heir eradicates that. I think your father wanted to exercise some control over your family. With your uncle's passing, they will choose the new leader next week. At the moment, his son Diego thinks he'll be taking over."

"But you want to." My emotions switch back to the reasons this villainous man wants me.

"Now that I've found you, I *will take* over. This is happening, Gwen, whether you like it or not. You can either come along for the ride willingly or fight me. It doesn't matter to me one way or the other."

"You think because you're some big badass secret society jerk, you can just claim my choice? All because I owe you? This is what you're taking for payment?"

"I'm taking *you* for payment." His voice deepens.

"Maybe so, but you're taking my choice and freedom. You're holding me here so I can't just walk away. Or run away."

"That's right." He inches closer. The scent of his cologne makes my stomach flutter. "That's exactly what I'm doing, and if you ever think of running, there's not a goddamn place on this earth you can run where I won't find you. Do you understand?"

A lump clogs my throat and my breath hitches. As

attracted as I am to him, he scares the shit out of me, mostly because I know he's serious. He's not screwing with me.

"Answer me," he prods.

"I understand." Yes, I understand that the only way forward is his way.

He sits back casually, but the threat of his words still hangs in the air.

"As for your choice, don't fucking tell me that a billion-dollar company with the ability to make more than it's worth doesn't sound attractive to you."

I can't argue with that. Only a fool would refute him. Of course, it's attractive, and I want it.

I could do everything a million times over with that money. I would never have to worry about Grams' medical bills ever again. Or anything else. Most of all, I could make my dreams come true of setting up my own physical stores in whatever city I wanted to.

I could be free, but would my father's family allow that?

Would Malik allow it?

"Are you really going to give me my share and let me go in six months?" I don't want to be screwed over again, and I don't want to allow myself to get involved in this only to end up with nothing.

"Yes. You get to keep what you're supposed to keep, and in six months' time, we go our separate ways."

I hold his gaze, searching for that spark of truth I've grown accustomed to. It flickers for a fraction of a second and instils hope within me.

It's six months. *Only six months.*

Compared to what I had planned, getting a billion-dollar fortune is beyond everything I've ever dreamed.

I can do six months for that.

"My father's family isn't just going to hand over everything to you because you found me. You know that, right?"

"You don't need to worry about that part. Leave that to me. Right now, we just have to focus on getting married. Okay?"

Married. Me. Like many other things he's said, the idea of marrying him still sounds strange to my ears. In three days' time, I'll be his wife.

"Yes." My answer sounds like my signature on an unwritten contract.

"Perfect." He issues me with an uncanny smile. "Now give me your left hand."

"My hand?"

"Yes, give it to me now."

I do with hesitation. He takes it, then pulls out the most beautiful diamond ring from his pocket and slips it on my ring finger.

Shock steals my senses at the sight of it. I wasn't prepared for an actual ring but here it is. It's as real as the ready-made fiancé sitting next to me.

A ring symbolizes shit just got real and I'm engaged to the devil.

The oval cut diamond is glorious, sitting on a thin gold band. It sparkles in the sunlight and the glint ripples on forever like an echo of a voice across a mountain range.

This is the kind of ring best reserved for royalty or girls like the Hiltons. But I have it on my finger.

"You will not take it off. I must see it at all times." It's as if he's taking some kind of pleasure in this.

Really Gwen? This ring is a mark of ownership. Of

course he's taking pleasure in this. Men like him like the idea of owning a person. It's not that much different to the collar around Sebastian's neck.

Malik releases my hand but I stare at the ring for a few more moments. It truly is beautiful.

Did he go out and buy this for me?

It doesn't matter. This isn't real. The ring is just a prop.

I place my hand back on my lap and stare back at him. There are more important things I need to know. "Do I have to live here the whole time? For six months?"

"Yes. You will stay here with me. It's safer this way. Once we're married the doors will be opened to all sorts of threats."

I believe him. "Does that mean you plan to keep me locked up in this house every day?"

His lips arch, revealing sinful dimples. "That part is entirely up to you. When I think I can trust you to keep playing nice outside of my watchful eye, we'll talk some more about you leaving the property."

I stifle a groan and hold my tongue. I'm walking on thin ice here with him, and I know I have to play his game to get what I want, but I can't allow the people and the things I care about to suffer.

"I work," I begin, keeping my tone measured while I level him a stare. "I work with Dru. We have plans that can't be put to the side for six months. Regardless of what I get at the end of this, my business will suffer. And so will my grandmother for not seeing me." Grams has already forgotten me. That night I left the nursing home, I planned to see her every week, so I need to see her.

He gazes at me for a moment, and I hope he's considering my plea.

"We'll talk about all that in a few weeks."

"*Weeks*? Dru might be able to hold down the fort for weeks, but by the time I see my grandmother again, she won't remember who I am."

The spark of something human flashes in his eyes and softens his expression. "I'll arrange for you to see her as soon as I think it's safe. You have to be in Boston for the moment so I can keep things tight and under control. We're meeting with Diego and Esperanza on Monday. That's where everything will change."

I sink my teeth into my bottom lip. There's just so much to think about.

I didn't realize we'd be meeting with them so soon. And I didn't think we'd have to actually meet with Esperanza in such a way at all.

"Okay." My nervousness echoes in my voice. "Why does Esperanza have to be there?"

"She's the head of Astori."

Great.

He sighs. "There's some paperwork we have to sign after breakfast." He changes the subject. "Jeanne will show you around then, and you can make your calls. I'm sure I don't have to tell you to watch what you say to Dru and Gilman when you speak to them."

"No."

"Good. At midday, Jeanne will take you shopping for some clothes and a dress for the wedding. I've arranged for your things in Wilmington to be brought here, but they won't arrive for a few days."

"Wow, you really planned all this with everything in mind." My voice is taut.

"I did. Now eat."

Eat?

This conversation was a lot to process, and my stomach feels like glass. I worry it might shatter into a million pieces if I eat, or even if move too much.

The news has left me weak, but somehow, someway, I need to find the strength to do whatever I need to secure my legacy.

Step one: Marry Malik Volkova.

Chapter Nineteen

Gwen

"This is so exciting." Dru's voice reverberates through the phone in a high-pitched tone of electrifying Dru energy. "I can't believe it's all worked out so well. This is one hell of a dream come true."

"It really is." I infuse my voice with as much excitement as I can muster, hoping she doesn't hear the underlying tones of fear hiding behind my words. "I'm so glad I followed your advice to be spontaneous."

"Yes. Thank God you listened to my always trusty advice. I am ecstatic. I think I might actually combust with happiness."

I can just imagine her glowing with happiness; it makes me feel worse for my lies.

I've spent the last five minutes telling her about the fake but not business opportunity of a lifetime that will change our lives.

I called her straight after I spoke to Gilman, who was happy to hear I was taking some time to myself to work on my business. I followed up on what Malik told them both but added a little more to the story for Dru. I told her the investor I'm working with—*aka me*—wants to discuss owning a share in my mother's original lingerie designs. Also, I'd be looking at property for us to set up our store. I knew the store was the only excuse I could use to explain this situation and stop her from wanting to come and find me.

Although the result of this will indeed change our lives, this is the biggest lie I've ever told her. One that's worse than not telling her who my father is. At least with that, she could assume the same thing most people did. That my father was never spoken about because he was either bad or some high-profile person.

This lie is different. The words came from my lips, and I had to withhold the marriage part. Dru and I have been planning our weddings since we were five. Now I'm getting married in a few days without her to a man I barely know.

I'm telling myself that it will be okay because I'll make it up to her big time. I'll pay off her debts and give her some money to do whatever she wants. The biggest bonus will be working together.

"Are you staying in a hotel?" Drew asks with the same bubbly enthusiasm.

I stare out the window at the lavish setting before me and think about how to answer that.

I'm sitting on the steps by the alcove that overlooks the Olympic-sized swimming pool.

Jeanne showed me around earlier and blew me away

further when I took in the rest of the house and surrounding grounds.

Earlier, when I thought the house was grandiose, I hadn't really seen anything yet of the stunning ten-bedroom mansion with its stately gardens and the beach.

The vast expanse of grounds by itself was enough to fit a small colony of people on it. The more I saw, the more I wondered why Malik owned such a massive home for just himself. I imagine him more at home in a high-rise penthouse apartment in the city. Then again, I could also see him sitting on a throne in Hell with infernal fires billowing around him and a host of poor unfortunate souls at his mercy.

It would be easier to tell Dru I'm at a hotel, but it's not plausible for a stay as lengthy as I've described. I've made it sound as if I'll be away for several weeks.

"I'm staying at a guest house," I decide to tell her. "It's easier to get to all the places I need to be."

"Wow, a guest house in Boston. It sounds like they're really taking care of you." Dru giggles.

"They are. I'm just so glad for the opportunity and how everything worked out. Most of all, no more Conrad." There is no pretense there. I genuinely am glad I don't have to deal with Conrad anymore, and hopefully will never again.

"This is so exciting. I just wish I could be there with you."

"I know, but soon." Sadness pulls at my heart. I don't know when I'll be seeing Dru again. This is like when we parted ways to go to college, but not. At least back then, we could arrange weekend visits or meet somewhere in between. I'm not calling the shots here. Malik is.

"Is there anything I can do? I don't want to be a sitting duck or like I'm dragging along for the ride."

"No." I shake my head even though she can't see me. "I've got this part covered. Besides, as it is, you've done so much already, so just keep doing what you're doing. I will keep you updated every step of the way." I sound so convincing, I almost believe myself.

"Are you sure?"

"Yes. Absolutely. I've got everything we need under control for the moment. If anything changes, I'll let you know."

"Okay, cool. That sounds good."

"I should finish up the designs for the new line by the end of next week, so I'll send those over to you." I should have plenty of time to do that. All I need is a notebook for the sketches, material to create the mock-up designs so the team back home can follow them.

That's what's going to keep me sane here.

Who knows what's going to happen after Monday when I meet my father's family?

"Perfect. Alright, enough business talk. Tell me more about Malik. You haven't said much about him."

I glance down at the ring on my finger and my entire body feels weak as if I've been drained of all the years of my life. I figured the less I say about Malik, the better it will be.

"He's been great."

"What's he like, though?" Her voice comes out in a hurried rush, like a child rattling off their Christmas present list. "Please tell me this is not just business. We both know it's not."

As far as Malik goes, Dru doesn't even know I slept with

him. I told her I went to see him to thank him for taking care of me and then he put me in touch with someone here who could help me set up the store. I also made it sound like he had to rush back here for his own work.

"There's nothing really to tell." I can feel my nose growing with every lie.

"Please tell me you've kept in touch and haven't just ditched him."

Again, I think of what the hell to say. "Well, he's busy, but we've agreed to meet up tomorrow." *And get married.* God, this is so crazy.

Dru scoffs. "Well, at least it's something, and thank goodness you weren't shy about telling him what you wanted to do with your life. But clearly, the seriously hot guy likes you, Gwen. Please don't allow the hot lieutenant to escape your grasp."

"Dru, you and I both know I need to be careful when it comes to men." That's my now old mantra, which is completely useless to me because I wasn't careful in the least.

"I know. But I just don't want you to miss out, especially on a guy who has literally served up your dreams on a platter. But I get it. I do think this whole thing is strange, but I'm telling myself he's like the secret millionaire." There's an edge to her voice that sounds as if logic is piercing through the veil of our excitement and telling her this is all too good to be true. "What's his actual story apart from the Navy?"

Damn. I was dancing around that question, hoping she wouldn't ask.

"I don't know much, but I think his injury affected him a lot. He said he would still be serving if not for it. Now he's just trying to do something else he loves in his family business. They own a shipping company, so I guess that fills the hole leaving the Navy left behind." Wow, I actually sound like I know him, but hearing myself talk makes me realize Malik has only told me the basic details I needed to know. Or rather, what he allowed me to find out and ask questions about. I don't really know the real him, and I'm not so sure it would be a good idea to.

"Gwen, I wouldn't be a friend to you if I didn't say he sounded like a decent guy. Please, just keep an open mind."

Guilt pinches at my soul again. It takes a lot for a guy to win the stamp of approval from Dru. Malik has only received it because I left out all the gory details that would terrify anyone.

My lies would be fine if I were telling them to anyone else, but not her. I'm not sure how I'm supposed to keep this up for the next six months. Saying it will be hard is an understatement.

"Okay, I hear you. An open mind doesn't hurt." I chuckle light-heartedly, so I sound like I'm considering her advice.

"Exactly. Oh, darn it, someone's at the door. I gotta go. Keep me in the loop and let me know if you need anything. Anything at all. I mean it."

I think of one thing that would mean the world to me. "Dru, please, could you check on my grandmother? That's the only thing I really need. I feel awful I won't be able to see her this week. It might be a few weeks yet before I can."

"Of course, I can definitely do that. I'll go tomorrow and send you some pictures."

"Thank you so much." That will help me massively; I

already feel at ease although I know if Grams doesn't remember me, she won't remember Dru either.

"Anytime, and please don't feel bad. Your grandmother would want you to do this."

She's right. Grams would definitely want me to get my legacy. She was as careful as she could be with the money my father left for me, until she couldn't. She would want me to seize this opportunity and fight if I need to.

"Thanks again, Dru."

"Don't mention it. Okay. I have to go before whoever is at my door knocks it down." She giggles. "Well done again, girl, and I hope you have lots of sex. *Lots* of hot but safe sex. Bye."

She hangs up before I can even think of an answer.

It's a good thing she wasn't asking me if I had safe sex, since I didn't.

I gaze out the window and mull over all the things that are supposed to happen next.

Jeanne will come and get me soon to take me shopping.

As nice as she is, the idea of buying a wedding dress with a stranger for my impromptu wedding is a little unnerving. Then I'm supposed to be spending the rest of the day with her. I'm usually a great people person, but I'm not really in the mood to talk to anyone. I suppose at least I get to leave the property and I'm going with Jeanne.

During my tour earlier, I got to know her a little more as she told me about the property. But I noticed she was being careful with what she told me. That must have been Malik's instruction which was fine by me.

Of course I still have a ton of questions about him, but as I'm still trying to process the overload from this morning, I didn't ask too much either. I'm worrying about what will happen once I face my father's family.

Movement catches my eye outside the window, and the red-haired maid I'd seen at breakfast comes into my view.

Her name is Kelly.

Instead of her maid's uniform, she's wearing a floral robe and walking along the poolside as if she's the lady of the manor.

The first thing Jeanne did was make it her duty to introduce me to all the staff.

Aside from being someone Malik is clearly overly friendly with, what annoyed me most about Kelly is that she was genuinely nice to me.

Jeanne explained Kelly had practically grown up with Malik and his brothers. She and her family worked for his parents when they were younger, but Malik took her on to work here when he bought the house.

Jeanne spoke fondly about Kelly, but all I could think was Malik might have had other reasons for employing her that Jeanne is too respectful and decent to see.

Kelly takes off the robe, unveiling a svelte figure with a turquoise bikini painted on her body.

She sets her robe on the deck chair, and with the elegance and power of an Olympic swimmer, she dives into the pool, slicing through the water like a mermaid.

With that vibrant red hair, she could be Princess Ariel.

She does a few laps, and I can't help but watch her because I can't swim. I grew up in a beach town, yet I can just about float around in a pool and splash about in the sea.

About ten minutes go by, and to my surprise, Malik walks up to the poolside.

I didn't think he was still here, but then again, I wasn't told that he'd left. I just assumed he'd gone because he said he had a busy day and looked like he was heading out to work.

Kelly swims up to him; a bright smile lights up her face.

I can't hear what they're saying, but when he returns her smile with equal vibrancy, it pulls at my insides with that envy I experienced earlier.

They talk with the casual ease of lovers who've known each other for a lifetime, and I note the way he looks down at her with fascination. The easy laid-back vibe he's giving off reminds me of how he was back in Wilmington when he came to see me at the restaurant for lunch. That was an act. This isn't.

As if he can feel my eyes on him, he straightens and looks straight at me.

Suddenly, we're staring at each other, eye to eye. Kelly continues talking to him, oblivious to me, while he's looking at me. He stares for a few beats, then switches his focus back to her, and even that annoys me.

Was it because he told me what he showed me in Wilmington was real why I feel like this?

Or is it because I'm wearing his engagement ring and marrying him in three days?

Does it matter?

Does what I feel matter if I get a billion-dollar fortune at the end of this?

It shouldn't, and maybe it wouldn't if part of me wasn't still stuck on the guy I thought I met in Wilmington.

I liked him.

He made me feel, and I never expected to have any such feelings after the entire ordeal with Gage.

He made me feel and now I don't trust him. Or know him.

No matter what he says to me, Wilmington wasn't real.

The door behind me opening pulls me back to the present. I look around to see Jeanne coming toward me. She's dressed in casual clothes, which look good outside her maid's uniform.

"Ready to go?" The sunlight touches her eyes, highlighting the friendliness in her expression.

"Yeah, sure. I'm ready." I stand and give her a little smile just to be polite.

"Great. I think we'll be away for most of the day."

"It will be nice to get out."

"I thought so too. As we have free rein of what we do, I thought I'd take you to some of my favorite places in Boston."

My smile brightens upon hearing that. "I'd like that. I've never been here before."

"I think you'll love it."

Love might be a stretch for me right now, but I need to adapt to this thing I'm doing. "Me too."

Instinctively, I glance back at Malik and Kelly. When I look at Jeanne again, I notice her looking at them too, before she returns her focus to me and sympathy washes over her face.

"Come on, let's get out of here."

I follow her out and try to steady my mind, reminding myself that this is only business.

It has to be.

Nothing more.

Chapter Twenty

Malik

"V*ictorious warriors win first and then go to war. But the greatest victory is that which requires no battle."—Art of war.*

Day two is official done.

Two more to go before I greet my enemies and emerge as not just the victor, but their conqueror. I love it when people think they've gotten away with something and realize all they did was bide time.

I park my car in the garage and rest my head against the soft leather seat of my chair. I breathe in the cool night air flowing through the window and allow it to settle my mind.

Today has been one of those seriously long days where it's felt like a year or two have passed. It's almost midnight.

When I left earlier, I went straight to Volkova Inc. and worked non-stop. Most of the work I had planned for the next two weeks is done now. That includes Bratva business. I just have a few things to tie up tomorrow, then the wedding is Saturday. After that I have meetings straight through until Monday morning when we meet with Diego and Esperanza.

After I meet with them and lay down the law, the next plan is to go to Mexico for the literal cartel takeover, where I'll be meeting with the members of the cartel and their allies. Zakh will be joining me and we'll be taking our strongest men. Desmier is contemplating coming with us, too. As we'll be on the Navarro's turf, we have to be prepared for retaliation by taking our best skilled in dealing with men like Diego.

Now that I'm home and I don't have the distraction of work, my mind instantly drifts to my wife-to-be.

I imagine Gwen inside my bedroom.

Is she asleep in my bed?

Or is she up thinking about the wedding and everything else?

The latter would be understandable.

I've dropped several bombs on her over the last two days; everything I told her is a lot to process.

As ruthless as I am, even I know that with the promise of a billion-dollar fortune, this change to her life is going to be drastic not only for the next six months but forever, because now the Navarros will know who she is.

She knows that, too. When she told me about the threat her father was under, I understood more about why Santiago wanted to keep her secret.

I never factored in Esperanza as a threat, but it makes sense, and I get it because that's what happened to my mother and how Desmier came to be.

My father was in love with his mother, not mine, and he had the same sort of secret relationship Santiago did with Gwen's mother.

The fucked-up thing about that was, I knew my father didn't love my mother even though they acted like they were in love. I could always also tell when he was with Desmier's mother. I didn't know her, and I didn't know him, but by the time I was nine, I knew my father was having an affair.

Like Desmier, Gwen is the secret child born out of a forbidden romance.

The only difference between her and Desmier is, she doesn't want this life, and right now, she belongs to me.

Those two things alone are enough to keep the goddess awake.

The thought of what I could do with Gwen awake sends a rush of hot blood to my dick. But I tamp down my lust.

I'll admit that I took pleasure in seeing the obvious jealousy on her pretty face when she met Kelly this morning. At first, I wasn't entirely sure if I'd assumed right by thinking Gwen was jealous, but I got confirmation when I caught her watching us at the poolside.

Judging from the look on her face, I knew she was thinking there's something going on between Kelly and me.

There's nothing. There never was and never will be. Even if at times I felt Kelly wanted something to happen between us.

We grew up like family and hung out because we were the youngest in my home.

She wants to move to L.A. next year and open her own dance school. Until then she'll continue to work for me.

With a tired sigh, I get out of the car and make my way into the house.

It's as quiet inside as a graveyard with the lights dim. They're automatically programmed to fade after eleven.

Through the long glass windows, I spot two of my guards on patrol. Both nod to me, and I return it.

Out of principle, I don't have guards inside the house unless I need to, like yesterday when I needed to keep Gwen in line. Yuri and Vladmir live in the guest house near the beach.

The *no guards in the house thing* was something I picked up from Leif. He wanted his home to feel like a home, not a military base. Father was different. He had his guards everywhere he went, so living at home did feel like we were under constant regimented supervision.

I turn down the corridor leading to the main section of the house when that scent of honeysuckle fills me, seeping into my lungs like pure oxygen to my system.

It's her—*Gwen*.

I look behind me to see if she's there, but she isn't. She isn't anywhere.

There's no one around but me and the scent of the goddess I brought into my home against her will. She is my Persephone, and I am her Hades.

This is my underworld.

Maybe I have some kind of curse on me for taking something so hallowed.

Or maybe it's a spell.

I don't fucking know.

All I know is, I haven't stopped wanting her.

Hearing shuffling in the kitchen, I divert and make my way there. Jeanne is always the last person to retire for the night. She's a perfectionist but also an insomniac like me.

Staying awake late at night or getting no sleep at all comes from the time when her husband was sick and dying. He had cancer. I was fourteen when he died. He and Jeanne both lived at my parents' home.

Just as I pre-empted, I find Jeanne inside the kitchen. She's sorting through the cupboard, but pauses when I walk in.

"Hey," I greet her.

"Hi. I'm just finishing up some last-minute stuff. Gwen and I got back later than I thought."

"We have other people who could have sorted this out."

"I know. I just like to have things a certain way. Especially with everything planned over the next few days." She closes the cupboard door and walks toward me. "Is there anything else you need me to do for the wedding?"

"No. I think we're all set."

"And you really don't want me there?" She gives me a hopeful but cautious smile and sets her shoulders back.

The only people I'm having there are my brothers and Aleksander, the Pakhan, who'll be marrying us.

"You know it's not that kind of wedding, right?"

"But it's still a wedding, and you're getting married. It's just something I would have liked to see. I've known you all your life."

"I know. But it's important we keep this as strictly business."

"Okay. As you wish." She nods. "Well, you'll have a beautiful bride. I got her the best dress in the store."

"Did she like it?" I don't know why I bother to ask that question if I just told Jeanne this is business.

"She was trying hard not to." Her smile widens.

"Is she sleeping?"

"She went to bed a few hours ago but asked for a notebook to sketch her designs, so there's a chance she's still awake."

"Alright, I'd better go up. I'll see you in the morning. Please don't work all night."

"I won't."

"Good night."

"Good night."

I take my leave and head up to my room. Before I reach the door, I see the room light shining from underneath it, suggesting Gwen is still awake.

I open the door and find her sitting on the chair by the window, sketching something in her notepad. When she sees me, she lifts her head, instantly looking wary, but I'm not paying attention to that.

My eyes go straight to her shapely breasts in the nude-colored camisole top hugging her frame with tiny little straps going over her shoulders.

With her hair piled up on top of her head in a neat but messy bun, the tendrils of golden strands adorn her face and highlight her exotic cheekbones.

There isn't a man alive who wouldn't be attracted like fuck to her, and he wouldn't be foolish enough not to acknowledge that getting married to her will hold some meaning. Business or otherwise.

By lunchtime on Saturday, Gwen St. James will be my wife. She'll become Gwen Volkova, and no matter how many months we'll have to stay married, we'll still be husband and wife.

"You're up late." I speak first because I know she'd have no problem staring off with me all night if she had to. I move closer, thinking of all the other interesting things we could do with our time.

"I was working."

I'm not surprised she found a way to work. Creative people are often able to find a way to work under any circumstance.

"What are you working on?"

"The new pieces for my line." She watches me as I take off my jacket and undo the buttons on my shirt.

"Sounds good."

"Do I get to see you in any of this lingerie you're designing?"

"No." Although she sounds nonchalant, the flush in her cheeks shows she's nervous.

"Not even if I request it?" My gaze drops to the golden skin of her legs showcased in shorts that match her top.

"I think it's best if we remember the business parts of our arrangement, don't you?"

I grin back at her smart-mouthing me and think of the perfect thing to say to her. "Where you're concerned, business for me means whatever I want it to mean. So I could have you walking around all day in a thong if I wanted to."

Her cheeks turn red, and at the sight of her nipples hardening against the sheer fabric of her top, I push aside anything in my head telling me I'm not to taste her again.

"My mistake. How dare I forget." Her voice is sour with sarcasm and the attempt to be ballsy makes me want her even more.

Yesterday, I lost control when I ripped off her clothes and feasted on her pussy. I thought I did pretty well this morning. I restrained myself. But now that we're in this bedroom, back at the place we were yesterday, I can't do it.

"Come and shower with me." I keep my tone even on purpose.

Her brows knit together, and she looks even more flustered than before. Signs of a person trying to deny themselves something they want.

"I've already showered, thank you very much."

"But not with me."

"I don't want to shower with you."

I walk up to her. She cowers, again reminding me of a little mouse. She shrinks into herself when I bend until I'm an inch away from her lips. That scent fills me again. It's richer coming from the source and potent enough to make me crazy.

"Take your clothes off and get in the shower with me."

"Why?" She folds her arms under her breasts, pushing up the ample flesh.

"Why do you think?"

"I honestly don't know. Other than maybe you like wasting water."

"Okay, let me tell you." I'm the one in control here. If she wants to play games with me when she's already on the losing team, then so be it. By the time I finish with her, she's going to be as red as the flashing lights of a police car. "I want to look at your naked body under the water flow with your nipples hardening and the water running down your pussy while I decide if I want to jerk off or have your pretty little mouth around my dick."

She turns as red as I thought she would, and her mouth drops open.

"You are such an asshole."

"Yes, I am, and it seems as if you've forgotten you owe me."

"I'm already fulfilling my payment to you by marrying you."

"No, no, no, no." I move closer, brushing my nose over her soft skin.

She flinches. "What do you mean, no?"

"Although the debt and your inheritance are intertwined, the debt is a separate arrangement. Your hand in marriage is just one thing, but that doesn't stop me from requesting other things of my wife-to-be."

Her lips part, and I can tell she wants to give me a mouthful but is holding her tongue.

I take advantage of the moment to gather the hem of her top between my thumb and forefinger and tug on it.

"Off now, or I'll take it off for you." I release the top and straighten.

Frowning, she mumbles something about me being a first-class jerk under her breath, to which I smile wider and whip off my shirt.

Without looking at me, she takes off her shorts first, then the top, allowing her gorgeous breasts to bounce when she stretches her arms up.

I get a good look at her, leisurely scanning her body from head to toe before I point to the bathroom door. She proceeds with a nervous tremor in her steps, and like always, when I get the chance to stare at her ass, I do. To me, her perfect ass is a bonus to this little arrangement of ours.

When we're inside the bathroom, she steps into the walk-in shower, and I slide my pants and boxers down my legs, leaving me as naked as she is.

Gwen turns to face me, her eyes going straight to my already erect cock, which hardens even more from the desire in her stare.

When she looks away, I step in behind her, taking her hair out of the loose bun and allowing the long golden strands to fall down her back like a waterfall of silky rain. I switch on the shower, adjusting the water flow to a light spray of lukewarm water. Then I grab a shower cloth, squirt some shower gel onto it, and rub it over her chest.

At my touch, she goes rigid, like she might snap in half if I poke her too hard.

"Is this what the next six months are going to be like?" She speaks in the same stiff tone.

"Maybe."

"I would have thought you'd be spoiled for choice, so you wouldn't have to bother with me."

I simply give her a wicked grin. I know what she's implying, and if I wholeheartedly believed my mantra about business being business, I'd allow her to think whatever she wants.

"I'm not a cheater."

She faces me and her bright eyes become more rounded, surprised by my declaration. "No?"

"No."

"I hardly think you can call it cheating if you have an arrangement like ours, so you can be with whoever you want, and I can—"

"No," I cut her off with the sharp tone of my voice before she can even think to finish those words. There's no mother-fucking way I'm going to allow her to believe she can fuck around because we have a business arrangement. Catching her doll-like face, I lift her chin toward me and hold her so she can't look away. "When you become my wife, if a man does as much as look at you, he's fucking dead. And if I catch you looking at anyone but me, you don't want to know what I'll do to your pussy to remind you of who you belong to."

Her eyes grow wider, and once again, I can tell this good girl isn't used to dark, foul-mouthed creatures like me.

I'll give her time. She'll get used to me.

"Do you understand me?" I ask, angling toward her so I can inhale her.

"Crystal clear."

"Good girl. Now spread those legs wide for me."

Her breath catches, then her chest rises and falls in a staccato of disjointed pants.

"Malik—"

I stop her again, but this time with a kiss that shocks us both.

At first, I kiss her hard, my lips demanding a response from hers, which she gives me. Then, when her soft body melts into the granite hardness of mine, I push my tongue into her mouth, and that's when spirals of raw lust consume me.

Fuck me, the fucking joke is on me if I ever believed I could suppress my need for her.

The ache in my being for her intensifies when she slides her dainty hands up my chest, beckoning me to enjoy the thrill of her lips on mine.

I need her. All of her. I can't just simply taste her the way I did yesterday. It's not enough.

This is not enough. I need more. The hunger for her is driving me crazy.

My lack of concentration gives her an opening to pull away, but I catch her and bring her back to me.

"I want to fuck you. Let me."

She breathes hard and stares back at me. "I..."

"There's no point in denying yourself what you want, Malyshka. You want to fuck me as badly as I want you." I run my fingers down to her soaking pussy.

She's wet from the water flowing down on us, but the moisture that greets me when I slide my fingers inside her passage is different—she's wet for me.

I push my fingers in and out, allowing her sweet nectar to coat them.

She takes a quick sip of air, grabs my shoulders, and tries but fails to bite back a moan.

Gwen watches me with keen eyes as I bring my fingers to my lips and lick off her glistening juices. While her lips are agape in shock, I place my finger on the plump flesh and trace the outline.

"Taste yourself the way I taste you. You taste like heaven to me, baby girl." I push my finger into her mouth, then right back into her pussy while shoving her up against the granite wall.

"Malik..." Her breathy voice stirs the desire in my cock, turning it hard as fuck.

Another moan escapes her lips, and I know I have her exactly where I want her. She has me right there, too.

But then again, she always did.

Chapter Twenty-One

Gwen

As Malik pumps his fingers in and out of my needy passage, I want to tell him to stop and that I can't do this because being with him screws with my mind and my emotions too much.

I want to tell him I can't get close like this, even this one time—*one more time*—because every time I'm with him, he takes me to a place I've never been with anyone. And I know I can't fall for him.

But the words I'm supposed to speak drown in my mind before they can take form on my lips. Desire buries them deep down inside me, somewhere I can't find them. Somewhere I don't *want* to find them.

Did I ever stand a chance of resisting him?

How can I say yes when my body yearned for his touch the moment he walked through the door?

Resisting him might have been the sensible thing to do if

it were possible because we're neither here nor there. The two of us feel like an anomaly that exists outside the sphere of everything else.

In our own world, we're trapped in lust. I can never save myself when he pulls me in this forbidden place with him. All I crave is his touch and him inside me.

Every touch makes me hungry for more and more and more, as if I've been injected with greed.

Malik pushes me harder into the shower walls, finger-fucking me with such a force I see stars. I arch into the smooth slippery surface to take the impact, moaning as I hold on to him tighter.

He moves to my ear, nibbles on the lobe. I just barely hear him utter something in Russian to me that sounds dirtier than what he would normally say to me in English. Then he takes advantage of my position and lowers his mouth to my breasts to suck each one with the same intensity as the thrust of his fingers in my pussy.

I can't get enough of the friction of his hard, muscular body moving against mine. The connection sends me cascading into the arms of ecstasy.

Moments later, I come with a sob of wild pleasure, my body shuddering against him.

"Beautiful. Fucking beautiful." His voice rumbles in my ear, and as my juices flow, he swirls his fingers around my clit, stoking my arousal once more. "Next time, you're going to come on my dick, and we'll keep it that way for the rest of the night."

"All night?" I give him a wide-eyed stare.

"Fuck, yeah, Malyshka."

Malik grabs my hips and lifts me. I instinctively wrap my

legs around his waist. Then his cock is inside me, massive and powerful, tunneling into my pussy. Owning me.

Owning me the way he did before. I get no time to recover. He slams harder into me and starts fucking me against the wall.

My senses explode from the sheer possession and the length of him pounding into me as he grinds his body into mine.

Catching my face, he brings my lips back to his, kissing me hungrily and demanding I hold nothing back. It's not long before I'm returning his kiss with the same potent intensity of need, as if I can't survive the next minute without him.

How has this man managed to do this to me?

And how the fuck am I supposed to not want him?

Or this?

His possession overwhelms my body and the waves of never-ending pleasure tear my soul apart. Before I know it, I'm coming again.

"Fucking perfect and all mine." His growl of pleasure from feeling my arousal coating his cock shatters my senses.

He pumps faster into me, and I watch his eyes darken to obsidian pools of lust. Then there's a new roughness in his touch and he's fucking me harder. It's like he's trying to possess more of me and take more than I've already given.

"Oh my God!" I writhe against his steel-like grip, driving my heels into his back.

Oh God, the pleasure is consuming me. I like it too much, so much I wouldn't know how to stop liking it.

As if sensing my inner struggle, Malik tightens his grip on me, holding me there so he can deepen his thrusts.

"Give yourself to me, Gwen." His voice is rough and demanding, overflowing with sexual hunger.

A delicious fire burns through my core, and the sensation ripples through my body, mind, and soul. I'm cut adrift in this euphoric state of being until his hips jerk and he comes, too, flooding my passage with hot cum.

He pauses for a few moments and we both take short, shallow breaths, inhaling the poignant scent of our wild love-making. No, we don't make love. I'm not sure he knows how to. That was fucking. The cold, hard kind you'd expect from two people who are possessed by lust.

What is he going to do now?

What am *I* going to do now?

He said all night. Did he mean it?

Malik holds me closer and steps out of the shower, carrying me.

I get confirmation that he meant every word he said when he takes me to the bed, sets me down, and guides me to kneel on all fours.

"Ready again, Malyshka? I am." He grabs a handful of my ass and slams back into my pussy before I can answer.

I'm shocked that he's rock hard again, and so quickly, but I don't get to think.

I start feeling again when he picks up where we left off and pounds into me.

This position always feels so damn good, and the rhythm of his relentless thrusts jolting my body forward is like a forbidden dance of sweet pleasure.

His presence wraps around me and I'm consumed by him. *Malik Volkova.*

Time passes and still he continues fucking me with unwavering stamina.

I don't know how long he takes me this way, but I come, and I come, and I come.

I come until my nerves shatter into fragments and we both crumble, falling onto the bed.

Not a second passes before we're tangled together between the sheets and he's inside me again.

Not just in my body but in my head, wrapping his raw dominating presence around every thought and every neuron in my brain.

He doesn't stop touching me, and I'm the same with him.

But then exhaustion claims me. I close my eyes for what feels like a few seconds at most, but when I open them again, bright sunshine greets me.

It's morning.

The day before the wedding.

And once again, Malik is gone.

* * *

I get dressed and leave the room, opting to go to the library so I can avoid everyone. I'm not in the mood to see anybody today. Nor am I in the mood to sketch anything.

Yesterday I made quite a bit of progress on the additional designs for my line and I don't want to mess up my mojo with bad vibes.

I just need to be by myself today, somewhere I can think. I'm not even going to get Sebastian.

I know he's safe and happy. Jeanne showed me the little

area she'd fixed up for him near the sun room. It's bigger than what he had at home in Wilmington.

I've reached a point where I don't know myself.

Last night jarred me, and I don't think I can talk to anyone today. In fact, it

would be best if I avoid people altogether.

Ironically, whenever I've felt like this in the past, I'd call Dru. She'd ditch whatever she's doing and we'd drive out somewhere or take a crazy road trip.

But I'm alone in this.

Jeanne has been nice to me, but I don't know her or any of these people here.

I've been pulled from my world and thrust into the deep end of this one where I'm supposed to just swim.

I know I have to find a way. There's no question about that because I'm determined to reach the end.

What's worrying me is the journey and I don't know what to do about the lack of control I experience when I'm with Malik.

It's not normal.

None of it is. I can't explain how I can flip-flop from one emotion to the next for a man I hardly know. If we'd been together for years, I might understand because of the bonds you form with a lifelong partner. But this...

This is crazy.

Last night was insane and what worries me is next time.

What will I do next time he demands my body?

Whatever happens I have to be strong enough to resist him. Last night can't happen again. If it does, I don't know if I'd be able to stop my heart from falling deeper into this thing with him.

I wander down the wide corridor with large oil paintings adorning either side of the satin wallpapered walls.

This section is what I would call the quiet side of the house. It's also more private, which is perfect for me right now. It's a kind of ambiance you can get lost in and I can imagine it being purposely built this way so that you could slip in and out without anybody seeing you.

The paintings on the wall are all as exquisite as the rest of the house. All of them are either of old pirate ships or landscapes that look as though they are somewhere in Europe. I'm guessing because of where Malik is from, it's probably the Russian countryside.

The landscape is very green and lush, although I know in parts of Russia it snows. These types of paintings are pretty much the same throughout the house. Yesterday's tour took up about three hours and I saw everywhere except the inside of Malik's office and the garage.

The most prominent thing I noticed was that while there were paintings on the walls, there were no pictures of family members. Not like in the secret room.

I found it odd because at Gram's house, there are so many pictures of our family. I don't know if it's because my grandmother loved collecting pictures of her loved ones, but most people I know are like that. It's just something you do if you have family.

If memory serves me right, this is the first house I've been in that I have seen no pictures of relatives. It makes me wonder why, especially when there's a room with specific pictures.

When I get to the library, I look around the enormous

room. It's beautiful in here. It reminds me of Belle's library in *Beauty and the Beast.*

The walls and ceiling have that look along with the arrangement of books on the shelves and the stacks. Yesterday, the first shelf I noted was the one carrying all of the poetry books.

It surprised me because I didn't expect to find such books in this home. There is an array of books in here. The ones about ships definitely suit Malik, as do the books about engineering and technology, but the poetry stands out.

I make my way to the Elizabeth Barrett Browning collection and pull out a book with a selection of her best poems.

This is Grams' favorite poet, too. When I visit her at the nursing home, we always read something by her along with Shakespeare or anything by Wordsworth.

Grams and I are miles apart, but whenever I'm reading something she likes on my own, I feel close to her.

I find a spot near the window and sit. There, I allow myself and my mind to drift away into the magic of reading.

A few hours passed by and I've read through nearly the entire book when Jeanne comes into the library carrying a cup of coffee and a large shopping bag in her hand.

She greets me with that warm smile and I do the same.

"Hi," she says.

"Hey, there." I set the book down.

"I thought I'd bring you this, as you missed breakfast." She walks over to me and places the coffee down before me.

"Thank you for bringing this to me."

"No worries. A girl always needs her coffee."

I smile at that. "I agree."

"Malik left this for you." She holds up the bag.

"What's in there?"

She takes out a big box. My eyes widen when I see the picture of a MacBook Air on the front of the box.

"He said you might need this for work. He's also arranged for your grandmother's doctor to email you with a progress report on your grandmother."

Hearing that lifts some of the worry from my mind and I feel a bit more at ease.

"Wow, I didn't expect him to do that." I look at the computer box.

"I think he could see how worried you were. You may use the computer as you wish for work." There's a slight emphasis on the word work and I understand it straight away to mean, I'm not to use the computer for anything else.

“That's great.”

"He's also asked me to clear a room for you to work in. Of course, you can go wherever you wish in the house, but he felt you would prefer a room for yourself."

I'm impressed to hear that. The gesture is certainly better treatment than the other night when he chained me to his bed.

"I'd love that." I nod.

"Great." Jeanne smiles. "I'll get that set up for you straight away. If you could let me know what you might need, then that would help me even more. Your things should be here in the next few days, but if there's anything else you need in the meantime, just let me know."

"Thank you. This really helps. I'm in the middle of designing my new line, so having a room to keep my things would be very helpful."

"Sure. Is there anything you need now?"

"Not so much. I'm... just trying my best to get used to this idea of being here."

"That's quite understandable." She brings her hands together. "This is perhaps the best place to start. Many of the books in here have come from those who have loved them."

"So I was right in thinking that Malik didn't go out and buy them?" I smirk.

She chuckles. "Yes, and no. Believe it or not, he enjoys reading." She points to the sailing books. "Those are mostly his."

"Ahh, that doesn't surprise me."

She turns to the other books, which include the poetry and the classics. "Those belonged to his parents."

"They gave him their poetry books?"

A wealth of sadness fills her eyes. "It's more like he took them... after they died."

Instantly, my heart shrinks. I understand that type of grief all too well. "Oh my, I didn't know. I, um, don't exactly know much about him or his family." That's an understatement. I know nothing more than the bullet point details he's given me. It's very unnerving to think I'm getting married to this guy in less than twenty-four hours and I don't know him.

Jeanne pulls up the chair in front of me and sits. "Have you met any of his family at all?"

"Not officially. There was a guy in Wilmington I assumed was his brother."

"That would have been Zakh. Malik has..." She pauses for a moment to think and I wonder if this is her checking herself again. "He has two living brothers."

"*Living*?" As in there were more?

"Yes. You'll meet them properly tomorrow at the

wedding. Zakh is the one Malik's the closest to. He comes here a lot. Desmier is the oldest. Malik is the youngest of the three."

I remember Malik telling Conrad that he wasn't like his brothers. I sensed the warning in the declaration and took it to mean he had no ounce of compassion, but I'm getting more information to create the picture of what he meant.

"And they're all Knights?" I ask tentatively.

"They are."

"Are... the Knights a danger to me?"

She shakes her head. "No. Not with whom you'll be marrying."

"I don't know anything about them."

She pulls in a little breath. "When you turn on your computer, you'll see an icon on the desktop with a knight chess piece. Click on it and you'll be given all the information you need."

"Really?" I tilt my head toward the computer.

"Yes. Everything you need has been pre-programmed. It's a database designed for the wives of members who weren't raised in the Brotherhood."

Now that really sounds all secret society.

"Your password is your fingerprints, so no one else can access the laptop's files. I hope that will help give you more insight."

"Yes." I nod. "Thank you."

"I'm sure Malik will tell you the story of his parents and other things himself at some point. He's experienced a lot of death in his life. No one should have to live through that type of darkness, but such is the life we live."

"It seems so."

She stands and assumes her previous composure. "Are you going to be in here for a while?"

"If that's okay. I'd like to be."

"Alright. How about I prepare some sandwiches and bring them by so you can eat at your leisure?"

Bless Jeanne for her understanding. I like this little friendship I've developed with her. Yesterday, when she took me shopping, I noticed she was understanding then too. "Thanks, I'd appreciate that."

"No problem. I'll get that all sorted out for you." She gives me a curt nod and leaves.

When I can't see her anymore, I open the box and take out the laptop. I'm surprised to see it's actually a new computer but must just have the special programming on it for me.

I take off the wrapping and set the computer up, which doesn't take long, a minute, maybe two. Everything has been organized for me to get into whichever file or program I want straight away.

As I'm so eager to find out what Malik has set up with Dr. Perry, I access my emails. I'm happy to see the first message is from him. The subject line states-progress report.

I click into the message, read over his greeting, which is standard from previous emails he's sent me, then I look at the report

It's only a page, but it shows all the medications Grams is on, and all the therapy sessions in the treatment plan that has created for her.

Finally, there's a summary of how she's been doing since I last saw her.

Nothing has changed, which is sad, but I know that's

actually good news. At least I'm in direct contact with Dr. Perry and I can see what's been going on with my grandmother's care.

The report ends by stating that another will be sent at the same time next week, but if I have questions, I can always contact him whenever I need to on his cell phone.

The message gives me reassurance I desperately needed. Although I still wish I could see Grams.

I'll make it up to her on my next visit. Whenever that will be.

With the tension eased from my mind, I decide to venture to the little icon Jeanne was talking about and learn about the Knights.

The icon stands out on the far right corner of the computer screen. When I click on it, I land on what looks like a library of everything I need to know about the Knights of the Brotherhood.

My body feels tight, my scalp tingles. I want to know more, but I'm wary.

Not enough to stop me though, because I need to know what I'm marrying into.

I click into the first file. It gives details about the organization.

I read through everything about the history, which draws me in straight away because it explains that the Knights were formed during the Viking age by a group of Norsemen warriors who were led by a man called Raventhorn. The Volkovas ancestor was one of those warriors. I would never have thought the organization was so old. Or that the family I'm marrying into was one of such importance.

The Bratva elements came from when the Knights

moved to Russia after the war and saw the benefit in joining with other Bratva brotherhoods. So they created their own brotherhood—the Komarovski—and kept it as a separate body that would be run by the main structure and laws of the Knights. They have actual laws that govern everything they do and they even have schools and colleges, their heirs and those who ally with them can attend.

This database has made everything sound so normal.

While they haven't tried to sugar coat anything, what they have recorded is far too mundane for people with serious wealth who live outside the laws and norms of society.

It's difficult to conceive fitting into that, even for a few months. I feel like what I'm about to embark on is something I can't unsee or unlearn when I reach the finish line.

I definitely wouldn't have found all this on Google. And if I had, I might not live to tell the tale.

It's interesting and fascinating and dangerous all at the same time.

I read on and on, as if I am studying for an exam. Soon night falls and my head is spinning but I continue reading.

Now I'm looking at the details on the Volkovas and their importance to the organization. There's a lot because they run the Bratva, but what interests me most is who they are to the wider society.

Their company Volkova Inc. is a multi-billion-dollar company with branches worldwide.

Billionaires. That's what the Volkovas are.

Of course, that has me wondering again about why Malik would be so hellbent on taking over the cartel. He was hardly interested in the pharmaceutical company. It was all about the cartel for him when he first started telling me about his plans.

The answer must just be greed.

When I finish looking at the information about Volkova Inc. I scroll down to the family tree and I recognize pictures of two of the men that were in the secret room upstairs.

Their names are Evgeni and Leif Volkova. They are as I guessed Malik's father and his uncle.

The next branch of the tree shows his brothers and I see that Desmier is the brother with the most power in the Knights. He's the second in command to the leader. He's also Malik's half-brother.

Malik had another brother called Viktor. That's the one that died. There is no mention of how he died, just the date of death, which was over three years ago. He was also only a few months younger than Desmier.

Interesting. Did Malik's father cheat, too?

Like mine?

I'm finding more similarities between us by the day, so it's a strong possibility. Or perhaps I'm jumping to conclusions because of my own situation. Misery

often likes company.

Jeanne was elusive on purpose when she spoke about the Volkova family. It didn't take a genius to figure out there were perhaps dark secrets she couldn't speak about.

I've paused on the page that has a picture of the three remaining Volkova brothers. I stare at it focusing on the one I'm going to marry.

I stare and stare until the screen blurs and my eyes feel like they might fall out of my head, a sign my brain has taken in way too much.

It might be best to stop for the night. Especially with the wedding a little over twelve hours away. I have enough on my mind. There's no need to overload. It's not like I can't continue this another time.

I zero in on Malik again and wonder what he'll be like once we're married.

Maybe the thrill and fascination of us will end then.

Or maybe it will be worse. *For me.*

When I look up, I nearly jump out of my skin when I see him standing before me, as if he just materialized from the screen.

I was so absorbed with what I was doing, I didn't even hear him come in.

It doesn't matter. Now that he's here, round two has officially begun and we've just entered the lair of 'next time'.

Chapter Twenty-Two

Gwen

Malik gazes at me, his dark eyes gleaming with malice and a touch of fascination for startling me.

I try to compose myself, but my breath is trapped in my throat.

He comes closer to the desk and peeks over the laptop, browsing over what I'm reading. Or, rather, the picture of him and his brothers that's taking up the center of the screen.

His eyes flick back up to meet mine and the light of fascination dances in

his darkness.

I know I should speak, but when he looks at me with such open captivation, I can't help but conjure the memories of how we were last night. They cloud my mind, preventing me from thinking past the villain who walked into my life not a week ago and changed it every which way except the way I knew it to be.

I lift my chin and breathe past the arousal thickening my lungs.

I don't care if he knows I'm thinking about the way he took me last night. Or that he successfully managed to charm me out of my dignity again even when I knew what he was. No matter what I do, or what I have to do, I must never appear weak.

Tomorrow is our wedding day and it will be the start of this path we're on for the next six months. I have to survive it.

"Having fun with your new toy?" He finally speaks, tilting his head so a lock of his hair can fall over his eye.

"Thank you for getting it. I spoke with Jeanne."

"She told me."

Of course she did. I'm sure Jeanne has to report everything that happens throughout the day right back to him like a trained parrot.

"I've received a progress report on my grandmother from the doctor," I say, deciding to ignore my annoyance from my previous thought.

"How is she?"

I wish I could say he looks like he doesn't care, but his question seems genuine.

"She's okay. The same, so that's good."

"Well now you know."

"Yes." My voice is cold and sharp, obvious signs that I'm pissed off about something.

As we've already established that I'm staying here and going through with plans to marry him because I want the money and my inheritance, the only thing I could be pissed about is last night.

No, I haven't forgiven him for the lie he was in Wilmington and for kidnapping me, but now he's given me other problems I don't want to deal with.

With that in mind, I would prefer if he left me alone. Any further contact won't lead to anything good and it's always physical with him. We can argue like mortal enemies and the next second he's inside me, and I'm holding onto him like the spirits of long-lost lovers have possessed us.

"Is there anything else you need from me?" I ask.

"I'm trying to figure out what interested you more. Elizabeth Barrett Browning or all the intel on the Knights." His deep voice is low and dangerous but displays the depth of his interest.

"Elizabeth Barrett Browning is one of my favorite poets. She's never done anything to me."

The corner of his mouth slides into a sly toothy grin that would rival Jack Nicholson's in the Shining.

"Elizabeth Barrett Browning is one of my favorite poets, too. But it might not be wise to go making enemies with powerful people you don't know." He looks me up and down and his eyes darken. "Especially when you're getting married to one of them in the morning."

"How could I forget?" If we were in other circumstances, I'd walk away to save myself from getting dragged into an argument I'm not likely to win. But I have to stay.

I have to stay and take whatever he dishes me because as he said before, there's not a goddamn place I could go to where he wouldn't find me.

"Maybe I was just hoping you'd honored tradition."

"What tradition is that?" He levels me a stare.

"Of not seeing each other the night before the wedding. It's bad luck."

"We don't need luck." He straightens.

"Of course. I forgot you own the world and the people inside it."

The grin returns. "No, Malyshka, I just own you."

"I forgot that, too." My tone is sour.

"Don't make that mistake again." He seems amused by my witty comments. "Get up and come with me."

No. God, no. This was how it started last night. A shower I shouldn't have had with him led to one thing after another. What will happen tonight if I go with him?

"I was actually just going to check on Sebastian, then head to bed."

He arches a brow. "Baby, I think you know what I'm going to say to that, so how about we skip past the arguing and get to the part where you're supposed to do as I say."

Bastard asshole.

I grit my teeth and stifle a groan. There's no point arguing with him. There never is. If I continue, I'll be the one who suffers in some way. "Where are we going?"

"Just over here." He points to the long stained glass windows and the brick wall across from us. "Shut down the computer."

With a heavy heart, I do as I'm told and stand when he motions for me to.

Placing his hand on the small of my back, he guides me over to the wall.

I almost think he's going to walk me right into it when he

places his hand on one of the bricks and the wall slides open the way the other one did in his bedroom.

This one reveals a cozy looking room which looks more like an office, except it has a wall with rows of shelves displaying an assortment of wines and other liqueurs.

"Is this house full of secret rooms and passages?" I glance back at him.

"There are enough. It's for security." He stares down at me with a sly grin, contorting his handsome face with menace. "And privacy."

My body tingles from the hidden subtext in his words.

Malik ushers me forward. As soon as we step into the room, the door slides closed, sealing us in.

"What do you use this room for? I thought you already had an office."

"Entertaining private guests." He walks ahead, going straight to the wine.

"*Private guests*? Like strippers and high-end prostitutes?"

He takes down a bottle of expensive-looking wine with Russian letters on it, then he gives me a challenging stare. "Do I look like the kind of guy who needs to pay for women to strip for me, or for sex?"

The question couldn't be more rhetorical. I'm sure women throw themselves at him all the time. I did, which is why I won't give him the pleasure of an answer.

"What sorts of guests do you see in here?" I rephrase the question.

"The kind who can't show their faces anywhere else."

That must mean criminals and other people like him. "Oh." I give the simple reply because I don't know what else to say.

"The other passages in the house are for escape if we ever come under attack."

"Attack? You mean people coming on the property to hurt us?" Like Conrad did to me at Grams' house.

"To *kill* us, you mean, Malyshka."

"Oh, Jesus." My voice is a rasp, displaying the terror I feel for just imagining such a possibility. I want to tell myself he's bluffing and trying to scare me, but I know he's not. It's not as though I haven't encountered dangerous people who didn't attack me the first chance they got. My face is still hurting from where Conrad hit me. The attack Malik is referring to, however, is more like something you'd see in Rambo.

"Don't worry. That's why I'm always prepared. I'm just telling you, in case something does happen, you know exactly where to run." He's smiling as if he's talking about the weather. "I coded this room with security so it won't open the door for anyone it doesn't recognize. If they try, they're dead."

"Wow, I guess you really are prepared."

He takes out two long-stemmed glasses from the cabinet, then opens the wine and fills the glasses.

He hands me a glass, but I just look at it.

"Drink it. You'll like it."

"I'm not in the mood for drinks."

"Drink it." His voice is more demanding. "Drunk Gwen is a lot less tense. She also has a filthy mind when it comes to me."

My cheeks heat with the memory of our first meeting. "That's all the more reason I shouldn't have it."

"Afraid you'll want to fuck me again? Newsflash, it

wasn't the alcohol talking."

I roll my eyes at him and steel my spine. He's never going to allow me to live that down. It's fine. Fuck him. I don't have to stand here and listen to this.

"You are an arrogant asshole, Malik Volkova. I'm going to bed." I whirl around and march back to the door, then press my hand to the wall for it to open.

It doesn't.

Frustratingly, I push against it, but nothing happens.

Malik comes up to me and holds out the drink for me to take. "It will open when *I* tell it to. The same as you'll leave once I'll allow you to. Now, drink with me. Remember what happened last time you defied me."

God, this is so humiliating. I take the drink, give him the filthiest look I can summon, and take a sip of the wine.

The taste surprises me. It's sweet like oranges and something else that makes it tantalizing and quite unlike any wine I've had before. Even from the collection Duke labelled to be the best of the best.

"Like it, don't you?" He smirks, observing my reaction.

I decide against confirming that I do. "What is it?"

"Kuban-vino, from the Château Tamagne collection. It has a walnut and orange taste to it. Come over here." He takes my elbow and guides me back to the drinks section. Then he pours me some more wine. "Drink."

I drink and it reminds me of our first meeting all over again, just with more expensive liqueur.

"So, did you learn anything of interest from the Knights' database?" he asks, his eyes drifting between my eyes and my lips.

I learned several things. Most of which led me to more

questions. Jeanne said he would tell me the story of his parents and other things himself at some point. I'm tempted to ask about that. "I didn't know your family was so prominent or powerful worldwide."

"They are. I guess now that we know a little more about each other, it's put us on equal footing."

"I still don't know you. I don't believe a database or the web pages can tell you the raw details about a person." With people like him, such things show what they want others to see. Nothing deeper. "And just because you have whatever information you do on me, it doesn't mean you know me either."

"No?"

"No." I shake my head. "Reading something differs from hearing the details coming from a person's mouth."

"Then maybe I just caught glimpses of you when you told me about Gage Miller."

My mind skids to a stop at the mention of Gage's name. I'd actually forgotten that I had to tell Malik about him on the night things went crazy with Conrad.

I didn't tell him much regarding my relationship, but what I had to reveal was enough to stir the humiliation in my soul. I should have also preempted that Malik would ask me more about Gage at some point.

"He was a mistake I wish I never made." I try to keep asphyxiating memories of Gage from resurfacing in my mind.

"Did you love him?"

The question rattles my brain and I bite the inside of my lip. "I thought I did."

The darkness deepens in his eyes. "*Thought.* Either you did or you didn't."

"I did at one point. Until he screwed me over and I found him in bed with a stripper on my birthday."

"I see." He looks me over and seems to form some opinion because he nods. "He was your first."

I stifle a groan and press down on my back teeth. "How could you know that?"

"A good hunch, from your tone. I'm right, aren't I?"

"Yes."

"So it was love like that."

I hate calling it love because Gage thought I was a fool. In the end, he turned me into one. "It doesn't matter. I guess he fooled the wrong person." I sound cold-hearted. "He met his match."

Malik's lips tip into a half smile. "Was it you? Did you kill him, sweet Gwen?"

He can't be serious. "Me? Really? You think I could do that?"

He touches my cheek and trails over the skin right down to my neck. "No. Maybe I want to believe there aren't that much differences between you and me. That the good girl is a façade and you're really a bad girl who would kill a motherfucker for cheating on you and stealing your money."

I wrinkle my nose. "There is hardly any comparison between you and me, Malik Volkova."

He stares at me for a few beats, takes a sip of his drink and sighs. "Our fathers weren't that much different."

He sets his glass down and I stare at him, wondering if he's going to confirm what I suspected about his father. "Weren't they?"

"No." He leans against the table, keeping his gaze trained on me. "They both loved women they weren't married to and pursued relationships with them when they shouldn't have."

I was right. His father cheated.

Is he going to make me feel like the bastard child? I hope not. I don't think I could take that kind of grief from him when I already beat myself up about it all on my own.

"I'm not proud of what my father did to his wife. It was wrong. The older I get, the worse I feel, and I know it's going to be awful when I face Esperanza on Monday."

"I imagine so. But do you think she was a good person?"

"No, but that doesn't make it right."

"Maybe not, but things aren't always black and white or easy to explain. Sometimes you have to look deeper into the gray areas to make sense of things."

He doesn't sound like he's judging me. Or his father.

"How did you find out your father cheated on your mother?"

He taps the side of his head. "Officially, a few years ago, just before he died."

"I'm sorry he died."

"Me too. But to answer your question properly, I always knew he was cheating."

I shift my weight from one foot to the other when a shiver rushes through my body.

"You always knew?"

He breaks his stare and pours more wine into his glass. "Always. People think the youngest is the baby and they don't experience things the way the eldest does or the middle child. That might be true on some level, but they forget that the youngest is the observer. They see everything. They see the things you rarely want them to see. Secrets, lies, hard truths."

"That's what you saw?"

"Yes and more. But I never blamed my father. I just wish he'd done things differently. There's always a way to get what you want. He just chose the wrong path. The same way your father did."

"I've always felt that, too. If my father had done things differently, like leave his wife before getting involved with my mother, none of this would have happened. Then I wouldn't be the bastard child."

Malik sips more wine and stares at me over the rim of the glass. He puts it back down on the counter, but this time touches my glass, pushing it to my lips so I can drink.

"You aren't a bastard child, Malyshka." He catches my face and lifts my chin so I can finish the wine, then he takes the glass from me and places it next to his. But he's still holding my face. "The thing about the gray area is we'll never understand what really happened. But...one man's mistake is another's gain. If your father had been the good husband he was supposed to be, you wouldn't be here with me."

"I know. That's why I wish he'd been a better man."

"Well, that's where we have a problem, because I want you here. I want you exactly *here* and in this unfortunate position you've found yourself in for the next six months."

Heat coils down my spine and spreads over my body. I should be livid at his words, but instead, my traitorous body is gobbling them up.

My damn attraction to him is undeniable, and it scares me.

"That's because you're evil and you delight in the misfortune of others," I stutter, attempting to remind myself what he is and resist him.

Malik leans closer so that his warm breath is tickling my nose. "We both know it's not that. But there is one thing I definitely delight in doing to my wife-to-be." His gaze drops to my pussy and lingers there.

Instantly I'm wet, as if I didn't just spend the entire day telling myself about the dangers of being with this man and strengthening my mind to repel whatever temptation I knew he'd throw my way.

When he leans even closer, I try to pull away, but he tightens his grip on my face and spreads his fingers over my throat.

"Why are you fighting me, Malyshka?" He brushes his nose over mine.

"I... can't do this again." My pulse is racing. He's way too close for comfort, and the nearness is throwing my nerves out of sync.

"Do what specifically, babygirl?" That wicked grin comes back.

"You know what, so let me go."

He touches his forehead to mine and shakes his head. "I can't. Even if I wanted to. I can't."

"Why?" The question comes out on the edge of a nervous breath.

"Because, sweet Gwen, your body drives me crazy. When I touch you, I don't want to stop." His fingers slide down my neck. "I always get what I want. Right now, I want you. *Again.*"

His words are intoxicating and I'm trapped in him all

over again, so when he presses his lips to mine and kisses me, my body responds to his touch and I crumble.

His incessant lips coerce me into submission, and I submit. Fire burns everywhere he touches in the most delicious of ways.

And damn it to hell, I can't resist him. I can't do it. My body seems to have a mind of its own, and my attraction to him is too overpowering to fight.

The only way out is to succumb to the passion that's consuming me.

As Malik deepens the kiss, I moan softly, giving in to the sensations coursing through me, which ignite a passion I can't deny.

With his lips still on mine, he moves with me across to the table and shoves me against it.

His cock presses into me and I grab onto his shirt, yanking it hard because I want so badly to tear it off and touch his skin.

Malik pulls away and stares down at me with a deadly cocktail of malevolence and triumph in his eyes.

"There she is. The girl at the bar who wanted to fuck me."

"I..." Realizing I'm still holding onto his shirt, I let him go, but he catches my hand and puts it back.

"Go on, take it off. Take my clothes off, sweet Gwen. Show me what bad things you want to do to me."

At first I'm hesitant because I'm still trying to resist, then he presses my hand to his chest and nods his encouragement.

I start undoing the buttons and his smile grows with each one I do. Within seconds the soft cotton of his black shirt lays open exposing his muscular chest.

My mouth waters and I push the shirt down his shoulders until it floats to the floor.

"This next." He places my hand to his belt buckle.

Keeping my gaze on him, I undo his belt and the zipper on his pants.

Malik takes my hand again, encloses it with his and guides me to his hard cock straining beneath his boxers.

My lips part and he takes advantage of that moment to kiss me again while squeezing my hand around his cock.

While I massage it, he consumes my mouth and starts squeezing my breasts.

In the next breath, he whips off my top and my bra, then places me on the table to sit.

Pushing my skirt up my thighs, he grabs the lacey edge of my panties and tears them from my body. I gasp and grip on to his shoulders.

"That's right baby, just hold on to me."

That's the only warning he gives before he grabs his cock and slams right into my needy passage, pushing me right over the edge of madness.

I fall like a dying star from the heavens, glowing and full of fire, which burns my soul.

He starts fucking me and I realize exactly why I failed tonight.

I crave his touch.

That's the answer. I want it. I'm hungry for it. I need it.

I arch into him as he hammers into my pussy while he holds me in place to take everything he's giving to me. It's painful and he's too rough, but it makes it feel better. I can't explain why, other than the need he's showing in this possession.

I moan until my voice is hoarse and aching with desire. My orgasm is close. It's tearing at my groin and clawing at my insides.

"Malik... I..." I can't finish the sentence.

He chuckles and continues powering into me. Then he slows as if he's going to stop and grabs the back of my head, pulling me closer to him.

"How many men were you with after him?" His eyes bore into me.

"What?" The question throws me off kilter, and I'm suspended between pleasure and the agony of wanting to come.

"Gage. Who were you with after him? You were broken up for over a year."

I blink as the answers stalls in my mind, not wanting to reveal itself.

"Answer me." His demand is insistent and hurried, as if his life is reliant on the answer.

"Just you."

The tension on his face loosens and his eyes become open with evident surprise and what I think is shame. Regret? I don't know.

"Me..." It's not a question. It's a statement.

"Yes," I mutter, and he speeds up, pounding into me so hard I come.

Stars speckle before me as the white hot wave of pleasure swallows me whole and I cry out so loud I'm sure all of Boston heard me.

He stops pumping, although he's still rock hard and pulls out of me so he can take me off the table, and bends me over it.

I glance back at him in confusion when he lifts my skirt over my ass and squeezes my ass cheeks.

Before I can ask him what he's doing, he lowers his head and licks me from my pussy, right up to the tight rosette of my ass.

He licks my hole again, this time allowing his tongue to circle me before gliding back to my pussy.

I suck in a breath as the room spins. I'm drunk on pleasure and that feels so damn good I want more. But Malik doesn't give me more yet.

Instead, he pushes his finger into my asshole.

"Are you a virgin here, Malyshka?"

"Yes," I grate out.

I'm staring ahead, but somehow I know he's smiling and my answer is satisfying to him.

"Tonight this ass belongs to me. I'm taking it and you'll remember it's me who owns that piece of you. Not *him*."

I'm frozen as he gathers juices from my pussy and smothers it into my asshole, then I feel him. I feel the fat head of his cock pushing in. It's painful.

It hurts so much I grip onto the edge of the table.

"Malik, it hurts."

"Shh. Relax, baby girl. I promise I'll make you feel better soon."

He pushes deeper and it's more painful. My passage stretches to take his cock and he begins to move.

He pumps harder and faster and suddenly a burst of pleasure possesses me and I'm begging him for more.

He fucks me harder and when I come again, his cock pulses. It gets harder and he climaxes, filling me with hot cum.

A few seconds pass and he pulls out of me, then turns me to face him so he can pick me up.

I wrap weak arms around his neck while he holds me close to his chest.

"Where are we going now?" I pant.

"Bed. I think we both need more, don't we?" He runs a hand through his wild, messy hair. "Answer me."

"Yes."

"Good. Next time, I want your pussy on my face. You can ride me all night and day tomorrow."

"The wedding—"

"It can wait."

Chapter Twenty-Three

Malik

Warm fingers float over my chest, caressing my skin.

I stir from a deep, deep sleep I'm rarely used to experiencing without the added effect of nightmares. My eyes open and take in the silver moonlight filling my bedroom, then turn my head and look at the beautiful woman lying in my arms.

Gwen is resting on my chest with her hand splayed out next to her face.

Her golden hair spreads over her naked breasts like a cape and I'm holding her against my body as if I always want her to be mine.

It's a sign of the shift between us I could control no more than a bull in a ring gearing up to kill.

Logic tells me to pull away, but the man inside wants to savor the feeling of being with her for a few more moments.

Just a few more seconds, then I'll step back into the reality where I have to focus.

I lost control again last night. I know I'm fucked because I keep falling into the same trap.

All I have to do is look at Gwen, then I want her and it's like I can't remember why I shouldn't have her.

Last night was more intense than any other. Each occurrence has pulled me deeper into her and that thing between us grows, getting bigger, wider, larger.

That thing turned into last night. The colossal epiphany that it's not just physical between us.

It's not just sex. I won't lie to myself and pretend it is.

Or that I'm *only* crazy about her body. What's making me crazy is her.

There's something more to being with this girl that I can't control.

The force of it is overriding my ability to think and when I'm around her it's impossible to focus on anything that's not her.

Last night, I realized the severe error I made was thinking I could switch off when we left Wilmington. I thought I could forget that potent chemistry we had and the attraction that drew me to Gwen in the first place.

Here I am, proving I couldn't.

My watch tells me it's four a.m., mere hours before we get married and I unleash my plan on the Navarros.

There's nothing I would love more than waking my beautiful wife-to-be so I can have her again. Then the wedding and the world can wait while we spend all day in this bed indulging on each other.

But I can't have that.

Going down that path is something else entirely outside the realms of this plan that I mustn't entertain.

It's something that will change me and I'll lose myself in her.

This thing I feel for Gwen is the wildcard the Universe threw at me like a mystical curveball. She tempts me to want it—*happiness. Life.*

But I am still death. Not life, so that's where I have to draw the line.

Just like when I had to follow my orders in the Navy, I'm following my own now on a mission that must succeed.

I might not be able to control this thing I feel for her, but I have to control myself.

It starts now. I get up with that reasoning, shuffling out of her arms. She stirs for a second and I think she might wake up. She doesn't.

Gwen rolls onto her side and stills, her chest rising and falling slowly until she drifts back to sleep.

There was somewhere important I was supposed to visit last night before I saw her.

Although it's ridiculously early, it would help to go there now and renew my motivation.

I put on my clothes, take one last look at the beauty in my bed, then leave the room. When I get downstairs and go outside, I find Vladmir and Yuri smoking on the porch.

"You alright boss?" Yuri asks.

"Yeah. I'm just heading out."

"At this time?" Vladmir glances at the dark sky.

"Just checking in," I answer and the two exchange looks of understanding, knowing exactly where I'm going.

"Do you want us to come with you?"

I shake my head. "I'll be fine. See you at the wedding later. I'll send instructions for Gwen".

"All right, boss."

I leave them, head to the garage and jump on my motorcycle. Moments later, I'm speeding down the road. The last time I took this journey was just before I left for Wilmington.

It was with a promise in my heart to get justice. Fifteen minutes later, I pull up at Mount Auburn Cemetery, the final resting place of Jim and Brian Davison.

The usual opening hours are eight a.m. to five p.m., but places like these are always open to people like me. It's more of a forest with a beautiful garden surrounding it than other cemeteries I'm used to.

When Brian died, Sheila, his mom, wanted him buried here with his grandparents. I wasn't surprised to learn that they buried Jim right next to Brian. It would have been exactly what he wanted. They were close in life and I know they will be close in death too, probably sailing the seven seas.

I find their graves and I can tell Sheila has already been by in the last day or so because of the fresh dahlias laid out on the graves.

Jim had a running joke about dahlias. He said they were masculine flowers, so if he ever died, he never wanted roses or anything like that. To me, they were all flowers.

Seeing them on the graves hits me hard and my heart sinks the way it always does for observing the bitter truth that my friends are dead.

The awakening gives me what I came for and my motivation is renewed.

I nod and place my hand at my heart.

"I did it guys," I say, my tone sounding like I'm already taking my vows. "Maybe we'll all have some justice now. Maybe."

I sit on the bench nearby and wait for the sun to rise.

As the new day forms, I stand, ready to take on the next part of the journey.

It's time.

Time to get married, make Gwen my wife, and take over the Navarro cartel.

It's also time to shut my heart down again.

No great leader ever allowed his heart to guide him into battle.

I'm about to open Pandora's box and unleash my secret weapon—Gwen St. James.

My enemies won't know what hit them until I strike.

Chapter Twenty-Four

Gwen

I stare at myself in the full-length mirror of the guest room Jeanne prepared as a makeshift dressing room.

I'm gazing at myself in my wedding dress which has an elegant Grace Kelly vibe with its long laced sleeves and a stunning flowing skirt.

I look beautiful.

Jeanne is behind me staring at me with pride. She's just finished doing my hair and makeup. Both of which look amazing.

She's given me smoky eyes and placed my hair in a neatly twisted chignon with a row of white flowers surrounding it. The style matches my dress. And I'm a bride. This is really happening.

It's finally time to get married.

Before noon today, I will become Gwen Volkova.

This is a day most women dream of being the best in

their lives, but it's nothing of the sort for me. Nobody ever told me, I'd have to find a way to stop myself from falling for my husband.

How do you do that?

If there's a manual somewhere, I need to read it straightaway before I fall apart.

The twist of angst in my core reminds me of how my body betrayed me again last night.

Each time Malik took me, I knew I was only setting myself up for disaster, but I kept going, giving as much as he gave me as if I'd lost my mind.

I told myself I could indulge and deal with the consequences in the morning. But when morning came and I saw he was gone again, I felt worse than

yesterday.

Jeanne told me Malik had already gone to the venue, but I knew he would have left anyway. Then to add more salt over my open wounds she also told me she wouldn't be attending the wedding and that the guards would be taking me to the venue.

I don't know why, but I felt her absence was done by design to send a message that this isn't a real wedding so I mustn't have real feelings.

I haven't been around long enough to figure out the relationship dynamics here, but from what I've noticed, I can tell that Malik respects Jeanne the way you would an older relative. Almost like the way I am with my grandmother, or my grandmother's friends, like Duke and Marybeth.

Jeanne is someone Malik would want at his wedding if this were real. The knowledge gave me another rude awakening.

My disappointment in everything made me wonder if I was really broken.

Broken like Mom was.

Mom made all sorts of crazy decisions that no sane or normal person would make. But it was falling for a man she could never have that broke her in the first place.

The same thing mustn't happen to me.

Jeanne touches my elbow, pulling me away from my sordid thoughts. "You look absolutely beautiful, dear." Her eyes crinkle with delight.

I give her a grateful smile and try to pretend I'm fine. "Thank you. I love what you did."

"Thanks. I'm glad you like it."

"You should do this professionally."

She laughs heartily. "In another lifetime I did. I was barely eighteen years old."

"Really?"

"Yes, in Russia I worked in a theater. I was a makeup artist for the dancers on the stage shows. Then I moved to the States and married my Andrieu. Now I am here."

She's given me glimpses of her life over the last few days. The other day when she told me about her husband, who died many years ago, I noticed how she spoke about him as if he were still alive. Grams used to do that. She said it helped her deal with my grandfather's death.

"I'm glad I got to do your makeup," Jeanne continues. "The last time I did anything like this was last spring for my youngest daughter's wedding."

"How many daughters do you have?"

"Three." Her smile widens. "You'll get to meet my eldest tomorrow. My granddaughter is coming to visit for the day."

"It will be good to meet her." If nothing else it will be something different to distract me from everything.

Jeanne reaches out and touches my hand. "I know the circumstances of today are a little different to most weddings, but you do look truly beautiful."

"Thank you."

I return my gaze to my reflection in the mirror.

At least I look like a fairy tale princess. But without the fairy tale wedding or, honestly, Prince Charming.

Jeanne walks to the dressing table and picks up the bouquet of white roses. "This is the last thing."

"Yes."

There's a knock at the door. Jeanne glances over her shoulder then looks back at me.

"That will be the guards. Are you ready?"

"As I'll ever be."

She opens a door, and two guards are standing there. One is the guy from the other day. His name is Yuri. The other is Vladmir. They are Malik's personal guards. He has others, but these two are in charge.

Both look like they belong on a military compound. Thank goodness they don't have their guns out today. I'm sure they still have them somewhere; I'm just glad I can't see them.

Jeanne says something in Russian, and both guards nod in agreement.

I still haven't managed to pick up anything of the language, but it sounded like she was telling them to take care of me.

Jeanne comes back to me and gives me a quick hug.

"I'll see you later. You will be okay."

I'm appreciative of the assurance, but I don't really think I'll ever be okay, even with all that money at the end of this. I've already felt the sting of being dragged into the Volkova's world.

"See you later."

Yuri and Vladmir escort me outside, where I'm ushered into a black Bugatti.

Yuri gets into the driver's seat, while Vladmir sits next to me. There's another car behind us with more guards. Seeing them heightens my nerves.

Although this might be normal for them, I've never been around so many guards before. It instantly makes me wonder if they're anticipating some sort of attack.

I pray not. I wouldn't put something like that past my father's family, but to my knowledge, I should still be a secret.

We set off down the driveway then off the property.

Once we're on the main road, I gaze out the window at the scenery, which looks so different from Wilmington.

As beautiful as it is with the stately homes and greenery, it's not home.

Unlike Wilmington, which has a more lackadaisical feel to it, there's a fast-paced vibe in Boston that holds the promise of wealth and a sense of accomplishment.

It's ironic. Boston is exactly the kind of place Dru and I were thinking of heading for the future. Now she thinks that's a possibility, and I'm going to have to make up another lie to cover the previous one.

Thinking of Dru takes my mind back to Grams. Dru is supposed to see her today.

As far-fetched as today is, I wish they were both here with me.

Both stand to gain as much as me from this venture of mine, but I won't kid myself—I know I'm being used.

I never had any choice in the matter. Malik would have kidnapped me and forced me to marry him anyway—which is exactly what he did.

The other stuff is just fluff—the promise of a billion-dollar fortune of fluff—to make me feel like I'm agreeing to this willingly.

The money and wealth at the end of this is the goal I'm focusing on, but everything would just be so much easier if I felt nothing for Malik.

An hour later, we pull up in front of an office building next to the Civic Center.

I'm taken inside and enveloped in stunning décor that has a European aristocrat ambiance to it.

We get on the elevator, and I'm taken up to the fifth floor and then into a massive hall with stained glass windows.

There Malik stands at the head with his brothers on his right and an older man with short-cropped dark blond hair on his left.

I recognize the man from the Knights database to be Aleksander Ivanov. He's their leader. He has the same dark vibe as the Volkova brothers but with an authoritative presence that makes my spine go rigid.

They're all wearing expensive suits that make them look like they're getting ready to pose on the cover of GQ magazine.

Seeing them together is jarring, but what's worse for me is facing Malik again after last night.

My heart flutters just at the sight of him standing there looking so handsome in his suit, about to marry me, then memories of how he consumed me pour into my head with image after image of scandalous pleasure.

From the heat radiating from my cheeks, I know I'm blushing and showing my obvious attraction to him.

As we get closer, my eyes lock with his. But he looks different than the man he was hours ago when he devoured me.

He's looking at me as if he's never seen me before. As if he doesn't know me and I'm just some girl he picked off the street.

The man before me looks cold and uncaring with eyes so guarded, you'd need a key and a password to unlock his thoughts.

I don't know how he's able to switch between personalities and versions of himself so effortlessly.

He's able to disconnect from the sexual haze that held us captive, but I'm left behind.

Maybe the coldness comes with the job or experience of feeling nothing but darkness and desolation.

When we reach him, Yuri and Vladmir move to the side.

It occurs to me that was my wedding march, but like the broken fairy tale, there is no music or friendly faces who will be happy for me.

"Gwen, these are my brother's, Desmier and Zakh," Malik introduces them in a business-like tone, pointing to his brothers respectively. "And this is Aleksander Ivanov, our Pakhan and the leader of the Knights. He will be conducting our ceremony."

"Hello," I answer, trying to keep my voice from shaking.

Malik's brothers both give me a polite nod, but Aleksander just stares at me.

"Unless there are any questions, we're ready to proceed," he says with a hint of a Russian accent.

"There are no questions," Malik answers with his eyes fixed on me.

I'm sure he knows if I had any such questions, I'd still hold my silence. He's already told me that I've been given all the information I need to know, which I suppose I have. I'm also aware that I'm in the presence of dangerous men. The less I say, the better, so the one word I spoke is perfect.

"Good. Let us begin." Aleksander straightens and begins the ceremony.

I get lost in the words moments later as everything becomes real to me.

My mind fazes out, and it feels like I'm having an out-of-body experience.

Then, before I know it, Malik and I are being asked to say our vows.

I say mine, and he says his, repeating after Aleksander.

The rings are exchanged, then suddenly, we're being pronounced man and wife and I'm no longer Gwen St. James.

I'm Gwen Volkova.

Just like that, we got married.

"You may now kiss the bride," Alexander declares.

Malik lowers his head to kiss me. When his lips touch mine, I expect the kiss from last night and every other time he's kissed me.

I thought I would feel him again, but that guy isn't anywhere. It feels like I'm kissing a stranger.

He pulls away and I search his eyes to look for him, but I see nothing but a void.

I open my mouth to say something. I'm not sure what, but it doesn't matter because Malik cuts me off.

"Please take my wife back home," he orders his guards. "I have business to attend."

Business.

That word hits me, cutting me deep, serving as another reminder of what we aren't.

At Malik's command, Yuri and Vladmir come forward. Malik moves away with his brothers and Aleksander without another word to me.

It's like the passion we shared never happened, *we* never happened, and our marriage was equally unimportant.

We go our separate ways.

The same way we will in six months' time when we come to an end and this will be nothing but a memory that will fade.

Chapter Twenty-Five

Malik

Well done Malik. You've successfully managed to shut down and become the asshole who didn't give a fuck that he'd just married the most beautiful woman in the world. Fucking well done...

As I follow my brothers and Aleksander out of the hall, I look back at my wife being escorted away by my guards.

My wife... Gwen St. James is my wife.

She's Gwen Volkova now.

Those words sound odd to my being, yet the selfish part of me loves the melody of the thought ringing through my mind.

If I could truly do what I want, I would be taking her to some exotic island where the two of us could get lost in each other.

Gwen looks more beautiful than I could have ever imagined. Her wedding dress looks like it was made for her. It hugs her frame in all the right ways, showing off all her finest assets while making her look like she just stepped out of a dream a devil like me would never be able to reach.

That golden hair adorning her head is a crown of glory, and she is

the goddess I christened her to be.

Today, I'm sure even Aphrodite was jealous of her newest rival.

I steal a glance at the gold wedding band on my finger and remember the Gwen I first met. I remember the girl who ran to me because she thought I could protect her. I remember the girl who trusted me.

When we took our vows, she looked at me as if she was trying to find me.

I can't be found. I'm so lost that people only see glimpses of who I used to be. She got close, though.

My eyes rivet to her body until Yuri opens the double doors and they all walk out. Gwen is gone, yet in my head, I can still see her and despite my decision to get my dick under control, I'm still consumed by lust for her.

I force myself to push her out of my mind and unwrap her from each beat of my heart.

I need to, because the uninvited guest from the Navarro cartel we have chained up in the dungeon below is perfect evidence of how distracted I've been with Gwen. Our new friend is a perfect example of why I need to focus.

This is the Bratva compound where we hold meetings. It's also where we *question* people. Five percent of the people who come through here for interrogation get to keep their lives.

People from our world know what this place is, and they know *never* to come here or look in our direction unless we send for them. But hours ago, my men picked up a man trying to sneak into the building—one of Diego's falcons, a motherfucking spy.

From the pictures my men pulled from his camera, they've informed me that he's been following me for the last two days—literally since Desmier invited Diego to the meeting on Monday.

Diego got his minion to follow me specifically because, of course, he probably guessed we know they're responsible for my captivity.

As we have no dealings with the Navarros, his first thought might have been that, but he was dumb enough to stir the nest.

I was so blindsided by Gwen that I didn't even know.

The presence of Diego's guy here means war has already begun, and it's not going to be pretty. As this war is mine, it's imperative I don't fuck things up.

We walk out the door and into the foyer, there we stop.

Now that the wedding is over, Aleksander and Desmier will be attending another meeting to speak to the men in our alliance who have contracts with the Navarros.

Zakh and I will be joining them after we take care of Diego's spy.

"I trust you can deal with our *visitor* in a timely fashion." Aleksander directs the comment at me.

"Of course, Pakhan." I give him a curt nod. "My men

have already extracted evidence from him. I just have a few questions before I deal with him."

"Wonderful. We'll see you shortly."

He and Desmier leave while Zakh and I continue down the path.

"Gonna go home after?" Zakh gives me a sidelong glance. "It is your wedding day after all."

I don't look back at him. If anyone knows how conflicted I feel now, it's him. It's annoying sometimes that he can figure me out. Especially when I don't want anyone to.

"No, I'm going to the office to finish up my work. I want full clarity next week. It's safe to say Diego is already trying to fuck with me, and he doesn't even know what I have in store for him yet."

"Alright, brother, you know best. Just thought you might want to check on your new wife. That might give you clarity."

If I touch her or go anywhere near her, she'll ruin me.

I won't want to leave her. I know it.

"This is what I need." I point ahead at nothing in particular, but he knows what I mean.

Moments later, we're down in the dungeon. The guards down there are mostly made up of my enforcers. The best on this earth. Also the most dangerous people you don't want to fuck with.

Leo Novak, my second-in-command, greets us first with an uncanny smile. It was he who found our new friend. We've known Leo since we were kids. He's Zakh's best friend and close enough to me for me to consider him in the same way. He's also Zakh's wife's older brother, so he's family to us.

"He's pissed himself," Leo says.

"Shit, I hate it when they do that." Zakh grits his teeth. "What the fuck did you do to him?"

"Rough him up a little bit." Leo chuckles. "Don't worry, I left some for you guys."

"Is he talking?" I ask.

"He's talking, but he's not saying the right things. He's also pretending he doesn't speak English well and can't understand us. It's a lie. Some of the messages on his phone are in English."

"What language is he speaking?" Although Spanish is the language mainly spoken in Mexico, some of Diego's men speak Portuguese as he recruits from Brazil. It's no problem as I speak both.

"Portuguese."

"Name?"

"Manuel Gutierrez. He claims he's a humble tourist who got lost when he wandered onto the compound, but the cameras picked him up killing a homeless man in the park."

Typical cartel guy. "The homeless guy must have seen him trying to get in."

"Yeah. I got the clean-up crew to take care of him. The fucker also doesn't know we got the pictures off his phone yet. They were encrypted. We also have this. He hacked you Malik." Leo hands me a copy of my email correspondence from this morning to my guy in L.A. discussing the paternity tests I arranged for Gwen.

Fucking hell. Not only did I not know this motherfucker was following me, but I allowed him to hack me. Zakh takes a look and frowns.

"Did he send this to Diego?" I ask.

"No. He hasn't." Leo lifts his chin. "Nearly did though. The message was in his drafts."

"Do they know about Gwen?"

"No. Her name wasn't mentioned at all."

It wouldn't have exactly mattered now. I've already married Gwen, and everything is in motion. I've already won. It's just that their knowledge of what I'm up to would have made things a little more awkward. I want to bring war to their doorstep and not fight any battles along the way.

"Then time is still on our side."

"It is." Leo hands me a few of the pictures. "You can use these in whatever ways you see fit."

I take them. "I will."

"He's this way." Leo points to the cell door at the end of the room.

He leads and we follow. When we open the door, Manuel's eyes pop wide when he sees us.

He's chained to the wall with the blood and sweat from his face covering his white T-shirt. He looks to be in his late twenties, like me, with a shaved head and tattoos on his dark skin covering his entire neck and the side of his face.

This motherfucker is a terrible liar because the Navarro cartel's mark of the black widow spider is on the hollow of his neck. I'm almost offended Diego sent this guy to investigate me.

"Manuel Gutierrez," I state. He looks like he knows from the mention of his name that he's a dead man.

He stares at us for a moment then rattles off a series of words in Portuguese, repeating what Leo said and telling us his English is bad.

To his shock, I respond in kind, replying in Portuguese,

warning him not to fuck with me because I know who he is and I know he can speak English just fine.

His face goes pale at my warning. I take that as a sign to show him the pictures in my hand. I step forward and do just that, loving the way doom spreads over his already fucked-over expression.

I smile and point to the picture of me leaving Volkova Inc. last night.

"Okay, friend, looks like you and I are on the same page." I chuckle and tap the side of his head. "You don't want to play games with me, so this is the only warning I'm going to give you not to do it. Fuck with me and you die. Understand?"

"I understand." His answer in English without an ounce of an accent confirms to the others that I've broken him.

"Wonderful. Now tell me, why did Diego send you to watch me?" I nod.

"It was just to get a heads-up for the meeting on Monday."

"And why would he need that?" I'm screwing with him.

"He didn't know why the Volkovas would want to speak to him and Esperanza in the week he's supposed to take over the cartel. He also got a billion dollars' worth of new contracts lined up for next week and doesn't want anything to go wrong."

I laugh. "Oh, really?"

"Yes."

"And what does he think could go wrong if we've never done business before?" My voice takes on a chilling sing-song edge that sounds otherworldly even to my ears.

Manuel doesn't answer. He just stares back at me with

his eyes doubling in size. From the terror crawling all over his face, I suspect he's aware of what the Navarros did to me.

"It's me, isn't it?" I nod. "Do you know what Diego's father did to me?"

Manuel continues to be still and graveyard silent. He's not even breathing.

"Answer me, friend."

"Yes."

Wow. Outside those I've told about the evidence I found, this is the first acknowledgement I've received. Just a simple yes that means so much.

"I'm guessing some of those contracts are people who work with the Knights, and he doesn't want them to pull out." I poke him in his chest. "Am I right?"

"Yes. You are."

"Are you his tech?"

"Yes."

"Are there more of you?" I search his eyes for signs that he might lie but find none.

"No. I'm the only one here." Manuel stutters out the words.

I straighten and clasp my hands. "So, it's only you who has the information."

"Yes. Only me."

There's nothing more I need to know here. Everything is still in hand to go as planned.

"It's a shame you won't get to tell him that I haven't even gotten started with him yet and Diego Navarro has so much more to worry about."

"Please let me go. I swear I will say nothing."

Poor guy. He must have thought if he cooperated, I'd

release him and let him live. He's a fool. He doesn't know he was dead either way the moment he set foot on the compound. *We* were obviously going to kill his ass, but so would Diego.

Even though Manuel thinks he's alone, Diego wouldn't have just sent one guy to watch me. So, the others will tell him we captured Manuel.

"Sorry, Manuel, I'd prefer to show you what the Knights do to spies."

"Please, no." His chains rattle against the wall as he panics. "Please let me go. I won't say a word. I mean no harm."

"So was the man you killed this morning. How about a taste of your own medicine?"

"No."

"Leo." I glance at Leo, who nods at me and pulls out his gun.

Manuel doesn't get to say another word.

* * *

It's late again when I get home.

This time, I don't go anywhere I know people will be. I divert and make my way upstairs. When I reach the second floor, I'm tempted to go into my bedroom and see Gwen, but I don't.

For the first time since I met her, I bridle my desire and stop myself from thinking with my dick.

I keep going up the stairs and walk into my office. It's more like an apartment suite in here which is equipped with a separate bedroom and bathroom. It also has a separate set of stairs which leads down to the boat garage.

I'm in here every day, but I sleep in here mostly when I'm working from home and I don't want to interrupt my workflow. At other times, I use it to get away because I could be in here for weeks and no one would know.

I could head down to the beach and take out my boat and be out to sea without anyone bothering me.

I sit in my chair and grab a bottle of scotch from the cupboard behind me.

Tonight is my wedding night. Instead of being balls deep inside my fuckable wife in my bedroom, I'm here thinking of jerking off to one of her pictures.

It's pathetic, but today proved that staying away and keeping my ass focused is the right thing to do. I've come too far to screw things up.

But that doesn't mean I don't want her.

I switch on the video monitor and find the footage of my bedroom. There I find my wife sitting on the window bay with her little dog next to her.

She's wearing something similar to what she had on last night, but I love her best in nothing at all. Just her.

As I stare at her, completely unknowing that I'm watching, the truth dawns on me, and I know what's she's done to me.

It's not black magic, and it wasn't the Universe.

It was her all along.

She made me fall for her.

She made me taste love.

Love...

Jesus. That's what it is. Gwen reached past the beast

inside me and found the man who's been struggling to break free all these years and live.

She's not my pawn.

She's my fucking queen. The most powerful piece on the chessboard.

But one day, I'm going to have to give her back.

Chapter Twenty-Six

Gwen

I gaze out the long stained glass windows of the library, watching the rain fall onto the roses that have just started to bloom in the garden.

The sight is a beautiful break from the sketches I've been drawing all morning.

Even though I now have my own room to work in, I still like being in the library. It has a homely vibe to it that makes it the perfect place to work.

Sebastian likes being in here too. He's curled up by my feet watching me.

He's been running around a lot better now and doesn't need the bandages.

Although I'm still in a foul mood from my sham wedding yesterday, I'm happy I don't have to worry about him so much. I'm also pleased I've nearly finished my designs.

The goal was to create a hundred new designs for my

new lingerie line and release twenty every month for the rest of the year.

Before I met Malik and got in trouble with Conrad, I'd finished twenty. They were already up on the website and were the designs our newsletter subscribers pre-ordered.

As of two minutes ago, I completed my eightieth design. So, I have twenty to go before I reach the goal.

Normally, I take my time because different ideas come to me on a daily basis that inspire what I'm designing. Talking to Dru also helps. Her eye for color schemes and trends is key to me. Aside from that, she inspires me because she believes in me. That always encourages me to do my best. But the situation here has pushed me to lose myself in my work.

Malik didn't come home last night.

Or if he did. I didn't see him, and he didn't come anywhere near his bedroom. I was up for hours, unable to sleep.

Given the fact that our wedding was little more than a business meeting, his behavior shouldn't have surprised me.

I should have expected it after his lack of acknowledgement at the ceremony.

But it's me who's being silly again.

Men and women do this all the time—*this game.* They hook up when they need to have sex, and the next time they see each other, it's like nothing happened.

Like us, those types of people can get married to each other for convenience and still fuck around.

It's ironic I was the one looking for a one-night stand when I first met Malik, so I should feel nothing. No big deal. Right?

Except it is and being unable to detach is making me crazy.

Having his rings on my finger isn't exactly helpful either. Nor is the can of worms that will be snapped open after tomorrow's meeting when I meet Dad's family.

The time has snuck up on me and I'm not prepared to see them. Everything is bothering me, but every time I think of meeting them, the warning in my heart tells me to run away. Even with the end goal in my mind, I have a bad feeling about the whole thing.

It's not bad enough to stop me from wanting what belongs to me, but I know it's not going to be easy.

If my entire life wasn't easy because of these people who couldn't find me, how will it be easy when they can, and I take what they cherish?

The thought of seeing them squeezes my insides and my stomach churns.

The queasy effect pushes me to my feet, and I take a deep breath. I take several more then set my notebook down on the little table.

It's probably time for a proper break. I skipped breakfast earlier because I didn't want to see anyone. I came straight in here, and Jeanne, bless her heart, brought me some coffee and a few biscuits.

I'm starting to feel lightheaded, so I think getting some real food into my system will make me feel better. It's almost lunchtime anyway.

Sebastian lifts his head when I walk away and gets up, rushing to my side to join me. Having him here has been a huge help, although I know he's aware something is wrong with me. He also knows we're somewhere unfamiliar, and even though he's taken to Malik, Sebastian knows I don't trust him.

We head to the kitchen, where I hear voices and light-hearted laughter. One is coming from a child.

I recall Jeanne telling me her granddaughter would be spending the day.

I walk into the kitchen and find Jeanne with a darling little girl sitting at the high counter. She couldn't be more than six or so and is so cute she'd make anyone want kids straightaway.

She has white-blonde hair, rosy cheeks, and crystal-blue eyes. The little pink dress she's wearing makes her look like a doll. If I didn't know better I'd swear she was.

"We were just coming to get you," Jeanne says, picking up a pineapple from the stash of fruits on the side.

I force a smile. "Sorry, time got away from me."

"That's fine. I completely understand."

"Thanks." I glance at the little girl again and Jeanne's face brightens with pride.

"This is Zoe, my granddaughter." She points at the little girl, who gives me a radiant smile revealing missing front teeth, which makes her look even cuter. "Zoe, this is Mrs. Volkova."

Hearing the name is like a punch to my gut. It pulls at the fabric of my reality because my brain doesn't comprehend that name is me.

Shaking the feeling, I move closer to Zoe and put my hand out for her to shake. She takes it and gives it a little shake.

"Please call me Gwen." I nod.

"Hello, Gwen. You're very pretty."

That makes me smile because I feel like shit run over on the highway several times. "Thank you. So are you."

Zoe giggles then gasps when Sebastian pads over. "Oh my gosh, I love dogs." She gets off the chair and strokes Sebastian.

"This is Sebastian."

"Hello, Sebastian. You are so fluffy. My teddy at home would love you to death."

Jeanne and I look at each other and laugh.

Laughing feels good and strange at the same time with the conflict riding my soul.

Just then, Kelly walks in from the other entrance, stealing the reprieve the laughter gave me. She's wearing yoga pants, a baggy top, and her hair is up in a ponytail. It looks like she's been working out or at a dance class. Jeanne told me Kelly teaches Ballet and contemporary dance in her spare time. Apparently she wants to open her own studio one day.

A touch of envy tugs at my insides at seeing her dressed this way as her attire displays the kind of athletic frame men like Malik like.

My body is more willowy, but I have curvy hips that get curvier and boobs that get bigger when I haven't been exercising—which I haven't done for weeks.

"Hello, everyone," Kelly beams, looking at each of us.

"Hi." I give her a tightlipped smile.

Zoe, on the other hand, leaves Sebastian and darts over to Kelly in a ball of excitement.

"You're here," Zoe bubbles, hugging Kelly's legs.

"Of course. I couldn't miss seeing my favorite girl."

I just met the child, and Kelly is someone she clearly

knows very well, so I shouldn't feel the pang of jealousy that hits me. But I do.

And I know it's because I'm a stranger who shouldn't really be here.

"Can we please go to the bakery? Please, please, please." Zoe jumps up and down, clapping her hands.

Kelly looks at Jeanne, who nods.

"Sure, but not too many sweets." Jeanne points at Zoe, who crosses her little fingers and straightens as if she's standing to attention.

"I promise you, grandma, I won't eat too many sweets." She sounds so sweet I smile again.

"I'll hold you to that, my little darling."

"I'll have her back in a few hours," Kelly promises, then she raises her finger as if she just remembered something. "Oh, Malik called me earlier. He said he forgot to tell you there'd be a delivery after lunch."

Malik called her?

He was away last night, but he spoke to her earlier?

No one can tell me I shouldn't feel uncomfortable that my new husband was talking to another woman first thing this morning. Or that I shouldn't find it strange he spoke to her about a delivery instead of Jeanne, who's supposed to be in charge.

Wake up, Gwen; they're totally screwing around. He probably spent the night with her, too, and all the things he's said about his feelings being real was absolute fucking bullshit I fell for because...

Because what?

I'm desperate?

I was hoping to still hold on to the belief that I'm not

broken and could do better than Gage Miller who fucked my life up.

It turns out that I couldn't do better. I actually did a hundred times worse.

"Good, I've been waiting for that delivery for days." Jeanne chuckles, but she glances at me, and I can tell she's sensed the shift in my mood. "It's just the new shelves I ordered for the pantry."

"Oh, good. I love it when we redecorate." Kelly rocks back on her heels, pushing out one muscular leg. "See you guys later."

"Yayyy." Zoe skips when Kelly takes her hand.

I watch the two leave. When I turn back to Jeanne, I find her already looking at me.

"I've made us some sandwiches. Do you want to join me for lunch? We can sit out on the terrace under the gazebo."

"I'd like that."

"Good, let me grab everything."

"Can I help?"

"Sure, you can carry the juice." She points to the large jug of juice on the tray on the opposite counter.

I take down two glasses from the cupboard, set them on the tray, and carry it out while Jeanne carries her tray of delicious-looking gourmet sandwiches.

Seeing I'm in good hands, Sebastian trots away to his little room.

As it's still raining, we continue through the sunroom and make our way out to the gazebo. There, we place our trays on the little wicker table and sit opposite each other, wrapped in the fresh scent of rain and spring flowers.

"Eat. I think you're going to love these." Jeanne points to the sandwiches then pours us each a glass of juice.

I grab a sandwich and start nibbling on it. It's chicken with mayo, but there's a tangy flavor to it that instantly makes my tastebuds water.

"Oh my gosh, wow. This is amazing." I can't help myself. I grew up around people whose sole purpose was to create good food, so when I get some, I know the labor of love a person puts in to it.

Jeanne issues me with a satisfied grin. "I'm thrilled you like it. It's mango and herb chicken with homemade mayo."

Grams used to make her own mayo, too. She'd use the vegetables and dairy from Marybeth's farm because everything was organic. "It is absolutely delicious."

"Good," she says then gives me a cautious look. "I thought you might like eating out here. I also thought you looked like you needed to talk. I know a lot has happened over the last few days."

"It has."

I stare back at her, not really knowing what I should say. She answers to Malik. That's where her loyalty lies.

She's probably just taking pity on me because she's a decent enough person to do so.

"But it's okay if you don't want to talk. I understand that, too." She smiles. "I just wanted you to know I'm here."

"I appreciate that. I guess I understand, too." I think for a moment, and a few things come to mind that I wouldn't care if she reported back to Malik. "Malik and Kelly seem awfully close. Does she *just* work for him?"

"Yes." Her voice waivers. "To my knowledge."

The churn in my stomach tightens. "Oh. Thank you for being honest with me."

"Honesty is what you'll get from me. They're close because they grew up that way. Their relationship is different to what he has with everyone else."

"She can't like my presence here very much, then." I swallow hard.

"I wouldn't say that. And realistically, it doesn't matter. You are Kelly's employer, and she is to show you the same respect she gives Malik, which I think she does."

"She does. She's been as nice as you have been to me." I say that to be fair. "I think I'd just like to know if there's more going on. I don't make a fool of myself."

I glance at my wedding band, and she does, too.

"I understand completely." She nods. "And as far as I know, I don't think you have anything to worry about." It's encouraging to hear her say that, but at the same time, it doesn't make me feel any better.

"Thank you. I know you didn't have to tell me that."

"I could see it was bugging you before you even asked."

Hearing her correct assumptions makes me feel more at ease.

"How much do you know about what's happening with me?" I assumed she was already aware of certain things, but I don't know to what extent Malik has spoken to her.

"I know everything," she confirms in a gentle tone. "Aside from his brothers, I'm one of the few people Malik shares his many secrets with."

I hold her gaze. The declaration makes me think about his plans to take me.

"So, you knew he was looking for me in Wilmington and what he planned to do with me."

"Yes." This time, there's no emotion in her eyes.

"It's strange that he seems to have so much, and there's probably more I don't know, but he wants the cartel."

"I think that's a conversation better placed between you and him."

I take that to mean she either thinks it's not her place to talk about that with me, or Malik has secret plans I'm not aware of.

Either way, I won't get the answer, because Malik Volkova is a closed book of information no one will ever receive, unless he allows you to unlock him.

I look at the swirling patterns on the sandwich tray then back at her. "Meeting my father's family is going to change things for me. I never thought I would meet them, and I've never been sure if my father wanted me to. Until I heard about his will, I thought I was supposed to remain in the dark. Locked away from everyone."

"Do you think the darkness was better?"

I consider the peculiar question. Is it better to stay hidden?

To be hidden so deeply I could never share anything about where I came from with my best friend?

I'm lying to Dru now, but at some point, I know I'm going to have to tell her some hard truths. She'll be hurt that I got married and didn't tell her, and she'll want to know about the money. She questioned it years before when my life was better and the money Grams had put aside for me hadn't been spent yet.

Dru's family were so clean cut. They were people who

went to church and even taught Sunday school. How will she react when she finds out my father was a cartel king?

But he was the architect of my legacy and who I came from.

He loved me. I don't want to live the rest of my life trying to keep that secret from the world.

"No, the darkness wasn't better. But neither is the light." I pull in a breath to clear my head.

"Sometimes it's like that, and you just have to live with it."

"I just wish there were another way. I'm not ready for any of this."

"Many of us aren't." The reflection in her tone suggests she's speaking from experience.

"How did you get into this life?" I hope I'm not overstepping the line. "It didn't sound like you were born into it."

"I wasn't, but I fell in love with... let's say the wrong kind of man." Her eyes holds mine as if she's looking into the deeper layers of my mind. "But he was right in every way for me. I wouldn't have traded meeting him and my life with him for the world."

"That sounds beautiful."

"It was. My Andrieu was my life and love. He was one of the senior guards to the Volkova family. Back in Russia, a woman like me would never be lucky enough to get close to the likes of a man like him. Rich and powerful. Reserved for the best. But dangerous."

"Dangerous." My voice is low, with the same hushed tenor you'd speak in at a funeral.

She nods, glances away for a few seconds, then looks back at me. "Only the best men work with the Volkova family. That means the most dangerous. It has to be that way. But he had the kindest heart of anyone I've ever met."

"Sounds like he was a good person then."

"He was." She sighs with reflection. "He saved me. I came to this country looking for a better life after having nothing. My parents were dead and the only brother I had was a no good drunk who ended up in prison. I was never going to make a living doing makeup, so I thought if I could just get here I'd be able to figure it out. But my plans failed. Andrieu found me on the road practically begging on the street in the cold of winter. I'd just lost a job that never was, and I'd used up all my resources. I don't know how I didn't die."

"Oh Jeanne, I'm sorry." That sounds terrible.

"It's okay. It worked out for me. Andrieu found me somewhere to live and took care of me. But it was a year before he officially asked me out." She smiles wider. "Months later, we got married. That was fifty years ago. We were married for just over thirty-five years. He's not here anymore physically, but I carry him in my heart everywhere I go."

"Wow." I wish I could have love like that. "Your story is inspiring."

"So is yours." She reaches across the table and taps my knuckles. "Stay strong in your heart and mind, Gwen."

I nod. "I'll try to."

I know I need to do more than try. God knows I need strength.

* * *

Volkova Inc. is one of the massive skyscrapers dotted across Boston's city.

You can see the company's name and logo from afar.

Looking at it is daunting, but what awaits me inside is my fate.

It's time. It's Monday morning, and I'm finally going to meet Esperanza and Diego.

Yuri and Vladmir escort me to the fifteenth floor. My steps get heavier with every one I take, and my chest squeezes with the anxiety of someone having a heart attack.

I didn't see Malik again last night, but when I woke up this morning, the scent of him clung to the air and I felt his presence. It's clear he's avoiding me, but he's the least of my worries right now.

I seriously don't know what to expect from this meeting, and I know no one can tell me because they don't know either.

I've only seen pictures of Esperanza and Diego on Google from newspaper articles. I found them when I was trying to look up details on the cartel and my father's death. Since then, the image of Esperanza's face has stayed with me. I remember her looking strict and brazen-faced.

I didn't really take note of Diego other than acknowledging that he was ten years older than me.

We stop before a set of conference room doors, and Yuri opens them.

When he leads me inside the room, I see Malik sitting at the head of the huge boardroom table. He looks at me the same way he did at the wedding. With that arctic expression.

His brothers are next to him. Sitting opposite them are Esperanza and Diego Navarro. Both are looking at me.

Esperanza is in her late fifties but could easily pass for ten years younger with her flawless skin, long straight jet-black hair, and blood-red lips. She's wearing a well-tailored pants suit with shoulder pads in the sleeves of her jacket.

Diego looks like a high powered C.E.O. He doesn't look that much different to the Volkova brothers.

Given the fact they don't know who I am yet, they both look like they could eat me alive.

When the truth is revealed, they just might,.

Chapter Twenty-Seven

Malik

Gwen walks into the room with her shoulders back and that assumed confidence I know she doesn't feel. I saw the shift in her expression the moment she looked at Diego and Esperanza.

Yuri seats her next to me, right beside Desmier and Zakh. We look at each other briefly, and I know this is the last place she wants to be.

Her presence and what I'm about to do stirs that thing inside me again I feel for her along with guilt, but I push it away.

Guilt is the antithesis to revenge. It compromises you with compassion, or in my case, something more I never expected to feel for a woman I know I can't keep.

The moment I've been waiting for is happening.

It's finally happening now.

All the players I need are here. I just have to strike, so guilt is the last thing I should feel.

With that in mind, I stand, taking the lead.

Under normal circumstances, Desmier would open the meeting, but this is about me. I'm in charge today.

When Yuri takes his place by the door with Vladmir, I straighten and get ready to attack.

"Now that we're all here, we can begin." I look around at everyone.

"That would be great," Diego chimes in. "I'm eager to know what this is about. You guys have been quite secretive. Obviously, it's quite an honor to be summoned by the Knights, but I'm sure you can understand how things look to me."

I glance at Zakh, who looks at me, too.

Looks like it's time to cut to the chase. I prepared a file box with all the items I need for my presentation. I slide it in front of me, and the first thing I pick up is Manuel's ring. His finger was still attached to it when I hacked it off.

I was going to present it just like that, but when I remembered Gwen would be here, I decided against doing so.

She's scared enough. She doesn't need to see my more unsavory habits.

I place the ring right in front of Diego.

When he looks at it, his eyes fixate on the spider insignia on the front. This ring is worn by all the members of his crew, so he knows what he's looking at. And who it belongs to.

His gaze switch to mine, and I give him a warm smile. The kind you'd reserve for family when you see them during the holidays.

"How about we agree not to bullshit each other or lie." I nod.

He straightens. "What is this about, Malik Volkova?"

"*I'm* taking over the cartel. Not you."

At first, he looks at me as if I've lost my goddam mind, then he laughs.

"Is this some kind of joke? You, take over the Navarro cartel? I know you people think you're God, but you can't do that." His accent gets stronger with every word.

"I already have." The humor on his face falls with my declaration, and his eyes darken like the sky before a thunderstorm. "As of Saturday at six p.m., everything was transferred to me, including Astori."

"Impossible," Esperanza speaks up in a sharp accented voice that is too deep and rusty for the softness in her face. It's almost as if it doesn't belong to her. "This is entirely impossible."

"And yet here I am, because this is happening."

She switches her gaze from me to Gwen, and I know she's figuring things out.

They both should be by now because they know there's only one way I could have taken over the cartel.

"Who is this woman?" Esperanza spits, balling her hand into a tight fist as she stares straight at Gwen, who tenses next to me.

"This is my wife." It feels strange to say those words. I look at Gwen, and she stares back at me. "Why don't I let her tell you a little more about herself?"

Real fear brims within Gwen's eyes as she continues staring at me. I nod at her, giving her some reassurance and pushing at the same time.

She looks away and stares Esperanza in the eye. "My name is Gwen. Santiago Navarro was my father. I am his heir." Considering she looked so scared moments before, her tone is confident and sounds like a person who's been dying to tell a secret they've been burdened with for a lifetime. I suppose she has.

This must be the first time she's ever said those words. And to the wrong people.

I'm a bastard for doing this. But war is war, and this is how you bring down giants.

Esperanza is already giving Gwen a poison-tipped glare, but Diego is stunned. His dark skin has even gone pale.

"Santiago was the founder of the Navarro cartel, and everything you have belongs to him," I state. "According to his revised will, he left his entire legacy to his daughter. This woman here, my wife." I point to Gwen.

"What proof do you have that this is Santiago's daughter?" Diego presses a fist into the table and clenches his jaw so tightly the vein in his neck pops out as if it's going to explode.

"I have everything here. Starting with a paternity test." I pull the next documents from the files and hand them each a copy. It has details back from the lab confirming Gwen's paternity. I got everything back this morning.

Gwen gives me a narrowed look because she didn't know I did this.

Diego and Esperanza scan the test confirming Gwen's DNA match to Manolo's then look back at me. They both know they can't fight me, and if they try, they won't win.

Esperanza glares at me then at Desmier. "Desmier

Volkova, you truly sanction this? You are the second-in-command to your Pakhan. This is an outrage."

"I sanction it completely," Desmier answers with a firm nod. "The entire legion of Knights and our Bratva Brotherhood all stand by this decision."

Hearing that makes her eyes blaze. If looks could really kill, Desmier would be a memory.

"Why? Tell me, Malik Volkova, the youngest Volkova brother." Esperanza looks back at me. "Why now? You went through a lot to find my dead husband's daughter. A woman I could never find myself. What do the Knights want with our cartel and a pharmaceutical company? Why would you do this? You have an insurmountable amount of wealth, and you don't work with any cartel."

A quick glance at Diego, who has gone completely quiet, tells me he already knows the answer. Esperanza isn't privy to it, though. The woman is one hell of a bitch who can hold her own, but it's obvious she's been kept in the dark when she needs to be. That's okay. I have no problem bringing her up to speed.

"Taking what you own was the best kind of revenge for what your people did to me." I set my shoulders back and lift my chin higher.

"What the fuck did we do to you?" She throws back. "We have no dealings with you."

I chuckle off-key the way a psychotic madman would before he loses his shit.

"Where do I start? When your husband realized I was investigating his black-market dealer friend, Barabbas Jones, he came after me. His people killed my old Navy captain, Jim Davison. Then you took me captive for over a year in

Kazakhstan." Gwen's eyes are back on me the moment the words fall from my lips, but this time, I don't look at her. "Your animals kept me alive to torture me senseless, and no one ever knew who took me. I doubt you wanted me to be found, but I suppose you mainly wanted me out of the way and the torturing was just to teach me a lesson that even I, a Knight and a Volkova, can have my wings clipped. But here I am."

"I have no knowledge of this happening." Esperanza grips the edge of the table and takes in a slow breath.

"Well, now you know."

"What proof do you have that we were involved?" Diego asks, his voice more hesitant than when he last spoke.

This motherfucker is one nasty piece of work. He knows I have proof. He already suspected it when he sent Manuel to watch me days ago. But judging from the look on his face, he just wants to know what exactly I have so he knows what he's up against.

I take out the last item in my box. It's a tape recorder. It holds the evidence that set today in motion.

I press the play button, and the room fills with Diego's voice telling Barabbas Jones about how his father imprisoned me in Kazakhstan when they thought I was a problem.

The truth is revealed within that two-minute conversation, and the recording stops playing.

"I should kill you all," I say with ease, staring Diego down.

"I am not responsible for my father's sins."

"I don't give a fuck. I'm holding you responsible, and this is what I'm doing."

Diego's face hardens. "This is not over yet."

"Oh, but it is." I say that with confidence, but I agree with him. I know this is just the beginning. "All you need to do now is gather the men in your alliance in Mexico and prepare them to meet with us in a few days. I'll let you know what day and time."

"For fuck's sake, I bury my father this week."

"Obviously, I don't care for your father one way or the other. If you want to still be a part of this cartel, you will get what you need to get done and do whatever I tell you to do."

Knowing I'm not fucking around, he backs down like a subservient dog.

"Fine. I'll do it."

"Good. You may go now."

Neither like the way I've dismissed them, but they stand, gather the documents I've given them, then make their way out of the boardroom.

Esperanza is the first to leave, but just before Diego walks through the door, he glances back at Gwen, who is already looking at him.

In those silent moments of seconds ticking by, I almost see his mind working.

When he looks at me, I know I'm right. The motherfucker is already coming up with a plan.

We all know how this works and how it doesn't.

Everything goes back to my dear wife—the queen.

If she's married to me, we own the cartel.

The only way we don't have it is if she stops being married to me—as in we get divorced or if I'm dead.

Since I'm not getting divorced, the only option is my death.

If I die, they'll take her.

There's just one problem for them. I'm not going to allow that to happen.

Especially when the only thing I want more than the cartel is her.

So, they're going to have to come up with one hell of a plan to kill me this time.

But as the Grim Reaper and I are one and the same, not even death will stop me from protecting her from them.

Chapter Twenty-Eight

Gwen

Revenge.

Not once did it ever occur to me that this whole thing could be about that. Everything makes so much more sense now.

What else does a man who has the world at his fingertips and *unsurmountable* wealth want?

Revenge.

Malik's plan was about getting retribution and doling out punishment for what my *uncle* did.

My mind drifts to the secret room in his bedroom and I think of the pictures on the wall. I remember the older guy dressed in military wear and all the other pictures of him there. That must have been Jim Davison, Malik's captain.

Killed by my uncle's men. And Malik was taken captive and tortured for nearly a year. *God...*

I remember how the room felt like a shrine. Now I think

I'm right it is and I'm guessing everyone on the pictures inside there are dead.

His military uniform was inside there, too. A symbol of the death of a career.

And his Knights' tunic? That reeked of death. Like something death's harbinger would wear.

That's what he is. The black knight of death seeking the souls of those who wronged him and the people he loved and cared about.

It doesn't matter that my uncle is dead. Malik found a way to punish a ghost.

By using me.

I was the way.

Me.

That's why he took me. He hunted me down until he found me. Now the hunter has gotten his revenge.

As the same Navarro blood flows through my veins, am I his enemy, too?

Why am I even asking myself that question? Of course, I am.

I gaze at Malik. He's staring at Diego walking through the door. Esperanza never looked back, but Diego did, and I didn't miss that look in his eyes that promised lethal retaliation.

The same retaliation I feared because now that they know me, this will fall back on me.

The room is quiet for a few moments with a heavy silence. Not the kind of silence you get when you're thinking, but the reflective kind when everything is uncertain and life hangs in a balance of probabilities.

Desmier is the first to move, and Zakh looks at him as if for guidance.

"We'll double up on security," Desmier states. "I'll put eyes on them and check in with our allies in Mexico and Brazil."

"I'll send some men ahead of our visit," Zakh chimes in. "You need to stay here, Desmier. It's best."

"I'd feel better if I went with you."

"The bloodline mustn't fall. And you are our leader."

My God, it sounds like they're preparing for war. They're actually talking about dying. I didn't even consider that anyone would have to go to Mexico, but of course they would need to. The Navarro Cartel is based in Mexico, and those allies Malik told Diego to speak to are all there.

"The fucking bloodline won't fall." Malik finally speaks. His voice sounds like thunder roiling across the sky in the midst of a turbulent storm. "You guys are talking as if we're low level assholes who can't even use a gun."

"It's called being careful, Malik." Zakh gives him a hard stare. "We can't just declare war the way we have and not take preventative measures to minimize risk."

"They would not be that foolish to kill all of us. One of us, of course, but not all. The Knights would obliterate them."

"We still need to keep in mind that they could kill us all." Desmier looks at both of them with a dark warning in his eyes. It's the look of a leader who knows not to underestimate anyone or assume you're invincible.

It's the absolute opposite of Malik, who seems to not care about dying or death. That scares me. He had the same look when he faced off with Conrad and his men back in Wilmington.

Malik says something in Russian that sounds angrier than normal and Zakh snaps back at him in Russian. The two start arguing back and forth. I don't understand a word and that only amplifies my fear of what's going to happen next.

Desmier finally breaks up the argument with one sentence in a raised voice that shuts Malik and Zakh down.

That silence returns and I use the opportunity to cut in.

"What should I do?" My voice is so meek it sounds out of place.

Malik faces me. "You're going home now. Come, let's go."

He takes my arm and practically hurries me out the chair.

"But I—"

"Home, Gwen. That is all." He talks to me as if I'm a petulant child and ushers me out of the room as such, too, leaving Desmier and Zakh behind.

Yuri and Vladmir follow us as we walk down the corridor.

Everything that just happened crashes around in my mind as I try to process it and my heart starts racing.

I have so many questions but I don't know what to ask first.

We get on the elevator and make our way down to the ground floor.

When we reach outside and I see the car that's going to take me away from here without the chance to get answers to my questions, my brain pops back into focus.

I can't just go back to the house not knowing what's going to happen next.

We reach the car and I wrench my arm free from Malik's grip, glaring at him.

"Why didn't you tell me?" I blurt. There are so many things I want to throw at him, like how he got my DNA sample and why he never said anything about Mexico, but the question I asked is the most important one. "Why didn't you tell me what happened to you and your captain?"

I look him over and put more pieces of his past together. That incident was what ended his career in the Navy. The injury he said he got is from that. When he said he would still be serving if not for that, he did mean it.

"You didn't need to know." His voice is as emotionless as his appearance.

"Why wouldn't I need to know that?"

"You didn't, but now you do."

The look he gives me tells me to drop it. I don't want to, but I decide I will given the fact I just found out I'm on the wrong side.

I guess I now know why he's treated me the way he has.

"When are you going to Mexico?" I change the subject.

"Tomorrow."

My God. I didn't know it was going to be so soon. "When will you be back?"

"When I'm sure the job's done. Now get in the car. There's nothing more for you to worry about."

Nothing more?

Except him.

We stare at each other in an awkward silence.

I completely forget Yuri and Vladmir exist until Malik

breaks his stare from mine and Yuri taps my elbow, motioning to get in the car.

I slide in, and Vladmir gets in the driver's seat.

Malik starts talking to Yuri in Russian. His tone is harsh. They're both harsh with each other until Malik gets up in Yuri's face and places a finger to his chest.

Whatever command Malik gives Yuri next has him back in control. Then, with a stern face, Yuri slides in next to me.

Vladmir starts up the car, and we drive away.

I stare back at Malik, who to my surprise is watching us.

I look at him until I can't see him anymore, then I face Yuri.

"What did he say to you?" I wouldn't normally ask, but I want to know.

Yuri considers my question for a moment then sighs. "He wants me and Vlad to stay here with you instead of going to Mexico. And we're dead if we let anything happen to you."

On hearing his answer, I instantly think Malik sounds like the protector I wanted him to be. That was the man my heart told me to run to when I needed help.

But maybe he's just protecting his investment.

In the next six months, if I die, everyone loses.

* * *

Ten days have gone by since I last saw Malik. My worries have increased day by day, and I've become a zombie in the house waiting to hear something. Anything.

My only saving grace is that Dru has gone to see my grandmother twice and sent me pictures.

I've spoken to her several times but haven't over the last few days because her suspicions are growing.

It's my fault. If I didn't sound so worried and on edge, Dru might be fine. I might have bought myself a little more time, but I feel that she's only holding back because she understands that I'm trying to do my best.

Today, I created the last of my designs. I finished around midday, and I've been out here ever since, sitting on the beach with Sebastian.

It's in the breath between night and day. Since I haven't eaten anything, I should probably go inside for dinner because Jeanne will be looking for me, but I don't want to go in yet.

I hug my knees to my chest and watch Sebastian running along the shoreline with a twig in his mouth he found by the rocks.

It's been ten days since I last saw Malik, but today marks two weeks since I've been in Boston and away from the life I know. If I'm like this now, I worry what will happen when another two weeks go by. And the time after that.

By then, I'm sure if Grams had any traces of memory of me, it will be completely gone.

My phone rings in my pocket. I'm tempted not to answer it because I know it can only be Dru at this time of day, but I would hate to ignore the call. She could be calling with important information about Grams. I guess, though, if something did happen to Grams, the nursing home would call me.

I answer the phone, pressing it to my ear when the wind lifts my hair.

"Hey." I try to put on a chirpy voice, but I end up sounding hoarse.

"Hi, I was just checking in as I hadn't heard from you."

"Oh, I'm sorry I've been really busy. I finished the designs today."

"That's great." Although she sounds excited, I can tell something's off in her tone.

"Yeah. I'm excited to see what's going to happen. This is going to be our biggest year."

"I know. It's a little scary. It sounds like I can quit my job here soon, though, right?"

"Yes." Dru loves all things marketing, but she hates where she works. Her boss is a sexist pig who's constantly hitting on her and putting others ahead of her because she won't sleep with him. She's stuck it out this long with the hope that our business will take off and her profit margin will be close enough to her usual earnings.

"I was thinking of taking a week or two off to come and see you. I'd love to see what's happening."

Oh no. My heart shies away, and my mind slows, struggling to come up with another lie. Another excuse. Another explanation I'll have to apologize for when the truth comes out.

What do I say now?

What the hell can I tell her that will buy me some more time?

"It would be great to see you, but I think the investors kind of want to deal with me for now."

There's a moment of tense silence before I hear her sigh. "I see. Gwen, are you sure... this isn't your way of cutting me lose? I understand if it is. This is your gig after all."

I gasp and press the phone closer to my ear. I know she's annoyed, and I understand why.

"No, Dru. Not at all. I wouldn't do that to you."

"I know you wouldn't intentionally, but sometimes these things happen. I just want you to know I'd understand. Sure, I'd be pissed off, but I'd have to be okay with it. I'm just the marketing brains. Right?"

"You're the reason I have a business in the first place. Dru, without you, I wouldn't know what to do. I've always wanted to pick up where my mother left off. You made me see that I could."

"That's sweet, and I appreciate you saying so. I'm just... worried about you. That's what it is. I'm glad you were spontaneous enough to seize the opportunity, but I wish I had more info. Or that I were there. It doesn't help that you seem reserved and worried as well."

She couldn't be more right. "I'm sorry. It's just that so much has changed, and this is a lot for me to deal with."

"Then let me help you. That's what we do when there's a lot to deal with. We've always sorted it out together."

"I know. It's just that this time, we can't."

"Gwen, if you want to rendezvous with Malik, then just say so." She laughs, but it sounds off-key. "I'd be the first to say you need more sex in your life."

"I know you would, and no, this isn't about that."

A sigh of frustration crackles through the phone. "Gwen..."

"What?"

"You sound like you're keeping something from me. I'm sorry to say that, but you are. You sound like when..." Her voice trails off and she goes silent again.

"Like what?" I prod.

"Like when anyone mentions your father. I hate

mentioning him now because it's unchartered territory with us, but this situation with you being away feels like that. It's making me worry."

"You don't have to worry."

"Notice how those words are easier said than done?"

"I know, but you seriously don't. I promise." *Really, Gwen, you promise?*

Maybe I have lost my mind. I'm married to a man who's not only in the mafia but a secret society, and he's in Mexico taking over the cartel—*my family*—who are obviously planning some retaliation strategy.

That pretty much sounds like everything I could worry about in this world served on one very big plate of shit.

"I hope so, but honestly, I often wonder if we're really as close as I thought we were."

"How can you say that?"

"Because I know you. So, I know there's shit you're not telling me. This is how you get when you have some secret. You did this same thing with Gage until I dragged it out of you. Then Conrad and the debt. But worse, this is how you are about your father. Don't you think it's strange that I'm supposed to be your best friend yet you've never opened up to me about him? I don't know if he was good or bad or anything."

How do I explain to her that he was both? "I promise we'll talk about him one day."

"I get it if you don't want to. It's not my business, but what worries me is that I've always had this feeling whenever you've been in trouble. Is that what's happening here?"

"No." I hate lying. "I'm not in trouble."

Another bout of silence fills the space, and another sigh

leaves her lips. "Okay, I'll stop pushing you." The disappointment in her voice hits me hard.

"Hopefully, I'll have more info in a week or so." Here's hoping Malik will be back by then. I can't keep this up and continue lying to my friend.

"Okay. That would be great. I guess it is what it is."

"Dru, please don't be like that."

"I think you understand how I feel. Anyway, looks like I'd better go. Be safe."

"You, too."

She disconnects the line, but I keep the phone to my ear, listening to the hollow sound of separation.

Great, just fucking great. The last thing I need is to piss off my best friend.

Dru and I never stay mad at each other for long, but this is different. She's also never brought up my father like that before. It's ironic that she would now, when what's happening has everything to do with him.

I put my phone back in my pocket, then stay out for another hour until night falls.

I summon Sebastian, and we head back up to the house.

I hear voices when I reach the courtyard. One in particular that makes my heartbeat kick up a few notches.

It's Malik.

Just as I think of him, he appears across the distance on the terrace.

It is him. He's back.

Despite everything, relief washes over me for seeing he's safe. And just seeing him.

I'm about to continue up the path, but I stop in my tracks when Kelly walks up to him and gives him a hug.

He holds her for a few moments, then she runs her hands through his hair and takes his hand.

She leads him inside, right into one of the guestrooms.

I can see them through the sliding glass windows, so I stand there watching until she closes the door.

I guess I got the answer to the question I asked Jeanne about them being more. It sure looked like they were. How fitting that he should not only see her first when he's back, but be with her, too.

I am such a fool.

Seeing the two of them together is another rude awakening, reminding me that I'm being used and I can't feel anything for a man like him.

I might be getting a billion-dollar fortune, but it feels to me like he'll be getting so much more. He'll take his revenge, the assets, the cartel, and the parts of me I never wanted to get hurt ever again.

I hate him for that.

Chapter Twenty-Nine

Gwen

I didn't sleep last night.

The oh-so-stupid part of me stayed up thinking Malik was going to show up at some point.

When he didn't, I felt even worse, and throughout the night, I kept imagining him in bed with Kelly.

I kept thinking about how much better she is for him than me.

Aside from knowing him forever, she's someone he can trust. Her estranged family didn't kill anybody for him, or try to hurt him.

Most of all, she's not his enemy, or someone he would think so little of that he would use as bait to lure out dangerous men who could hurt her.

At this point, I'm not sure which of us would be classed as *the other woman*—her or me.

Since I have roughly a five and a half month expiry date, the answer is me.

When I'm gone, they can live happily ever after, and she'll benefit from Malik's share of my father's inheritance.

Just fucking great.

Hours ago, when morning broke, I couldn't believe I'd spent all night lying in this stupid bed that doesn't even belong to me thinking about them.

Why didn't he just come up here with her and give me my own room?

And do I seriously need to be here?

A knock at the door makes me sit. Jeanne walks in when I let her know the door is open.

Over the last few days she's checked on me whenever I'm late for breakfast.

"Morning. Are you okay?" she asks, giving me a little smile.

"Yeah, I'm okay, but I didn't really sleep so well."

"Oh, no. Well, I made a good breakfast."

I smirk. "You always make a good breakfast."

"I try my best. Malik is also back." The relief in her voice is evident. I'm sure she was worried about him, too. That day when I got back from Volkova Inc., I knew she was aware that I knew the whole story, but I never asked her about anything more. "He'd like for you to come down."

Hearing his order tightens my chest. Honestly, I would rather not see him. It would almost be better for me to go through the next few months without him in my life. But I need to know when I can see my family and friends. And when I can leave.

"Okay, I'll be down in ten minutes."

"Perfect. I'll make some more coffee."

"Thank you."

She leaves, and I get ready quickly, keeping my hair in a messy bun.

I head downstairs. When I approach the dining room, I see Malik inside.

He's sitting at the head of the table looking handsome as ever, dressed in a black button-down shirt with the sleeves rolled up his forearms. His hair looks slightly longer, and he's allowed his beard to grow a little fuller. It gives him a rugged yet sophisticated appearance.

I walk up to the door, and a weight settles in the pit of my stomach when I realize he's talking to Kelly.

The two are actually engrossed in a deep conversation which I can't understand because surprise, surprise, they're speaking in Russian. *Again.*

It takes nanoseconds for me to conjure the memory of how she was with him last night. Her hugging him and running her fingers through his hair.

Her taking him, the man who is supposed to be my husband, into the guestroom.

At least Malik looks at me and breaks the conversation to acknowledge my presence.

"Good morning," he says.

"Hello." My tone is stiff and he can tell I'm pissed as fuck.

I make a point of sitting next to him in an attempt to get Kelly to take a hint and leave us, but she drags Malik back into the conversation.

Jeanne comes in with coffee, pours me some, and glances at them talking.

Even she looks uneasy, but she doesn't say anything. I don't expect her to because she's not confrontational and wouldn't do anything that would make her seem rude. Definitely not to her beloved employer.

When she leaves, it doesn't surprise me.

Ignoring the coffee, I stare at Kelly and Malik until Kelly looks at me. It takes her a moment to figure out that I'm not impressed with her talking the way she is to my husband. I'm not impressed with him either.

"Oh, sorry, we tend to get carried away when we're together," Kelly bubbles as if the mere apology—as genuine as it seems—will suffice in absolving her.

"My goodness, you can actually *see* me sitting here. I totally thought I was invisible." I blink several times, amplifying my sarcasm. I don't care how I look. I'm sick of this shit.

Kelly looks stunned by my outburst. "I'm... sorry. I didn't mean to offend you in any way." Her words come out in an uncertain quiver. She looks caught off-guard. I should probably give her a break, but given my suspicion that she slept with my husband last night, I don't care.

"I find that really hard to believe," I throw back.

"No, I didn't mean to upset you."

"Okay, apology accepted." I intensify my gaze. "But just so you know, where I come from, it's considered rude and completely disrespectful to be so deep in conversation with another woman's husband when she's sitting right here. It's even worse that I don't know what the fuck you're saying to him."

"That is enough," Malik cuts in, giving me a hard stare.

"No, it's not enough." My brows snap together and I curl

my hand into a tight fist. "The two of you do this all the damn time."

"I said enough." His voice is harder, harsher. "Kelly, please leave us and lock the door behind you. It seems my wife and I have matters to discuss."

"Yes, sir." She bows her head respectfully.

I've never heard her call him sir before.

She looks away from the two of us, then marches out. It's not until the door closes that Malik sits forward and glares at me as if I've lost my mind.

"What the hell is wrong with you?" His gaze becomes sharper.

"Are you serious?" My shoulders almost snap as I flick my palms over.

"Yes, I'm serious."

I blow out a ragged breath. I'm not going to allow him to sit there and look at me as if I'm crazy. Or in the wrong. I know I'm not. "First, you go away for ten days, and I hear nothing. I'm just expected to sit and wait. Then you sit there, ignoring me while you're in some conversation with your maid that I don't understand."

"And you think it's okay to lose your shit with my staff?" He raises his brows.

"You think what she did was okay?"

"No, that's not what I'm saying."

"It's because it's *her*, isn't it? That's why you're being so defensive," I snap. "I saw you last night."

"You saw me what?" His eyes narrow.

"With *her*. I saw you going into the room with her last night. Did you sleep with her? Is that where you were all night?"

I hate it that he chooses this moment to give me that mocking smirk.

Yes, I know how I sound. Like the jealous brat of a wife.

Like he's broken me.

Like I've actually fallen for him and hearing he slept with Kelly would hurt me deeply.

Wouldn't it?

Is that why I couldn't sleep?

Is that why I hurt with everything else?

He leans forward so we're breaths apart. "Malyshka, didn't you practically tell me I could fuck anyone I wanted to?"

Oh God... he did sleep with her.

The stress of everything rolls into one giant ball and implodes in my chest. The detonation pushes my reasoning out of my mind, and my immediate reaction is to grab the closest thing to me, which happens to be a glass of orange juice.

When I shove the glass and the juice splashes all over his face, then trickles onto his expensive clothes, I feel nothing like what I did weeks ago when I slapped him. I don't fear the repercussions or the punishment, and I wouldn't care if he spanked my ass like he did before.

I simply don't care.

"I'm not doing this with you." The numbness stays with me when I stand, yank my wedding and engagement rings off my finger, and throw them in his face.

He seemed pretty calm up until that point, but the moment my rings clink against the marble floor, he gets up so fast the chair tips over and the glass closest to him falls and smashes.

"Not doing what with me, Gwen?" His face darkens, and there's a fierceness in his eyes that awakens my terror.

I find my voice and back away. "I want to go home. There's no reason for you to keep me here and treat me like shit."

Malik knocks the cup of coffee off the table. It joins the smashed pieces of glass.

I step back, and he bounds forward, knocking the other chair to the ground.

My instinct puts me in flight mode, and I ready myself to run, but if I've learned nothing else about this man, I've learned that I'll never be able to run away from him.

He catches me and walks me into the wall, shoving me against it then barricading me in with his body so I can barely breathe.

"Malik—"

He catches my face and I wince.

"You think I'm fucking my maid? Is that what you think, Gwen?" he snarls.

"Aren't you?" My accusatory tone confirms that's exactly what I think.

He tightens his grip on my face, digging his fingers into my skin. "No. I'm not. I already told you I'm not a cheater. I'm also not a liar."

I gasp, panting. His grip is threatening and almost at that point where it's painful. "You are the biggest liar I know."

He gets up in my face and pushes his body harder against me, forcing me into the wall.

I stare back at him, anticipation eating me alive as he searches my eyes. Then he presses his nose to my hair and inhales me. The action sends a shiver through my blood, and I try to figure out what he's going to do next.

"You know what, baby girl?" His voice deepens, becoming sharp like a blade, the words piercing into me. When he calls me baby girl in English, it's not normally a good thing. It's a signal that he's pissed. "You're not nearly as afraid of me as you should be, but maybe that's what I love most about you."

Blood rushes to my head as I absorb his words.

Those words—*what I love most about you...*

Love—that word.

I've never been with a man who loved me. Even the ones I thought might, didn't. They never even told me they loved me as a lie. I've just never had it in any shape or form romantically.

And here is this maleficent devil, speaking words of love to me.

But it can't be true. Malik Volkova is just screwing with me again. He's doing it because he can see the effect he has on me, and simply because he can.

This man is a god. He can do whatever the hell he wants and get away with it.

That doesn't mean I have to stand here and take it, or look like I don't have a spine or voice of defense.

"You are a soulless monster." My voice is small but firm. "You love nothing. You don't know how to love. Everything about you is selfish."

The light in his eyes dims, then he comes closer so we're a kiss apart. That mocking smirk returns to his face, along with an air of seduction. My chest tightens.

"You might be right, Malyshka. But I've never lied to you."

I frown. "When we first met, you didn't tell me who you were."

"But I never lied about what I did tell you. I just didn't tell you everything."

"It's the same thing. You led me to believe things that weren't true."

A dark smile dances on his sensual lips. "Like what? What did I lead you to believe that wasn't true?"

"I thought you were someone else. A normal guy who wanted me."

His grip loosens, then he runs his fingers down the side of my neck in a slow purposeful caress I feel deep in my core. His touch stirs the need in my pussy. I try to push the desire away but it only grows.

He moves to the shell of my ear and lingers there. "You seriously thought I led you to believe that?"

He moves so I can feel his cock pressing into my belly. I gasp.

His smile widens, and he pushes into me again. "Tell me, Gwen."

"Yes."

He lifts the edge of my skirt, rolls it up my thighs, then hooks his finger into the lace band of my panties.

Maintaining eye contact, he strokes the skin there, and my brain and body go still between his and the wall. Malik swipes his finger over my sex and pushes two thick fingers into my pussy, then swirls around my clit.

"You're wet for me. Just like always."

"No." The word comes out on the edge of a breath, stopping short in my throat when he starts pumping in and out of me.

"Who's the liar now?" One corner of his mouth slides into a devilish grin, and we're pulled back into that relentless game of predator and prey. Except this time, we're husband and wife. "At least one of us is trying to clear their name."

He pumps harder.

"Malik..." I moan out embarrassingly loudly and pray no one is anywhere near the door.

"Let me show you what truth feels like, Malyshka. Let me show you what's real," he growls into my ear. "Maybe when you fuck the soulless monster, you can tell me again if you think I misled you. But beware, to be with me is to taste death."

Molding his muscular chest to mine, he captures my mouth in a kiss that makes my bones melt with infernal fire. I part my lips for his tongue so he can taste me and for me to do the same to him. I want to taste him again.

When I do, I feel his darkness. It thrills me. He tastes like something I know I shouldn't have but want. The forbidden feeling spreads the fire over my body, consuming me the same way he does.

The rage and uncertainty that previously fueled me are forced out of my mind.

My blood sizzles. My brain is scorched, and all I feel are his possessive kisses which show me this is real. The prospect of such a thing makes me cling to his shirt to pull him closer.

I *need* him closer. I want to feel all he gives me. The thing I've never gotten from anyone else.

I want to feel him.

Lifting my leg, he moves my panties aside. Then he

shoves his pants down his hips and with one quick thrust, he slams his already rock-hard cock into my aching pussy.

Then there's no prelude to his fucking; he just starts hammering into me. Hard.

It hurts like it did the other night, but I like the bitter sweetness of pleasure and pain.

I scream against his lips, and his mouth slides to my neck, nibbling against the hollow while he fucks me.

"YA sobirayus' trakhnut' tebya tak sil'no, chto ty ne smozhesh' khodit'," he sneers, licking the side of my face.

I touch his bearded cheek. "Tell me what you said."

"Are you sure a good girl like you wants to hear such dirty words?"

"Yes. Tell me," I stutter.

He grips my hip harder, increasing his pace, stealing my senses. "I said I'm going to fuck you so hard you won't be able to walk. Okay?"

"Ye...sss."

He ruts into me with desperation, and all I can do is grip onto his wide shoulders, my fingers burrowing into his skin through his shirt.

Every thrust of his cock pushes me to lose myself in him, and I come. My delicious release leaves me calling his name and moaning my pleasure into the hot air encasing us.

"Yes!" I scream.

The sound seems to fill him with more energy and he devours me. Then suddenly, he laces his fingers through mine and strokes my ring finger with a gentle caress that makes everything inside me stop and pay attention.

The gesture shifts the air between us, and we feel different. *He* feels different. Like he's making love to me.

Malik presses my hand into the wall and keeps it there while he seems to push deeper inside me, then he stops kissing me and just stares into my eyes, telling me without words what he feels.

What he feels for *me*.

We're pulled into another kiss. This one is sweeter. Too sweet, too tame, too normal for him.

The moment he seems to realize it, he changes the tempo and switches us back to fucking.

My body convulses and my walls squeeze around his cock, milking waves of hot cum into me when he comes, too.

When his pumps slow, he holds me, keeping our bodies pressed against each other.

His heart beats rapidly against me, and just as I begin to savor the sound, he pulls back.

"Malik—"

He presses a finger to my lips.

"Don't. Just come with me. Up to our bed. You and me." He speaks in a low sensual timbre. "We leave everything else down here. You hear me?"

"Yes."

Chapter Thirty

Malik

The second thing I shouldn't love so much about my wife is how she looks when she's riding my cock.

I shouldn't love the way she fits me. Nor the way the darkness surrounding my heart unravels the instant I touch her.

We're in the hot tub now, fucking like animals during mating season.

God knows what time it is. We came down here after we officially christened the bed as a married couple. Night had fallen by then, so we'd been in that room all fucking day.

Water splashes over our bodies as Gwen bounced up and down my cock, the queen of my body.

I can feel that entity expanding between us as she moves. It's hungry for our need.

She needs me. And I need her.

As long as we keep going, it will grow and grow and grow.

I shouldn't want it to, but I do. The selfish part of me wants it all when it comes

to her. I realize by such an admission that I've lost the game.

I did everything I said I wouldn't do.

I gave in, and now I can't stop.

Squeezing her lush ass, I pull her body closer so her breasts can bounce in my face. I suck on her gorgeous tits and when she moans, the sound heats my blood with raw, primitive lust.

I fuck her pussy recklessly, leaving her screaming with pleasure, and I just keep wanting more of her.

The more I taste her and take her, the more I feast.

Every time we come to a stop, I come up with one more way to take another piece of her. Pieces I want to keep for myself forever.

Gwen is the thing I never saw coming until she was already swimming in my blood and infecting me like delicious poison. Or life.

She crept inside me and breathed new life into the remnants of my soul, allowing the man inside to taste humanity.

Now I fear what I know will happen when we stop. I fear I'll never have her again like this.

Those thoughts only drive me to take even more. My fingers dig into her ass cheeks, and I pound up into her body. We both groan in wild ecstasy, uncaring of who might hear us.

I pay my people enough to stay the fuck away when I

need them to, so no one should disturb us. If they hear us, it's pretty clear what we're out here doing.

When Gwen climaxes, she digs her fingers into my shoulders, and we kiss. I come, too, sharing the release.

I kiss her ear and tell her in Russian that she's beautiful and I want to feast on her forever. Words I'd never utter so she'd understand.

"What did you say?" she whispers over my skin.

"You're beautiful." I leave out the rest of it.

"Sounded like you said more than that." She giggles.

"I did, but you've had enough of my secrets for one night."

"No." She runs her fingers through my hair. "I want more."

"Okay, then this one's easy. I want more, too."

We kiss again, and that fuels another session. Eventually, we end up in the bed again, but now we're lying next to each other, gazing at the stars through the window.

Her back is pressed to my chest, and we're cocooned in the still silence of the breath between night and day.

I'm lying here with her acting as if this is our life and I don't have a care in the world besides pleasing my wife.

Nothing is further from the truth. Mexico was a success, but only for now. The heads of the cartels in the Navarros' alliance only folded and signed their allegiance to me because they had to.

No one had the time to prepare a counterattack to my vengeance, so they essentially had to sign on the dotted line if they wanted to live. The only thing left to do now is to implement the strategies of my leadership and roll it out. My duty to the Knights must come first, especially since I take care of the defense system for our entire organization. That means I have to delegate but also make sure I show my presence.

Zakh and I were only in Mexico for so long because there was a lot to do and a lot of people to speak to. We were also keeping tabs on the men and making sure everything was under control. The last thing they needed was a mutiny. You don't bring shit like that to the Knights without real fire.

Diego and all those men are just like me, so they will only bow when they need to and plan to rise up and fight the first chance they get.

That's what I need to prepare for because the prize is still her.

Gwen.

My wife.

"What are you thinking about?" Her soft voice pierces the silence.

"All sorts of things. What about you?"

Gwen pulls in a slow breath. "I'm always thinking about my grandmother, but now I have one very pissed-off best friend to worry about."

I should have known she would say something like that. Of course, she's worried about her grandmother. Worried sick. And it was inevitable that Dru would start getting annoyed. Gwen's been gone for a while, and Dru doesn't have much information.

"You'll get to see your grandmother soon," I promise.

Gwen twists in my arms to face me with hope in her eyes. "Really? When?"

"Soon. I just need another week or so. We have a few meetings with the executors and lawyers. Once that's done,

I'll have a clearer picture." Before I even contemplate sending Gwen back to Wilmington, I also want to finish getting everything sorted out with the cartel and keeping tabs on Diego. *And* Esperanza for that matter. I don't want to scare Gwen, so I won't tell her those parts. "Is your grandmother okay?"

"She's the same, so neither good nor bad." She tucks a lock of hair behind her ear, allowing the moonlight to catch her face properly. "Dru has been checking on her while I've been here, but I miss her. And I really don't want her to forget me. She didn't know who I was last time."

I can't imagine how awful that must be. Loving a relative who can't remember they love you.

"Her heart remembers you even if her brain can't."

She smiles with appreciation. "I truly hope so. My grandmother is my world. She protected me all my life. I want to do the same for her. I would have kept her at home if I could have provided the right care for her, but she got so bad she needed to be in a home. I've always felt guilty for that."

She dabs away a tear with the heel of her hand and blinks to stave off others. Apart from that night I dealt with Conrad, this is the first time I've seen her cry.

"You did the right thing for her. Keeping her home without the proper care she needed would have made her health worse."

"I know. It's just hard for me, and I've had to accept that this is it. She's not going to get any better from here onwards. All we'll have is memories."

This is the first time Gwen has spoken like this.

I cup her face and stroke her smooth, silky skin. "Memories are the most powerful thing we have. That's where we love all the people who have ever been in our lives."

"That's a nice thought. I guess regardless of what's happened to me, I've had good memories and good people."

"Me too." I have quite the story to tell, but I've had the greatest people in my life, and I would never trade that for a different life that could have been better. "What's happening with Dru? Did you guys argue?"

"Yes. She's onto me. I don't know how long I can keep up my story."

I think for a moment. She's going to have to tell her friend something soon. Now that the cards have been laid out and everyone who's party to this plot knows what's happening, Dru isn't a threat. Not anymore. We're no longer at the stage where Gwen could have told Dru she's been kidnapped and involve the police or anyone like that who would create a mess I don't want to clear up.

"She's just eager to get our dream," Gwen adds. "That's what I sold her. She thinks I'm here setting up the beautiful store the two of us have dreamed about since forever. It was the only thing I could tell her. I figured I'd be able to sort it all out in six months when I get my inheritance. But I worry about what will happen to us along the way."

"Do you trust your friend?"

"With my life."

"Then the next time you speak to her, tell her whatever you feel comfortable to share."

She gazes at me for a few beats, surprise filling her pretty face. "You're seriously allowing me to tell her what's going on?"

"I'm sure you'll think about what you believe she needs

to know." Gwen isn't going to put her friend in danger, and she'll only talk about the things she knows she can trust her with.

"I will. Thank you."

"It's okay."

She continues to stare at me, and I can tell she's thinking about my past. She has the same look in her eyes that she did when she first heard my truth.

"What actually happened to you, Malik?"

I smirk. "Story for another time, Malyshka."

"Will you ever tell me?"

"Yes. It's just difficult to talk about, and it's not just one thing that happened to me." My captivity and Jim Davison's death were just a part of the bigger picture of shit. There was also the disaster with my parents, Leif and Viktor. My head is fucked because all of it was just too much for a person to deal with. "Let's just say, life wasn't exactly kind to me."

She holds my gaze. "That room. The secret room with all the pictures on the wall. Those people are all dead, aren't they?"

My heart pinches at her recognition. I nod slowly. "My father, my uncle, my old captain, and his son who was my best friend. All of them are dead. I keep everything that represents death in that room." Including my uniform and my Knights tunic.

"I'm sorry."

"It's okay. It is what it is." I decide to change the subject slightly. "Kelly and I were talking about my uncle. It's an emotional topic because he was murdered. That's what you saw the other night."

She gasps. "Oh my God. I... didn't know."

"No one told you, so you wouldn't have known. My uncle Leif helped her family out a lot. The room we went in is where I keep some of his things. She'd redecorated and wanted to show me what she'd done." I care enough to explain that.

"I overreacted."

"You didn't. I would have done far worse if it were you."

A little smile pulls at her delicate mouth. "Would you?"

"You already know the answer to that." I press a soft kiss to her lips. "I'd kill any man who touches you."

"What if I don't like people touching you? Even if they are friends you grew up with and are close to?"

I chuckle. "Okay, let's do this. How about for the next six months, we just touch each other."

"Really? Are you sure Kelly can keep her hands off you for that long? I'm not exactly buying the friend thing."

I brush over her nose. "A deal is a deal, and I'm a man of my word."

"Okay, I'll hold you to that."

"You do that. Now, come here."

She returns to my lips, and we fall into that cycle again where we can't stop.

The next few days pass by, and each one sees us the same. When I'm away from the house, it's only for a few hours, and I can't wait to get back.

The changes in me become more apparent to those around me who know the beast who likes to shut himself down from the world. Gwen has me doing things I don't normally do that feel natural again. Things I forgot that were a part of me.

On Saturday evening, I have her sitting on top of the

piano in the hall while I play Bach and Debussy and teach her Russian. The last time I played the piano was long before I left for the Navy. The one I have is mainly for Jeanne because she always plays.

Today, Gwen has on a pair of short-shorts and a tank top that shows off her breasts. Her hair is down and draped over her shoulder in a sexy side swoop. My wife is fucking gorgeous, and I like looking at her like this—carefree and mine.

Gwen giggles when she gets the pronunciation wrong of the Russian words for good morning. The giggles turn into a hearty laugh. A sound I can't get enough of.

"It's dobroye utro." I said it slower that time so she could pick up the pronunciation a little better.

"Dob bo bo utto." At first, she looks really serious, then she starts laughing again at her terrible attempt. I do, too. Like really laughing, something I never do.

"My God, woman. You're gonna need a lot of extra lessons."

"I know, but I'll get it with practice." She sounds determined.

"You're going to need a lot of that."

"You won't stop teaching me, will you? I know I totally suck."

"I won't. It turns out I love the way you suck other things on me, so you're good." I wink at her and she blushes. "Come here to me."

I stop playing the piano and pick her up, setting her into my lap, where she slips her arms around me and we fall into a kiss.

It's only when we hear someone clearing their throat behind us in an exaggerated manner that we pull apart.

I already knew it wouldn't be any of my staff, and only one of my brothers is jovial enough to do that.

Zakh is leaning against the doorway, watching us with an amused expression on his face.

"Sorry to interrupt you newlyweds." He straightens, casting me an I-knew-you-wouldn't-be-able-to-keep-your-hands-off-her smirk.

"It's okay." I clench my jaw and try to compose myself. "We were just wrapping things up here." As in, I planned to take Gwen upstairs and spend the rest of the day buried inside her. That will have to wait, because Zakh wouldn't be here if he didn't have anything important to tell me. We've already spoken this morning, and he didn't mention he'd be stopping by.

Gwen blushes and gives Zakh a nervous smile of acknowledgment. She knows Zakh is here about business.

I stand. "Baby, why don't you go help Jeanne and I'll come find you in a few minutes."

"Okay."

When she leaves, I turn back to Zakh.

"What's going on?"

"I tracked Diego to Uzbekistan. He's talking with Ilya Imarov, the leader of a militant rebel group. Seems like he's gathering forces to come up with a plan."

We expected this, but I didn't think Diego would go to that part of the world to seek help.

"Ilya Imarov?"

"Yeah. We've got eyes on them, but something is coming, Malik. I just wanted to prepare you. At least we have a heads-up, but it's not everything I can track. Diego and his people are like us. They also know we're watching and to be cautious. He'll try to come at us with something solid."

"We'll be ready for him whatever it is." I nod. "I'm not going to allow that motherfucker to take my wife."

Zakh's expression softens, and he glances toward the direction Gwen went. "I didn't think so, brother. It also seems like you want more than just revenge now."

I shift my weight from one foot to the other thinking of a response.

He's right. I do want more than just to be the punisher.

"Maybe."

"You look happy with her. You look alive. Would it really be so bad to keep an open mind?"

He's asking me to consider if this thing I have with Gwen could work.

Could it?

At the sixth month mark, when it's time to let her go, how will I feel then?

Can I let her go?

I don't want to.

"Maybe not." My answer surprises him.

"Then maybe it won't be so bad."

Having an open mind isn't the bad thing.

It's me.

Chapter Thirty-One

Gwen

I'm working all day. Go and see Jeanne when you wake up.

I left something for you,

M

P.S.- Don't you fucking dare take your rings off ever again.

I've just woken up to this note from Malik lying next to me in an envelope on his pillow. My rings were also back on my finger, feeling as if they always belonged there.

Jeanne brought them up days ago and handed them to Malik. I thought he would give them back to me then, but he didn't. Not until now.

Seeing them on my finger didn't surprise me nearly as much as finding the note.

God help me, when I saw it, my silly girly heart skipped through the meadow to *The Hills Are Alive* with the *Sound of Music* beat ringing through my head.

The thought of him leaving a note for me touched me in a way I can't describe.

There's so much going on around us to worry about, but we've been in that sphere of passion for the last week where it's just been us.

It's been nice and I've selfishly wanted to hold on to those moments for as long as I could. Especially when I've attempted to speak to Dru.

She's been giving me the silent treatment since we last spoke even though I sent her a message days ago letting her know I needed to speak to her. She's either responded to my follow-up messages with short answers telling me she's busy at work or told me so herself on the off-chance she answered my calls.

I'm glad I've been given the go-ahead to speak to her, but I'm honestly struggling to think of where I'd start spilling the truth. I'd have to tell her about my father, which feels harder than anything else because it would show that I was keeping big secrets from everyone all these years.

Regardless, I am going to speak to her. It's time to, and perhaps had this thing with Malik not occurred, Dru would never hear the truth from me.

I get off the bed and get ready, then go downstairs to find Jeanne. I catch a glimpse of her in the kitchen, but I also see Kelly in the living room fixing the flowers.

I stop by the door, and she sees me, too, but looks away quickly, avoiding eye contact like she has been since my blowup.

I know I owe her an apology, but I've hardly seen her to attempt to offer it.

She doesn't come into the dining room at breakfast anymore, and when she does, she says nothing to Malik other than good morning and asks him what he wants to eat. In English.

Of course, she's not exactly difficult to find, and I could have sought her out to tell her I'm sorry, but I haven't because I still maintain that it was rude for her to carry on her deep conversation with Malik.

I'm also still not overly fond of her closeness with him.

But that's my jealousy I have to deal with. I guess I just hate whatever relationship she has with him because she's a part of his life and shares pieces of him I can't reach.

I no longer think he sees me as an enemy, but there's an expiry date hanging over our heads that I know will hurt me more than anything else.

Kelly stops what's she's doing when I walk in and looks at me. I can already tell from the tension in her shoulders that she's only addressing me because she believes she has to if she wants to keep her job.

"Mrs. Volkova, is there something I can do for you?" she asks.

Until our falling out, she called me Gwen.

"Please call me Gwen again."

"I thought it would be more respectful if I addressed you... properly."

"I know, but you were respectful before. I wanted to apologize for how I spoke to you."

She looks completely surprised. "That's okay. It was my fault. Because I grew up with Malik, I tend to forget sometimes that I work for him. I can definitely see where it was disrespectful toward you and I am sorry."

"How about we start over? I'd hate for us to have this tension between us for the next few months."

She smiles. "I'd like that."

"Good." I dip my head. "I'll see you later."

"Sure."

I leave her and head to the kitchen. There I find Jeanne putting a pie in the oven.

"That's for supper later." She beams.

"It smells delicious."

"It's apple and rhubarb."

"My favorite." I rub my hands together.

Jeanne laughs. "I know."

"Malik said I should see you about something."

"Yes. After breakfast, Yuri is going to take you into the city."

I narrow my eyes. "What for?"

She shrugs. "Malik didn't tell me that part."

"Okay. I guess I'll find out. I hope it's not some kind of meeting with my *lovely* relatives." I pray it's not. If it was, I think I would have known before this morning and Malik would have told me outright. At least I hope so.

I couldn't stand to see Diego and Esperanza again. I would be quite content not seeing them again for the rest of my life. I will never be able to shake the way Esperanza looked at me out of my mind. I sense we'll cross paths again before this is over. She looked as if she wanted to give me a piece of her mind.

"I don't think it's anything to worry about." Jeanne gives

me a hopeful smile. "As soon as you've finished eating, give me a shout, and I'll get Yuri."

"I will."

As I'm eager to see what this is all about, I just grab a few pieces of toast and a cup of coffee. I'm finished within fifteen minutes and on my way into the city with Yuri, who also couldn't—or *wouldn't*—tell me anything more than he was given instructions to take me to the city.

It's just him today and as he doesn't say much anyway, we drive in silence.

An hour later, the Boston skyline comes into view, and minutes later, we're on Newbury Street, one of the trendiest shopping areas in Boston.

We slow down and I consider that maybe I'm going shopping, until my eyes lock onto a beautiful boutique called Brash. Of course it catches my eye because that's the name of my company.

At first, I think my eyes are screwing with me because I've had this dream for so long, maybe I've lost my mind and am seeing things. But no, it's there, along with my floral logo in pink and black swirls, calling to me.

"Yuri, what's going on?" I ask when he pulls the car to a stop right outside the store.

He reaches into his pocket, pulls out a little key, and holds it out for me to take. "This is for you. I'll be out here until you're ready to leave. Vladmir is already inside."

"Is this seriously what I think it is?" My entire body is buzzing with energy and disbelief. Malik didn't seriously buy me a store. *Did he?*

"Why don't you go see." He offers a rare smile I don't recall ever seeing.

I take the key and get out of the car, then walk up to the store front to look at it.

Although the display windows are bare, it has that less-is-more contemporary effect I love. When I open the door, that feeling of accomplishment fills me with hope.

I walk inside and look at the stylish décor of shelves on the wall, clothing rails, and mannequins. All waiting for my designs to be placed on them.

"Oh, Malik, I can't believe you did this for me."

Footsteps draw my attention away from the décor. I turn toward the sound coming from the doorway in the corner. I expect to see Vladmir, but when Dru walks out with the brightest smile on her face, I grab my chest and tears of joy instantly flow down my cheeks.

"It's really something else, isn't it?" She chuckles.

"Oh my God, you're here." I fly straight into her awaiting arms, and we hug as if we haven't seen each other in centuries, not just the few weeks I've been missing.

My tears keep flowing, and my heart swelling. Malik is supposed to be the devil, but he seems like an angel to me.

Dru looks me over when we pull apart and smiles.

"Well, I can see married life is treating you well."

Oh God. "You know?"

"A few things." She nods. "Malik explained I guess what he thought would be the harder parts to me."

"You saw him?" I bring my hand up to my mouth.

"Yeah. A few days ago, I woke up to find a hundred grand in my account and a seriously hot Russian guy on my doorstep requesting my presence in Boston for a top-secret mission. I got here to a penthouse apartment and a body-guard, and this place." She squeals with delight. "I saw Malik the next day. That's when we spoke. I've been decorating the store ever since."

I can't believe what I'm hearing any more than I can that Malik would do this for me. For *us*—Dru and me.

"You've been here for *days*?"

"Yeah, sorry I couldn't talk properly. There was no way I could speak to you for more than two minutes and not spill the secret surprise, which was one hell of a secret surprise. So, this was what I was busy doing." She motions around the store while I stare back at her open-mouthed.

"I'm in shock. We have our own store?"

"Yes. We have our own store."

We stare at each other for a few seconds. And then we scream and scream and scream and hug again. And cry. We both cry because we've wanted this so badly.

"Oh my God, we have a store." I gasp, bringing my hand to my mouth.

"We do. I'm still in shock. Needless to say, I quit my job and I'm here at your beck and call to work."

"Oh, Dru, thank you so much. And I'm so sorry. I'm so truly sorry. I lied to you."

She rests her hand on my shoulder. "We've been friends forever. I know you didn't mean to, but I am interested to hear the rest of the story, and for the record, I'm pissed I missed your wedding. But all is forgiven because you did good and your husband is totally hot."

I shake my head at her. "Same old Dru."

"If it's not broken, there's nothing to fix." She gives me a sassy one-shoulder shrug, then sighs, and the seriousness returns to her face. "We should talk, though."

"Yes."

"I'm guessing Malik isn't just your ordinary ex-Navy lieutenant, is he?"

"No." I release a heavy sigh. We haven't really started talking properly yet, but this feels good.

"Come, let me take you to your office."

I have an office. This doesn't feel real.

We walk through the door she came through and head down the passage, which smells of fresh paint and vanilla-scented candles.

When we reach the end of the corridor, we turn into a large room with a white table and matching leather chairs.

"This is amazing," I gasp.

"Wait until it's done."

We sit on the leather sofas by the window, and there I tell her everything. Absolutely everything, leaving nothing out.

She listens and holds my hand like the good friend she's always been whenever I needed her.

"I'm so sorry, Gwen." Her voice is soft and reflective. "I really wish I'd known more over the years about your father. But I understand why you couldn't tell me."

"There were many times when I wanted to. Especially when he was alive. Then when he died. I was so broken because I'd just lost both my parents."

"I can imagine. At that time, I hadn't lost mine yet. When I did, I felt like the world ended, and I've been somewhere else ever since living someone else's life."

"Me too, except I was always someone else, never allowed to just be Gwen Navarro." I've tried out the name many times before. Never out loud.

"It suits you, but I like Volkova better." Her eyes twinkle and the light brightens her face.

"I do, too." I bite the inside of my lip. "But in a few months' time, I have to give it back."

"Gwen, I don't know a man alive who would do what Malik has done for you and be willing to let you go in a *few months' time*."

I don't know any, either. "I know."

"I mean, look at this place." She throws her hands up in excitement. "We dreamed big of having a chain of stores in every major city. This is a start we never saw coming, and it's a gift."

"I know," I repeat, sounding more dreamy.

"Good, because the fact that it's here and not exactly in Wilmington says he wants you for longer than the next few months."

I don't want to get ahead of myself, but it does look that way. "Staying together wasn't part of the plan."

"Plans change sometimes."

"They do."

* * *

Dru and I spend the rest of the day catching up and decorating the store I still can't believe we have.

At nightfall, her car came to take her to her luxury apartment, and Yuri took me home.

Jeanne told me Malik is out on the terrace, so I make my way there.

I find him sitting on the balcony looking sexy as hell in a button-down shirt with the top buttons open and the sleeves rolled up. He's smoking a cigar, and his hair is a boyish mess. Sebastian is resting by his feet and merely acknowledges me with a lift of his head.

Malik gives me a seductive grin, and his eyes take me in with lust-filled desire.

"I'm not sure where to begin to thank you." Although the words come out, I'm completely choked up.

"Did you like it?"

"Of course, I did. I..." My voice trails off as I'm overwhelmed again by emotion. "You gave me my own store with my best friend inside, who has a penthouse apartment, a bodyguard of her own, and a hundred grand in her bank account. That's..." Tears stream down my cheeks, and my voice catches in my throat.

I can't talk. It feels great to cry over something good. It's just that this is so much more than just *good.*

Malik puts out the cigar and moves toward me.

"It's a gift for someone who deserves it."

I pull in a breath of the still night air. "I can't thank you enough. There's more to you than what meets the eye, Malik Volkova."

"Is there, Malyshka?"

I nod, stand on the tips of my toes, and kiss his chin. "You say you don't have a heart, but I can see yours."

His eyes gleam with a sheen of purpose. They're dark and unfathomable yet magnetic and compelling, as if he's holding on to the meaning in my words.

"Maybe there's a reason for that," he finally says, breaking the stare.

"There is still the matter of that pie I keep promising

you. You haven't tasted that yet." It feels easier to joke with him now. We feel the way we did when we first met.

"Oh, I still want pie, Gwen Volkova. I'm just crazier for the taste of you."

He cups my face with one large hand and gently guides me to meet his lips for a long leisurely kiss that promises forever.

The promise instills hope in my heart and makes me wonder if I could have that with him.

If I could, I would.

Chapter Thirty-Two

Malik

I never thought I would live to see this day, where I'd be attending one of the annual charity fundraisers with my wife.

Gwen and I are standing by the bar area in the grand hall of the Langham Hotel. We're with my brothers and their wives, Anastasia and Lorelai.

Zakh is regaling us with tales of one of his crazy adventures, and everyone is listening and laughing.

Last week, I introduced Gwen to Anastasia and Lorelai properly because I felt it was time to. I knew they would be fascinated with her, and they were.

Like mother hens, they took Gwen under their wings. Within an hour, no one would believe they'd only just met that morning.

It's been the same tonight.

This year, Volkova Inc. partnered with Monsoon Tech to raise a million dollars for the Children of Tomorrow, a children's charity that takes care of children with cancer and rare diseases. Every year, we sponsor a different charity and this event is usually held at Volkova Inc.

I'm used to attending events like these a few times a year. Each time alone.

I don't always leave alone. In fact, I seldomly lack for a woman on my arm. But it was clear to everyone that I intended to be the perpetual bachelor.

Until now.

Dressed in a suit like the rest of the men here with my wife at my side, who's wearing an elegant black gown that hugs her perfect body, I feel like I've evolved into something else. Something much more than the man I was supposed to be.

Something the men I hold in my heart as the highest examples would have been proud of.

My father, Uncle Leif, Jim and Brian.

Brian would never believe I found one actual woman I adored enough to give my name, no matter the reason. Nor that when I look at my future, I can't imagine having one without her in the picture.

It's been a little over a month since she's been in my life and been my wife, but so much has happened it feels like several lifetimes have passed. For each, I've had her at my side, taming the beast inside me and restoring what I once felt when my heart used to beat on its own. Now it just seems to beat for her.

Gwen laces her delicate fingers with mine, and I glance

at her smiling up at me. Even though she's in her heels, the top of her head only just brushes my shoulders.

When we look back at Zakh, I notice Lorelai and Anastasia exchanging curious glances.

I know exactly what they're thinking because I've fascinated them, too. I'm usually the least talkative of my brothers and the guy who seems cold and calculative, a little scarier than most because no one can figure me out.

But tonight, it's been no secret that my wife means more to me than a contract or any cartel.

Zakh starts talking about the trip he and Desmier took last summer to Denmark, then the upbeat music changes to something old and sentimental. It's a 1940s jazz song I recognize but don't know the name of.

It seems to mean something to Gwen, though, because she stares out at the couples gathering on the dance floor across from us and her hand sways gently in mine.

She looks back at me, and her face lights up.

"My grandparents used to dance to this." She chuckles lightly.

I lean close to her ear. "Dance with me."

"Really? I'd love to, but do you dance?" She gives me a quizzical stare.

"Watch me."

Before she can comment, I lead her out onto the dance floor, leaving Zakh, who stops mid-sentence in his story.

They're all looking at me, but I'm focusing on Gwen.

I take her into my arms and dance with her, pulling more surprises from the proverbial bag.

At first, she beams up at me, excited to be dancing with

everyone else. Then she rests her head on my chest, getting closer.

This feels like the dance we should have had at our wedding. It feels like the first of many others I want with her.

Damn me. I can't remember the last time I tried to resist the urge to love her.

Or the last I attempted to put things into perspective and remind myself that this was just supposed to be about getting the cartel and doling out punishment to the Navarros.

More and more I feel myself slipping into the valley of obsession as I wonder if this could truly work.

Gwen lifts her head, and our lips find each other. I kiss her right there with everyone watching me and wondering, and I feel like kissing her forever would never be long enough.

We part and smile at each other, then the intensity of eyes on me breaks the serene haze covering my mind.

I'm aware several people are watching us, but this is different.

When I look ahead up toward the second-floor balcony and see Diego Navarro standing in the shadows, I understand why.

Gwen is content in my arms, safe with me, and none the wiser of his presence which has shifted the air around us.

I anticipated something like this. It was just a matter of when I would see him.

A few days ago all the legal matters in securing the Navarro empire and the cartel were wrapped up. Gwen and I own everything now, and I'm the new leader.

Diego's new leader.

But he's not here to greet me as such, or he wouldn't be watching me the way he is.

Diego doesn't move, meaning he wants to talk.

I pull Gwen against me and purposely wait until the song ends. My girl wanted to dance with me, and I'll give her that.

When the song ends, another begins with equal sentiment, but I have to deal with the looming threat.

"Malyshka, let's come back out here in a few minutes," I say, ushering her away. "There's something I have to take care of."

"That's fine." She giggles. "I had fun."

"We'll have more fun later, I promise."

I take her back over to Zakh and Desmier, placing her right next to Zakh.

Then I lean close to him and mutter in old Norse, telling him that Diego is here. I speak in that language because the girls don't understand it. It's the language the Knights use to send secret messages or in times like now when I want to keep things under wraps. Desmier hears, and he and Zakh both glance up at the balcony where Diego still stands.

Zakh nods, and I set off to find Diego.

The motherfucker must have some death wish to come here.

At the moment, we know he's planning shit. We just don't know what, and if I end him now like I want to, I won't find out.

I also don't want to end his ass when I don't have solid evidence on him because it would fracture the relationship we have with our allies.

The motherfucker knows to keep under the radar in such

a way that we can't figure out his movements. But I knew what I was up against when dealing with this family.

One and the same took me captive for all that time and no one knew who was responsible. It's people like that who can give people like me and all the tech the Knights hold at their fingertips a run for their money.

But the moment I find out what Diego is up to and contain it, he's fucking dead. I'll make an example out of him.

I reach the top of the stairs and see him. He's moved away from the balcony now and is standing by the long casement windows.

There's no one else up here because the area is sealed off. But it's not off limits to us.

Diego has his hands in his pockets and is staring out at the Boston skyline.

He looks at me with a smirk on his face when I reach him and turns so his back is against the glass.

I think of how easy it would be to kick him through it. He'd fall fifty feet straight to his death.

"Señor Volkova, what a lovely night to be out." His voice takes on a sing-song edge of mockery I don't like.

"Indeed." I keep my voice measured and my focus sharp.

He grins back. "Wives are interesting creatures, aren't they?" He inclines his head, gesturing toward the dance floor.

"They are."

"I met my Giuliana when I was eighteen. We got married a year after. I would have married her the first moment we met, though. I knew she was the one." He smiles wide, takes out a cigarette, and lights up, blowing a ring of smoke toward me.

"Good for you." I look him up and down, sizing him up.

If he's here for a fight, he won't win because although he's the same height as me, he doesn't even come close in muscle.

"Diego, please don't fuck with me. I didn't come here to talk about how lovely the night is, or your wife. So, cut to the chase. You know I hate bullshit."

He laughs. "And there I was trying to be civil with you, my new leader. Maybe trying to make up for the past sins of my father."

I step closer and draw in a deep breath. "You know what, you say sins of your father, but for all I know, you could have been there, too. As far as I'm concerned, you were. You knew about it."

"Isn't that a little farfetched? I have receipts that state I was either in Mexico or Argentina for pretty much the whole time. I knew nothing about your captivity until my father told me a few years ago. I swear to you, amigo, that is the truth."

I press my lips together then blow out a ragged breath. "You know what? It doesn't matter to me one way or the other. The results are still the same."

"For you. I give you credit. You set out to do something, and you did it. Punished us whether we deserve it or not. Just like a Knight. But I lost more than you know."

"In what ways, *amigo*?" I borrow the word and the care-free tone he used to address me.

He inches closer. "Let me let you in on a secret. You see, to everyone else, my father had a terrible accident.

People believe his heart gave out as he was admiring the view of his villa. But they don't know I was with him. I injected him with a solution that causes momentary paralysis and leaves no trace behind after an hour. It was just enough to give him the little push he needed when he fell through the window." He raises his palms as if what he's just confessed is nothing more than a discussion of the weather.

This asshole killed his father, and the psycho is staring back at me with a bright smile on his face.

"You killed him."

"Yeah. My father was a nasty son of a bitch, so I would say we have an enemy in common."

"How so?"

"The cartel was always the goal. We've all wanted it. He was jealous that Santiago created it and rose to power the way he did. My father was having an affair with Esperanza and pulling all the strings in the background, so fuck knows what he did to Santiago. I had my suspicions about that but kept quiet because I didn't want to screw myself over. Then I found out he raped my wife. I wanted the cartel, and I believed I was going to get it, but when I confronted him about what he did to my wife, he took steps to write me out of his will so my cousin would get everything. I wasn't going to allow him to do that to me. The Navarro empire was always supposed to be mine, so I took my vengeance. Except now, *you* have it."

I see where he's coming from. And like any other man who loves his wife and vows to protect her, I do feel something for hearing his was raped by his own father. But that's as far as my sympathy goes.

"You have it, Malik Volkova, and there is no need for it to be so."

"I beg to differ. I chose the mode of punishment for the crimes against me. You should be lucky you get to keep your life."

"It is not luck why I am alive. We both know that."

This is going fucking nowhere. "Like I said before, cut to the motherfucking chase. What do you want?"

He puts the cigarette out. "I have an opium field in Argentina. Check it out. The land itself is worth a few million. The business even more. We have notable buyers we have a good rep with. You can have it if you divorce Gwen and hand back the cartel to us."

If it's one thing I know in life it's this: if an enemy is willing to offer you something of worth for something you have, you should never give what you have away.

Not that I would.

"And what happens to Gwen? She has to marry a man of your choosing whom you can control? And after the cooling period, what will you do to her, then?" I make it sound as if I'm considering it.

"Those are things you don't have to worry about. She is Santiago's daughter. My cousin. I will personally take care of her and make sure I find her a good husband who will look after her for the rest of her life."

He must think I'm an idiot to believe his lying forked tongue.

If Santiago believed for one minute that his daughter was going to be safe with these people, he wouldn't have moved the heavens and earth to keep her a secret.

The translation to what Diego is telling me is, he'll find

some asshole who won't kill Gwen until the time is up. Then they'll kill her because they won't allow her to keep her share of the ownership or inheritance. They'll get everything and my beautiful girl will be nothing but a memory. She'll join the other ghosts in my life.

"No." That one word feels like I just signed my life away, but then again, there was always a target on my back. It was just a matter of when someone would pull the trigger.

"No, Señor? Are you sure?"

"One hundred percent."

"She doesn't belong in our world. You know that, right?"

"Of course, I do. But you think I'm going to hand her over to you?" I raise my brows.

"What if we could promise to ensure she returns to her normal way of life?"

"You need to stop now because I don't believe a word you say."

He feigns innocence, pretending to be hurt by my comment. "That's below the belt."

"I told you no bullshit."

"Okay, well, it was worth a shot." He shrugs, brings his hands together, and pretends to applaud himself. "Next time you see me, I might not be so nice."

"I look forward to that day, friend."

"Just remember, amigo, it's not always good to show devils like me your weakness." He glances back to the dance floor and a shiver laces through my blood, cascading from my head to my feet. "There is always a way to get what you want. You just have to find it."

Dipping his head, he walks away.

I watch him until he's gone.

His visit here must mean whatever plan he's concocting isn't working as quickly as he'd hoped. But that doesn't mean he's not looking for a way, as he said.

I look down at the dance floor and see my girl talking away with Anastasia and Lorelai.

Nothing good can happen from here. I can feel it in my bones, but I can't allow anything to happen to Gwen.

I *won't*.

Even if I die trying to protect her.

Chapter Thirty-Three

Gwen

"I should be in Wilmington next week for the entire week," I tell Dr. Perry.

I'm in my office at Brash, getting ready to go home. Dru is out on the shop floor with Jeanne, who has been coming by to help us set up.

"It's good to hear you'll be here for a while. It will be great for your grandmother to see you."

And me, too. I miss her like crazy. "I'm looking forward to seeing her."

"I know you are. In the meantime, please try not to worry."

"I will."

With everything wrapped up with the cartel and my father's inheritance, it's opened the floor for me to go back to Wilmington and visit Grams.

I can't wait. What's even better is, Malik is going with

me. I know it's because he's being protective. There are things happening in the background he hasn't made me aware of. But it's nice to know he'll be traveling back with me so I can introduce him to Grams.

"She's responding well to the care plan I've placed her on, so everything is as okay as it could be on our end." Dr. Perry sounds pleased, which is always a good sign. "But we can go over any questions you may have when I see you, or please feel free to email me."

"That would be great. I'm just glad Grams is doing okay. Thank you so much for taking such great care of her."

"You are most welcome. It's my duty as a doctor to provide her with the best care, but as a friend, it means a little more than that to me, so rest assured she's in good hands."

"I know she is."

"Okay, see you soon." There's a smile in his voice and I imagine his easy-going presence.

We hang up, and I stare at the phone in my hand for a few minutes thinking of how sad it will be that there's every chance Grams won't recognize me when she sees me. She also won't feel or understand the real depth of knowing I got married.

But it's okay. I have to appreciate what I have.

Even if Grams can't remember me, I still have her. She's still alive, and if Malik is right—which I believe he is—her heart will remember me.

Dru sashays into the office wearing a stunning black cocktail dress. Her bob has been trimmed into a blunt cut with a long fringe that frames her face.

She looks like she's just finished doing a photoshoot for some fashion magazine.

She has a date later. She disappeared to the bathrooms downstairs earlier to get ready. She stops at my desk, gives me a model-like pose and a vibrant smile.

"My God, you look absolutely fabulous." I bring my hands to my cheeks and look her over.

"I thought I'd do myself up a little more for Tony tonight." She beams.

"This is what you call *a little more*? Girl, you look like you're ready for the cover of *Vogue*."

She laughs. "I do my best.

I couldn't agree more, but I don't know how she does it. Dru has the ability to jump through hoops the average woman would find difficult and just make whatever she's doing work. Especially when it comes to men.

She's hardly been in Boston for week, and she's managed to snag a guy—aka Tony, no last name yet—who's impressed her enough to take her out three times. Tonight will be date number four.

"I give you credit."

"Says she who is married."

I bite the inside of my lip. "Okay, we both get some credit."

"I should think so. And look at this place." Excitement bounces between every syllable of her words. "The way things are going, we'll be ready to open the doors in two to three months.

"God, I hope so. Regardless, it's exciting."

"And entirely possible. We have the team in Wilmington working their asses off to make the designs you sent over, and we've outsourced a team here. I see no reason why we can't plan for a grand opening by the beginning of summer."

That gives me goose bumps. "I think you're right. I just keep pinching myself to check if this is real."

"It's real, and it's happening, my friend."

It is happening. It's unfolding day by day right before our eyes. Our plan is to set things up here, then once we're finished, we'll open another branch in Charlotte, New York, and L.A., just like we planned, but by the end of the year.

"Anyway, see you later, girl. I'm not going to keep my man waiting. You mustn't keep yours waiting either."

"I won't. I'll be done in about ten minutes."

"Cool."

"Have fun."

"Oh, you know I will." She winks at me and gives me a mischievous smile, then practically waltzes out of the room with a bounce in her step.

The circumstances of me coming to Boston might not be the best in the world, and the threat of danger is looming over my head, but I'm glad my strange adventure has brought both of us good things we would never have had if not for being here.

And knowing Malik.

This is all him, and when he said he would take care of things, he did. My staff have all been paid at the restaurant, Grams' treatment is all paid for, and then there's this place. And they're all gifts.

From him.

* * *

Ten minutes later, I finish, lock up the office, and head out to the shop floor, where Jeanne has just finished packing away her things. She was working on the shelves today. I wanted them painted blue like the backdrop. We have painters and decorators helping us, but Jeanne insisted on doing this part.

"Ready to go?" she asks.

"Yeah. Thanks for helping out today. This looks great."

Jeanne chuckles. "You know I love any excuse to be creative. I'm also at your service for as long as you need me."

"It's great having you here."

"Happy to help. Let's go, then."

I appreciate her support, but I know her presence here is also Malik's way of keeping an eye out. The guards are always on the premises, inside and out, but I've come to know that he trusts Jeanne more than anybody else on his team.

I turn off the lights and Yuri comes to lock the place up, then we're on our way home.

Before we reach the house, I get a text message from Malik saying:

Meet me on the boardwalk when you get in.

It makes me smile and I wonder what this man has planned for me tonight.

I text back:

Sure. I'll be home in a few minutes.

When we arrive, I drop my things off inside and head to the boardwalk.

Before I even turn the corner at the stone wall separating the garden from the beach, I see Malik at the end of the boardwalk loading a bag onto a large sailboat with magnificent white sails billowing in the wind.

He has another two boats moored on the other side of the boardwalk, but they're both motor yachts I've seen before on my walks out here. The one near Malik is a sailing yacht. The type many of the sailors in Wilmington would use for fishing and boat races.

My steps quicken toward him, and he turns to face me.

He's wearing a fitted white T-shirt and black slacks. I'd be freezing in anything like that. The temperature dropped earlier, so I kept on my jacket. My legs are still a little cold, though, because I'm wearing a wrap over skirt.

When I get closer to Malik, I can't help myself—I skip into his arms and sink into his hard chest as he pulls me in for a kiss.

"Damn it, why do you always taste so fucking good?" he rasps against my lips.

"Maybe because I always want you." Listen to me talk; I stopped holding back days and days ago, and now I'm literally spilling out my heart.

"That's always good." He gives me a grin when he releases me and the moonlight turns his teeth silver.

I look at the yacht and point at it. "Where did this come from?"

"It's old. I was fixing it up along with a few others in the garage."

A normal garage would house a few cars and other vehicles. His has boats, too. I've seen the cars, but there was another section that I haven't seen yet. I'm guessing the boats are there.

"How many boats do you own?"

"Five. This one's special, though. I built it with my uncle when I was sixteen."

My mouth drops, impressed to hear such awesomeness. I've never met anyone who could build a boat before.

"You built this?"

He looks proud. "Yeah. My uncle was a hands-on craftsman. He loved the old Viking ways of doing things, so he made it his duty to learn how to build everything, including boats. He taught me to do the same."

"That's really impressive." I'm deeply fascinated, but I also notice that he's talking about another member of his family apart from his brothers and his father.

It's all a mystery to me and a closed book of wonder just like him.

"Want to go for a ride?" He gives me a wolfish smile.

"When?

"Now."

"Now?" My heartbeat picks up.

"Yeah, now."

"Oh my God, really? But it's so late." I can't imagine going out on the waters at this time. And it's so dark. For a person who can't swim, that makes everything even scarier.

"We'll be fine. I can sail any boat with my eyes closed. In fact, I have." A deep chuckle rumbles in his chest. "The moon and the planets align tonight. We can get the best view at sea."

That sounds mesmerizing. "The moon and the planets?"

"Jupiter and Venus. Look." He points at the clear night sky toward the moon and what looks like two bright stars below it. I can tell they aren't just stars, though, because they look different from the others.

"That's really Jupiter and Venus?"

"Uh-huh, come with me, and we can get a closer look."

He stretches out his hand to take mine. I give it to him, and we both get on the boat.

I shudder when my feet touch the wooden flooring and the boat rocks.

Pushing away my fears, I focus on Malik and the prospect of sharing this adventure with him.

"Hold on here." He places my hand on one of the silver rails on the side of the cockpit, then leaves me to switch on an old-fashioned light and undo the ropes holding the boat moored to the boardwalk.

Malik lets out the main sail, allowing it to capture the wind. A thrill races through me as it puffs out and propels us forward with a force I didn't expect. I've seen this before in Wilmington, and I've always thought it looked intriguing. As if the sails have come alive and are taking their first breath of life.

As apprehensive as I am, being onboard is definitely more exciting.

I hold on tight, watching him with interest to see him in his element outside the world of the Knights.

Moments later, we're adrift. I look back at the boardwalk to see it's far, far away. I'm surprised how quickly we got out to sea. It's barely been a few minutes.

Malik comes back to me and brushes his finger over my cheek. Then he retrieves a handheld telescope from the bag he loaded on and looks through it.

"There we go." He smiles wide, aiming the telescope toward the sky. "Have a look. The brighter one is Jupiter."

He reaches for me and slips an arm around my waist, then holds the telescope out so I can see, too.

Everything instantly looks a hundred times brighter, closer and absolutely stunning.

"Wow," I gasp. "This is amazing."

Jupiter and Venus look like giant balls of diamonds beaming in the sky, and the crescent of the moon is sharper. There are also several bigger stars beside one of the planets.

"I knew you'd like this. The other things you can see are four of Jupiter's moons."

I glance back at him. "This is unreal."

"I know, right? Space is so extensive it makes you wonder about all the things that are out there."

"It feels like a whole other world."

"It is." He nods. "And it just so happens that it's always better when you stargaze from the sea, like the sea captains of old who used the sky as a map."

He lowers the telescope.

"Have you always done this?"

"Always." His face brightens. "I can't remember not doing it. I blame it on my uncle. We used to play pirates whenever he'd come to visit me, which was practically every day. He and my father were close."

"That must have been nice, having them both around."

"It was. My father was strict with all of us boys, so Uncle Leif was the fun adventure guy. I took to him like a house on fire."

I giggle. "I take it he was the one who encouraged you to join the Navy."

"It all began with him, and he set me on the path."

We crest a wave, and I stumble into him, squealing and grabbing his shirt as if I'm going overboard.

Embarrassed, I laugh at my silliness. "I'm so sorry."

"Don't worry about it. Come, let's go sit over there. We'll stay out for a little while until the fog rolls in." He points at the padded leather seated area. "You'll be less scared sitting down."

"That sounds good." It's dark, but I know he can see I've gone pale. It's the anticipation of being out here.

Malik guides me over to sit with him and twists to face me.

"Sorry I'm so squeamish." Nervous laughter falls from my lips. "This is my first boat ride."

"I could have guessed that, but that does surprise me given you come from Wilmington and live right by the boats."

"I know, it's so embarrassing. What's worse is, I also can't swim."

Surprise fills his eyes, and he shakes his head. "No way."

"Yes, unfortunately." I shrug sheepishly, the same way I do when I make that confession. "I can float a little, but that's it."

"Don't worry, I know people who live on islands who can't swim."

"That definitely makes me feel better." I smile.

"I'll teach you to swim." His face brightens at the idea.

"Thank you, but please don't teach me tonight."

"Are you sure?" He leans forward for a moment and presses his nose to mine. "My unit in the Navy believed the best time to learn to swim is at night. You become one with the water because you have to trust it. Trust the waves, trust the current, trust the sea."

"Sure, if you're a fish."

He laughs. It's a real laugh, like he actually found what I

said funny. I've never heard him laugh like that before, and I find myself wanting to tell some kind of joke so I can hear that laugh again. Except, I know that was probably a once-in-a-while opportunity. Hearing that laugh in such a natural way again and so soon would be as rare as seeing a unicorn fall out of the sky.

"Okay, no night swimming, then. How about we schedule some daytime lessons?"

"I'd like that even more."

"Any reason why you don't swim?" He quirks a hard brow.

I press my lips together and think back to when I'd witnessed the cruel hand of the sea and decided water was evil. "I saw someone drown once on the beach near the restaurant. It was an old man who'd dived in to save someone else's child. The current was too strong, and I don't think he was a good swimmer. But I suppose it was instinct that made him jump in. I remember watching the paramedics trying to save him, but they just couldn't."

"That's awful."

"It was. I've never forgotten it either. I was seven years old. Watching death at work like that was almost like a prelude to what awaited me. The year after, everything changed in a massive way."

He holds my gaze, staring deep into my eyes, as if he's looking into my soul. "Death is a force no one can reckon with."

"I know." I look away and gaze out at the shadowy waters ahead of us. "I always worried something was going to happen to my mother. Then it did. I was young, but I felt I was prepared for it. My father, on the other hand, got me the most. I've never been able to accept that he killed himself."

"No one is ever able to do that. We can never know what people are going through when they make that decision."

I return my focus to him. "I've tried thinking that way as I've gotten older and attempted to understand it. Except the warning in my heart will never allow me to accept and respect that's what happened."

"What does the warning tell you?" He searches my eyes.

"That he didn't do it. That someone killed him and made it look like he took his life. It just doesn't make sense that he would leave me alone when he promised he was going to take me to live with him."

Malik studies me intently, as if weighing my words. "The difficult thing about being in our world is, secrets stay buried until they're ready to reveal themselves."

"What if that never happens?"

"Most times, it doesn't. I'm not sure if that's good or bad. To be ignorant, I mean."

"How can it be bad?"

"Because the truth always hurts worse than the lie." His voice holds an air of wisdom that can only come from experience.

From the moment I found out what happened to him to set him on this course, I've been curious and eager for more details. Of course, I got the gist of what happened, but I care about him enough to want the whole story.

I've also realized there was more than just that event that hurt him. *Broke him.*

I'm broken, too, so I spotted the signs practically straightaway.

I want to know what created the monster.

"What truths hurt you more than the lies, Malik?"

His eyes darken dangerously, but the sensuality that's always there whenever he looks at me is still present.

He looks away, and I wonder if that's his way of ending the conversation.

Then he looks back at me, and in the still moonlight, I notice that the guard he usually keeps up isn't there anymore.

The openness I'm witnessing reminds me of a child. He has that lost little boy look. It's so different than the man, and the beast.

"I'm not sure where to begin. I don't know what hurt me more."

"Maybe just start."

He sighs and presses a fist into the seat. "My mother helped kill my father and my uncle. That hurt like nothing else."

My mouth drops. "Oh my God."

"She was in league with Viktor, my older brother. She wanted him to take over the Volkova empire. To do that, she needed my father out of the way. She plotted with people who wanted my uncle gone, too. Everything blew up, and I lost them all within a matter of days." He pauses for a moment then continues. "I will never forgive my mother for what she did, no matter her reasons. She took away two men who meant everything to me. Losing my father and uncle pushed me over the edge. I was barely hanging on anyway because I blamed myself for my old Navy captain's death."

"How can you blame yourself? That sounded like it was an attack."

"It was, but the cartel and whoever the fuck they aligned with were after me. Not him. He got caught in the crossfire trying to save me. To them, he was expendable, worth nothing." His shoulders sag. "I grew up with him and his son, Brian, who was like a brother to me. When Brian died the year before, I promised myself I'd take care of his father. Then when his father died, I promised Brian I'd do what he couldn't and avenge his father's death. All that time I was held captive, revenge was the only thing I wanted to live for. This is where I'm at."

I understand him better now, and my heart grips when I think of what he must have gone through.

"Did you get justice?" What I'm really asking is if taking me was worth it.

He pulls in a deep breath, keeping his eyes fixed to mine, then he shakes his head slowly in reflection.

"I'm not sure if I ever will. That part of me that had to go through it all is still dead inside, and so are they. But..."—he lifts my chin toward him—"maybe I got something else I didn't deserve. Something valuable, something precious, something good."

Me. He means me.

I've never considered myself valuable, precious, or good before. To hear him say such things about me lifts my soul.

As I look at him, I know I'd say similar things about him. He saved me. He's been good to me, and he's been the only man I've ever loved.

Love.

I might never have been in love before, but I know in my heart that I love him without question and without end.

"Maybe I got that, too."

He covers my hand and gives it a gentle squeeze. "No, Gwen. You ended up with a very bad, broken man who's just a shell of the person he used to be."

"Because something happened to you."

"I was born bad. It was encoded in my DNA to be bad, but the things that happened to me created the heartless monster."

I place my hand over his heart and savor the rapid beat. "You're not a monster. I can feel the real you inside alive with every beat of your heart. It's just like mine."

His eyes bore into me, bathing me in fascination and hope.

Malik touches my face and feels over my cheek the way a blind person would if they were trying to commit something to memory with their fingertips, then he lowers his mouth to my lips and gives me a soft kiss that sends spirals of ecstasy through me.

His kiss becomes slow and exploratory, the opposite of the ravishing, possessive ones we're used to. Then he lifts me onto his lap and kisses me harder, more demanding this time, like he's trying to take all of me.

I kiss him with the same eager need.

It's me who pulls at his shirt first to feel the hard muscle pressing against my body, then he whips off my jacket and top in one swoop.

The coldness I felt is replaced with the heat of our lust and his greedy touch.

Those slow passionate kisses become the same, and soon we're naked, our bodies pressed against each other with me bouncing up and down on his cock.

I ride him like I want to possess him, too, but he takes back control, thrusting up into my body to fuck me.

Every thrust and touch leave my body burning with imprints of him onto my soul in a way I know I'll never forget. Not even after death.

It doesn't take long for us to both come. As I do, he catches my face again and holds me even closer, lacing his fingers through my hair.

"You are life, Gwen." His husky voice is filled with awe and compassion. "You fill my dead soul with life."

And he feels like home.

"You make me feel like I could try." He sounds like he means trying for everything. Trying to live. Trying for *us*.

"Then try."

He nods, and my heart sparks with hope, then he kisses me again. And consumes me again.

In my world, under the stars and the aligning planets, the only thing that exists is my husband.

Malik Volkova.

* * *

I flip through the files again, this time taking my time.

This would be my third attempt to go over these invoices. Every time I reach the middle of the stack, I get stuck and have to start all over again because I can't get my head out of the clouds.

Last week, Dru and I set up this filing system so we could keep a check of all our paperwork. As Invoices are the worst for us, I was supposed to sort them by due date so we could keep track of everything.

Normally, I can do things like this with my eyes closed, but my mind is stuck on the wild night I had with Malik. Like a teenage girl who's just gone on her first date with the popular boy she's crushed on all year, I haven't been able to get him out of my mind for longer than two minutes to concentrate.

Today, it's become clearer to me than ever that I'm a woman who's falling deeper in love with her husband. I'm falling for the man who stole me away from my home and forced me to marry him.

That's crazy, right?

Under normal circumstances, the down-to-earth level-headed version of myself would think it was absolutely ludicrous. Like one of these whacked stories you'd hear in the tabloid news.

Yet here I am, thinking of all the ways I can find to stay with my captor.

I don't think I can call it Stockholm Syndrome. How can it be if I wanted him before he took me, and I want to be with him even more now?

Jeanne walks up to the door and gives it a little tap although it's wide open and I'm looking at her.

"Almost done?" she asks.

"Nearly. I think maybe another hour."

She chuckles. "You're gonna get me in trouble with the boss, Miss Lady. It's already well past the time you'd normally leave."

She's right. It's nearly nine. I've been leaving at around six or seven. Dru's already gone, but I allowed her to leave early because she had another date with Tony.

"I promise I'll be done soon." I clasp my hands together, and she laughs.

"Okay. Well, I've finished decorating and painting that whole area. Come up and have a look if you want a little break and some coffee."

A break might be good, and I'm eager to see what she's done. It looked amazing when I last checked. "Give me five minutes, and I'll be up."

"Okay. I'll get the coffee ready. Yuri got us the good stuff."

When she leaves, I set the invoices I've finished to the side and label a Post-it note with instructions on what I need to do next so I can pick up where I left off easily after my break.

As I walk out of the office, a chill from outside hits me. A look to my left shows me the fire escape door has been left open. The guards wouldn't normally do that.

As I'd be freezing later if it stayed open, I divert to close the door.

Just before I reach it, I stop mid-stride when my gaze falls on Jeanne lying on the floor by the stairwell.

There's blood running down her forehead.

"Jeanne!" I rush to her side and check her. She's breathing, but faintly.

I'm about to get up to call Yuri and Vladmir, but something sharp wedges into the side of my neck.

I turn and come face to face with Esperanza smiling down at me as I sink to the floor and whatever the hell she just gave me numbs my body.

"Aww, there, there Princesca," she coos in a sugary voice, her Spanish accent stronger. "It's funny, though, and ironic. I should have known you were Santiago's daughter from the moment I saw you. Seeing you now like this, with desperation in your eyes, I see the resemblance. You look just like your father before he died."

Her words die in my mind just as they begin to process, and I realize what she means. Then darkness covers everything, swallowing me whole.

Chapter Thirty-Four

Malik

I slam my fist into the wall next to me, leaving a crack and bruising my knuckles. The pain that shoots through my fingers is welcomed. It gives me something to feel other than rage.

They took Gwen.

They fucking took my wife and hurt Jeanne.

Diego. He's a dead man when I find him.

But damn me, I left my best men here to make sure shit like this didn't happen, yet it happened anyway.

Fucking shit like that isn't supposed to happen when you have top-notch security.

I don't even know when she got taken.

Yuri called me half an hour ago to drop the news I never wanted to hear, and I rushed straight to the store.

He told me that he discovered Gwen was missing and

Jeanne was hurt when he'd come inside to check what time they were planning to leave.

What he found was Jeanne on the ground, barely conscious, and Gwen gone.

Jeanne's in the hospital now. She maintained she was okay because she wanted to help find Gwen, but I insisted she get herself checked out.

I have my brothers and my men looking for Gwen. I'm going out on the street, too, but I've been here at the store with Leo and a few others from my senior team searching for clues.

Now I'm in Gwen's office again, rewinding the CCTV footage from before the fucking cameras were tampered with. I want to see if I can spot something else I might have missed.

I start the recording and watch with my focus keen on the screen, but I see nothing more than I did before. The cameras only picked up the alleyway where the bins are kept and Vladmir waiting at the back. That's it. Then nothing. I don't fucking know if Vladmir walked away.

Or fuck, if he helped the enemy.

I hate casting suspicion on my own, but this isn't normal. And I have to face the fact that my guards practically had the place surrounded, so the only thing I can think is that someone helped them.

Someone who works for me. A fucking rat.

I assume the said person switched off the cameras so Diego's people could have slipped in. I think they entered through the shop next door, which is an empty space for purchase like this was.

Other than my assumptions, which could be wrong, I have nothing.

Not a damn thing, and in my heart, I know it's not going to be easy to find Gwen.

Footsteps echo in the hallway, tearing me away from the screen when the footage ends.

I whip around hoping it's someone coming to tell me they've found Gwen, but I'm met with a tearful Dru, who rushes in and flies into my arms.

She cries against my chest, and I feel so much worse.

I haven't really spoken to Dru since I got her to Boston, but I know she trusted me enough to come here, and more importantly, she trusts me to take care of her best friend. I feel worse than shit that I'm supposed to be the man I am and I couldn't even do that.

When Dru pulls away, she can barely catch her breath. She places a hand to her chest to calm herself down.

"I just got the news," she stutters in garbled words. "I left Gwen here to go on a date. I feel so terrible. I should have stayed. God, I should have. If I'd known she was in so much danger, I *would* have stayed."

I rest my hands on her shoulders and try to act like I'm not about to lose my shit and tear the city apart to find my girl.

"It's better that you weren't here." I never shared with her the parts of this saga that involve Diego and the Navarros, but I assume Gwen did.

"No. I should have been here, Malik. Maybe I could have done something. Like call the police or raise some alarm or call you."

The latter of those options would have been the only

ones she had. The police would have been defenseless against Diego's men. And they would have probably killed her. Jeanne got off lightly with a blow to the head that could have killed her. My guess is she wasn't killed because they didn't get the chance to do so.

"I need you to go back to your hotel. I'll double the guards."

"No, I need to help look for Gwen."

"Trust me, Dru, it's going to be better if I know you're safe. I'm heading right into the heart of danger. I can't let anything happen to you. Gwen would never forgive me."

More tears come and she nods. "Okay. Please get her back, Malik. Please. She's family to me. Wherever she is, I know she'll be scared. She'll be terrified."

And I won't be there to protect her. The thought spikes my blood, and I feel like ripping off my skin.

"Please don't worry. I'll search every corner of the earth until I find her," I promise.

"Thank you."

I don't bother to tell her that I might not have to do that, or anything at all for the matter. My silence makes me feel like a hypocrite.

The next part of this plan is for the enemy to come knocking at my door and put an end to my existence. My death frees Gwen to marry someone else of their choosing.

I can't let that happen. I can't go to the other side, leaving my girl to suffer at the hands of her enemies.

* * *

"Any news?" Jeanne asks when I walk into the kitchen at home.

"No." The word sounds hollow, just like my heart.

It's nearly two in the morning.

I've looked everywhere I could for Gwen. We've tried all the places Diego would go to in Boston and interrogated his allies. And still, we have nothing.

Jeanne looks shaken. She has a bandage on her head where she was struck, and her skin is pale.

She's sitting at the breakfast table with a cup in front of her and her hands shaking.

I move toward her and plant a kiss on her forehead.

"I'm sorry you had to go through that," I say. "I never wanted to put you in that kind of danger."

A tear runs down her cheek. "It's not your fault. I feel awful and useless because I can't help. I don't even know who hit me. I went to close the fire escape door because it was open. I thought one of the guys left it that way. I didn't think. I should have suspected that something was up, but I didn't. Now they have her."

"Jeanne, please don't blame yourself. If there's anyone to blame, it's me."

There's no way I could excuse my sins in this. No matter which way anyone looks at this, it's all my fault. All of it.

Gwen shouldn't even know me.

"How can it be your fault? You took every step necessary to make sure this didn't happen."

"You know I'm right. This isn't just about last night. It's everything."

She shuts down because she can't argue with that fact.

Jeanne was the first person I ever shared my plans with

when I discovered Santiago had a secret daughter. I knew she didn't agree with my evil scheme, but like always, she went along with whatever she's told to do. All members of our staff know you never defy the Volkovas when you've been given an order.

Jeanne places a hand on mine. "You'll find her. I know you will. I have faith."

"Thank you for believing in me."

"Always."

"Go get some sleep. I'll let you know if anything changes."

She dips her head and leaves.

I head to my office, where I stay until morning, doing all I can to hack every camera in the city to see if I can pick up Gwen. Desmier is contacting our allies in South America who can keep a look out for us and get information a little quicker than we can if Diego takes Gwen to Mexico.

At seven, I summon Yuri and Vladmir, whom I benched yesterday until I knew what to do with them.

I had Zakh and Leo check out their whereabouts throughout yesterday and dig deep into their correspondence over the past few weeks.

Nothing untoward came back, but that doesn't mean shit. More and more I suspect someone screwed me over to take Gwen.

Zakh and Leo arrived with them a few minutes ago. We're in my office now.

Zakh is sitting next to me, while Leo is standing in the corner. Yuri and Vladmir are standing before us.

I have guards outside waiting for backup in case we need it.

Yuri looks at me first. Judging from the crease in his forehead, I know he must have guessed he and Vladmir look like they're working for the other side.

"Before you even say anything, boss, please remember who we are," he says, but those words mean fuck all to me. "Our loyalty has always been to you and your family."

"You know I suspect you two, don't you?" I get straight to the point.

"Of course." Vladmir sits straighter and gives me a hard stare. "And whoever did this knew that's exactly what you would do. After all, we were there. Your wife got taken on our watch."

"She did, and there's no trace of any clues."

"And things have been fucked for us to even try to find any," Zakh adds, staring them both down.

He's like me when it comes to giving people chances. We don't.

"Boss, we told you what happened," Yuri jumps back in. "Vlad and I were at our usual posts, guarding the place and keeping watch. Neither of us noticed any unusual activity. Not a fucking thing until I found that door open and Jeanne on the ground. I checked out the place, looking for Gwen. When we couldn't find her, we called you. That is what happened."

Vladmir nods, agreeing with Yuri. "That is exactly how it happened."

I look at Yuri and Vladmir, finding it difficult to conceive that either of them could have betrayed me. They've been my fucking guards since I was born and obviously with the Knights long before that.

But I can't rule it out. I also don't want to get it wrong and kill them when they could be telling the truth.

"Give me your keys and passes," I demand, and they frown.

"Seriously, Malik?" Vladmir speaks to me, using my first name the way he used to when I was a boy.

"Yes. You will go with Leo to the Bratva compound and stay there until this is sorted out."

Jail. I'm practically sentencing them to jail. But it beats death.

Without any further arguments, the two of them hand over their security passes and keys to Volkova Inc. and my property.

"It wasn't us, just know that." Yuri dips his head and stands.

Vladmir stands, too, and Leo leads them out, glancing back at me with apprehension in his eyes, suggesting he doesn't want to do this.

They leave, and I look at Zakh, who's already swiveled his chair around to face me.

"They didn't do it," he states.

"I don't fucking know. I just want her back."

"Malik—"

"Zakh, I want my wife back." I'm an octave down from shouting. "I want Gwen back. I don't care who I offend by trying my fucking best to find her. I just want her back, so please don't tell me how wrong I am when I already know I'm fucking everything up by the minute and that this whole plan is fucked up."

He sighs, then tips his head, agreeing. "Okay, calm

down. We'll keep looking. That's all we can do. Everyone is on this. It's all hands on deck. We'll find her."

"I have to, Zakh."

I have to find her. Then I have to fix things in whatever way fixing the situation means.

Chapter Thirty-Five

Gwen

I'm still surrounded by darkness. Except now I'm awake and sitting on a cold dank floor.

Once again, I've been taken captive. I'm a prisoner. But Esperanza and whoever helped her take me are not like Malik.

When I thought he was cold and uncaring, I was so very wrong.

This is what cold and uncaring is. Me in darkness with a chain attached to my ankle, holding me to the wall.

I'm being kept in a room. A small, small room. That much I know.

It feels like I'm in the basement of wherever I am, and maybe the more fitting description of this room is a dungeon. The feel of it reminds me of watching those TV shows about prisoners of the past like in Robin Hood days.

Judging from the funky smell of death emanating from

the corner to my right, I think something died in here, too, or there are remnants of rotten flesh. There are also rats or some sort of vermin. I've heard them scuttling across the floor, nibbling and squeaking.

I try to keep moving. Alternating between sitting and standing so they don't come near me. But I don't know if that will continue to work and for how long.

I know wherever I am must be absolutely filthy, so I would have opted to keep standing, but I've been awake for what feels like several hours.

Standing was exhausting, and I woke to a sharp pain scattering through my head. Most likely from whatever drug Esperanza gave me to knock me out.

The pain hasn't left me. Nor has it distracted my mind from going over that powerful morsel of information Esperanza gave me before I blacked out.

That it must have been her who killed my father.

I haven't even allowed myself to think about how the hell I was so easily taken from the store with all of Malik's guards surrounding the place. I've just been thinking about my father and what Esperanza did to him.

Growing up, I've always hated that my instincts were right. I've even gone against them many times to try and prove that they could be wrong. Every time, I get screwed.

Like now, although that information is screwing with me in a different way.

I feel like I should have known Esperanza had something to do with Dad's death. But I didn't factor her in because she loved my father. Or so we were led to believe.

Maybe she did. Maybe that was true.

Maybe he approached her with the subject of taking care of me after Mom died and she flipped out.

Whatever it was, something definitely happened to push her to do it.

Until I'm told what that was, I'm left to wonder what the hell happened.

And what could have been. Learning my father didn't kill himself has opened my mind to all the things that could have changed for me. For us.

Dad meant what he said about taking care of me. Knowing that means so much to the little girl inside me who's still waiting for her father to find her. To come home.

He meant it, and everything he planned for us was taken away by a cruel, evil woman who wanted to destroy us.

She's won now because she has me.

As I've had no contact with anyone since waking, I don't know who is part of this plot, but I'm sure Diego is undoubtedly in line with this.

Another bout of time passes by until I hear the shuffle of footsteps in the distance that draws closer and closer.

A soft light comes on, and I can see around me. The room is as small as I guessed it to be. But God, I was better off in the dark. This can only be described as some sort of torture chamber. I have to stifle the urge to scream.

There's blood splashed over the gray walls which have chains hanging from them, and spikes. And in the corner where the smell is emanating from, there's a blob of gunk dried up on the floor. A few rats and mice scatter underneath the wall. I hold my breath and my thumping heart.

The door ahead of me has a little glass window. I knew there was a door there from earlier when I tried to walk around and see how far I could move with the chains on my ankle.

A man's face suddenly appears through it, and he smiles when he sees me looking on.

God, what is this now?

Something is happening.

I stand, not wanting to place myself in a more vulnerable position.

The door opens, and Esperanza waltzes in with two guards behind her. The scent of her perfume wafts in too when she moves closer to me, dulling the stink.

"Leave us," she orders in that hoarse voice that reminds me of a cross between a frog and a hundred-pack-a-day smoker who's been at it for years.

She flicks a perfectly manicured fingernail at the door, and the guards leave, closing the door behind them.

Esperanza looks me up and down like she's sizing me up for a fight.

I'm sure I could take her if it came to that, but not chained up like this and with her guards outside.

A sardonic smile spreads across her red-painted lips, and the humor spreads into her dark unfathomable eyes.

"Look at you. Imagine this." She laughs. "I can't believe I spent all those long years looking for you, and here you are, chained to a wall without daddy dearest to protect you, or your Knight."

"You are one nasty piece of work." I know my comeback is lame, but I have to say something.

"I am. You have to be in my line of work, where people take advantage of you. You are weak if you don't fight back."

"Is that what you were thinking when you killed my father?"

"Partly. By then I felt he deserved to die. I had no love left for him and no remorse when I watched him take his last breath."

My heart aches at hearing this. "I thought you loved him. We couldn't have him because he was bound to you. How could you shoot him in the way you did?"

"That part was his brother. I was far cleverer. I'm a biochemist, so when I kill you, I'll make you suffer in ways you only hear about in nightmares. I swapped his allergy medication for something that would screw with his brain and dissolve it from the inside out. Manolo shot him just to make it look more legit."

This woman is pure evil. I can see it in her eyes and oozing from her just like the scent of that sickly sweet perfume.

"Why? Why then?" That is the question I'm desperate to get an answer for. "Why did you kill him then? Why not before?"

She releases a short sigh and gives me a haughty glare from under her thick lashes. "Two reasons. Two things happened. First, he'd extinguished the threat I held over him to stop him from leaving me. He managed to find his enemy and kill him. So, my threat to expose Santiago for killing his enemy's brother, no matter how accidental it was, was worth nothing. He came to me with divorce papers again. It was at that moment that he found me in bed with his brother."

"Wow, I guess you had to have them both?"

"It wasn't that as such. Santiago didn't love me, but his brother showed me some sort of love. Even if he didn't love me either, he didn't plan to leave me in the wind with nothing the way your father did." She smirks and brings her hands together. "That brings me to the second thing."

"Which is?" My voice is demanding and imbued with a confidence I don't really feel.

"Santiago changing his will. Before he found out his brother was sleeping with me, he trusted him like none other. Not enough to tell him about the identity of his mistress or the secret child he had with her, but he trusted him with the business. Until then." She shifts her weight from one foot to the next, and her heels scratch against the floor. "Manolo was always second-in-command to him. The agreement was if anything were to ever happen to Santiago, Manolo would take over. The revised will's existence fucked everything up. Santiago intended to rule by himself, but we put a stop to that. We couldn't change the will because it was tied legally to the pharmaceutical company, but what we had was better than nothing. It was unfortunate that Manolo died, but Diego planned to ensure I was never without. Then Malik Volkova happened, and he unearthed the one thing that could destroy us."

"Me." I stare back at her feeling the cold of her Arctic stare chilling my bones.

"You. Gwen."

Now I have the answers, my body feels like it might turn inside out and never stop until there's nothing left of me.

"Weeks ago, when we learned about you, I looked up your mother and her death. Things made more sense." Esperanza inclines her head. "The *timing* made sense of when Santiago set everything up the way he did, and so quickly. As well as his grief he never shared with anyone.

The love of his life died, and he was going to take care of his little girl."

"You took that away from me."

"You talk to me as if I care. As if I should. As if I'm supposed to feel some compassion for you. Don't you realize you shouldn't even exist?"

Those words sting my soul because I've thought them before.

"You are a bastard child who should have been killed," she spits. "You and your pathetic mother, who thought it was okay to spread her legs wide open for a married man. My entire life was created to marry that man, and I hated that I loved him."

"I apologize for my mother and father's infidelity, but it has nothing to do with me. I exist, and I'm a person."

"Of course, spoken like a true princess." Her mocking tone is full of venom. "I might have been able to accept your father's betrayal because I couldn't have children, but he just didn't love me. The harder I worked to find out who you and your mother were and where you were, the harder it became to find you, the more I realized how much he loved you both. He invested his life trying to protect you. In our world, most men don't want their families to be involved in the business, but he was protecting you from us. From *me*."

The breath in my lungs stills, like it's been switched off, and my heart aches even more for my father.

Malik was right, like with most things. He said the truth hurts worse than the lies. It does, and there's nothing I can do about it.

I want to take the time my soul needs to grieve and process this, but the real question now is, what next?

Right now, I'm in a situation my father died trying to protect me from. No one who loved me would have wanted to see me here helpless like this and at the mercy of my father's wife.

"What are you going to do with me now?" I hate how feeble my voice sounds.

Her face lights up as if she was just served a million dollars on a silver platter.

"We're flying back to Mexico later. Then we'll kill that meddling husband of yours. After that, we'll figure out the other details, like replacing your husband and planning your death when we no longer need you alive. That is what is happening next."

I knew death was in the cards, but hearing it spoken shakes me to the core.

Of course, I worry for myself, but when I think of Malik dying, it feels like the world around me will turn to ashes and fade away.

I can't let him die.

What can I do, though?

Look at me.

"You won't get away with this." I sound pathetic, and that's exactly what Esperanza thinks of me.

"My dear, I already have. As powerful as your Knight is, we can match whatever technology he has to cover ourselves and stop him from finding you. By the time Malik Volkova gets to you, he'll be dead."

"You are one evil bitch."

"And I take that as the highest compliment." She flashes pearly white teeth.

"I'll come back for you later."

She walks out and slams the door.

The light stays on, so I rush forward and look out through the glass window on the door.

Esperanza is still out there giving the guards instructions to watch me and not give me any food or water.

What a fucking bitch.

I'm about to back away but stop when a tall man with graying hair walks up to her and I realize I've seen him somewhere before.

"Make sure you kill Malik Volkova this time," he orders in a gruff voice.

"Don't worry. We will." Esperanza chuckles. "We will not make the same mistake twice."

"Good."

When he turns to walk back the way he came and I see his face properly, I remember where it was I saw him and my head spins. For a moment, I wonder if I'm seeing things. Or if I've gotten my memories mixed up.

But no. I don't have anything mixed up.

The man I'm looking at is definitely who I think it is. His picture hung on Malik's wall in the secret room.

He is Captain Davison.

He's alive.

Chapter Thirty-Six

Gwen

Make sure you kill Malik Volkova this time.

Those words are still ringing through my mind, and the deepest shock has consumed me.

It was hours ago now that I saw Captain Davison alive in the flesh speaking those wicked words.

Hours again of waiting. But this time, I had so much more to think about.

Captain Davison is alive. And not just alive—he's working with the same people who were responsible for capturing Malik and torturing him.

The same people who Malik swore vengeance on for killing Captain Davison.

I don't know what the fuck is going on.

None of it makes sense. I get why *I'm* here and why I'm needed. But him?

Jesus Christ, Malik thought he died. He blamed himself and told me he lived to seek revenge.

But his ghost is alive and wants him dead.

Why?

Since Esperanza left, my mind has flit between trying to process the shock of everything I've learned and praying that by some miracle, I can come up with an escape plan.

Obviously, there's something more at work here, and I need to find a way out.

Even if my sole goal is to warn Malik and give him another truth that's going to hurt worse than the lie.

I've been hoping Esperanza would return and get me, then I could see exactly where I am and who's around me. But time has joined my enemies.

I wait for what feels like another forever, until finally the door latch moves and it opens.

I want to be relieved because it's something different than the nothingness and angst of wondering when they'll be back. But this is where the next chapter begins and I'm going in blind.

The guard from earlier, who was smiling at me, walks in and jingles the keys before me.

"Hola, chica." He looks at my breasts and continues speaking in Spanish. I don't need to understand the language to know he said something filthy that would disgust me.

"Give me your hands," he orders in broken English.

I want to slap the smile off his face but instead, I give him my hands.

He secures a pair of handcuffs around my wrists then crouches down to undo the chain around my ankle.

It comes free, and I realize the skin has chafed from rubbing against the metal.

I want to kick him and run out of here, but this guy is as big as Malik's guards. He would knock me to the ground and do God knows what else to me.

"Move." He grabs my shoulders and shoves me forward. "Keep walking one foot in front of the other."

I do as I'm told, walking on trembling legs.

He takes my elbow, digs his fingers into my skin, and leads me out to a corridor with the same stone flooring as the room I was kept in.

There are dim overhead lights running down the whole passage until a brighter light meets us at the end and we walk up a set of stairs which lead to carpeted floors and wallpapered walls showing pictures of the English countryside and fox hunting.

This has to be someone's house or a hotel of sorts.

We get onto an elevator that takes us up to the third floor, and when we step out, I lean more toward the idea that this is a house.

It has that homely vibe to it although I haven't seen anyone walking around.

It's the décor.

The guard stops in front of a bedroom door and opens it.

Esperanza is inside talking on her phone.

She signals him to leave me to the side, and he does, then he walks over to her, hands her the keys for the cuffs, and leaves us.

Esperanza continues talking on the phone heartily, as if I'm not here. She swaps between speaking Spanish and English.

If I didn't know any better, I would swear she looked normal. She probably is to everyone else, until you peel away the layers of her skin and find the horns and dragon scales.

"Yes, yes. We'll close the deal on Monday. The representative from the FDA will be coming by to discuss the next steps for the drug approval." She smiles away.

When she turns around, looking away from me, I take the opportunity to assess my new surroundings.

The room is exquisitely decorated. Everything from the gold-framed paintings on the wall to the little ornaments doting around the room could be categorized as collectable works of art.

A wooden four-poster bed sits in the center with a chandelier hanging over it, and there's an archway leading out to the balcony. Since I can see a set of chairs out there, I consider that the area might be big. But we're up on the third floor.

Nevertheless, could that be a way to get out?

If I managed to flee through there, what would await me?

More guards with guns?

It doesn't matter. I have to be brave enough to try.

The first thing I need to do is find a way out.

Esperanza has a phone and the keys to my cuffs, two things that could help me immensely.

If I can get those, I can call Malik.

"Okay, see you very soon," Esperanza chimes. "I'm flying back in an hour."

She hangs up and slips the phone into her jacket pocket. She keeps the keys out, looping her finger through the ring.

When she returns her gaze to me, she resumes her normal self, becoming the devil again.

"You need to bathe and get out of those stinking clothes." She wrinkles her nose in disgust. "There's no way you are going on my jet smelling like shit."

"Maybe if you didn't put me in a room that smelled like *shit*, I'd smell different."

She chuckles without humor. "No, my dear, come to think of it, I believe that stink is your natural scent. You came here smelling of it. It's the sort you have when you shouldn't exist. It's like the world has rejected you and cursed you."

When she steps closer, I glance at the lamp on the desk on my right.

It has a soapstone base. If I could get my hands on it, I could use it as a weapon.

I look back at her quickly, so she doesn't follow my gaze.

"Say whatever you want." I lift my chin higher.

"I will, of course." She walks to the dressing table and takes out a set of clothes from the drawer. It's a T-shirt and yoga pants. "You will wear this."

"Am I going to get my hands free to put them on?"

She smirks. "Obviously. I'm sure I don't have to tell you not to try any funny business. The guard is just outside the room, and the grounds are surrounded. I need you alive, but you don't have to be conscious or functional. Not dead, in whatever capacity that means, will work."

Not dead. "Like Captain Davison?"

Realization forms in her eyes. "My dear Gwen, you see too much. There are things at work you don't understand. Debts to settle that can never be monetized."

"I see."

She grabs my hands and plugs the key into the lock.

This is my chance. Everything I do next has to be

executed with precision. If I get it wrong, everything will go to hell.

The lock comes undone with a quick snap, and my hands are free.

"Go into—"

I don't let her finish. I throw a punch straight into her face, grab the handcuffs out of her hands, and hit her with them.

She yelps, and I worry the guard will have heard that, but he doesn't rush in.

"You little bitch. You'll pay for that." She lunges at me, but I'm already going for the lamp.

Raw instinct takes over, and I grab it from the table, then slap Esperanza straight in her head as hard as I can when she reaches me. I hit her again and

she doesn't make a sound as she drops to the ground. Not even a whimper.

In an instant, blood seeps from her head, running down her face.

The way she looks... like she's just shut down. I think I killed her.

Oh God... I think she's dead.

I took a life.

The thought feels dirty in my mind; I want to rip it out and purify my brain with the strongest detergent.

I look down at the woman who committed so much evil. She killed my father, and she was the reason we could never be together.

She's captured now, but if I continue to stand here, I'm going to miss out on this opportunity. Malik will die.

That thought moves me. I crouch down and grab Esperanza's phone, then I rush out to the balcony, which is as big as it looked from inside.

No guards have come yet. I'm hoping like hell that means no one heard anything. I also don't think there are any cameras in the room.

That doesn't mean I have forever. Someone is going to check soon if we're supposed to be heading to Mexico in an hour.

I dial Malik's number and hide behind the alcove with the potted plants. It will be a good hiding space until it's not.

Malik answers on the second ring, and I savor that voice.

"Malik, it's me," I blurt.

"Oh, Jesus, Gwen where are you, baby?"

"I don't know. I managed to... I think I killed Esperanza." I pant. "I think I killed her."

"Baby, please don't worry about that. Are you safe?"

"No." I hold back the tears threatening to pour out of me. "I'm in a bedroom. There are guards outside. It's only a matter of time before someone comes in. We were supposed to fly to Mexico in an hour."

"Okay, listen to me carefully. I'm going to track your location. Stay on the line for one minute. You're going to stay where you are and keep the phone on. As long as you have it with you, I'll find you. Okay?"

"Okay."

The line goes quiet for a minute, but I can hear him breathing.

"I got you, Gwen. You're about thirty minutes away from me, but I'm sending whoever is closest. I'm still coming, though."

"Okay, thank you."

"Baby, you don't have to thank me. Stay hidden, okay? We're on our way."

"Malik..." Suddenly ,everything stills around me, and I feel like I'm going to fall apart from the inside out.

"Yes, baby?"

"I'm scared."

"Don't be. Just think of me. Think of me. I will always protect you. I'm on my way."

"Okay." I nod, and we hang up.

I stare at the phone in my hands then press it to my heart as I crouch down lower, making myself small among the plants. The mixture of wide leaves and the shadows of the night conceals me.

I wait with hope in my heart. I'm sure fifteen minutes must go by before I hear the door open.

Heavy footsteps track in, followed by voices.

It's the guards. They found Esperanza. They're speaking Spanish, but I heard them say her name.

Next, a cluster of footsteps fills the room, along with hurried voices.

They're looking for me.

"Where is she?" That's Diego. I recognize his voice.

He starts shouting in Spanish, coming closer to where I am. He walks out onto the balcony, and my heart jumps in my throat when I see him. But then gunshots ripple through the air. The sound is coming from the ground below.

Diego looks over the balcony and swears.

"Damn it! Fucking hell." He moves away, and the next thing I hear is the same cascade of footsteps rushing away from the room.

The gunshots continue, along with the cries of dying men, sounding like I've been pulled into a warzone.

It seems to go on forever. Then everything goes still. A quiet that settles over the air that makes me scared to breathe.

My chest rises and falls with the weight of fear clutching at my lungs.

Suddenly, more footsteps approach. They track straight toward me, and I swear I experience the meaning of true happiness when my gaze falls onto my love.

I stand, and he sees me, then he rushes toward me, and I do the same to him.

Malik folds me into his arms, holding me like he'll never let me go, and I pray he won't.

"Gwen," he speaks into my hair. "You are with me now."

"You found me." I'm so happy to see him my soul is leaping with joy. But then the image of Captain Davison pops right into my mind and I remember this isn't over yet.

Chapter Thirty-Seven

Malik

We just got home.

My men led a full-on attack that barely gave Diego's men time to retaliate or escape.

I wanted to kill Diego, but the motherfucker managed to escape. The house they were staying at is owned by a black-market collector who normally remains off the grid like most friends of the Navarros.

I got him in for questioning, but I don't expect to get much out of him.

It's fine. I will find another way to kill Diego. At least the other half of the brains behind his operation is dead.

Gwen killed Esperanza. I haven't told her, Esperanza is dead yet.

I know she feels bad enough as it is. There will be time enough to tell her. Right now, I can't believe I have her back.

When we walk into the foyer, Jeanne is the first to greet

us, followed by Kelly, who has been here taking extra care of Jeanne.

I called Dru when we were on the way back, so I assume she'll be on her way over here soon.

"Oh my God." Jeanne takes Gwen into her arms and hugs her tightly. "I'm so glad you're home."

Jeanne has been a wreck the entire time.

"Me too."

"Please let me make you something, anything," Kelly offers.

"Thanks. I need a moment to speak to Malik first," Gwen says. She's been on edge from the moment I got her back.

"Gwen, you should have something to eat," I insist.

"It can wait. I really need to speak to you in private."

The first thing I think is that something more happened to her. Something worse.

"Okay. Come, let's go into the living room."

I slip an arm around her and guide her away, glancing back at Jeanne, who has gone paler, and Kelly, who looks even more worried than previously.

The moment I close the door behind us, I turn Gwen to face me and cup her cheeks.

"They didn't touch you inappropriately, did they?" God, if they did, I don't know what the fuck I would do.

"No, it's not that. I saw something. Someone."

I narrow my eyes, wondering why this is relevant. "Who?"

"Captain Davison."

My hands drop to my sides, then my chest caves, filling

with shock unlike anything I've ever experienced. It clamps a tight fist around my heart.

Surely, I couldn't have heard her right. What she said is entirely impossible. "Say that again."

"Captain Davison. He's alive, Malik. I saw him talking to Esperanza."

"Gwen, that's impossible. It must have been someone who looked like him. I watched him die."

"No, Malik. No. He's not dead, and it's really him. I remembered him from the pictures on your wall."

Disbelief has me shaking my head. I pull out my phone and search through my pictures to find the last one of Jim before he died. It was taken weeks before Brian was killed in the car crash. We were still in Afghanistan.

I show Gwen the picture. "This is him. Is this the man you saw?"

"Yes. That is definitely the same person I saw. Malik, something really strange is going on. He said to Esperanza she should make sure you die this time."

The ache in my chest is unbearable. My heart is exploding, and tendrils of blood-curdling rage engulf me.

What the fuck is Gwen saying to me?

What did she just say?

Make sure I die this time.

I bring a heavy hand to my head, feeling like I'm going to shatter into a million pieces.

Gwen presses dainty fingers to my chest. "Malik, he was working with them."

Yeah, he was fucking working with them.

He set me up.

* * *

"They're going to try and get to Gwen again," Desmier points out, glancing at Zakh.

We've gathered in my office to discuss the next steps. It's just past nine.

All I've been able to do is call my brothers to fill them in on the recent developments about Jim Davison.

My fucking brain is numb, so I haven't been much help with anything else besides looking like I'm alive.

I take a drag on my rollup and allow the potent mixture to work its way into my mind.

I needed something strong to help me move past the shit and try to focus.

Gwen is upstairs waiting for Dru to arrive, and we're here trying to figure this out.

"Malik," Zakh prods.

"I want them all dead. Every last one of them. But leave Jim Davison to me."

I look at Zach, and I can tell from the wealth of concern in his eyes that he's worried about me. He thinks I'm gonna go crazy. That I'll flip out and lose my mind worse than I did when they got me back after the attack.

I might. I just might this time. He knew Jim. Desmier didn't, so Zakh will know exactly how I must feel.

This is the worst type of betrayal, possibly worse than anything I've experienced, and I want to know why.

The man I knew and revered my entire life would never do this to me. My entire mission was to avenge him, but he's alive and rubbing shoulders with my enemies.

I just wish I knew why.

Why did this happen?

What the fuck did I do to Jim for him to want me dead?

What the fuck could have happened for him to have staged his death?

"We need to get more men on the street to figure out where they are," Desmier states. "They're still grounded as far as we know. I haven't had any record of anything going out to Mexico. But we still need to be mindful."

"Yes. Diego seems to have many friends in high places. But so do we," I sneer. "If he's in the air, we also have time."

Even if they took a private jet, we still have a few hours if they're heading to Mexico.

Diego and his entourage only have about an hour and a half head start on us. I think he fled the scene the moment he realized he was vastly outnumbered.

"We also have people waiting in Mexico to get to him if need be, providing he lands where we can reach him." Zakh nods.

"I think he's still in Boston. I think he's still here hiding out somewhere." I can feel it in my gut. I have what Diego wants in the palms of my hands. He's not going to leave to go anywhere without Gwen. That wouldn't make any sense.

"Then we'll find him."

"We will."

"Hey." Desmier reaches across the desk and taps my knuckles. "Maybe we should call it a night. It's been a long day for everyone."

I nod. "Yeah. Let's leave it for tonight."

"You got your wife back."

"Yes." I nod.

"We'll come by first thing in the morning," Zakh promises, standing.

Just then a message comes through on my phone. I pull it out from my back pocket, and my temper instantly flares when I see the message is from Diego.

On the home screen, the preview is showing that he sent an image.

I click into the message wondering what the hell this could be.

The moment the message opens and I see what it is, my blood turns to ice.

It's a picture of Dru.

Dru with a gag around her mouth and her face stained with tears, blood, and bruises. I nearly break the phone when I read the caption beneath.

I want Gwen. I'll exchange for her friend. Call me by midnight, or the girl is dead.

Jesus Christ, this isn't fucking happening.

I ball my hand into a tight fist, digging my fingernails into my palm as I look from Zach to Desmier, who are both staring at me.

"What's happened?" Desmier asks.

I open my mouth to answer him, but the fucking words don't come. How do I say that the situation just got so much worse?

How do I tell Gwen that her best friend has been taken and her life is in danger?

Chapter Thirty-Eight

Gwen

From the moment I see the ghostly pale look on Malik's face, I know something is wrong. Something more.

He walks into the bedroom, closes the door behind him, and pulls in a deep, haggard sigh, looking even paler, if possible.

Of course, the news of Captain Davison's betrayal cut him deeply, as anyone could imagine.

Earlier, just as I tried to talk to him, his brothers came by. I thought it would help him more to speak to them, so I came up here to clean off and eat the sandwiches Jeanne and Kelly made me while I waited for Dru to arrive.

I look him over. The dullness in his eyes is different to how he looked when I dropped the bomb on him.

What else could have happened now?

And so soon?

"Hi." I shuffle against the stack of pillows behind me on the bed and sit up straighter, waiting for him to fill me in on what's happening, but a few awkward seconds of silence pass by and he says nothing. "Has something else happened?"

"Yes...Gwen." The regret in his tone suggests I'm right. Something else has happened, but when I think of all the shit I've been through since yesterday, I can't imagine what else could have gone wrong.

"What's going on, Malik?" I swivel my legs around, so my feet are on the floor.

"We have to talk."

Hearing that only exacerbates my anxiety.

"What's happened?"

"Dru's been taken."

I jump off the bed and nearly split out of my skin.

"What?" My voice is so high I'm surprised the windows don't shatter. "No. Please no. Tell me it's not true."

Oh, Dru.

"I'm doing everything I can to find out where Diego has taken her. I've got everybody out on the streets trying to find her."

My heart is beating so fast I can't catch my breath and my head feels like it's going to explode.

"What happened to the guards? Dru had at least four bodyguards." She told me Malik had sent extra men.

"They're dead."

My hand flies to my mouth. "Oh my God. All of them?"

"Yes. They were found in their car dead."

Every muscle in my body goes rigid and fear prickles my scalp like a colony of ants scattering over a nest.

"How? How did that happen? How did *I* even get taken? It was so easy." I'm the last to cast blame or doubt, but this is too much now and too obvious. "Somebody is working with them."

"I know."

"Who is it?"

"I don't know yet, but rest assured they will be dealt with. Right now, I'm trying to focus on finding Dru."

Dru.

Tears tip over my lids and stream down my cheeks.

Dru was taken. This shouldn't have happened to her. We shouldn't even be having this conversation with her name in it.

Diego has kidnapped Dru.

But... he doesn't want her. She's nothing to do with him and is of no benefit to him other than leverage, because he wants me.

That's the only reason he would do this and hopefully to exchange.

"This is because of me. Diego wants me. Has he contacted you?"

Malik is silent. "Baby, please allow me to handle this."

"Malik, don't do this to me. Don't shut me out. This is my best friend we're talking about. I need to know what's happening."

He stares back at me for a few moments then bites down hard on his back teeth before balling his hand at his side.

"He has contacted me. He wants you in exchange for Dru. I have until midnight to get back to him."

"What happens at midnight if you don't?" My voice is so small, clothed in fear, it's like I've barely spoken.

"I'm not going to allow anything to happen to her."

My eyes snap wide. I know the answer even if he won't give it. Diego will kill Dru. That's what's going to happen at midnight if Malik doesn't get in touch.

There's only one way out of this. Just one way. The way it all began.

With me.

"I'm going to him." I nod with determination.

"No." The vein in the side of his neck pulses. "That is out of the question."

"It's the only way and the only answer to fix this."

"And you think he's going to let Dru go just because you're there?" His eyes bore into me.

"I'm praying he will. The other option is no option. In two hours, it's going to be midnight. What if you don't find them? Esperanza told me they have their ways of staying hidden."

As badass as the Knights are, they aren't gods, and I have to acknowledge that if I hadn't called Malik, I would be on my way to Mexico now.

"I will find a way. We have technology, too, and I've called in all the stops."

"Dru shouldn't even be a part of this. This has nothing to do with her and everything to do with me. I don't think you can fight this. I don't know what the hell I'd do if something happened to Dru."

He rests his hands on my shoulders and stares into my eyes. "Please allow me to do what I'm doing. I can't let you go. I can't. So, there has to be another way. I'm going back downstairs to see what my hackers have found so far. I'll let you know what's going on as soon as something comes up."

He releases my shoulders and backs away, then he leaves the room with sagging shoulders, his head dipped slightly as if the worst has already happened.

When the door swings shut, I collapse back onto the bed and break down, crying with everything inside me, my tears growing stronger with every second that passes.

My phone buzzes with a text, and I grab it from the nightstand.

It's from an unknown number.

I open the message and read the text. It says:

Hello, cousin,

Well done on your grand escape. It was very impressive, and I'm sure you took some joy in killing Esperanza.

We both know your husband isn't going to let you go, so how about we take care of this problem ourselves?

If you want to come to me willingly, I promise you I will hand over your friend unharmed. Let me know how that sounds to you.

I should say I am going to kill her at midnight if you don't reply.

Diego.

Earlier, I felt dirty and inhuman for what I did to Esperanza, but now I feel nothing hearing I killed her. As far as I'm concerned that was for my father.

Now the only emotions I feel now are rage and terror. I know Malik won't let me go, and now I know in my heart that it's not because of some ulterior motive.

It's because of me. Because he wants me. When I look at him, I see love.

I may never hear those three words many dream of, but I see it in him, and that's what I will hold in my heart.

I'll keep it there and pray that something else can be worked out, so he doesn't die. When I was in that cell, I wanted to warn him. I've done that. He has a sufficient heads-up to save himself.

Malik has his legion of Knights and allies in the Bratva and other criminal organizations.

All Dru has is me. She's always come through for me.

Now it's my turn to do the same for her.

I'm already typing back my reply to Diego before my brain can fully process what I'm doing.

I text back:

I will agree to come to you in exchange for my friend unharmed and your promise not to kill Malik. You have to find another way to get the cartel back.

I cross my fingers and toes he'll agree.

The blue dots jump below my message, and Diego's reply appears.

You have my word. Your friend will not be harmed, and I won't kill your husband. My little undercover assistant will knock on your door in one minute. You are to go with them. They will bring you straight to me, and we'll make the exchange. You are not to alert anyone, or the deal is off. Understood?

. . .

My breath stalls at the thought of meeting the traitor in our midst, but I bridle my emotions and type back: *Yes.*

I stand, tamping down the terror churning in my soul, and wait for exactly one minute, holding my breath.

I release it when there's a knock on the door, but I still feel like I'm suspended in time.

"Come in," I call out, my voice shaking.

In that split second as the door starts to open, all sorts of questions fly through my mind:

Who is this person?

How could they betray Malik?

How could they betray me?

What are they getting out of this deal with Diego?

What if Malik catches us?

Can he see us now?

What if his other staff come by and intervene?

I disqualify that last question when the door opens fully, and I see Jeanne standing before me.

Suddenly, things that didn't make sense start to.

Judging from the guilty look on her face, I know she's not here to intervene.

She's Diego's undercover assistant.

Chapter Thirty-Nine

Gwen

It's perfect, really.

All so perfect.

Malik is a man who doesn't trust easily.

Many who tell you they trust no one will still have one or two people they keep close to their hearts.

That is what happened here.

This is how you get to a powerful man like Malik Volkova and his people. It's not coming to his home with guns and threats.

It's this. You find the person they trust more than anything and anyone, and you get them to betray your target.

No one would ever suspect Jeanne.

No one would suspect her for helping the enemy take me because she was attacked herself.

And no one would suspect Jeanne for helping the enemy take Dru because as she served me sandwiches and watched me talking to my friend, all the woman showed was sympathy.

No one is suspecting her being in my room now because she's always going backward and forward. We spend hours talking and sharing life experiences.

No one would simply suspect Jeanne just because she's Jeanne.

The Jeanne who took care of me. The Jeanne who taught me about this world of the Knights.

She's the Jeanne who is always just Jeanne, like a blanket of comfort you hold close at night when you need reassurance to help you fall asleep.

She is the traitor.

The perfect, perfect traitor

"You." My voice is broken with regret.

"Yes." Her tone is apologetic.

"You did this to us? They hurt you?"

"They wanted to make it look legit. They didn't kill me because they needed me to keep watch."

That should have been the first clue.

People like Diego will kill you just for looking at him the wrong way. It should have been clear that the only reason he kept Jeanne alive was because he still needed her.

"Why? Why would you do this?" I want to shout at her and tear the skin off her face I trusted because she helped me not feel lost.

Tears slip down her cheeks and shimmer against the light. "They have my granddaughter. My Zoe."

A steel weight drops in my stomach, and I flounder in conflict. Jeanne is the traitor, but her little granddaughter was her price.

"When did they take her?" I bring my hands together.

Jeanne lifts one trembling hand to her face and wipes away more tears that pour out of her like a broken tap.

"A week after Malik came back from Mexico."

"My God, that was weeks ago."

Jeanne nods and tries to catch her breath. "Yes. I've been trying to hold it together, hoping against hope that a way would be found to resolve this. They threatened to sell her on the black market if I didn't help them, and they said they would kill her if I told Malik. I couldn't let them hurt her. She's just a child. My family are besides themselves with worry, but I just want to die. I'm so sorry."

"It's okay." None of this is okay, but it is what it is, and I have to find my way through it.

"They said they'd give her back if I can get you to them."

"How are you going to get me off the property?"

"I know the secret passages leading off the grounds. I have the password for the surveillance down there. Once I switch it off, we can get off the property without being seen. My car is on the other side."

It's all been planned out.

"Okay, let's go." Those words recruit me into the list of people who have betrayed Malik's trust. At this moment, I'm no different because he expected me to trust him to take care of this. Part of me wonders if he would be able to figure out where Dru is, and that's most likely why Diego is making the deal directly with me. But I can't take the chance and play with Dru's life.

"I'm so sorry, Gwen. I didn't mean for any of this to happen."

I don't know what to answer and say, so I keep quiet and pray to whomever will listen for help.

* * *

Ten minutes later, we're on the road heading off to meet Diego—*my doom.*

We got off the property so smoothly and quickly I had to wonder if it was all really happening.

It was only when we got in Jeanne's car that I snapped out of my reverie.

We drive in silence, something usual for us. I've never been around her and kept this quiet. Even when I didn't know her, we were talkative, as if we'd known each other for a lifetime.

Thirty minutes go by until we approach the opened gates of what must be a private airport.

There's a private jet off in the distance and two warehouse hangars right by the river.

The sight of the plane has my insides in a twist as I wonder what will happen to me once I'm in Mexico.

We drive right in, and men with machine guns approach, along with Diego.

One of his men is holding Dru. She's tied up and gagged, and she's been hurt.

Jeanne stops the car beside Diego, and when he sees me sitting next to her, he claps, cheering loudly like he's at a national football game and his favorite team just scored a touchdown.

"Well done," he praises Jeanne. "If in doubt, always go

with the help. Look at this superstar here. Step out, my dear."

Jeanne glances at me then opens the door. The door on my side is opened by one of Diego's guards. I step out, praying like hell things go the way I need them to go and Dru is freed.

I straighten and look at my friend, who is shaking with terror.

Will they allow her to leave with Jeanne?

Is that what they're going to do while we fly to Mexico?

I switch my focus to Diego when his guard grabs my arm.

"I'm here now. Let her go." I imbue my voice with strength I'm summoning from deep within.

"Of course. I'm just going to ensure you both held up your end of the deal first," Diego answers, displaying the wealth of his arrogance. "Search them."

"I don't have anything on me." I shake my head.

"*Search them*," Diego repeats with emphasis on each syllable, directing his words at me to show we're going to be searched regardless of what I say.

"Arms stretched out," the guard orders me.

I do as I'm told, stretching out my arms. He inspects me with a leery smile, taking pleasure in feeling up my breasts then patting me down.

By the time he's finished with me, my stomach churns with scorching bile.

The guard nods at Diego after he's looked at my phone and scanned over it with a device that looks like a pricing gun.

Jeanne is searched, too, except with less sneaky sexual

harassment ploys, but when the guard searching her looks at her phone and scans it, he shouts something to Diego.

Jeanne glances at me wide-eyed. She seems to understand Spanish just fine.

"It seems I spoke too soon," Diego barks. "You switched on your emergency tracker. Now all the Knights know where we are."

When I notice that she hasn't denied his accusation, that terror brewing within me rises like a pressure cooker.

"I'm not a traitor," Jeanne stutters. "Malik should be just behind me, and he will deal with you."

Hope lifts my heart for all of two seconds. But in those brief moments, three things happen. First, my heart leaps at the thought that Jeanne has helped us and Malik should be on the way. She provided a way for Malik to find us.

The next thing that hits me is the gravity of what Jeanne just did. She can't save her granddaughter now, and Diego will find some way to punish us.

Before my brain gets the chance to process any of that, Diego snarls, whips out his gun, and shoots Jeanne in her chest.

"No!" I scream.

I lunge forward to go to Jeanne, but I'm held back by the guards.

Jeanne drops to the ground screaming with pain.

"So shall it be." Diego laughs like a madman and looks down at Jeanne. "This is fine. Let Malik Volkova come. Killing his ass is the easiest and best option, so let's kill two fucking birds with one stone. His trusted assistant can be the first breadcrumb in the trap."

God, what's going to happen now?

Chapter Forty

Malik

I drive onto the grounds of the private airport where Jeanne's tracker has led me.

I have an entourage of men, along with my brothers who are in the car with me. We're ready for war.

Never underestimate the enemy...

That's one of the first things we're taught as Knights.

I've always prided myself on following such teachings, but tonight, I'm guilty of being human.

Did I ever suspect Jeanne?

Of course, I did.

I'm not a fool.

It would have been foolish of me not to suspect her when all arrows pointed in her direction. I just didn't want to believe it.

Sometimes, the thing that makes sense is what doesn't.

It's the parts of the shit that don't add up because it's staring you in the face like a wolf in sheep's clothing.

My first clue was that she wasn't killed when Gwen was taken.

All the while, as I sat in my office, sentencing my men to the outer limits, Jeanne was on my mind.

It wasn't just her not being killed, though, that triggered my suspicion. It was how she looked during the entire time.

That aside, Jeanne was the perfect person to deliver Judas' kiss on my cheek. She has all the passwords. She can walk around like a ghost on and off my property and other places without being seen. She had the passwords to Gwen's store surveillance, so she knew when to turn off the cameras.

Most of all, being in my home and working as my custodian, being close to the Volkova family all made her the perfect candidate to betray me.

I just can't pinpoint when she started playing devil's advocate for the other side.

I don't fully know what's going on right now, but I got the notification of the emergency tracking alarm. All members of staff who work for the Knights use it when in danger and in need of backup. The message goes out to everyone. When I realized it was Jeanne's and saw she was missing, I went upstairs to find Gwen.

Realizing she was missing, too, and suspecting Jeanne pushed me to fill in the blanks and do the math.

Then I knew like Jim, Jeanne had stabbed me in the heart.

My blood heats when I spot Jeanne's car ahead.

I pull up next to it, but when I see her lying on the

ground in a pool of blood, I jump out of the car and panic propels me to her side.

Betrayal or not, I didn't want this for her.

In the moonlight, her pale skin makes her look like a ghost, but to my surprise, she moves. Zakh and Desmier join me, staring down at Jeanne's bloody form.

"Jeanne." I look her over, and my heart squeezes when I notice the wound in her chest. "Guys, call an ambulance," I blurt, but Desmier is already dialing 911.

"See if you can wake her," Zakh says.

I scoop her up and hold her. "Jeanne."

She opens her eyes and blinks several times, but it looks like it takes her great effort. "Trap. It's a... trap." Her voice is weak and barely there. "Diego discovered that I set off the alarm. They're hiding, waiting for you. They have Gwen and Dru in the hangar. I'm so sorry for what I did, Malik."

"Let's talk about that later. We're going to get you to the hospital."

"Please wait. I have to tell you why I betrayed you." She coughs blood, and my chest seizes. "They took my Zoe."

Fuck. I knew there had to be more to this because it would take a lot for Jeanne to betray me the way she has. Now I understand why, but I wish she could have found a way to come to me. "Do you have any information about where they're keeping her?"

"No." Tears slide out of her eyes. "Diego threatened to sell her if I didn't help him. I'm so sorry, Malik. I didn't know what to do. I ... also didn't know about Captain Davison until tonight. When I saw things were getting out of hand, I had to do something to fix it. I'm... I'm..."

The words fade in her throat, and her eyes close.

"Jeanne, no. Please."

Leo walks up to me with two of his men.

"You guys go with the rest of men to get Gwen and Dru," he says, taking charge. "We'll take Jeanne away from here and wait for the ambulance to arrive, then we'll join you."

"Yes, let's do that." Desmier nods.

Leo picks Jeanne up and carries her to his car, then I watch him drive back the way we came. I pray that wasn't the last time I got to see Jeanne alive.

Forcing myself to focus, I look back at Desmier and Zakh then at the two gigantic hangers in the distance by the river.

A jet is parked on the landing strip, looking like it was getting ready to leave.

That's not going to happen tonight.

"Let's go," I declare, seething from deep within.

We move toward the closest hangar. The doors are already open, and there's a plane inside.

There are about a hundred of us here with all sorts of skills to end this once and for all. I'm not going to allow Diego to get away with what he's done.

The instant we step inside the hangar, bullets start flying and men emerge from their hiding places.

Zakh and I take cover behind a stone pillar while Desmier does the same across from us.

We don't get time to think before more bullets rain down around us. This is crazy, but we knew we were going into this blind, so we just have to conjure our natural battle skills.

"Look," Zakh says, pointing ahead of me.

I look. When I see Diego standing on the balcony across from us with Jim Davison holding a gun to Gwen's head, a crimson haze of rage surrounds my vision and unrelenting fury boils my blood.

Diego shoots at me, but he can't get a clear shot from where he is.

I steal a moment to look at Jim. He's looking at me, too.

My brain can't comprehend this and won't accept it's real. But it is, and right now, I don't have time for my brain to catch up.

They have Gwen, but really, they want me.

"That's where I need to go," I tell Zakh.

"I'll cover you. We move on three."

Zakh counts, and we run out. He shoots the guys in front of us, and I do the same behind.

He covers me until I reach the stairs, then we get separated while he deals with a bunch of guys who jump him.

I turn back to help him, but he waves me off.

"Go. I got this."

Seeing he can handle himself when he takes down three guys, I keep going.

By the time I reach the balcony where Diego, Jim and Gwen were standing, I see them heading out the exit door at the end of the platform. I'm sure this is another trap. They want to lure me out to somewhere we can either fight or Diego can get a good shot at my head.

I follow, going through the exit which leads to another set of stairs that looks like it goes up to the roof.

I take that, too, and see I'm right.

As soon as I step onto the roof, a force that feels like a fifty-ton truck slams into me.

It's Diego.

The force of him crashing into me sends us both to the ground, and we drop our guns.

He manages to land a fist in my face, but that's all I allow. I do the same to him, knocking him back enough to get him off me.

"Don't think I can't take you, Malik Volkova." He sounds like a wild animal caught in a snare.

"Come on, then, let's see you try."

He comes at me again, and I have to give him credit. He's not exactly muscular, but he can fight. Fight dirty like they do in the streets where you don't get any formal training. But I can do the same and more.

I batter him with my fists, and he still keeps coming. Until he can't.

I spot the moment when he realizes he's not going to beat me. It's in his eyes.

At that moment, his gaze darts to the guns near us on the ground, and I know he realizes that's his only way out.

He's close to the guns, so if he gets one of them, he would have that chance.

Diego dodges my punch, and instead of coming back at me with a counterattack, he lunges across and grabs the gun.

I follow him, doing the same. But I don't reach for my gun. I grab my knife from the sheath on my side and plunge it into his neck just as he is about to cock the hammer on the gun.

The fool doesn't realize what's happened until blood spurts from his neck.

His eyes go wide with disbelief. It's as if he really thought he would kill me.

"Not today, amigo." I shake my head. "Or any other."

I slice the knife right across his neck, nearly separating his head from his body. He's dead before his body hits the floor.

I don't spare him another glance.

That was just round one.

Round two just commenced because there is Jim, standing by the edge of the roof with that gun at my love's head.

He must have been behind the column. That's why I couldn't see him before.

I grab my gun and rise to my feet, never taking my eyes off him.

In my periphery I catch sight of Gwen, crying and shaking against the gag around her mouth. My heart wants me to run to her and hold her so I can tell her I will never let anything happen to her, but I can't do any of those things until I get her away from a man I didn't know was my enemy.

"Hello, old friend," Jim greets me, taking hold of Gwen's arm.

"Do not use that term with me. I am not your friend."

"I suppose not."

It's strange hearing him talk when I remember being told about his funeral. Just the other week I visited his grave.

I wonder who they buried, and who's in that grave. Maybe it's empty.

It also makes me wonder who else is in on this plot.

"Where have you been all this time, Jim?"

"South America. It turns out to be quite the place to go to when you want to stay off the grid. It does help, too, when you work with people like the Navarros."

Motherfucker. "Give me my wife." Enough talking about shit. As badly as I want answers, I need Gwen safe first. "Give her to me."

"No. I'm not going to do that."

"Because you want the cartel?" This is absurd.

"No. I don't care about the cartel. That was Diego's gig. All I wanted was for you to suffer. You haven't suffered nearly enough yet. Not the way I have."

Now I have to know why this man hates me so much. "What happened, Jim? What the hell happened to you? What the fuck did I do to you? Tell me. I think I should know."

"You were the reason Brian died."

His words are like a gunshot to my heart. It pierces into me, then the shrapnel finishes me off by shattering my nerves.

"*Me*?" I give him a narrowed look. "How? Brian died in a car crash. How the fuck is that my fault?"

"He was run off the road when he was leaving your house. Your father's enemies came after you, but they mistook him for you."

"What?" I can't fucking believe what I'm hearing.

"A foolish but honest mistake as you looked so similar. Remember how people used to say you could have been twins? That's what happened that day. They thought Brian was you. When he died, the reports came back showing that the break wire in his car had been cut. I knew then he was murdered, and I didn't stop until I tracked down his killers. I got the truth out of them before I killed them. But then I realized the problem wasn't just them. It was you."

I stare back at him stunned into a stupor of silence. All

this time, I never knew more blood had been spilled because of me.

Brian's blood.

He died because of me.

My God, I've been completely mistaken.

"Why didn't you just tell me what happened?" I stutter.

He shakes his head and rubs the barrel of the gun along Gwen's temple. "The time for talking had passed. Just looking at you enraged me because it should have been you who died." He's shouting now. "You, Malik. It should have been your father who buried you. It should have been him who tracked down your killers. It should have been... it just fucking should have been you. Yet here you are, still alive while my son never stood a chance."

"I'm sorry." I am. I wouldn't say so otherwise. I am sorry it wasn't me. Brian didn't deserve to die in place of me.

"Keep your fucking sorrys. I could have accepted if my boy had died at war fulfilling his duties, or even if it truly was a car crash. But not what happened. A mistake in identity. I was always against you joining the Navy because I worried about what *could* happen. I thought your father's enemies would use it as an advantage to get to you. That's exactly what they did when a deal went wrong and your father pissed off the wrong people."

"I would never have known that."

"It doesn't matter. It happened anyway, and your family should have factored in the dangers of bringing your world to ours. But you all think you're gods and you can take whatever you want." His eyes blaze like a feral animal's. "I sought my revenge on you. I wanted you dead, but I wanted you to suffer first. When Diego's father found out what I was doing, he approached me with an offer of ten million dollars and a plan to take you. He didn't want you to ruin his billion-dollar business plans with your investigation. The Navarros saw an opportunity when they met me and offered me the same. We both took what was mutually beneficial to the other. The only downside was faking my death."

The truth is like venom in my soul. Poisonous and deadly, waiting to consume me.

"Why didn't they kill me? They had me for nearly a year."

"I wanted them to torture you and break you down bit by bit until there was nothing left. I wanted you to feel my pain for losing my son. I wanted you to beg for death, but I'm told you didn't. Instead, you survived to avenge me. Look at us now."

"Yeah, look at us. What happens next, Jim?"

He gives me a sadistic smile. "She dies while you watch."

"No."

Gwen shudders against him. I step forward, freezing when he cocks the hammer on the gun.

"Yes. It seems like the perfect punishment for you. Brian never got to have a wife or a life. And here's the thing—I don't care what happens to me now."

Blind panic pulses through my brain and every nerve in my body. How the fuck am I going to get Gwen out of this situation alive? I barely have seconds to come up with a plan to save her.

"Jim, let's talk about this. You can't think this is right. She's an innocent. She has nothing to do with us. Why don't you just let her go and kill me? That's what you want, isn't it?"

He laughs. "I did until I saw the way you looked at your wife and realized death still wasn't enough."

"*Malik, I don't have a clear shot of Captain Davison, but I'm going to provide a distraction.*" That's Zakh's voice in my earpiece on the communicator.

Hearing his voice gives me some hope.

"This is wrong." I try to keep Jim talking until Zakh gives me the distraction.

"Fuck you, you—"

Suddenly, a round of bullets hits the floor near Jim. It gives me that split second of an opening to do something.

I shoot him right in his heart, the place he was supposed to have been shot during the attack in Uzbekistan. Except this time, *this* bullet will kill him.

Jim drops his gun, and Gwen makes a move to run toward me, but before she can take one step, Jim wraps his arms around her and pulls her back to him.

Everything crushes inside me as I watch them both fall off the roof, going over the side into the dark abyss below.

Chapter Forty-One

Malik

Gwen went over the side.

No, no, nooo.

The terror of watching Gwen falling catapults me forward, and I almost run off the roof in an attempt to save her.

I barely manage to stop myself from plunging into the river below, but it's like I'm still going. My hand is still stretched out trying to reach her, and my cry of anguish is still clinging to the wind.

Gwen went over the side. I couldn't save her.

I couldn't stop her from falling.

That fucking fall must have at least been forty feet, and I don't know how deep the river goes. Or what's down there. There could be rocks, or it could have been too shallow to swallow the fall.

I don't know if there's even a chance that she could have

survived.

No. I can't stand here thinking shit like that.

Love pushes the thought out of my mind and fuels my body with determination. I can't give up. I have to try and save her.

I race back the way I came, practically leaping across the roof.

"I saw them fall!" Zakh shouts in my ear when I reach the stairs. "I'm heading there now."

Fuck. Thank God. "Zakh, she's tied up and can't swim."

"I'm getting in the water now."

The battle is still going on inside the hangar when I reach down there, but I manage to get past the gunfire and run outside.

I use every ounce of strength I have to run as fast as humanly possible, but it's taking too long.

I'm taking too long.

Minutes later, I reach the riverbank. My sense of hope awakens when I see Zakh emerging from the dark waters with Gwen in his arms, but there's blood seeping from her head.

"She hit her head," Zakh calls out. Blood covers his shirt, too.

He gets out of the water and sets Gwen down on the grass. When I join them, I pull out my pocketknife to cut away the gag from her mouth and hands.

I check her vitals. Terror fills me again when I notice Gwen's not breathing.

"She's not breathing, Zakh." I can't remember the last

time I sounded so panicked and afraid. "She's not fucking breathing."

"I'll call the ambulance."

While he does that, I start mouth-to-mouth resuscitation.

I try to calculate how long she must have been in the water. It had to be around five minutes. Maybe a little longer.

The minutes are amplified by the fact that she can't swim, and she couldn't even try to with her hands tied up. The gag on her mouth would have let the water in instantly, so it would have happened quickly.

With every rescue breath I give her, I pray it will bring her back to me.

But it doesn't.

Like a doll, she's motionless in my arms.

The world fades into the background, and the shadow of death draws near. I'd be the one to sense him first. After all, the Grim Reaper and I are one and the same being.

But still, I can't give up.

I won't.

I don't, but it's the hardest thing in the world to focus on what to do when Gwen isn't breathing.

When I start CPR, I promise on my soul that if I get her back, I'll do right by her this time. I'll do whatever I need to do to ensure she gets everything she ever wanted in life, including a chance to just live and be herself.

Gwen St. James.

Not Gwen Volkova. The woman I turned her into.

The angels must smile down at me because as I have that thought, she coughs up the water. It spurts from her mouth and her eyes flutter.

She's breathing again. Praise God. I expect her to wake up and see her beautiful green eyes staring back at me, but she doesn't.

She's remains unconscious.

* * *

Two hours later, I'm sitting by Gwen's bedside at the Massachusetts General Hospital, holding her hand.

The doctors have finished taking care of her and have allowed me to see her.

Aside from a few broken ribs, Gwen is in a coma. The blow to her head was significant.

The doctors have said the only thing that can be done now is to wait for her to wake up on her own.

No one knows when that will be.

Jeanne is here, too, but still in surgery. I've been told to prepare for the worst.

In all honesty, I know the same rings true for Gwen because there's only so much anyone can do if she doesn't wake up.

I remember years ago, after the showdown with my mother and Viktor, Desmier got shot trying to save his wife. He was in a coma for weeks, and there came a point where we didn't know if he was going to make it, but he pulled through.

I always believed it was his love for Anastasia that brought him back. As if he fought death just to see her again.

I'm hoping Gwen will do the same. If not for me then for the people around her who she knows need her alive.

But most of all, I'm selfish. I want her to fight death to come back for me.

I stare down at her beautiful face marred with bruises but still so beautiful. Just like her soul.

Gwen is a lover. She cares for people, putting them first above herself. That quality shines through even now, making me love her even more.

It shouldn't have come to this for me to accept the depth of that love, and now I feel like I'm too late.

Footsteps tear my eyes away from her face.

It's Zakh. Desmier was here earlier then went off to check in with Jeanne's doctors.

He looks from me to Gwen with hope. I shake my head, and he moves closer.

"I'm sorry." He speaks respectfully low.

"There wasn't any more that we could have done."

"No, I don't think there was." He pulls in a breath. "Dru is staying with us. I figured she'd need support. We also managed to get Zoe back. Leo was able to track her down."

"That's good. And a relief. Was Jim Davison found?"

"Yes. This time, he's truly dead."

I haven't told anyone the truth about him yet, but I will. "I'll fill you in on him later. Right now, I need to thank you for saving her."

God knows what would have happened if Zakh didn't get to Gwen when he did, and he jumped into the river to save her without any hesitation.

I couldn't have gotten her or retrieved her in time.

For a start, the fucking river is dark. By the time I would have located the emergency kit and lights, then find her, it would have been too late.

She would have been under water for too long and suffered more severe brain damage.

"You know you don't have to thank me for that."

"I do, because I could have lost her for good. The way it looks now, I... still could."

He rests his hand on my shoulder. "You can't think like that. You have to have faith that she'll pull through."

"I'm trying. I just don't know if I have any right to getting her back when all I did was ruin her life."

"It wasn't all bad, Malik."

"But it was mostly bad. Remember when we were in Wilmington, and you asked me if I couldn't just accept that Manolo's death was enough? I should have at least thought about it. There were several moments when I had the power to change this course of destiny, but I didn't. Everything I did was fucking selfish. Now look at her."

He gives my shoulder a gentle squeeze. "Think positive, Malik. We all look back with regret when things don't work out. But think of the positive."

"I'll try."

* * *

The next two weeks go by, and Gwen remains the same. I'm with her every day and mostly all night. I've also been helping Dru where I can and liaising with Dr. Perry about Gwen's grandmother's care. Last week was the week when we would have been in Wilmington.

I was hoping that maybe Gwen would pull through at the prospect of seeing her grandmother.

Jeanne woke up after her surgery but has been under

supervision and on a lot of medication.

This morning, the doctors called me to let me know she was up and about, so I'm going to see her now.

When I reach her room, I notice the door is open.

Jeanne is sitting in a wheelchair, gazing out the window at the falling rain.

She looks at me when I walk in. This is the most lucid I've seen her since the accident.

"Hi," she says in a weak voice.

"Hey. Look at you sitting up." I walk toward her and plant a kiss on her forehead as if nothing has happened between us.

She seems surprised by the gesture.

"I hate hospitals, but I was trying to move around a little more so I could visit Gwen. How is she?"

"The same."

Her eyes dims on hearing that. "I'm sorry."

"Yeah, me too. How are you doing?"

This is the most we've said to each other since she came out of surgery.

"I'll be okay. I'll be in here for another two weeks then rehab. Other than that, I'm okay."

"Looks like you'll be away for a while." I haven't thought about us and what I'm going to do about her working for me. I understand why she did what she did, but it doesn't change the fact that she betrayed me.

"Yeah. Thank you for getting Zoe back for me. My entire family is indebted to you. I don't know what I would have done if anything happened to her. But by choosing to do what I did, I betrayed that sweet little boy I watched grow into a man, who used to trust me with his life."

I stare back at her wanting to continue this conversation but being mindful that she's barely been out of her sickbed for a day. I don't want to stress her out.

"Perhaps it's best if we have this conversation another time. You're still very weak."

"And guilt is eating me alive."

"Jeanne, you were shot." My voice rises more than I want it to. "You were shot. No matter what you did, you nearly died. That takes precedent over everything." Because I dragged her into this mess, too. Like dominos falling against each other, everything I did had a rippling effect.

"But it doesn't. I know what my job is. I've worked for your family for decades. I know the danger. I'm aware of what can happen. But I broke the one term of my contract that was the most important—breaking trust. And with that said, I'll make it easier for you to fire me because I know I can't go back to work for you."

Our eyes lock. I want to say that she's wrong. I want to tell her that we can forget this and move on, but I can't do either of those things. Trusting the people I work with keeps me and the people who depend on me alive.

Jeanne broke that trust. If she were anyone else, she would have been killed, if not by me then under the Knights' law.

I should be quick to agree with her, but I don't know if I could be without her, especially since she came through for me in the end. She provided a way for me to find Diego quicker than I would have, therefore getting to both Gwen and Dru faster. For as skilled as I am with all the resources at my fingertips, I lacked time that night in a big way. Time was my enemy again.

"Maybe we could meet somewhere in the middle," I suggest.

She reaches out and takes my hand, searches my eyes, and shakes her head. "I don't know if I can. You do realize what could have happened because of me."

"Yes."

"I tried my best to alert you, but it just wasn't possible. And even if I thought of something, I was terrified of what they'd do to Zoe. At the airport, I took a gamble I knew I'd get punished for, but I hoped something would work out."

"So, you gave me a chance," I fill in. "Jeanne, my life has just turned to shit. I don't think I can lose you yet. If you're ready to retire because it's all too much for you, then no one can fault you. I would be selfish to stop you. But if it's not that, then let's go with you gave me a chance. Can we do that?"

I feel some sense of relief when she nods. "We can do that."

"Thank you."

She ruffles my hair like she used to when I was a boy and smiles. "Gwen has to pull through, Malik. She loves you. She will come back because of that."

"I hope so."

* * *

The following Saturday, I visit Gwen with flowers and Sebastian, who looks excited to see Gwen.

He barks then whimpers when he realizes she's not moving.

I set him down next to me while I sit at her bedside, and

I read from the poetry book I saw her reading in the library at home.

Night comes, and I stare at her lying there still in her deep slumber.

It's nearly time to go, but I can't bring myself to leave her yet and spend another night like this.

If Gwen is still in a coma by the end of next week, it will be a month. The doctors are talking about different things now. Things like she might eventually become brain dead, and if that happens, there are decisions to consider that I don't want to think about.

I'm still holding on to hope.

I stare at her and decide on one last poem, then I'll go. I pick one of her favorites by Elizabeth Barrett Browning.

"How do I love thee? Let me count the ways. I love thee to the depth and breadth and height my soul can reach, when feeling out of sight for the ends of being and ideal grace. I love thee to the level of every day's. Most quiet need, by sun and candle-light..." I pause for a moment then continue reciting the poem.

I don't need to read from the book anymore. The words come from my heart.

When I finish and stare at her, something wet drops onto my lap. It's water. A teardrop. Coming from me.

I didn't know that was possible, but it shows even the devil can cry when he's in love and he can't help the love of his life.

Suddenly, Sebastian starts barking loudly. I speak in Russian, telling him to stop and soothe him by stroking the top of his head.

"I thought I told you to stop talking to my dog in Russian," comes a soft but groggy voice.

I've gotten so used to not hearing anyone else speaking around me when I'm in here that the voice throws me, until I realize it's Gwen.

I look at her hoping like hell I didn't just imagine hearing her. My soul lifts when I see her moving her head from side to side.

I move closer, and she opens her eyes to look at me.

My God, she's awake. She's actually awake.

"Malik." She says my name with fervency and relief.

"Oh my God, Gwen, you're awake." I press my forehead to hers and relish the warmth of her skin.

Her fingers flutter over my chin, and I look at her.

"What happened?"

"Terrible things."

She swipes a finger over my cheek. "Baby, you're crying."

Baby...

She's never called me that before. I like it. I could listen to her call me baby forever.

"I'm okay," I assure her.

"I dreamt I was lost, and I knew that if I found you, I'd be okay. I found you now."

I take her hand and kiss the tops.

"I got you."

I press her hand to my heart and savor the moment, because I know what I have to do next.

I have to let her go. It's the first right thing I've done in years.

I have to let her go and set her free.

Free from me.

Chapter Forty-Two

Gwen

An entire month has passed since I woke from my coma. Two of those weeks were spent in the hospital and the last at home with Malik.

With the three weeks that I was completely out of action, it's been a total of seven weeks.

I know I came close to death. The thought is terrifying.

Everyone has been milling around me offering their support. Dru has barely left my side, and I've even seen Jeanne several times. Every visit displayed the sorrow she felt for the part she played in my injury.

I forgave her a long time ago, but I know going forward, things have changed.

Then there's Malik.

He's been a class all on his own. Just like always.

I know he's happy to have me back and has gone above and beyond to take the greatest care of me. Like Dru, he's barely left me to do anything, but I can tell something's not quite right. I know it's completely crazy to think that given all we've been through because, of course, things are still a mess.

His old Navy captain he was seeking justice for came back from the dead, and Malik found out everything he believed was a lie. That was enough to mess him up.

I remember Captain Davison recounting the details of how his son died and why he sought vengeance on Malik. It hurt my heart to watch Malik crumble because I knew he would blame himself. The same way I know that he's blaming himself now for what happened to me.

He's not talking about it, though. And that's the thing that worries me, because he's not talking about *anything*. Not the accident, not anything to do with Captain Davison, the cartel, or my inheritance, and not us. Above all, the latter is what is getting to me most.

We're supposed to be going to Wilmington in two days' time because I've been so eager to see my grandmother. But Malik hasn't even packed yet.

I know we still have time, but I sense that's by design.

My suspicion grows the next day at lunch when I return from the store and Kelly tells me Malik wants to see me in his office.

When I reach the office, I walk in through the already opened door and find him standing by the long windows with his back turned. He's looking at the sea ahead. It's the perfect weather for sailing or simply being outside in the warm sunshine. But a chill lurks in the air in here.

Or the coldness could just be coming from me. From that icy tendril of anticipation a person experiences when they're not sure what's going to happen to the thing they value most. In my case, it's my relationship with him.

Malik faces me and offers a little smile that doesn't quite reach his eyes. I've been with him for long enough to know that's one of his tell-tale signs that his mind is unsettled.

I close the door behind me and walk up to him, stopping a few paces away.

"How are you feeling today?" he asks, holding my gaze.

"Better. I feel better every day."

"Good. And you're always a pretty sight, right from hello." He speaks in a low voice.

"Thank you. I think."

"That's always going to be a compliment."

"I know, but it just now sounded like it was a distraction of sorts. Was it?"

He touches my cheek and traces the line of my jaw. "Maybe."

I glance around the office, taking note of how everything looks like he's ready to work for days on end. The only other time I've been in here, the place was in pristine condition.

Just like everything else, it doesn't feel like he's getting ready to go anywhere. I look back at him, deciding I can't stand the suspense anymore.

"You're not going to Wilmington with me, are you?"

He continues staring at me for what feels like years then finally shakes his head.

"I think it's best that I don't." His answer comes out on the edge of a breath. The words are soft and simple, yet they feel harsh and sharp to me, like the blade of a knife.

"Why?"

"Come, let's sit over here." He slips his arm around me

and guides me to the leather sofas by the window. On the little coffee table in front is a brown envelope with my name on it.

Once we sit side by side, I look from him to the envelope, not comprehending where this is going and what's happening.

"What's going on, Malik?"

He pulls in a deep breath and keeps his gaze fixed to mine. "I've made arrangements so that when you go to Wilmington, you'll be going back to your home there, and that's where you'll stay."

My chest tightens, holding on to the air in my lungs. I sensed his apprehension, but I never imagined this. "You're sending me back?"

"Gwen, you don't need to be here anymore. We only need to stay married for six months to fulfill our legal obligations, but that never meant we needed to live together. At first, I wanted you to stay with me for safety reasons, but now the threat is gone. Even if there are more threats, I can send my best men to stay with you."

"Oh... I see." Suddenly, my skin is on fire and my temper flares. God, I feel foolish for forgetting the fine print. "The legal obligations. I forgot that's all I am to you."

"You're not."

"Oh, really?" I don't bother to try and hide my sarcasm. We've gone way past the time for tiptoeing around my feelings, and too much has happened.

"Gwen—"

"No. You played me right from *hello*, Malik Volkova. And like an idiot, I fall for you every time. All you do is screw with my mind, and I'm sick of it." I can't help the anger lacing through my words any more than I can the stupid love I feel for him. "Why the hell would you do all you've done for me then let me go?"

His eyes fill with a mixture of regret and tenderness I've never seen before. "Because I love you."

Like a bolt of lightning, those words pierce my frustration and replace it with shock. But not the usual kind of shock you experience when you see or hear something that surprises you. It's the other kind. The kind that works its way into every single cell and organ of your body as it restructures the fabric of your reality.

I stare at him, understanding those three little words I feel like I've waited my entire life to hear from him, but yet I don't understand because he wants to let me go.

"I love you, too." My heart takes over to speak those words, but only for a moment. I need my brain now because I can't imagine being without him. "If we love each other, shouldn't I be coming back to you after my trip? Shouldn't we be staying together?"

"No. Love isn't enough."

"How can you say that?"

He gives me a strong-willed stare. "Everything about me has been selfish. It's monsters like me who your father tried to protect you from. I'm not exactly that different from Diego or Esperanza, who tried to use you for their gain."

I understand what he's saying, but our feelings must count for something. "But you were different."

"Yes, I am, because I was the worst one of the bunch, and I won. I'm the one sitting here with the prize. I married you, and that gave me the cartel." His voice hardens with bitterness. "I was the one who found Santiago's daughter, a woman who was never supposed to be found. Then I used you as a weapon in a fight where I was the fool."

"You didn't know." My voice is weak because my brain knows I'm just making excuses for him that don't actually excuse what he did.

"It doesn't matter. I behaved the way I did because that's who I am. That's how I was raised. To be ruthless and merciless. To not think with my heart. And the biggest mistake I made through all this was thinking I was invincible. Me being me nearly cost you your life. We were lucky, by mere seconds. I'm a danger to you, Gwen, and that's why you can't stay with me."

He keeps my gaze captive. I can't look away from his dark foreboding eyes.

I want to argue with him and tell him he's wrong. I want to tell him things changed along the way. That *we* changed. I want to give him all the reasons we should stay together. But I can't.

I can't think of anything solid that would refute his arguments, because everything he's saying is true.

It's all true. All of it

Every last word is a slice of truth from the pieces of his plan for revenge.

All I can do is look at him and try to figure out what else we can do, but nothing comes, besides what I feel in my heart.

"I don't want to leave you." My chest heaves at the thought.

Malik dips his head briefly. When he looks at me again, that deadness I witnessed weeks ago is back.

"If I love you the way I say I do, then the only way for me

to show that is to set you free. I need to let you go so you can live the life you would have had if you didn't know me. No one who claims to truly love you would want to put your life at risk, especially when it's already happened. You know what I'm saying is true, so there's no point arguing."

"I don't see it that way." I blink back hot tears but fail. One slides down my cheek. He catches it, then holds my face.

"That's the way it has to be. This *way*." The tenor in his tone is final.

"So, this is it?"

"This is it. In a few months' time, we'll start the divorce proceedings, and we won't see each other again."

My soul weeps at the thought of not being his wife anymore.

Releasing my face, Malik picks up the envelope from the table and sets it in my lap.

"That's an agreement for me to transfer my share of the assets we received after we got married."

"You're giving that to me?"

"Yes. I think your father would have wanted you to have it. The cartel will stay among the Knights, so you won't have to worry about that. However, all profits will go to you. You'll also get half of what I own personally."

My lips part. I'm already choked up, but I'm more so at this gesture.

"That's too much. You've already given me my dreams."

"Well, this will ensure that you can do more than that."

It's more money than I'll ever need in my life, but I want him more.

"What if all I want now is you?"

He shakes his head. "No. The guy you should be with will always put you first. He'll spend every day trying to be the man you deserve, and most of all, he'll protect you with his life. This is the right thing to do. You may not see that now, but it's right."

He sounds so convinced, as if it's the only truth, but it feels as wrong as lies to me.

Chapter Forty-Three

Malik

4 months later…

I've heard it said before that winning isn't everything.

I never fully understood the saying until I lost Gwen.

Over the centuries, people have said so much about how to defeat your

enemy and how to stay strong when you are weak.

But very few, if any, teach you what you're supposed to do once the war is over and you ended up losing along the way.

No one teaches you how you're supposed to act when you end up being the loser in the end, nor what you're supposed to do when you've fucked everything up and the vision you had of winning has been tainted by the hard truth of reality.

To say that my life has been a pile of shit since I lost Gwen is an understatement.

My mind is constantly stuck on all the memories I have of her and how much meaning she gave to my life. Everything I do now feels pointless.

I walk into my office at home and try to ignore the remnants of her that are still here.

It's been four months, but I can still smell that scent of life Gwen left behind, and I can still feel her warm skin on my fingertips.

That was the last time I was in here.

I left for Russia the same night, so that little meeting where I broke up with my wife was the last I saw of her.

I've been away ever since, not wanting to be here or near anything that reminded me of her.

We've gone over the six-month mark now, so we've reached the time to get divorced.

Zakh is supposed to be coming by tomorrow with the paperwork and particulars from the lawyers.

When all is said and done, I'll be heading back to Russia. I plan to stay there for a while and take care of the Volkova Inc. branch in Moscow. That office usually sees me once a year even though that's the branch I take care of. Now I'll be there fulltime.

No sooner have I set my bag down than Jeanne walks in with a tray of food.

It's only her special sandwiches, but they smell divine and like coming home.

"Welcome back," she greets me.

"Thank you."

Her smile widens when she gets closer and sets the tray down on the coffee table. "Did you have a good flight?"

"As good as can be. How've you been?"

"Good." She nods and smiles, but I can see it in her eyes that she's sad that I'm not with Gwen anymore. "How long do I have you for?"

"About a week or two. Give or take. Maybe more, maybe less."

Her smile falters. "Oh, okay, well, I'd better make the most of it."

"You know I'm just on the end of the phone when I'm away." I smile.

"It's not the same."

"I guess not. Is everyone else okay?" I hate that I'm secretly hoping she'll tell me if she saw Gwen. I'm aware they've been in touch whenever Gwen has come to visit the store here. Dru mostly runs the store, while Gwen has been in Wilmington setting up the branch nearby in Charlotte.

"Everyone is good. Kelly and I went to the opening of Gwen's store last week." She searches my eyes. I try to remain guarded.

I'd heard the opening was soon, and I wanted to send flowers, but then I stopped myself. I also forgot the date on purpose.

"I'm sure it was great."

"Would have been even better if you were there."

I'm surprised by her bluntness. It's unbecoming of her, but at the same time, her candor is fitting for the moment.

"I suppose so. How was she?"

"She was okay. She was happy to be opening her store, but I think she was hoping you'd be there."

The knife already plunged into my heart twists. "Was she?"

"Yes." Jeanne rests her hand on mine and leans a little closer, as if she's going to tell me a secret I need to know. "You need to think about what you're doing before you do something you'll regret for the rest of your life. I owe it to you to make sure I tell you that."

"It's safer for her to—"

"No. Stop. When I say think, I mean think with your heart. Not details and all the reasons your mind will give you, so you lose her forever. I want you to think, Malik. I know I messed up and parts of you will never trust me again, but please, trust me with this." She releases my arm, nods, and leaves.

I stand there, staring at the path she just left behind, her words circling my mind, filling every corner.

Think with my heart?

Gwen awoke it and gave me purpose.

Think with my heart...

What if I already know what my heart wants?

I never stopped wanting Gwen. I just wanted to do the right thing, but I feel more wrong than I've ever felt for being without her.

* * *

The next day, I'm trying to get my head to align with my heart.

I'm sitting on the boardwalk by the boat with my legs hanging in the water.

Zakh should be by any moment now with the dreaded divorce papers.

If I sign them like I planned to, I'll be sticking to my guns and setting her free, but that selfish seed has taken root inside me again, and I've started thinking of ways around this.

When I hear footsteps, I look down the path and see Zakh approaching me. There's a manilla envelope in his hand.

He lifts his chin to acknowledge me, and when he reaches, he sits on the ground, joining me.

"I thought you'd be in your office. Jeanne said you were out here," he states.

"I was thinking."

"Thinking? Did those thoughts have anything to do with this?" He holds up the envelope and gives it to me.

"Yeah." I take it and pull the divorce decree. Just seeing those words with my name and Gwen's twists my insides.

"Are you going to tell me what those thoughts were?" He hardens his gaze. "You kind of look like a man who's about to sell his soul to the devil."

"I think I already sold him my soul. This is so fucking hard, Zakh. It's so damn hard. I feel like I'm about to fuck things up again, or more than I have."

"Because you're allowing fear to rule you. That will never feel right."

"You saw what happened to her. You were there, and if you hadn't been, fuck knows what would have happened. The whole damn thing happened because of me."

"That is the sequence of events that transpired when

things went wrong," he points out. "You talk about putting her in danger, but you forget all the good things. You forgot she was in danger when you met her. If she didn't know you, what the hell would she have done then?"

Only God knows what Conrad would have done to her because Gwen wouldn't have been able to pay her debt. She wouldn't have gone to the police either. If she had, Conrad is the kind of guy who would have killed someone she loved from the bars of his prison just to teach her a lesson.

I did help her, at a time when I didn't have confirmation of who she was. But that doesn't make things right.

"We live dangerous lives. Yes, she was in danger, but this isn't her world. I can't lose her again like that."

"I'm not saying you're completely wrong. I just think with all the things that can happen to us in life, you can't base your decision on that alone."

"Isn't it enough?"

"No. It's not. I love my wife. Desmier loves his. We both have kids. We know what can happen. We've seen what can happen and lived it, but neither of us would have it any other way. Not us, nor our wives. It's not living, Malik. To reject love is death."

The conviction in his tone grips me. It cuts away the layers of my fears and reaches the place inside me where I need it most.

"You, Desmier, and I are Knights, and we have a duty to the Brotherhood." His gaze is unwavering. "At the same time, we're supposed to carry on the legacy of the Volkova line and run the empire. But the most important thing we can do, above all of that, is vow to protect the ones we love with our lives. If you don't think you can do that, and if you believe that time can help you move on from whatever you feel for Gwen, then forget her. Wish her well and forget her. But if you think time will make you live with regret, then don't this. Don't sign those damn divorce papers."

I make the choice simple because it is, and my answer is the latter. I would spend the rest of my life protecting her, and if I lost her, every moment that passed without her would kill me slowly.

The wind picks up, and the papers lift in my hands.

As I allow the answer to process in my mind, I release my grip and allow the wind to carry the document away from me out to sea.

I look back at Zakh. He's smiling.

I am, too, and I make a new vow.

A new promise to myself.

To do whatever it takes to get wife back.

Chapter Forty-Four

Gwen

Grams smiles in utter fascination as I push her wheelchair into the radiant sunshine.

The sun is beaming down on every rose in the garden, making them sparkle as if they've been sprinkled with magic.

Sometimes, I love watching Grams take in these moments because she looks at things as if she's never seen them before. Then I remember it *is* like that for her.

As her condition has worsened, everything is new to her.

Even me.

Every day I visit is like we're just meeting for the first time, but I get to form that bond with her all over again.

We head to the willow tree. It's between the duck pond and the water fountain. I place her in the shade and sit on the bench in front of her.

"How about we read some Shakespeare today?" I hold up *Romeo and Juliet,* and she smiles.

"I'd like that, dear. You're very kind to read to me while I wait."

"I'm happy to spend time with you." I nod.

"Only if it doesn't take up too much time."

"I have as much time as you want."

Her smile brightens. "Thank you. My relatives will be here soon."

This is something new she started doing the other day. She knows she's supposed to be waiting for her family to visit —*me*. But she doesn't know me.

She thinks I work for the hospital and I'm just doing this because I'm kind. I've started telling her stories about herself, but she doesn't know the woman I'm talking about is her.

It's heartbreaking, but I do it anyway, for her and for these moments we get to spend together.

In a twisted way, I've found myself thinking that perhaps it was best she didn't remember me during the time I was away. If she had, she would have worried herself sick. The shit I went through might have pushed her into an early grave.

I open the book and start reading, allowing my voice to become animated just the way she likes it. My mediocre attempts to act as if I'm on a Broadway stage entertain her, so it's worth it.

For the last four months, I've been coming here a few times a week. Sometimes, I stay in the hotel nearby so I can be close. That week when I first got back was like that.

I'd returned to Wilmington heartbroken. Nothing had changed except everything about me and my heart. I left here a single woman who'd just found out her ex had been murdered and returned as a married woman who'd just split up with her husband. All in a matter of weeks. It's the sort of outlandish drama you'd hear on some daytime tv talk show.

In my sorrow, I needed to be near Grams, whether or not she remembered me. Seeing her during those times helped even more. But as soon as I was by myself, Malik would return to my mind.

He's there again now that I've gotten into the play and I'm reading from memory.

I keep wondering if something is wrong with me. Why can't I let go of Malik?

I went through so much shit just knowing him. From being kidnapped to alerting Dad's family about my identity, then walking the thin line between life and death.

But I can't forget him. My heart won't allow me to, and my soul forbids it.

I love him...

I fell for the devil and I can't unlove him, no matter how hard I try.

He's the guy you can't forget. Even when death was calling to me, I was trying to find him. I believed if I could, I would have everything.

When I went back to Boston for my store's opening, I knew he wouldn't come.

Malik Volkova locks himself off to the world, but there are things about him I can figure out. That was one of them. Yet, like an idiot, I looked out for him. Every time the door opened, I hoped it would be him. When I saw Jeanne and Kelly walk in, I hoped he wasn't too far behind. Each time, disappointment buried itself deeper into my heart, and I accepted the sad truth that I might not be able to move on.

As the evening wore on, I realized that truth was something I was going to have to live with if I had to live without him.

It's awful that I have unimaginable wealth now, but not the one thing I want.

Before I left Boston, Dru and I made arrangements so she'd take care of the store there while I'd drop by from time to time, and focus on opening our others.

Honestly, I doubt I'll be able to go to Boston at all. If I do, it will just be if I absolutely need to. I don't think I'll be able to wrap my head around being there and not see him or be with him. Or worse, I would hate to run into him and his new woman. Or God, his new wife, if he decides to remarry.

I can't do it.

Grams suddenly gasps, and I look away from the book. She brings her hands up to her cheeks, then places one at her heart.

"*Rafe*," she mutters my grandfather's name. Hope sparks in my heart. This is the first inkling of a memory she's had since I've been back.

"Grams. Do you remember him?"

"There!" She points across the garden. I follow her gaze.

When I see Malik standing by the roses, my breath staggers and my heart trips over itself.

"Rafe," Grams repeats with awe filling her voice.

It's Malik's hair. He has the same blond hair as my grandfather, and I suppose they were roughly the same height, too. From here, if I didn't know better, he could pass for a younger version of my grandfather. From when he was in the Air Force.

What's he doing here?

Yes, I know that as of last week, we'd gone over the sixth-month mark. I was gearing myself up to receive the divorce papers any day now, but I never actually thought I'd see him again. And *here?*

What is he doing here?

My nerves spike when he walks over. Grams smiles wider, convinced she's looking at my grandfather.

"You came back," Grams says heartily.

Malik glances at me. I find myself lost in those eyes I never thought I'd be staring at again.

"Sorry, she thinks you're someone else," I tell him.

"No, it's really him," Grams insists. "My Rafe. The war must be over." Grams stretches out her hands toward Malik.

I'm about to tell her again that she's mistaken, but to my complete surprise, Malik moves toward her. He walks over and takes her hands, holding them both in his.

"Hello," he says in that deep voice that first enchanted me.

"You're back, just like you promised." Grams scans his face.

"I am," he tells her, surprising me further.

She sighs. "Our poem is in my mind. *How do I love thee? Let me count the ways. I love thee to the depth and breadth and height my soul can reach, when feeling out of sight.*"

My mouth drops. That's nearly an entire verse from Elizabeth Barrett Browning's *How do I love thee?*

I'm shocked further when Malik says, "*For the ends of*

being and ideal grace." Then he continues reciting the rest of the poem. The words pour out of him as

if he's some famous poet and he's done this a million times before.

When he finishes, Grams is beaming from ear to ear.

"You remember?" she gasps.

He gives her hands a gentle squeeze. "Always."

I can't look away from them. What he did for my grandmother just now is sweet and shocking and...one of the best things anyone has done for me in a long time.

And it's him again. Doing something sentimental that only he can do to show me that even in the darkness of gloom, there's light and hope.

Malik glances at me. I realize how I must look gawking at him, so I try to compose myself.

Grams smiles at him, but then her smile fades and confusion sets in. Having witnessed that expression on a daily basis, I know exactly what's happening. She's forgetting.

"I'm sorry. Who are you?" Her gaze roams over his face. "I think we were talking, but I can't remember."

"I'm a friend," he tells her, then looks at me again, realizing what's happening to her.

"Oh. I'm sorry, I just can't remember."

"That's okay." Malik releases her hands. "Would you mind if I speak to Gwen for a little while? We won't go too far."

"Not at all."

He stands and focuses on me. "Will she be okay by herself for a moment?"

"Yes, she'll be fine." I nod and give Grams the book I was previously reading her.

"Romeo and Juliet." She smiles again. "I haven't read this in a while. I love this story."

"I know." Although my heart is breaking, I put on my best face. "I'll be back in a minute."

"Okay dear." She opens the book and starts reading.

Malik and I walk over to the terrace, stopping away from everyone. So it's just us.

Now that we're by ourselves, my previous question resurfaces.

Why is he here?

Does he have the divorce papers with him?

I expected them to come in a biggish envelope with some sort of seal, but maybe I'm wrong. Maybe it's a slip of paper.

I look him over, quickly scanning what he's wearing. He doesn't have a jacket on, only a black button-down shirt and black slacks. I suppose if it is a slip of paper, he could fit it in his pocket.

"I didn't know her illness was so bad." His voice breaks into my thoughts. I was so deep in concentration that I have to think for a few seconds about what he's talking about.

"Yes," I answer. "She doesn't remember me at all, so that was a good moment. Most of her long-term memories from before I was born are still there, but they're fading. Thank you for doing what you did."

"I'm glad I helped. I didn't know what to do, so I just went with it."

"That's okay."

He stares at me with those compelling magnetic eyes that I want to get lost in, but I get a grip of my thoughts so I can stop myself from falling for this man all over again.

"Why are you here, Malik? I never expected to see you

again." I blow out a ragged breath and try to relax my tense shoulders before they snap. "I thought we might just do the divorce documents by post or whatever. You didn't have to come."

His expression becomes more open and there's something that looks like desperation in his eyes that I recognize, because I feel it too.

"I'm not here for that."

I give him a narrowed look. "Then why are you here?"

"For you." The low tenor of his voice is like a gentle caress on my heart.

His words fill me with the hope I've been trying so hard to push away all these months of not seeing him and trying to accept that this was going to be my new normal.

"Me?" The word barely comes out of my mouth.

"You."

"But you said this was best."

"Was it best for you?" The intensity of his gaze ensnares me, anchoring me to the question.

"No," I rasp out. There's nothing to think about.

"Me neither. The divorce papers came and I couldn't sign them. I couldn't do it because it felt wrong. But I realized *everything* I did felt wrong because it was. So I thought I'd do something right for a change and start over."

"Start over?" I search his eyes.

"Right from the beginning, except this part could be the beginning. Right here and now, where you are my wife and I am your husband. And we stay that way."

"Really? So no divorce?" I step closer and he brushes a finger over my cheek.

"No divorce. Instead, I tell you I love you with my entire

soul and I promise to spend the rest of my life protecting you and being the kind of man you deserve. I couldn't stop being selfish when it came to you, Gwen, because I want you in my life always. I can't let you go and I can't stand by and watch you be with someone else who's not me."

Emotion overwhelms me and I lift my trembling hand up to my cheeks. "Oh, Malik... do you mean that?"

"I've never been more serious. You are life, Gwen. My life. When I found you, I found life and love and all the things I didn't know I could have, but wanted. If you give me another chance, I'll prove every single promise to you and make you love me again. Can you give me that chance?"

My heart explodes with the deepest joy and I fly straight into his arms, wrapping mine around his neck, and he holds me.

"Yes. Yes, a million times, yes. I never stopped loving you, Malik Volkova."

He presses his lips to my ear. "And I loved you at hello."

Epilogue

Gwen
One month later...

Malik's biggest idea of starting over was getting married again.

We did two days ago on the Carolina Beach Oceanfront in Wilmington, where he gave me the wedding of my dreams.

This time, everyone I know and loved was there. Grams, Dru, who was my maid of honor and all my friends and friends of my grandmother.

All of Malik's family were there, too.

It was a beautiful ceremony, but most of all, it was magical.

As we took our vows and promised to love each other forever, I thought about how far I'd come and where I began.

My story began with my parents, who just wanted to be together and have a family. They had me and the most important thing they both wanted for me was happiness. I'd like to think they both looked down on me and saw that I found it in my husband. I found love, and it's everything I ever wanted.

Malik and I started with a chance meeting in a bar that was almost normal.

I was drowning my sorrows, and he was the deadly, handsome, mysterious stranger who walked in.

He had that dangerous air about him I was always warned to stay away from, but his charm captivated me.

All it took was one touch and I couldn't resist. That spark led me here.

Now we're on our honeymoon in Barbados. We arrived yesterday morning.

We have a beach house all to ourselves with a slice of the scenic beach greeting us at our front door. The beauty of the island is one that lures you to explore, but we've spent the time indoors exploring each other.

Just like we are now.

It's just gone lunchtime, and I finally made him my famous apple pie.

He started eating a slice, then halfway through he got other ideas and set me on top of the table.

Now he's kissing his way up my leg. *Slowly.* Oh so slowly, as if he wants to savor the taste of my skin.

"I thought you were supposed to be eating my pie, sailor." I giggle when he reaches my thighs and parts my legs.

He lifts his head and looks at me. "I am, I'm just greedy. I want everything, including tasting you."

I'm about to come back with something witty, but my voice cuts when he buries his face between my thighs and thrusts his tongue right into my pussy.

Pleasure tears through my veins, pumping fire inside me that scorches everything from my mind. Everything but my husband and the way he's consuming me as if I'm a goddess.

I moan into the incredible sensations produced by his tongue, exploring my inner passage. It races over me, leaving me weak. I'm a rag-doll in his arms by the time he stands and pushes his cock into me.

"You're all mine Mrs. Volkova. All mine." He kisses me hard.

"I am. You're mine too."

"I am and I plan to devour you for the rest of forever."

"I'll hold you to that."

Our lips meet again and as our hearts beat as one, I know I'll never be lost again because we have each other.

* * *

Malik

Three months later

I never thought I'd ever have Christmas at my house. I was always the one going to somebody else's place.

Now everyone is here with me.

As I looked at all of us sitting around my table at dinner, I thought about how my brothers and I started the family line again. Almost with a new legacy.

We each have wives now and two of us have kids.

It will be interesting and exciting to see where we go from here. It's definitely the first time that I've looked forward to the future.

While Desmier is entertaining everyone with Viking stories the babies absolutely love, I thought I'd steal a few minutes away from everyone.

There's something that's been on my mind for a while now and I feel like I need to sort it out today.

It's the room. The secret room, as Gwen calls it.

I make my way upstairs and into the bedroom. What I'm doing won't take up too much time, but it's what it represents for me.

I open the room up and go inside. After I found out about Jim, I came in here and took down his pictures. With them gone, I realized how morbid the place felt, so I took out my Knight's tunic and left everything else.

It wasn't until a few days ago that I realized why the room still feels the way it does. It's Brian's pictures. All of them. Keeping them up there is like hanging on to a ghost and holding on to guilt.

He died two days before Christmas. That's why I felt like I had to do this today. So I won't drag his ghost into another year.

I'd gotten a special album to put them in. I grab it from the shelf behind me and start taking the pictures down. As I remove each one, I try not to think of the memories behind the images.

"Are you okay?" The gentle voice of my wife soothes me.

I look at her standing in the doorway. I was so absorbed in what I was doing I didn't hear her.

"Yeah, I'm fine."

She walks in. Even though I just saw her moments ago, I can't help but look at her as she approaches and revel in how lucky I am to have her in my life.

"You took the pictures of Brian down?"

"I needed to. You called this place a shrine once. It became exactly that and reminds me of everything I lost. I don't think it's healthy."

"No it's not." She places her dainty hands on my arm.

"I didn't want to take it into tomorrow. I wanted tomorrow to be a fresh start." I smile down at her.

"Did you have something in mind?"

"A walk-in wardrobe for my beautiful wife."

Gwen's face brightens. "Really?"

"Yeah. Seeing as how you had one in Wilmington, I think you need the space."

"I do, but I have a better idea." She gives me a mischievous smile and stands on the tips of her toes to plant a kiss on my chin.

"What's this idea of yours?"

"A nursery." She nods. "I hear it's better for babies to be closer to their parents in the first few months. This room would definitely make a great nursery."

"Sure, but why would we need a..." My voice trails off as I realize what's she saying to me and I smile. "Gwen, are we in need of a nursery?"

"We are. I'm pregnant."

"Oh my God. You're serious? We're going to have a baby." My God, I won't just be Uncle Malik anymore.

"I'm serious. I'm only three weeks, but I'm pregnant."

"Oh Gwen." Joy fills my heart in a way I've never felt before and I pick her up, spinning her around.

"You're happy?" She cradles my face.

"I'm happy. Happy to have you and happy for all the things we're going to do with our lives together." I was right. She is life. "I love you Gwen."

"I love you too."

* * *

THANK YOU SO MUCH FOR READING.

Also By Faith Summers

Series

Dark Syndicate

Ruthless Prince

Dark Captor

Wicked Liar

Merciless Hunter

Heartless Lover

Ruthless King

Dark Odyssey

Tease Me

Taunt Me

Thrill Me

Tempt Me

Take Me

Original Sins

Dark Odyssey Fantasies

Entice

Tease

Play

Tempt

Savage Legacy

Devil's Kiss

Duets

Blood and Thorns Duet

Merciless Vows

Merciless Union

Cruel Secrets Duet

Cruel Lies

Cruel Promises

Novellas

The Boss' Girl

The Player

Standalones

Deceptive Vows

Deadly Games

Acknowledgments

For my readers.
Always for you.
Thank you for reading my stories.
I hope you continue to enjoy my wild adventures xx

About the Author

Faith Summers is the Dark Contemporary Romance pen name of USA Today Bestselling Author, Khardine Gray.

Warning !! Expect wild romance stories of the scorching hot variety and deliciously dark romance with the kind of alpha male bad boys best reserved for your fantasies.

Be sure to join her reader group - The Dark Odyssey

https://www.facebook.com/groups/462522887995800/

Made in the USA
Monee, IL
18 April 2023

32073553R00301